"What hau

Matt drew in air. "Too much."

"How did your brother die?" she asked.

"He was a soldier...and was shot. It's my fault he died. I didn't protect him."

"Ah." Laney snuggled closer, her fingers tightening on his. "Even if you couldn't have protected him, that must hurt."

His breath caught. The fact that she hadn't offered platitudes or not-your-fault statements warmed him. He felt what he felt, and the fact that she acknowledged his reality made her unique...even more unique than he'd thought. "I like you."

"I'm imminently likable." Her gaze dropped to his lips. Her lids fluttered to half-mast. "This is *not* a good idea," she murmured. She bit her lip, leaving a little indent he wanted to lick.

"Talking to the choir here." His entire body went into overdrive. He needed her to push him away, to be smart enough for the both of them.

But her eyes shut completely as she swayed toward him. No force could prevent him from leaning into her and brushing her lips with his. Soft, so sweet, her mouth was a temptation a man couldn't resist. Especially a damaged man with a ticking clock over his head. So he fisted her hair, tethering her, and went deep...

Praise for
Forgotten Sins

"4½ stars! Top Pick! The rich world of romantic suspense gets even better with the first in Zanetti's tremendous new paranormal-edged series…[A] rapidly paced, clever thriller… Zanetti pulls together a heady mix of sexy sizzle, emotional punch, and high-stakes danger in this truly outstanding tale. Brava!"
—*RT Book Reviews*

"*Forgotten Sins* is the first book in what looks to be an extremely promising series…I'm completely captivated!…I feel like a kid in a candy store who just discovered a new favorite candy—and discovered they're sold out of it. Bring on the next book!"
—RomanceJunkiesReviews.com

"[Zanetti is] an auto-buy author for me…Her world and characters captivated me, and she has maintained her grasp across three different romance subgenres. *Forgotten Sins* was no exception…I am really looking forward to Zanetti's future stories with the Sins brothers."
—TheBookPushers.com

"Lord, I loved this book. From the first page to the last, this one left me trying to catch my breath after each action-packed page…Zanetti will always be a fixture on this reader's bookshelf!"
—Ramblings from a Chaotic Mind
(nikkibrandyberry.wordpress.com)

"Amazing…The reader is pulled into a story of mystery and suspense that is only matched by the heat and passion of sexual attraction."
—TheReadingCafe.com

SWEET REVENGE

Also by Rebecca Zanetti

Forgotten Sins
Blind Faith

SWEET
REVENGE

||||||||||||||||||||||||||||||||||||||||||||||||||||||||||||||||||

REBECCA ZANETTI

FOREVER

NEW YORK   BOSTON

Copyright © 2013 by Rebecca Zanetti
Excerpt from *Blind Faith* copyright © 2013 by Rebecca Zanetti
All rights reserved. In accordance with the U.S. Copyright Act of 1976, the scanning, uploading, and electronic sharing of any part of this book without the permission of the publisher constitutes unlawful piracy and theft of the author's intellectual property. If you would like to use material from the book (other than for review purposes), prior written permission must be obtained by contacting the publisher at permissions@hbgusa.com. Thank you for your support of the author's rights.

Forever
Hachette Book Group
1290 Avenue of the Americas
New York, NY 10104

www.HachetteBookGroup.com

Printed in the United States of America

Originally published as an ebook

First mass-market edition: June 2014
10 9 8 7 6 5 4 3 2

OPM

Forever is an imprint of Grand Central Publishing.
The Forever name and logo are trademarks of Hachette Book Group, Inc.

The Hachette Speakers Bureau provides a wide range of authors for speaking events. To find out more, go to www.hachettespeakersbureau.com or call (866) 376-6591.

The publisher is not responsible for websites (or their content) that are not owned by the publisher.

For Tony Zanetti, because no hero in any book will ever come close to you. I love you.

ACKNOWLEDGMENTS

I appreciate the assistance I've received in getting this book to readers, and I hope I didn't forget anybody. If I have, I truly apologize. Many people worked hard to make this book happen, and I am very grateful.

As always, big thank-yous go out to Tony, Gabe, and Karlina, my family. Thanks for the support and fun! Thanks for giving me the time and quiet to write at the lake this summer up on the deck...and feeding me throughout the day as I finished this book. I love you!

A big thanks to my agent, Caitlin Blasdell, who works so hard and has such wonderful insights...and who has the tough job of reminding me to relax and enjoy the moment just when I need to hear that. Thanks also to the whole group at Liza Dawson Associates. I'm honored to be part of the Dawson gang.

To my brilliant editor, Michele Bidelspach, thank you for the wonderful edits—and for searching out the places in the book that required more emotion. I like that you push me to go deeper into the characters and their emotions, and I hope the final book shows how hard we worked. Thanks to Megha Parekh for all the timely updates, and thank you to copyeditor Janet Robbins and production editor Jamie Snider for the excellent work. Thank you also to everyone at Grand Central who has worked so tirelessly on getting this book to readers.

Thank you to Kelly Mueller at *Books-n-Kisses*, Sue Brown-Moore at *GraveTells*, and Joy Harris at *Joyfully Reviewed* for hanging out with me at conferences, and also for your support. I love talking books with you ladies! Also, thank you to Carla Gallway for your hard work.

Thank you to my street team, Rebecca's Realm Runners. You are so much fun, and you give me so much support. I can't tell you how much it means to me to have a soft place to land on Facebook.

Thank you to Dr. Robert Holman, Dr. Richard McLandress, and Dr. Fred Ambrose for answering my many, often bizarre, questions about medicine and the body. Also for keeping me alive and well during surgery. Any factual inaccuracies in this book are mine and mine alone, because sometimes fiction has to leave reality behind, even for a little while.

And as always, thank you to my constant support system: Gail and Jim English, Debbie and Travis Smith, Stephanie and Donald West, Brandie and Mike Chapman, Jessica and Jonah Namson, and Kathy and Herb Zanetti.

SWEET REVENGE

PROLOGUE

Southern Tennessee Hills
Twenty Years Ago

MATT STOOD AT ATTENTION, the cold block walls sending chills to his bones. Yet he stood straight, shoulders back, face blank. Based on his size and strength, he figured he was about twelve years old. He'd killed, and he'd almost died for reasons he didn't understand. Now he'd earned answers.

Another boy stood next to him, also not moving.

The commander glanced up from his metal desk, black eyes flashing. "You demanded to see me, Cadet Matthew?"

"Yes, sir." Matt relaxed his stance, arms behind his back. Fatigue weighed down his limbs, but he refused to show any weak emotions. He ignored the woman sitting at the corner table as she furiously scribbled in her ever-present notebook. Dr. Madison did nothing but poke around inside his head, and he was tired of her.

The commander nodded at the other boy standing at attention. "Cadet Emery, your hand-to-hand fight yesterday was excellent, but you nearly killed another cadet." The man's tone held respect and...pride. Yeah, that was pride. "We don't want our own cadets killing each other."

Emery was probably a year older than Matt, and his voice had already dropped low. "If he didn't want to die, sir, he should've fought harder."

The commander chuckled. "You make a good point, young man. You're dismissed."

Matt fought nausea. Emery was an asshole who liked to hurt people, and he acted like his younger brothers were expendable, and only there to back him up. The commander seemed to enjoy the psycho's exploits. If the bastard came after one of his three brothers, Matt would take him down. Hard.

The reality of how far Matt would go nibbled away at his façade of calmness. The line between right and wrong had been blurry ever since he could remember, but now the division didn't exist. To protect his brothers, he'd become the monster the scientists had engineered. That truth squeezed his lungs as strong as any grappling clinch hold.

Emery saluted and pivoted to leave, slamming his shoulder into Matt's arm.

Matt growled. Someday he and Emery were going to have it out. But for now, Matt had another problem to deal with. "I saw the transfer orders for Jory."

"So?" The commander lifted one dark eyebrow.

Unease slithered down Matt's spine. The knife in his boot warmed while his heartbeat thrashed in his ears. Still, he kept his voice calm. "I want to know where my youngest brother is being sent."

"Wherever I choose to send him. Dismissed." The commander returned to his paperwork.

"No." The word rang through the barren room.

Dr. Madison gasped. The commander stilled and then slowly lifted his head. "Excuse me?"

Matt's mouth dried up. He shifted his leg forward three centimeters in case he needed to go for the knife. "I said no."

Metal scraped when the commander pushed away from the desk and stood. "Cadet Matthew, you are dismissed."

It took every ounce of will Matt had to remain in place and not run from the man who stood at least a foot taller than he. For now. A sick sense of dread accompanied dots crossing his vision. "I'm not leaving until you tell me what's going on with my brother."

The commander's lip twisted. He narrowed his gaze, and silence wrapped around the room. "Fine. Jory is too small and not strong enough to be a cadet here. So we're sending him to another camp."

"Bullshit." The word shocked Matt as it slipped out of his mouth. His teeth ground together. "We both know what happens to *cadets* who don't make it here. Don't we?"

The commander smiled in a way that rolled Matt's gut. "You don't know anything, Cadet."

Yeah, but he had an idea. Kids who disappeared never showed up again. Maybe there was another camp, most likely not. Regardless, he couldn't protect his family if they weren't with him. They genetically came from the same father, had the same gray eyes, and the same build. There was no question they were family, even though they had been created in test tubes and had never met their parents. "You are not taking my brother." He enunciated each word, careful to coat over the Southern accent that got them shoved in the brig. His legs tensed, and his shoulders drew back in a fighting stance that came naturally to him.

For his brothers, he'd kill *now* if necessary. Good thing he'd brought the blade.

Dr. Madison returned to her notebook, pursing her lips as she wrote. "This is interesting," she mused.

"You have two other younger brothers to worry about, and considering Shane's last blade-fighting test, you'd better worry about him." The commander stalked around his desk. "Nathan, on the other hand, is quite safe here."

Nathan had fighting skills beyond anybody else at camp, but his obsession with perfection from himself and everyone around him was going to get him killed. Matt feared the day he exploded. "You get all four of us, or you get none of us." His shoulders tensed and wanted to shake. "Jory is only around seven years old. He will grow, and he'll get stronger. I'll make sure of it."

In the corner, Madison's heart rate picked up. Matt tuned in his enhanced hearing to check out the commander. His heart rate and breathing remained calm and normal. Nothing ever shook the soldier.

The air shifted—and Matt knew the commander would move before he did so. In fact, Matt knew exactly where he'd go and how far he'd move. Someday Matt would take his special ability to perceive movement, one the commander remained unaware of, and kill the man. Without question.

The commander stepped closer and peered down. A gleam lightened his fathomless eyes. "You have a deal. If one of you fails at training or on a mission, you all get... *transferred*."

Fear tasted like thick dust. In that moment, Matt learned the reality of making a deal with the devil. "I understand." Turning on his heel, he exited the room, not waiting for permission to leave. He made it to the barracks he shared with his younger brothers before dashing into the latrine and puking out his guts. He finished on hands and knees, body heaving.

A towel appeared on his shoulder.

Wiping his mouth, he turned around and sat on the freezing concrete, his back to the stall door. Through the tears in his eyes, he studied Nate.

Nate leaned against the door frame. At about ten years old, he was tall and skinny, but he had the same build as Matt, and would probably soon fill out. He lifted his chin, gray eyes swirling with terror. "Well?"

"Jory can stay."

Nate breathed out. "Good. Okay. That's good."

Matt shook his head. His pulse raced, and he made an effort to slow down his heart so he wouldn't puke again. "Maybe, maybe not. If one of us fails in a test or on a mission, all four of us are dead."

Nate jerked back, and he frowned. Tilting his head to the side, he slowly nodded. "Okay."

"Okay?" Heat roared through Matt's lungs as he shoved to his feet. "How is any of this okay?"

"Family is all we have. If one of us goes, I want to go, too." Nate smiled. "Besides, we're the Gray brothers. Even though we don't have a last name, we're brothers, and we ain't going nowhere."

"Say it right," Matt snapped.

Nate straightened. "We aren't going anywhere. Sorry."

Matt closed his eyes. Even his skin hurt. He couldn't worry about last names right now. Someday, when they found freedom, they'd choose a real family name. "It's not okay. Not anymore." His lids flipped open, and his voice went hoarse. "I'm gonna have to train them, train you, until you guys hate me." That idea scared him more than the commander killing him. All he had were his brothers.

"We won't hate you." Nate grabbed his arm. "I trust you, Mattie. You're better than the commander."

God. Nathan's blind faith was as difficult to face as Jory's innocence or Shane's hope. But Matt had studied psychology the last few years in training, and he understood Nathan's need to believe. If Nate believed Matt was invincible, the kid could sleep at night—at least for a while. Responsibility weighed like cinder blocks on Matt's shoulders, and the urge to escape narrowed the room into a tunnel. But that wasn't who he was, and he wouldn't leave his brothers. "I won't let anything happen to you, Nate. I promise. The four of us... We're *never alone*. Ever."

"*Never alone*," Nate repeated, standing even taller.

"Has the commander discovered any of your abilities

beyond the special senses?" Matt asked, his mind calculating plans and a possible future for his family.

"No. He knows we can hear and see better than most people. I haven't told him or Dr. Madison about anything else."

"Good. From now on, we don't tell them anything." Which would probably get them killed if the commander found out they were hiding information. With the commander almost sending Jory away, he'd put himself on Matt's enemy list. There was no returning to ally—Matt's world had to be absolute or he couldn't survive it.

Nate nodded. "I won't tell the commander shit, and now we'll train Shane and Jory—make them tough, too. Someday, we're getting out of here."

Matt exhaled. He'd do his best to find freedom for his brothers, but it wasn't going to be easy. Heartburn tingled up from his gut. "I need your help."

Nate's chest puffed out. "Anything."

Matt rubbed his chin. His mind cleared, and his body relaxed as he committed fully to his plan. "I'll push them and train them, but you need to protect them. If I go too far, you have to tell me."

Nate sobered, his eyes darkening and making him look years older. "Is there any such thing as *too far*? In *our* lives?"

"Probably not." Matt shoved up his sleeves, mentally listing drills for the rest of the day as he hustled to grab his gear from the barracks. "I guess we're about to find out."

CHAPTER
1

Present Day

S TAB WOUNDS HURT worse than bullet wounds.

Crouched on asphalt in the dark, Matt Dean leaned against the brick building and scanned the vacant alley. Garbage cans lined the doorways of the now-closed businesses. The place smelled like honeysuckle.

What kind of an alley smelled like honeysuckle?

He'd been stabbed in Dallas two days ago and had to get as far away as possible from what now must be a bloody crime scene. The staples he'd used to keep his flesh together had all fallen out during the last hour after riding over rough roads, and blood stuck his T-shirt to his skin. Time to staple again.

Two of the men in Texas who'd jumped him would never jump, much less breathe, again. The other two might wish for death when they awoke. How the hell had they found him?

His phone had been damaged in the fight, and he'd had no choice but to continue on the mission, hop on his bike, and ride across three states. Out of their reach.

Time to break into one of the businesses and call his brothers.

He shook off his leather jacket and glanced at his destroyed shirt.

A door opened several yards down. He stiffened, reaching for the knife in his boot. At two a.m., nobody should be in the alley.

"Eugene?" a female voice whispered.

The tone shivered right down his spine. Sexy and frustrated, the tenor promised heated nights. He'd always had a thing for a woman's husky voice.

So he turned his head.

She stood in the moonlight in a compact yoga outfit, her mahogany hair up in one of those clips. Damn, he'd love to let that mass fly. Tiny but toned, she reminded him of a pretty figurine he'd seen in a store once. Feminine and mysterious.

Blood loss must be getting to him.

"Eugene?" the woman called again, holding the door open with her hip. She glanced down the far alley, alertness in her stance. "Your walk should be finished by now, and enough is enough. Your moodiness is getting to me."

Who the hell was Eugene? It was a matter of seconds before the woman noticed Matt, and he didn't have the energy to fight the mysterious Eugene. Irritation grated along his skin at the sudden, albeit beautiful, distraction. He needed neither witnesses nor questions right now.

She gasped when she saw him. Pretty green eyes widened, the pupils expanding. Her heart rate sped up enough that he could hear each thump with his enhanced hearing.

Great. Now she'd run inside and call the police.

Except she didn't.

The woman rushed toward him, dropping to her knees. "Oh my God. You're hurt." She swallowed several times and levered away. Her eyes were the color of an emerald he'd stolen from a Colombian drug lord years ago while on a mission. "I'll call an ambulance."

Surprise kept him immobile for two seconds. She wanted to help him? Why? He narrowed his gaze and caught her arm, careful not to break the delicate bones. "I'm fine." Pressing his other palm against brick, he shoved himself up and helped her along. "Though I'd accept an aspirin."

She looked up, way up, toward his face. "Um—"

He tried to smile. "I won't hurt you." Yeah, right. He was at least a foot taller and a hundred pounds heavier than her, found bleeding in her alley. All he needed was duct tape and a ski mask to be a bigger threat to somebody so small.

"Right." She swallowed and shook her arm free. "You're harmless. Anybody could see that." She stepped back, her gaze darting around.

Damn, she was cute. He assessed her, figuring out how to get an invite inside so he could use the phone. With a harmless shrug, he tilted his head toward his motorcycle. "I'll just get on and leave you alone. Sorry to scare you."

"I reacted before thinking." She frowned and rubbed her forehead as she studied the bike. "Did you fall?"

"Yes," he lied smoothly. "Hit a pothole and basically landed on my head. I was tired and not watching the road."

Indecision crossed her classic face. She leaned forward to eye the tattoo on his arm. "You were in the marines?"

"Yes." Yet another lie. He'd been undercover as a U.S. Marshal, then as a marine, and the tat was temporary.

"Oh." She exhaled. "My brother was a marine."

"Was?"

"Yes. He didn't make it home."

Matt's chest thumped. Hard. "I lost a brother, too." Finally, a truth he could give her. "Hurts like hell and always will." Five years ago, he and his brothers had escaped the military camp in which they'd been raised, but they'd never found freedom. Not completely. In searching for freedom, they'd been on missions. It was Matt's fault Jory had died two years ago, and Matt had been paying for it ever since.

Besides, he'd broken the one promise he'd always made. Jory had died alone. *All alone.* For that, Matt would never be whole again. The pain gripped his heart, and he gritted his teeth to keep his expression calm.

Some souls were meant to be damned, and he deserved the agony of hellfire.

The woman sighed, resigned wariness filling her eyes. "Well, I can't leave an ex-marine in the alley. Come in and we can get you cleaned up, but if you're injured too badly, I'm calling an ambulance." She levered under his arm, her slender shoulders straightening to assist him.

Intrigue and an odd irritation filtered through him. "You shouldn't help strange men, sweetheart."

"All men are strange." The grin she flipped him warmed him in places he thought would always be frozen. "Besides, I'm armed."

There wasn't a place for a weapon in her little yoga outfit. He nodded anyway, pleased to be getting indoors. "Okay. Then I'll behave." Perhaps he should let her call for medical help, considering he was in town to find a doctor. The woman he'd been hunting the last five years. But he wanted to be on his game when he found the bitch. "What about Eugene?"

Matt's rescuer bit her lip. "I'm sure he'll be along shortly."

Who the hell was Eugene and what kind of a threat would he pose? Matt tuned in his senses but failed to hear any footsteps. A couple argued several blocks away about who should drive home. They both slurred their words, so neither should drive. For now, Eugene was absent, and Matt needed to get inside and call his brothers.

He released the woman and forced his feet to move toward his bike. He'd lost too much blood. "Do you mind if I park my bike inside? I'd hate for anybody to steal my baby."

She chuckled. "In Charmed, Idaho? Nobody will take your big motorcycle." Yet she opened the doorway wide. "You can park inside to the left."

He rolled the bike inside an organized storage room holding toiletries and cleaning supplies. "What's your name?"

"Laney Jacobs." She locked the door and gestured him toward another doorway. "Let's get you an aspirin."

He stalked through another storage room that held all types of alcohol and into a closed bar. A sports bar with wide-screen TVs, pool tables, and dartboards. He glanced down. "You work at a bar?" He'd figured her for a yoga instructor or a teacher. Not a barmaid.

She gently pushed him onto a wooden chair by a worn table. "I *own* a bar." Her pretty pink lips turned down as she glanced at his demolished T-shirt.

"Oh." He frowned. The woman was much too delicate to be closing a bar by herself. Whoever the hell Eugene was, he needed a beating for leaving her alone at night like this. "By yourself?"

She lifted a shoulder while walking behind the bar and returning with a first-aid kit. "My brother and I owned it together." Her eyes remained down.

He understood that kind of sorrow. "I'm sorry, Laney."

She blinked and met his gaze with those amazing green eyes. "Me, too." Taking a deep breath, she straightened. "Let's see what you did to yourself."

He gingerly tugged off his shirt.

Her cheeks paled from rosy to stark white in seconds. Emeralds shimmered when her eyes opened wide. "You're really bleeding." Her eyelids fluttered, and she swayed.

He caught her one-handed before she hit the floor in a dead faint.

What the hell?

Easily picking her up, he glanced around the bar. The booths were circular at an odd angle, and the chairs were hard. He could either place her on the bar or on a pool table. Gently, he laid her on a pool table, warmed by how nicely she fit against him. Indulging himself, he removed her hair clip so it wouldn't poke her and allowed the curls to tumble free.

She was pretty, and she was sweet, and no way in hell should he be touching her. Her kindness in asking him inside had been without any ulterior motive, and that just confused him. Even so, he ran a knuckle down the smooth skin on her face. The softness mellowed something new inside him.

He'd been without a woman much too long.

Now was not the time. Yet he couldn't help taking a moment to appreciate her classic features. Delicate and soft women were a mystery to him and something he'd only seen on television. He believed they existed but definitely steered clear.

This one? This one needed protection, and he'd have a nice talk with Eugene when the bastard finally showed up.

For now, he'd lost enough blood. Flipping open the lid of the medicine kit, he frowned. Not what he needed.

Prowling behind the bar, he searched the low shelves. *Aha.* A rusty tackle box rested in the back. Inside, he found thick fishing line and flies with hooks. Bending one, he poured whiskey over it to kill germs and threaded it like a needle. He took a swig of the alcohol, allowing the potent brew to slam into his gut and center him.

Minutes later, he'd successfully sutured both wounds. The one on his upper chest took twice as long as the wide gash along his ribs. The guy who'd stabbed him knew how to use a blade.

So did he.

He glanced at the stunning woman on the pool table. How long did a fainting spell last, anyway? The phone behind the bar caught his attention. He slapped sterile pads across his wounds and reached for the phone to dial in a series of numbers while peeking into a tidy office behind the bar. A second doorway revealed a modern kitchen.

"Swippy's Pool Hall," a man answered.

"Deranged Duck 27650," Matt said.

Several beeps echoed across the line as it was secured. Finally, silence ensued.

"Where the hell are you?" his brother growled.

Matt wiped a hand down his face. Shane sounded worried. "I'm in place. Had some trouble in Texas, however."

"What kind of trouble?" Shane asked, computer keys clacking in the background.

"Jumped by four men—well trained. They found me in Dallas as I was heading out here." How had the commander found him in Texas? He'd been there only a week, to gather intel on the woman he'd been searching for. After helping his brothers to escape the commander five years ago, Matt had set out to find the doctor who'd implanted deadly chips near their spines—chips that would explode in several weeks, killing them. It had taken this long to track her down, but he was close. He could feel it.

"No mention of a problem on any police forces or news outlets." Shane sighed. "They covered up the scene quickly."

Which meant the commander had new resources in the government. Terrific. "Are you sure the woman is here?" Matt asked.

"Yes. We finally traced her to Charmed, but we don't know who she is. I've narrowed it down to a family practitioner, a veterinarian's assistant, or the coroner." Shane clicked more keys. "My money is on the coroner."

The woman they hunted had been a top-rated surgeon and biochemist before disappearing and hiding. Chances were she was still cutting into people. Most surgeons couldn't let go of playing God. "I'll boot up my laptop tonight and have you send me the files." Matt's gaze caught on a HELP WANTED, PAY PLUS BOARD sign in the window. "I may have found my cover while in town."

"Good. She went by the name of Doctor Peters while working for the organization, but I haven't discovered her real name yet. When she went to work for the commander, they wiped her past."

Yeah. The commander was a master at making reality disappear. "Keep on it," Matt said.

"I will. Stay in touch, Mattie." The line went dead.

Matt rubbed his chin, his gaze on Laney. Pouring a glass of water, he maneuvered over to her. Now all he had to do was get her to hire him.

Laney slowly opened her eyes and tried to ignore the bar swirling around her. What in the world?

A man stood over her, and her memories crashed back.

She shot up, her hand going to her aching head. "What happened?"

"You fainted."

The low rumble of his voice matched his battle-scarred chest. A tattoo of some type of symbol gracefully decorated the area above his heart. Even with two pristine bandages, old wounds lived among the hard ridges and ripped muscles. And the guy was *ripped*.

A warning flutter rippled through her abdomen. She kept a line of sight on the exits. This is what happened when her routine was interfered with, damn it. Her bouncer and main waitress had eloped the previous week, leaving her high and dry . . . and on deck to close the bar at night.

A pounding set up in her temples at even thinking of the next two weeks. She and Smitty, the bartender, would never survive the rush of bikers riding through town. Desperation swirled through her brain.

Her visitor cleared his throat. "You're drifting off, sweetheart," he said.

Her gaze swung back to the injured soldier. Actually, she was heading for a full-on panic attack at the stressful nights still coming her way. "Um, I'm fine." Though being alone with the muscled stranger might negate that assurance.

As if he'd read her mind, he set a glass of water on the pool table and took several steps back. Giving her space.

"Drink," he said.

Not a man of many words, was he? She took the glass and sipped, allowing the water to cool her heated throat. The pool table was surprisingly comfortable, the gaze studying her, not so much. She knew better than to let strangers into her business when she was there alone late at night. "Who are you?"

"Matt Dean." He rubbed a hand through his shaggy hair.

He still had dried blood on his impressive abs, and she shoved down the panic rising inside her. The mere sight of blood made her pass out within seconds. She shook her head and tried to focus. The man didn't seem like he wanted to hurt her. If he had, her passing out would have been a prime opportunity. Even so, she eyed him for possible weapons. "Why are you in town?"

He shrugged. "After the marines, I decided to tour the country for a while. I find nice places to visit, work for a bit, and move on afterward."

Sad. The guy was obviously running from old horrors. "Is it working? I mean, the traveling?" Maybe she should take off and just run.

"Yes."

The blood disappeared as his physique took center stage. Wow. Strong, broad, and naturally cut, his body defined *male*. Intriguing gray eyes studied her with a knowing intelligence. The new warmth drifting through her veins had nothing to do with caution. Tension emanated around him with the promise of fire and passion.

The kind of guy who'd burn a girl, but it'd be worth it.

He gestured toward the sign in the window. "You need help?"

Always, and right now from her own libido. "Um, no."

Hell yes, she needed help. But from a wounded soldier who veiled his expression so well? She had enough problems. "Thanks, though."

He grinned, and the air somehow thickened. "You have a 'Help Wanted' sign in the window."

"Yeah, but I don't know you." Even though he was half-naked.

"Hmmm." His expression shifted into wounded. "Don't like hiring soldiers, huh?"

Her back straightened, and she studied the battered planes of his strong face. Was he for real? "My brother was a soldier," she reminded him quietly.

"Then why?" he asked softly.

She swallowed. The truth wouldn't do, and she couldn't think of a good lie. "This bar is my life, and I have to be careful with it." In fact, the business was all she had. Of course, if she didn't find help for the next two weeks, she'd never make it. Talk about being in a difficult, crappy spot.

He grimaced and leaned back against a table.

Her heart fluttered. "Are you all right?"

"Yes." He paled. "Just a bit of pain."

She bit her lip and glanced around at the clean bar. The man had kept her from hitting the floor and then given her space to get control of herself. If he'd wanted to hurt her, he would've already done it. Plus, she was beyond desperate, and this was just temporary. "You need money?"

He pressed his lips together and shook his head. "No. I'm fine."

Crap. She'd embarrassed him. The guy was probably a war hero, and now she'd made him feel bad. Her throat thickened with the need to make things right. "Have you heard of the Rally in the Mountains?" she asked.

He frowned. "The motorcycle rally in southern Oregon? Yeah, I've heard of it."

She took a deep breath. The least she could do was temporarily help the soldier. The guy had neither taken nor hurt her while she'd been defenseless, so that wasn't his goal. "Well, the rally is in two weeks, and many of the bikers from the east drive through town. We're incredibly busy for those two weeks." She eyed him. At several inches above six feet and broad, he'd be a deterrent to any problems. He'd seen war—the guy was definitely wounded.

And tough. He'd be able to handle any disputes. In fact, with that hard gray gaze taking in the room, the bikers wouldn't mess around. Of course, with Matt's thick black hair and strong-boned face, he'd draw in the women. The face of a fallen angel and eyes that had seen hell were an intriguing combination. As an amateur photographer, she itched to take his picture. To capture those shadows on film.

The man needed help, and she needed a tough guy in her corner. Plus, he'd served his country and was one of the good guys in a scary world. "I need a bartender/bouncer for two weeks."

He smiled, revealing strong teeth.

She swallowed again. Wounded and scowling, the guy was handsome. Smiling and charming, he was downright devastating. Her heart rate picked up again.

His smile widened. Why? It wasn't like he could hear her heart.

Frowning, she scooted to the edge of the pool table. Strong hands instantly banded around her waist to lift.

She gasped, not having seen him move. "You move fast."

He settled her on her feet and waited until she regained her balance.

She tilted her head back—way back—to glance at his face. This close, a masculine shadow covered his jaw.

His hands remained at her waist, warm and strong.

"No," she murmured.

His eyelids creased. "Why not?"

"B-because." She couldn't help but focus on his full lips.

"A woman who ventures into a darkened alley and helps a stranger is brave and likes to take chances." Challenge and something darker lurked in his eyes.

He smelled like the forest: wild and free.

Heat washed down her torso, and she tried to breathe slowly. What in the world was going on? She liked safety, and she liked security. Plus, she loved her daily routine. This guy would blow that to bits. "I hate taking chances."

His mouth quirked as he studied her. "Somehow I don't think so."

"I do." She pushed away from him.

"Okay." He turned and drew a shirt from the bag he'd tossed on a table and pulled it over his head. Dark gray, it matched his eyes perfectly.

A yowling set up outside the entrance door. He pivoted, shielding her.

Her skin chilled from his removed hands, while her heart warmed at how quickly he'd moved into protector mode. "It's all right," she said, stepping around him.

One hand banded around her arm and tugged her back as the yowling increased in volume. "What is that?"

She chuckled. "Let me go."

"No." He released her and moved toward the door, gingerly unlocking it to open a crack. A heartbeat later, he stepped back, surprise lifting his dark eyebrows.

Matted brown fur came into view first before a battered face. Eugene meowed at seeing her. She dropped to her haunches. "There you are." *Thank God.*

She rubbed his thick fur, careful to avoid his scars. He'd been wounded when she'd found him, and she was the only person he'd allow close. For a brief moment, she'd feared he was in danger again.

"Thank goodness you're all right," she crooned.

Matt locked the door and leaned against it, muscled arms crossed. "I take it that's Eugene?"

"Yes." She smiled as Eugene purred like a diesel. "I thought maybe—" Oh. Too much information to the stranger. "Nothing."

Matt frowned. "Maybe what?"

"Nothing." She relaxed. "He's fine."

"Why wouldn't he be?" That gray gaze narrowed on her.

She cleared her throat, feeling suddenly like a specimen on a slide. "Life isn't always smooth, even in a small town." Her life was nowhere near peaceful. Life was also too short to spend time dumping her problems on a guy who had enough of his own.

"Are you in trouble, sweetheart?" he asked softly, pushing off from the door.

Yes. Definitely. Trouble with all capital letters stood before her like every dangerous fantasy a girl had about tattooed bad boys on motorcycles. "No. So, how about you start tomorrow?"

He rubbed his chin. "The sign says 'Pay and Board.' Where's the room?"

Heat flushed down her torso. "Um, no room." No way, no how.

"Oh." He blinked and took a deep breath before wincing. "Okay. The forests look decent around here. I'll head out and find a nice campsite." He lurched off of the table, his face paling further.

Thunder rolled above them as if on cue.

She sighed. God, when had her heart gotten so darn soft? "Fine. There's a room upstairs you can rent by the week while you're here. I'm across the hall, and I have not only triple locks but a couple of guns I know how to use." As a threat, it was accurate.

Matt stepped into her space, bringing warmth and the scent of male. One knuckle tipped up her chin. "Sounds perfect. You saved me in the alley, and I owe you."

The absolute strength and determination across his face

should scare her. Lava burned through her veins instead of fear. While she had issues, no doubt the biggest threat stood before her with hard muscles and bloody jeans—because against all caution, she wanted to avoid reality and jump into the heat.

That's how a woman already in danger got burned.

CHAPTER
2

LANEY UNLOCKED THE apartment door and gestured for Matt to come inside as Eugene waited by the stairwell. "There are two apartments here on the second floor, and mine is across the hall. I own them both along with the bar downstairs." The scent of male wafted by her as Matt surveyed the small living room.

She pointed him toward the sparse kitchen and wandered past him to open the bedroom door. Habitually, she glanced at the windows to make sure they were still secure. "The sheets are clean, as are all the appliances."

He leaned over her to view the bed. "It's very nice. Thank you."

"No problem." She had to get away from his body before she tried to lick his smooth skin and tackle him to the navy blue bedspread. She ducked under his arm and hurried toward the hallway before turning. "The tattoo above your heart? What does it mean?"

He followed her and put one broad hand on the door's edge. "Freedom."

Ah. Perfect for a soldier. "That makes sense, considering you fought for freedom."

His eyes darkened to the gray of the sky before a storm hit. "You have no idea."

The low rumble of his voice gave her all sorts of ideas, but she had enough trouble.

"Okay. I'll see you tomorrow," she said.

"Laney? Why do you own a bar?" he asked.

She paused, studying him. Nobody had ever really asked her that question. "I was raised by an alcoholic."

He cocked his head to the side, eyes narrowing. "Interesting. Why buy a bar?"

She shrugged. Her mother had battled booze her entire life, often leaving Laney to raise herself. While safe and clean, she was often lonely and afraid of the world. "I learned early that alcohol controls you, or you control it. This way, I win."

Intrigue creased his cheek, and those eyes warmed. "Fascinating."

Her belly flopped. Why had she told him the real truth? Ignoring the sizzle in the air, she turned to the matching door across the hall. "Well, I'm in there. If you need anything..." God. She hadn't just said that.

One second he was glancing at her door, the next moment, he'd grabbed her waist, turned, and planted her behind his hulking form.

"Whoa—" she sputtered. Who moved so fast?

His back all but vibrated, the muscles shifting. "Did you leave your door ajar?"

"Um, no." Dread ripped down her spine. She peered around him to her quiet doorway. "Why?"

He crossed the hall, dropping to his haunches. "It's open."

She tiptoed toward him, her mind spinning. Leaning over his shoulder, she squinted. "Are you sure?" The door appeared closed. But the thought of somebody waiting inside dropped a hard ball of terror into her stomach. "We should run." She grabbed his arm and tugged.

He didn't move. "No need to run."

Fear surged through her veins and clogged her throat. She couldn't move him. She'd been on guard for so long, she never would've left her door unlocked. "Please. Let's go."

For answer, Matt set a knuckle against the wood. The door coasted open.

She gasped, and he turned toward her.

Eugene chose that moment to jump for her knee, and she tumbled into Matt. Heat, toned muscle, and male warmed her palms as he pivoted to keep her from falling. Her hands skimmed down to his abs. He grasped her upper arms, steadying her. She swallowed, glancing up at his hard-cut face, and tried to retreat. "Sorry." Run. They had to run.

He gently pushed her toward the other apartment and bent to draw a wicked knife from his boot. "Go in there and lock the door."

At the sight of the blade, her mind cleared. "That's quite a knife."

"Yes." He gestured her toward his apartment.

The knife...the blade. Her brain flashed back to his wounds. There had been no gravel or dirt in the gashes... and they were straight. Somebody had cut him. "You weren't in a motorcycle accident." She backed into the wall.

He surveyed her, no expression on his face. "No."

"I, ah, think you should leave." She should run into the other apartment and slam the door.

"Listen, Laney"—his voice dropped to smooth and soothing—"it looks like somebody might have broken into your apartment, and they might still be there. How about I check, and afterward I'll leave?"

"Who are you?" Her voice trembled, while her mind listed the items she needed to pick up on the way out of town.

"Exactly who I said." He waited patiently, not making any threatening moves.

The man appeared more than trained, more than capable

of dealing with an intruder. If she heard one wit of a fight, she was heading for her car and speeding for the next state. She slowly nodded and was rewarded with a charming smile that didn't come close to lightening his alert eyes.

He turned. "Stay here," he whispered.

Right. Two choices. Stay in the hall and let a strange man wander her apartment, or go into her apartment *with* the strange man. No way. There was no choice. She sidled back toward the empty apartment in case she needed to jump inside and lock the door. A tiny voice whispered in the back of her head that a locked door wouldn't stop a man like Matt Dean. So she'd head for the window the second after she locked the door. There wasn't an escape rope in the guest apartment like she had in her place. Jumping two stories would be difficult, but she could do it.

He emerged from her place minutes later with a bouquet of red roses and an unopened card. "I think these are for you."

Relief filled her so quickly she sagged. "Oh." Ripping open the card, she shook her head. The script was short and sweet. *Laney, I'm sorry our date didn't work out. Please give me another chance. Greg.* "You're kidding me."

"Problem?" Matt frowned.

"Not really." Laney blew out a breath and took the flowers. Her hands shook as the adrenaline fled her body. "Just a guy who doesn't understand we don't mesh." The mild-mannered pharmacist had been a complete bore the night they'd gone to dinner. "He probably thinks this is romantic."

Matt eyed the roses. "That is creepy. He had to have keys in order to have navigated the lock and two dead bolts."

"Unbelievable." How had the creep gotten her keys? Her mind reeled. She was usually so careful. Suddenly, she felt small and vulnerable. "I guess I'll need new locks."

"How about as part of my rent I replace your locks as well as mine?" Matt leaned back against the door, arms crossed.

God, he was big. She swallowed. "Who stabbed you?"

He studied her until she wanted to squirm. So she lifted her chin. "Well?"

"I don't know." He lifted one muscled shoulder. "I was in a bar fight in Colorado that got out of control. A guy pulled a knife and stabbed me."

"What about him?" she asked quietly.

"He may have been knocked out." The flash of teeth was quick. "But he's still alive, if that's what you're asking."

She shuffled her feet. Her problems were apparently getting worse, and having an ex-marine in her corner would be a huge bonus. What if Matt was the dangerous one? Her instincts weren't the best, but she wanted to trust him. At least, her suddenly raging libido wanted to trust him. Plus, she really needed him in the bar for the next two weeks. During that time, she'd make enough money that maybe she'd move on. It was probably time.

He waited, not moving, his endless patience intriguing.

Finally, she nodded. "You can stay. But lie to me again, and you're out on your butt."

"Fair enough." He slipped toward his doorway. "Do you want me to have a discussion with this Greg person?"

She couldn't stop the quick laugh. "Ah, no. He'd probably die of a heart attack if you threatened him. I can handle it."

Matt pivoted at his door. "If you say so." He paused in shutting it. "If you have any other problems, you call me." Not waiting for a reply, he shut the door.

Laney stared at the silent door. Her heart rate kept galloping. "Yeah. Right."

Matt leaned against his door and waited until Laney had shut and locked her door. The three locks were impressive and meant business. The woman was smart, so how had she lost her keys?

His brief tour of her apartment had taught him quite a lot

about his new boss. She was meticulous, liked bold colors, and had created a bedroom made for passion. Sprawling bed with a sensual sapphire-colored bedspread. There were several bookshelves scattered throughout the small home shelving books ranging from classics to modern romance novels.

Different digital cameras had been lined up on a bookshelf along with a few scrapbooks. Black-and-white photos of buildings, rivers, and stormy skies had decorated the walls—pictures he'd bet had been taken by Laney.

She'd also taken many pictures of her brother, whom she'd apparently loved. The young marine had been featured in several pictures throughout.

Matt should feel guilty about how easily he'd manipulated her into giving him the job and the apartment. Yet he was exactly where he needed to be right now in order to complete his mission and find the damn female doctor who'd guaranteed his death.

Time to get down to business and forget the appealing woman next door. Matt pulled his laptop out of his pack and followed his nightly ritual of pressing play on a well-worn DVD. They'd discovered it in a raid of an off-grid training facility a month ago.

The scene came up, the one that gave him nightmares. Even though it hurt like a hot poker to the spine, he tuned in all his senses, hoping this once, he'd see something different. A clue as to what had really happened to his youngest brother, and more importantly, where to find him. Dead or alive, but most likely dead.

On the DVD, two years ago, Jory sat, hands tied, bloody and battered. Fire was in his gray eyes, showing a rare but deadly temper. Then the silhouette of a woman had showed right before several shots were fired into Jory. He'd fallen, gray eyes wide in death.

The screen went blank.

No clues, nothing new pierced Matt's brain. Failure and

raw agony swamped him. He'd left his baby brother to die alone. Tears he'd never allow anybody to see spiked his eyes like acid. He'd lived with fear, he'd lived with pain, but failure was just too much. Now, with Jory's face in front of him, his hands shook and his vision clouded. "I'm sorry," he whispered, his voice raw and hoarse.

He wanted to rail at the fates and lose himself in the process. But despair was a luxury he couldn't afford until he saved his two remaining brothers. He'd promised them as children that they'd survive their captors and find freedom.

A month ago, his other brother, Shane, was sure he'd seen another DVD where Jory had moved after being shot. But Shane had fought with a head injury, with amnesia, and the other DVD had never been found. Shane thought he remembered seeing Jory blink after being shot, but he couldn't be sure. Even now, with his memories returned, he didn't know if Jory blinked or if it had been a trick of the lighting.

Matt swallowed and fought down rage. The recording didn't lie. Jory was gone. He repeated the mantra, trying to shove down desperate hope that he was wrong.

Taking a deep breath, Matt tugged a worn postcard out of his back pocket. He'd stolen the card from a woman in Texas, the grandmother of a nurse who had supposedly befriended Dr. Peters, the woman he now sought, at least according to what Shane had been able to discover from the few medical personnel they'd tracked down.

Medical personnel who used to work for the commander and the organization—the group still hunting Matt and his brothers. The nurse had somehow died while working for the organization, and Dr. Peters had initially sent a sympathy card. Once Matt had been able to track down the dead nurse's grandmother, they'd watched her for years…breaking into her quaint home every once in a while to go through her correspondence and computer. A month ago, they'd finally hit pay dirt. Dr. Peters, whoever she was, had sent money along with a postcard. The card was blank except for the address, and it featured a picture of the small town of Charmed, Idaho.

The doctor had to be in Charmed.

He punched in a series of codes on his laptop to ensure security. Finally, he opened the e-mail from Shane. Current pictures of the possible targets living in Charmed came up—three women, all blond. That made sense. While they had never found a picture of Dr. Peters, the medical folks he'd interrogated confirmed she'd been a brunette. A woman on the run would change her hair, and blond seemed like a good choice. He would've gone with red, but he was probably better trained.

The laptop dinged, and Shane appeared. His brother's brown hair brushed his shoulders, and his eyes were tired. "Made contact yet?"

"Not in the last thirty minutes." Matt rubbed his chin as he studied his younger brother, the one who'd fought his training the hardest and yet had brought the most hope to them all. The one who'd taken a chance on love with his wife, Josie, and actually won, giving Matt one more family member to agonize over. Matt couldn't imagine his family without her now. "My money is on the family practitioner."

"I'll take that bet. It's the coroner." Shane peered closer, his gray eyes identical to Matt's. "She'd still be able to cut into people that way but would be hard to find."

"Perhaps. Give me what you know on the nonexistent Dr. Peters." He'd rather hear the rundown about her than see it for the first time.

Shane stretched his neck. "She's in her late twenties, a highly trained doctor, no family, and no close friends I could find. Her one and only contact is where you found the postcard. She's a loner, I think."

"Sounds like a sweetheart." This was the kind of woman he was used to—cold, determined, and merciless.

"Yeah. The bitch is a neurosurgeon with a specialty with the spine."

That made sense, considering she'd implanted triggers beside their vertebrae that would sever their spines in less than two months if the correct code wasn't entered into the chip. As soldiers, they were often in surgery, and it had been easy to knock them out and implant the devices. They'd also had sperm harvested while they were out, but according to the records, no babies had ever been created. "Are you sure she assisted with the surgeries?" Matt asked.

Shane nodded. "According to the files I've hacked, she at least assisted Dr. Rodriquez with the surgeries."

"Rodriquez created the devices, right?" Matt bit back a wince when his homemade stitches pulled.

"Yes, and we killed him when we fled the operation." Shane sighed, no regret in his dark tone. "Our only chance is finding this woman, Matt." Desperation filtered through the words.

"I know." He'd find the woman, and he'd make sure she helped them get rid of the triggers before they blew. Shane needed to live to protect Josie. In fact, they all did. Death hung over them like a talisman. "How did you narrow our target down to three women?"

"Once we narrowed the search to Charmed, I hacked every governmental database I could find to investigate the citizens. Thank goodness Charmed is a small town. I've only done a surface search, and so far, these three women are all off the grid and have some sort of medical background. Red flags." Shane shook his head. "No records past about five years ago...which is odd. I guess if you're running from something, Charmed, Idaho, is a good place to go."

Maybe. But the doctor couldn't hide from Matt. "I'll find her. I promise."

Shane frowned. "I've also been trying to find some information on Emery since we learned he's still working with the commander."

Matt stretched his neck, his gut churning. Josie had been taken by the commander only three months ago, and during that time, she'd discovered Emery was still with the enemy. Thank God Matt and his brothers had rescued her before she'd been really hurt. "When we blew up the compound and escaped the commander five years ago, I knew we should've killed Emery." The guy was crazy and enjoyed inflicting pain. He always had.

Shane shook his head. "Emery had a right to find freedom for himself and his brothers, just like we did. He was raised and trained in that hellhole, too."

Yeah, but as the leader of the brown-eyed family of brothers, Emery had enjoyed the hell. "If we find confirmation that he's still working with the commander, I'm taking him out," Matt said.

"Fair enough." Shane leaned closer to the monitor. "You're pale. How badly are you wounded?"

"I'm fine. Ah, how's Josie?" The thought that Shane was actually married still threw him. Especially since Josie was a sweetheart and much too soft for their life.

"She's working hard on the books for our security company." When they'd escaped from the commander, they'd set up a security business that provided jobs for ex-soldiers in protection, infiltration, and other methods the government didn't condone, but still used. They'd made a nice sum of money without anybody, including their employees, knowing their names or locations. Good enough money to buy excellent equipment to hunt the group still hunting them. Shane rubbed his chin. "Josie is adjusting well to life here."

His brother was too well trained to state their location, even through a secured line. But Rebel, Montana, was a perfect place for their home base. "I'm glad. Really." In fact, the relationship fascinated Matt. How in the world could it work? Kind and soft women were anomalies in their lives. "Tell her hi for me."

"I will." Although haggard, Shane looked happier than Matt had ever seen him. Good on him.

"Has Nate checked in?" Matt asked.

"Yes. He's following the lead on the lost DVDs— hopefully the one I saw before losing my memories." Shane leaned closer to the camera. "I still don't remember anything else except the end of the video when Jory may have moved. He may not have, Mattie. I might be wrong."

Chances were that Shane was wrong. Matt hadn't seen any movement when he watched his video. "Jory is dead, Shane. Stop hoping and let's deal with the facts."

Shane nodded, a veil dropping over his eyes. "Okay."

What a load of crap. "I mean it." Matt put bite into his order this time.

"Yes, sir." Shane instantly slipped back into early training. Then he bit off an expletive. "Stop it. We're past that."

"We're not past that until the commander is dead."

"Whatever. Did you find a place to stay?" Shane asked.

Matt glanced around the tiny apartment. "Yes, and I found a job. With these injuries, I'll seek out the family practitioner tomorrow. Also, I may have a way in with the vet." Well, perhaps. Eugene probably wouldn't let Matt take him in for a checkup. Either way, time was running short, and he needed to find Dr. Peters so he could stop the chips from exploding and taking out their spines. Six weeks wasn't long to live.

Wispy blond hair came into view, and Matt's sister-in-law elbowed her husband out of the way. "Hi, Mattie." Her smile was pure sweetness.

"Hi." He forced good humor onto his face.

"What's wrong?" She frowned, angling closer to the camera.

"Nothing." He opened his eyes wider.

"You're pale. Did you get hurt?" She took Shane's arm, and his face ended up next to hers. As a couple, they were striking as opposites. Shane was all angles and hard strength, while Josie was tiny and soft. She squinted. "We can be there in a few hours."

Warmth wandered through Matt's chest. "I'm fine, I promise. You stay right where you are." He admired Shane for taking such a risk with Josie. Matt was merely her brother-in-law, yet the idea of keeping her safe kept him up at night. How the hell was Shane sleeping? No wonder the guy looked tired. "We're going to finish this and stop running, Josie. I promise you'll be safe."

She rolled her eyes. "We'll all be safe. Now, you get some sleep, or I will head over there."

"Yes, ma'am." With a genuine grin this time, he shut down the laptop. Oh, Josie could be tough when needed, but Matt hoped she'd never be in danger again. What would it be like to have somebody so kind in his life? His mind shot instantly to the woman who'd ignored all safety and rushed to his aid in the alley. Of course, within seconds Laney had fainted from the sight of blood.

She was truly a temptation, but the last thing he had time for was rescuing a petite bartender with a voice that heated his cock. Besides, warning tickled the base of his neck from her reaction upon discovering Greg the pharmacist had stolen her keys and broken into her apartment.

Without a doubt, that had been relief in her pretty eyes.

CHAPTER
3

LANEY STRAIGHTENED THE fork on the napkin, bustling around the long table in the party room of the bar. She'd moved the tables together the previous night and now needed to set up the tableware for the luncheon.

She loved her routine and relied heavily on it. Maybe now that Matt could take over as bouncer, she could get back to normal. The need to stick to the familiar had grown in her childhood, since she'd never known if her mom would be the cookie-baking fun mom, or the passed-out-in-the-backyard drunk mom. So she created a list of tasks every day to show that life could be orderly. And controlled.

She'd loved her mother desperately, and her mother had loved her right back. When she'd died from liver failure when Laney had been seventeen, Laney's world had collapsed.

At that point, after years of hiding her mother's illness, she'd vowed never to hide the truth again.

How wrong she'd been about that.

She glanced around her orderly bar, and light from the back window cast interesting shadows across the wood. Great dimension. She tugged a small digital camera from her pocket and snapped a couple of shots. Taking pictures, snapping a moment in time, calmed her like nothing else.

A shadow crossed the entryway before Matt's spicy scent of male and soap wafted her way. She jumped and then quickly calmed herself. He wasn't there to hurt her.

Her abdomen heated. She turned, curious.

Yep. The man was just as sexy in the daytime. A rough shadow covered his jaw, and he filled out his dark T-shirt and faded jeans in a way guaranteed to earn him decent tips.

He ran his hand through his thick hair and prowled closer. "What's all this?"

She fought the urge to capture him on film and slipped the camera back into place. With a shrug, she finished sliding the last knife into place while battling down her libido. "The Charmed League of Businesswomen has its monthly meeting here for lunch." As a member, she gave the group a discount on lunch but still made a modest profit each month. "I need you to help serve drinks and bus the table during the luncheon."

Those odd eyes focused on her. "Why were you taking pictures of the floor?"

She coughed out a laugh. "The light and shadows intrigued me." Shrugging, she tried not to feel like a complete dork.

He frowned and eyed the floor. "Light and shadows, huh?"

She bit her lip. "Yes." Enough of opening up to the ex-soldier. "How's the apartment? Do you have everything you need?"

"Yes. It's a great place." His smile warmed her right up. "Did you speak with Greg the burglar?"

They needed to get lines drawn, regardless of sweet smiles. "Um, while I appreciate your help, I'd like to keep this professional."

One dark eyebrow rose. "Okay. I don't understand what that has to do with breaking and entering."

An intensity poured off the man in a way that sped up her

heart rate, and she didn't have time for confusion right now. "What I mean is, I'm your boss, and now your landlord, and I, ah, can handle my personal life myself."

Amusement lifted Matt's lip. "Somebody breaking into the place where I work and now live *is* my business."

The guy was a force of nature. "If Greg breaks into your apartment and leaves you flowers, I give you full permission to deal with him." Laney couldn't help the small smile. "Other than that, I'll take care of my own issues."

"No problem." A veil dropped over those eyes.

For the briefest of seconds, regret filtered through her. Matt was strong and solid, and it'd be nice to have somebody in her corner. But he was also a complication she wouldn't risk. "Good. Thanks."

He eyed the quiet bar. "What do you want me to do?"

Get naked and busy? She shook her head. "First, are you hungry?"

"Not really." The words were calm, but the hunger in his gaze as it traveled her form told another story.

Such blatant male interest set up a humming in her blood. He stood close enough that his wild scent surrounded her, pricking up the hair on her arms. "Stop looking at me like that."

"Like what?" he said softly, challenge curving his lips.

Like he wanted to spend days exploring her head to toe. She held still like a rabbit caught in a snare. "You know."

"You're beautiful, and I can't help it if I notice."

The words sent an annoying thrill through her. He thought she was beautiful? Her face heated. "You're very kind, but again, let's keep this professional."

"I'm nowhere near kind."

She needed to develop some sort of protection against the desire he so easily sparked, so she turned her voice crisp. "There are three pitchers behind the bar. Would you fill them with iced tea, Diet Coke, and water?" The outside door opened, and Laney turned. It was too early for the group to show. She sighed, irritation heating down her spine. "Excuse me."

She wove through the tables and chairs to outflank Greg. Instinct told her Matt would try to discuss breaking and entering with him, so she moved quickly to prevent them from clashing. Now wasn't the time for a brawl.

Greg glanced down his patrician nose, his brown eyes sparkling. "Did you get the flowers?"

She forced annoyance away from the surface, her attention squarely on the too-quiet man across the bar. But the last thing she needed was one more enemy in town, and she could end things nicely with Greg. "Please give me the keys to my apartment." She held out a hand.

He frowned, confusion crossing his handsome face. "You didn't like the flowers?"

Temper tickled the back of her neck. "I didn't like you stealing my keys and breaking into my apartment. Now give me my keys." She'd learned early to deal quickly with bullies and with morons. Greg seemed a bit of both.

"I thought it was romantic." He rubbed his smoothly shaved chin. The slight cleft in the middle had initially intrigued her, and now it was a nuisance.

"Leaving flowers in a woman's home might be romantic to someone you've dated a couple of years and who trusts you completely. But to somebody who you've only been to dinner with once? You're lucky I didn't call the cops." Yeah, right. Like she'd ever call the cops. But the pharmacist didn't know that.

He dug into his back pocket for the keys, which he dropped into her hand. "You're very complicated."

No kidding. "How did you get my keys?"

"I copied them one day when you were working." He shrugged, his button-down shirt moving with the effort. "I apologize if I've upset you."

"No problem." She stuck the keys in her shirt pocket, planning to get new locks anyway. Then she turned toward the room she needed to finish getting ready. "Well, bye."

Strong fingers wrapped around her wrist and pulled her back around. "Wait a minute," Greg said.

Something slammed behind the bar, and they both looked toward Matt. Awareness prickled down Laney's spine.

He leveled his gaze at Greg. "Release her arm."

Greg straightened his six-foot frame. "Or what?"

"I'll break yours." The tone remained casual, but the smile Matt flashed promised pain.

Greg snorted air. "New bouncer?"

"New bouncer." Laney extracted her wrist, sidling several feet away from Greg. Her instincts stretched awake and guaranteed Matt wasn't a guy who bluffed. Greg was a puppy who wanted to be petted, while Matt was a German shepherd who wanted to bite. Now she was comparing men to dogs. Enough of this. "I believe you should probably go."

"I wanted to invite you to dinner tomorrow night." Greg tucked his hands in his dress-pants pockets. "Maybe to make up for my flower gaffe?" Good humor curved his lips, while his gaze remained focused on Matt.

"I don't think so." She tried to soften the rejection with a pat to his arm. Greg's confidence in facing Matt actually impressed her, but it could be the guy was just clueless regarding self-preservation. Who knew? Either way, she was a master at protecting herself. "I'm not looking for romance right now, and I think we should remain friends." *Lame line, Laney.*

He clucked his tongue. "Friendship is nice, but I'm not giving up. Plus, I'll see you at the carnival, right?"

The town carnival was a huge moneymaker for the bar, and of course her doors would be open. "I'll see you around." Turning, she dismissed him. Waiting until he'd left and the outside door had closed, she put her hands on her hips and tried to sound professional. "You threatened bodily harm on somebody you don't know."

Matt lifted a shoulder in a way that flexed the muscles in his chest. "I didn't like him grabbing you."

Her chest peaked into action in response, her nipples pebbling. "Too fucking bad." Yeah, she threw in the expletive to catch his attention, and by the firming of his jaw, she'd gotten it. "You're an employee, and I can be sued for what you do while at work. So no more threatening anybody unless it's necessary to protect the patrons."

"You want to talk law? Grabbing a woman equals battery. Period."

The man was trying to protect her, and a sweetness lived in the smooth soldier that tempted her far too much. She was touched that he'd tried to protect her, and the thought of someone actually being on her side intrigued her. But she couldn't take the risk right now, and she had to draw clear lines. "I appreciate your concern, but my brother was a marine, and believe me, he trained me in self-defense. I can handle myself, Matt."

"How tall are you?" Matt's voice softened to a tone that licked across her skin.

"Five six." She lifted her chin.

He cocked his head to the side.

"Fine. Five four, and if you ask me my weight, I'm going to throw something at you." She bustled toward him to grasp the water pitcher and ignored her weakened knees. "I don't see your point."

He leaned over the bar, his intense gaze holding her captive. "You're small and weigh nothing. Do you really think a few hours spent learning cross blocks and hold breaks from your brother would help you against somebody like me?"

Not a chance in hell. "Yes."

His grin turned him into pure charm that turned him

from intriguing to far too appealing. "Fine. How about I train you while I'm here? Say in exchange for rent?"

Grappling on the mat with that body? She'd want his clothes off within minutes. Swallowing, she tried to keep her voice level. "Thanks, but I'm set. I appreciate your intent to take over for my brother, but I think he did a good job already."

Matt studied her, amusement dancing in his eyes. "If you say so. Just to be clear, I feel anything but *brotherly* toward you, Laney."

Life would be easier if Matt could view the petite bar owner like a family member or even an employer, but as he watched her deliver another pitcher of tea to the women gathered around the table, he realized that was impossible. She laughed at something one of the women said, and his cock hardened. Again.

The woman had spunk, intelligence, and a heart-shaped ass. Of course he wanted her naked and sweating beneath him. That confused as much as irritated him. She was the exact opposite of what he usually looked for in a woman. Temporary, tough, and unemotional worked best, and the idea of being with someone soft and kind scared the shit out of him.

Laney was right to keep him at a distance.

The new phone he'd purchased early that morning buzzed, and he glanced down at his first text message of the day. Nate had texted that he was safe and would check in later. Relief relaxed Matt's shoulders upon reading that his brother was all right. The guy hadn't been out on a mission for years, and Matt had been worrying about him. Maybe Nate would finally heal from falling in love and being betrayed.

If anybody could throw a dose of cold water on Matt's desire to pursue Laney, it'd be hard-assed Nate. He perceived only black and white, danger and safety. There was no safety in seducing Laney...for anybody. She wasn't the woman Matt needed to find in Charmed.

Plus, as much as the idea turned Matt's stomach, if he had to seduce the elusive Dr. Peters to secure her help, to save his brothers, he'd do it.

Of course, the family practitioner was the one woman who wasn't sitting around the table. He'd paid special attention to the coroner and the veterinarian's assistant, and the vet's assistant was currently checking him out behind wire-rimmed glasses. Bright eyes showed intelligence and an interesting wariness. He shot her a smile.

Her cheeks pinkened, and she half turned to talk to the woman on her right.

Laney, sitting across from the vet, instantly shot a look his way, delicate eyebrow arched. He met her stare evenly, pleased when her high cheekbones filled with color. The fact that she kept his gaze with challenge in her eyes, even while blushing, pleased him even more. The polite thing to do would be to grant her a reprieve and look away.

Too bad he wasn't a polite guy.

Laney should learn not to challenge him.

Her chair scraped back, and she muttered something to her friends and then calmly maneuvered around tables toward him, hips swaying...keeping his gaze the entire time. His shoulders went back, and his blood started to hum. Who was this woman so full of surprises?

She reached him, her eyes sparking in irritation. "Would you please stop turning the most successful businesswomen in town into simpering morons?" she whispered.

He blinked. Damn it. He focused down a foot at her irritated face. "What in the world are you talking about?"

Her body remained relaxed, but he could hear her heart thumping, and her expression was quickly transforming into anger. She kept her face angled away from the women at the table. "Stop smiling, stop flirting, and do your job."

He lowered his face just enough to make her eyes widen. "You sound jealous."

Ah. There was the fury. "I'm not, you jackass. Keep the charm in your pants, and stop flirting."

Okay. He may have poured on the charm with the two women he needed to investigate, but he'd been trained in subtlety and covert action. "Why are you suddenly interested in what's in my pants?"

Laney's gasp heated him in all sorts of places. "If I have to tell you again to knock it off, you're fired."

The little spitfire had better be careful who she threatened. "So you want me unavailable to those women?"

Satisfaction filled her pretty face. "Exactly."

"Okay." He grasped her hip and covered her mouth with his. The kiss was hard, quick, and enough of a taste to make him crave more. He lifted away to gauge the shock on her face. "There. Now they think I'm taken."

The air vibrated as her hand closed into a fist, and he shook his head. "You don't want to hit me."

"Why not?" she ground out.

For the first time, he let his mask slip so she could see the predator the government had created. "The second you make contact, I'll have you on that bar, held tight, my cock pressed between your legs, my lips on yours until you beg for more. Even fully clothed, I may make you come—and I won't care who's watching."

Her sexy mouth dropped open. Surprise and fury lit her eyes...along with desire. She tried to mask it, but he was an expert at reading people, and the woman was intrigued. "You egomaniac. I'm not remotely interested," she whispered.

Surprising anger shot through him. "You want to threaten me? That's fine. Challenge me? No problem." He stepped even closer and into her space. "But don't you ever lie to me. Ever, Laney."

She pressed her hands against her hips, confusion blanketing her features. "We just met."

The woman was correct. He had no right to demand a damn thing from her. For all she knew, he was a bad guy. But this once and with this woman, against all rational training and thought, he truly didn't give a shit. He didn't understand it, sure as hell couldn't explain it. So he went with his gut. "Yeah, we did just meet. Those are the ground rules. Period." He lowered his chin and waited for her to challenge him, anticipation lighting his veins.

CHAPTER
4

THOSE ARE THE GROUND RULES? Oh no he hadn't. Laney scrubbed the table clean in the quiet bar after the luncheon, her mind spinning, her legs wobbling. After her *employee* had laid down the law, she'd refused to rise to the bait in a crowded room. Keeping her dignity, she'd returned to lunch and the interested glances from friends. Yes. The hottie had kissed her.

Bastard.

Who the hell did he think he was? Even worse, why was she still turned on by the kiss? He was just a guy.

She snorted. Matt Dean was nowhere near a normal guy. Normal guys didn't fill out their shirts like that...nor did they make her world explode with one little kiss. Hiring him had been a colossal mistake. She'd lived her early years with somebody else's moods controlling her life, and she refused to do so again. No person, no matter how sexy, would ever set ground rules for her.

Of course, the women at lunch had all declared they were coming back for a business drink during the upcoming weekend. Yeah, right. They were coming back to ogle the new bouncer. The fact that he'd kissed her seemed to entice them even more.

How dare he kiss her.

"You're gonna rub the sealant on the table into nothing," a guttural voice said from the doorway.

She jumped and turned around. "Darn it, Smitty. Don't scare me like that."

Smitty grinned, and his gold front tooth glittered. He'd combed back his gray hair and donned green suspenders to keep his pants up. "What has you all tangled up?" Hitching his belly, he sauntered around the bar to begin cutting lemons.

"Nothing." She stretched her back, turned, and threw the dishrag at him.

He caught it one-handed. "Uh-huh."

She blew out air. Smitty had been her first hire three years ago when she'd opened the bar, and she couldn't run the place without him. "By the way, I hired a backup bartender and bouncer for the next two weeks." If she didn't kill Matt first.

"Good." Smitty turned toward the limes. "We need help with those bikers. Tell me you hired a badass."

"I hired a badass." One with the body of a god and the ego of a demon. "I'm sure he'll come in handy." She nearly choked on her casual tone of voice.

"Good." Smitty kept slicing. "Did you remember the Jack Daniel's?"

Darn it. She sighed. "No. Completely forgot." Hustling to the bar, she fetched her purse from the bottom shelf. "The shipment will be here tomorrow, so we need...what? Two bottles?"

"Make it four. The bikers arrive today." Smitty gathered the slices to place in containers. "Drive carefully. There's a storm coming."

She nodded, her keys already in her hand as she headed out the back door and down the alley to her compact. Clouds rolled high above, and the wind scattered leaves against the brick buildings. Hopefully she'd make it back before the storm hit—and maybe she could get a couple of great pictures of the action. Hopping inside her car, she quickly drove through the small town to the liquor store to the west. After making her purchases, she headed back to her car and stopped short.

The hair stood up on the back of her neck.

The left windshield wiper secured a piece of paper flapping in the wind. Her breath heated, and she scanned the empty parking lot. Most people had headed indoors before the storm descended. Swallowing, she looked inside the car to make sure nobody was waiting. The backseat remained empty, so she opened the door and slipped the bag of alcohol onto the floor. Steeling her shoulders, she shut the door and marched around the car to retrieve the note.

I've been watching you. Hastily scrawled letters covered the paper in black ink. Fear slithered down her back, while bile tried to climb up her throat. If the note spoke the truth, then somebody was probably watching her right now.

No way would they want to miss out on seeing her reaction.

She was smart enough to know their motivation for leaving a note was to make her feel vulnerable and haunted. So she hardened her eyes and looked around. Forest land sat to the west and north, while town sat to the south. Wind slapped leaves against her boots and shot a chill down her spine. If they wanted to see fear, they were out of luck.

She forced a smile onto her trembling lips and flipped off the forest.

If some coward wanted to leave her anonymous notes, no way was she going to let him know he scared her. Could it be Greg? Just as soon as the thought crossed her mind, she discarded it. If Greg had wanted to leave her a note, he'd write a bunch of silly, purple prose in it. This note was threatening and definitely not from Greg. She slid inside the car, locked the doors, and drove away from the store, her hands shaking.

Confusion clouded her thoughts. The people after her wouldn't leave threatening notes. In fact, she doubted she'd even see them coming. Everyone had secrets, and she'd done what she had to do in order to buy the bar and settle down in safety. The small town had given her a home, and the bar had given her security. Looking back wouldn't do any good. Even so, that's exactly what she did while driving back to the bar. Nobody followed her.

Dragging the booze in, she slapped the note on the bar in front of Smitty. "Apparently I'm being watched."

The bartender tugged spectacles from his back pocket and squinted as he read. His eyes widened. "That's creepy. Have you noticed anybody weird around?"

"No." The only new person around was Matt. She set a bottle of Jack on the shelf behind Smitty and stacked the rest on shelves under the bar.

"Think it's the pharmacist?" Smitty shoved a gnarled hand through his hair, concern wrinkling his forehead.

She tossed her purse to the back. "Not really."

"Hmmm. You should go to the cops."

"No." Dread stuck her feet in place. "You know I can't go to the police."

Smitty sighed. "Calling the cops might not be the risk you think." His faded blue eyes narrowed behind the glasses. "Though, since this isn't a threat, we could probably wait it out."

She'd let it slip one night while drinking that the money she'd used for the bar had come from a dubious source. "I'd like to wait."

Smitty grimaced. "Since the bar is now flush, have you ever thought of paying back the loan shark? I mean, I know your brother borrowed the money, and you have a different name from him, but still, the guy may find you someday. Even though he's a loan shark, you still kind of stole from him. You could be arrested."

"The compounded interest would be too much, and after all this time, the guy probably wants me dead." She tucked the note in her jeans and turned to open the front door. The less Smitty knew about her past, the better.

He wrinkled his nose. "I promised I'd keep the secret, and I will. So let's forget about it."

"Good plan." She unlocked the door.

Matt strode into the room and headed for Smitty. "Matt Dean."

"Smitty Jones." They shook hands, sizing each other up.

Laney leaned against the door, her head tilted. Would Smitty like Matt?

Finally, Smitty smiled. "You any good behind the bar?"

"I do all right." Matt cut his eyes to Laney and back. "What kind of trouble are you expecting from the bikers?"

"Depends how much they drink." Smitty wiped down the bar. "For the most part, they're good guys. But somehow we attract troublemakers during this week. I figure you can handle yourself."

Apparently the sizing up was over. Laney sauntered over to the bar. "We'll need you to back up Smitty, deliver drinks if necessary, and step in if anybody gets rowdy. Feel free to card anybody who looks younger than twenty-one. All right, handsome?"

Matt nodded. The fire in Laney's sparking green eyes glowed with both irritation and desire. Matt had been trained to read people from day one. The woman had enjoyed their kiss earlier.

Yeah, it had been stupid kissing his boss, especially since he had a job to do. Problem was he'd like to do it again, and right now. The challenging tilt of her chin spurred him in a way he hadn't felt before, and a force inside him wanted to explore the idea. To explore her.

Which, of course, would be a disaster.

Even so, his gaze tracked her tight hips as she kept moving toward him. Finally coming to a stop, she put her hands on her hips. The move tightened the material across her breasts.

He swallowed, his brain slipping from calculation to male interest. The pain from his wounds lessened, and the fierce rein he kept on his emotions unfurled. He hadn't realized how tight he'd been wound until he'd allowed her ample chest to distract him.

His jeans were suddenly too tight. Damn it. He needed to get a grip on reality instead of the beauty in front of him. So he leaned over the bar to fetch another dishrag and stopped as a noise sounded outside the door. A shuffling noise... two heartbeats, one heavy breather. Emphysema, if he had to guess.

The door opened, and two elderly men shuffled inside. Worn, leathered, the duo had obviously made an effort to straighten up tattered clothing, their gray hair slicked back. The one with the breathing problems coughed. "Are we late, Laney?"

Laney shook her head. "You're right on time, Rufus." She gestured toward the bar. "Have a seat. Boys, this is Matt, and he'll be helping out for the next couple of weeks."

Rufus lifted an eyebrow lined with a deep scar as he hitched himself up on a bar stool. "New bouncer?"

"New bouncer," Laney affirmed as she hastened behind the bar. "I'll be right back."

"I'm Aaron," the other man said, hopping onto a stool, his faded blue eyes sweeping Matt. "A Thunderbird, many years ago. You serve?"

"Marines." Matt lied smoothly.

"Thought I recognized a grunt." Rufus leaned his elbows on the bar.

Close enough. There wasn't really a name or rank for who he was, so Matt nodded.

Laney bustled back out from the kitchen, two steaming bowls of soup in her hand. "Okay. This is the new chicken noodle recipe, and I'm worried about the spice content. Taste for salt as well as the undefinable." She set the soup down in front of the men and whipped spoons out from a drawer. "If you're not too full after this, I have a new bread recipe I'd like you to try."

The men dug in with happy murmurs.

Laney grinned at Matt. "Rufus and Aaron are the best tasters in town. They pretty much saved my chicken cacciatore recipe."

"Too much oregano," Rufus said around a mouthful of noodles while Aaron sagely nodded.

Matt's heart thumped. Hard. The little bartender was feeding the down-and-out in a way that spared their dignity. Just when he thought she couldn't get any sweeter, she knocked his knees out from under him.

Another two heartbeats thumped from outside, one fast, and one slow. Now who was coming for food? He turned as the door opened and an elderly woman hitched inside followed by a toddler, who skipped around her and rushed toward Laney.

Laney caught the boy and picked him up, smacking noisy kisses along his cheek. "There's my favorite boy."

"I caught a frog." The kid grinned and revealed a gap in his front teeth.

"I love frogs." Laney set him down, and a quick flash of sorrow flashed in her eyes to be quickly banished. "Go sit by Rufus, and I'll get you some special soup."

Did the little boy make her sad, or did all kids sadden her? Matt narrowed his focus and tried to read more of her movements.

Smitty set down the glass he was cleaning and pivoted to head into the kitchen. "I'll get the soup."

The kid held up a finger wrapped with a bandage. "I cut my finger, but don't worry, Laney. You can't see the blood because Granny covered it up."

So everyone knew about the woman's fear of blood. How many times had she fainted, anyway? Matt rubbed a hand through his hair. Laney was so delicate she actually couldn't stand the sight of blood. He'd spilled it, and he'd lost plenty of it. They couldn't be more different as people.

Somehow, that made him want her even more.

"Good. No blood." Laney rubbed the kid's wild hair.

He grinned. "Where's the cat?"

"He's out hunting for squirrels." Laney pointed across the room. "If you look behind the bar, there's a bag with your name on it, Phillip."

The kid gasped and dashed around the bar, his little legs pumping. Out of sight, he made plenty of noise until running back around with a bright green backpack. "It's from the general store. For school." Delight lifted his small lips.

The elderly woman shook her head. "You shouldn't have."

"Of course I should have," Laney said, her eyes softening. "Every kid should have a new backpack for the school year."

"You're too nice." The woman tugged a stack of papers from her pocket. "I have the forms to get reduced-price lunches for Phillip at kindergarten next week, but I can't figure out how to fill out Section C." Her eyes widened as she focused on Matt. "Oh my."

Laney gently led the woman over to a bar stool. "June, this is Matt."

"New bouncer?" June asked, her papery cheeks turning pink.

"New bouncer," Rufus and Aaron said in unison.

Smitty returned with two more bowls of soup, which he placed in front of the newcomers.

Laney took the papers and spread them over a free spot on the bar. "Let's take a look at Section C, shall we?"

Close to midnight, Matt finished busing a table, his attention on two guys at the far pool table. They'd finished several shots of whiskey, and their voices were rising. He figured somebody would throw a punch after another drink or two, but using his enhanced senses, he could tell they weren't quite ready to rumble. So he shot them a look that should make them behave for a few minutes and grabbed a garbage bag to run outside.

An old wound in his ankle pounded. Inflicted by Cadet Emery during a knife-fighting exercise, the injury reminded Matt daily of his nemesis.

Emery had broken protocol and tried to stab Shane in the heart during the exercise, and only Matt's quick reflexes in kicking out had saved his brother. He'd taken the knife to the ankle and still tackled Emery to the ground, whispering that if Emery ever made such an attempt again, he'd die. Instantly. Emery had snarled that someday he'd kill Matt with great pleasure.

Now it seemed as if Emery wouldn't need to even try, considering the chips would soon detonate. Matt shook himself back to the present, taking several deep breaths to ground his concentration. He didn't need to spend time in the past; the present was dangerous enough.

Yet he found himself calming and appreciating the serene moment.

Late at night, the alley was quiet and peaceful. He'd spent the entire night quelling arguments and avoiding grabby female hands. His ass had been pinched more than once, and each time it had startled more than irritated him. While he wanted to stay in the alley, the drunks inside were probably ready to fight each other, so he headed back toward the door.

It opened, and Laney barreled into him, a garbage bag in her hands. He caught her arms to prevent her from falling back. Nicely toned muscle, warm and feminine, filled his palms.

His groin shot into instant awareness.

She settled herself, blinking those gorgeous eyes up at

his. In the darkness, his enhanced sight noted her dilating pupils and increased heart rate. She swallowed and licked her lips.

He wanted to lick those lips.

She cleared her throat. "What are you doing out here?"

"Needed some air." He took the garbage and tossed the bag in the Dumpster across the alley.

Her eyebrows lifted. "Nice aim."

"Thanks." Why did the pint-sized bar owner affect him like this? Feelings for her would lead to weakness, to a vulnerable spot his enemies would blow wide open. Even so, his fingers itched to brush a curl off her face, so he tucked his hands in his pockets. "Seems like the business is doing well tonight."

"Yes, although I'm glad we close in thirty minutes." She smiled, her eyes twinkling. "My ratio of female to male customers seems to have increased rapidly."

He frowned. What did that mean? "Um, okay."

She drew in a deep breath and tilted her head to the star-filled sky. "This is my spot, you know."

Matt glanced around the quiet alley. The place was clean and still smelled like honeysuckle. "I get that."

"Sometimes I need to escape the noise and people." She pulled his hand from his jeans to tug him down to sit on the steps. "Close your eyes and listen."

Her touch calmed the turmoil always in his head, and his shoulders relaxed. It had been so long since he'd allowed someone to touch him, since he'd taken a moment to appreciate the energy of a woman. From the second he'd learned about Jory's death, he'd started to close himself off from anything but revenge and survival.

His constant companion of pain lightened its choke hold.

Her hold lessened, and he knew she was going to pull away. He didn't want to be left cold, and he didn't want the pain to win again. Not yet.

Panic rippled through him, and he tangled his fingers through hers in an innocent touch that felt like so much more. Who was this woman? If he wasn't careful, he'd forget completely about the woman he really needed to find. Yet he kept Laney's hand, and he'd fight to the last breath to keep it a few more moments. "Listen to what?"

Laney glanced down at their entwined hands and then up to his face. Knowledge and a shared loneliness curved her pink lips. "To the quiet. Now listen." She closed her eyes and sighed.

A pathetic gratefulness filtered through him at being allowed to keep her hand. The soft moonlight played across her classic features in a way that made his chest hurt. She wore scuffed boots, faded jeans, and a dark tank top, yet she looked like a princess from a fairy tale. He'd met real princesses. They didn't come close to this woman.

"Are you listening?" She kept her eyes closed.

"Always." The night wasn't quiet for him. He heard people blocks away, cars a mile away, and even animals prowling the forests far away. There was no true quiet. "That was nice earlier—you feeding people who needed food."

"Making soup is no big deal, and you sound...sad." She opened her eyes and turned toward him, studying him. "What haunts you?" she asked softly.

He drew in air. "Too much."

Her chin lifted. "Yeah."

Was she haunted, too? By the death of her brother, or by something else? He tried to read her eyes, to get those answers he was beginning to need as much as want. Deep and green, they glowed with a vulnerability that made Matt want to draw her close, when he should be turning away. Losing her brother seemed to have taken a toll, and as much as Matt wanted to heal her, he couldn't. He didn't know how. "Do you suppose some people live without ghosts haunting them?" he asked, keeping his voice low.

"I'm not sure." She sidled a little closer as a breeze swept by. "Was the brother you lost your only brother?"

Training dictated he lie. "No. I have two other brothers." Who'd kill him for issuing that statement, as they should. He'd just met this woman and knew better than to trust anybody.

"How did your brother die?" she asked.

"He was a soldier...and was shot." Close enough to be the truth. What Matt didn't know was if Jory had really died, or if he was still alive, as Shane believed. Chances were, the youngest Gray brother was buried in an unmarked grave somewhere. "It's my fault he died. I didn't protect him."

"Ah." Laney snuggled closer, her fingers tightening on his. "Even if you couldn't have protected him, that must hurt."

His breath caught. The fact that she hadn't offered platitudes or not-your-fault statements warmed him. He felt what he felt, and the fact that she acknowledged his reality made her unique...even more unique than he'd thought. "I like you."

"I'm imminently likable." Her gaze dropped to his lips.

Bad idea. Very bad idea. Keeping her hand, he turned more toward her and tangled his free hand through her hair.

Her lids fluttered to half-mast. "This is *not* a good idea," she murmured. Her voice deepened to a tone beyond sexy. She bit her lip, leaving a little indent he wanted to lick.

"Talking to the choir here." His entire body went into overdrive. He needed her to push him away, to be smart enough for the both of them.

But her eyes shut completely as she swayed toward him. No force could prevent him from leaning into her and brushing her lips with his. Soft, so sweet, her mouth was a temptation a man couldn't resist. Especially a damaged man with a ticking clock over his head. So he fisted her hair, tethering her, and went deep. Much deeper than he had any right to go. He kissed her hard, sweeping his tongue inside for a taste.

That one taste shot through his skin, through his heart, and settled strong. She tasted like honey and hope.

She whimpered in the back of her throat, and the vibration of sound almost snapped his control. He could get lost in this woman. Going even deeper, he slid his free hand beneath her shirt, almost groaning at the heated skin along her delicate ribs. He wanted to kiss each one, to lick his way down to—

The door opened behind him, and he released Laney to jump up between her and danger.

Smitty stood there, garbage bag in hand, eyebrows raised. "You two takin' the night off?"

Jesus. Matt hadn't heard his footsteps. He'd been so involved in the kiss he'd let down his guard—something he'd never done. Ever. "No. Just getting air." Without looking back, he brushed by Smitty and headed into heat and noise—away from temptation. It would take hours for the hard-on he was sporting to go down. He was on a mission, damn it. His brothers and their survival trumped whatever feelings clawed through him. No matter how sweet and appealing Laney became.

CHAPTER
5

LANEY'S KNEES WOBBLED as she hurried back into the bar. Actually wobbled. Matt's kiss had been like a shot of hard whiskey—warming her everywhere and stealing her breath. Her body ached, and her mind spun.

Even worse, when he'd held her hand so tightly, her heart had softened. Just for him. The wounded, lost soldier was a temptation she had to resist. Her life was in disarray, and allowing a broken man into it was a horrible idea. Especially since she fought to keep herself from breaking again.

But that kiss.

Searing, sexy, and searching, he'd conveyed more than simple desire when he'd held her in place.

He'd made her want more than just the moment, more than just the physical release he all but promised her. The combination of restrained strength and deliberate gentleness had reached down deep in her heart and taken hold.

The man was as wounded as a man could be and as temporary as a storm. He wasn't a guy who stuck around.

He'd leave soon, but maybe she could capture a piece of him to keep her company. She needed more than ever to get a couple of pictures of him before he left. The dangerous hollows in his face combined into a lethally handsome combination with all shadows and light—a true temptation for any photographer. For any woman.

Kissing him was stupid…Anything more would be disastrous.

Her body didn't care about disasters and only wanted the relief he'd promised in his kiss. A tidal-wave, hurricane-sized, orgasmic relief.

She ducked into her office to grab some aspirin. A folded note on her keyboard caught her eye. What the heck? Her hand trembled as she opened the paper: *I can't wait to see your eyes glazed over with passion. I'm still watching…*

Terror and fury roared through her. Some asshole had violated her private office? Her sanctuary?

How was this even possible? There had been people in the bar all day. Whoever the note maker was, he masked himself well.

She crumpled the note and shoved it in her pocket. The idea of going to the police held some merit, but she couldn't take the risk of exposure.

Raised voices toward the dartboard brought her up short. Turning, she sighed. Two burly men stood nose to nose and shouted profanities—something about a borrowed trac-tor. She was *so* not in the mood. Steeling her shoulders, she marched out of the office and up to them.

Just in time to duck as a beefy arm swept toward her head, the fist aimed at the other guy's face.

Then things happened too fast to track.

A hard arm banded around her waist and set her out of the way. A heartbeat later, Matt had both men on their knees, one with an arm behind his back, one with an odd hold on his neck.

Both men whimpered, and one drooled.

Wow. Laney blinked and shook her head. That was unreal. She held both hands out to diffuse the situation. "Whoa, there. Let's calm down." Her gaze rose to Matt's face, and she froze.

The man was beyond calm. No anger, no fear, no expression. He'd put down two hulking men with minimal effort and no emotion. "I believe these gentlemen were heading home," he said.

One guy gurgled his agreement. The other guy whimpered again.

"It's good we agree." Matt released them, and the two scrambled to their feet, almost running each other over to get out of the bar. A step forward, and Matt manacled her arm in an unbreakable grip. "Boss? I'd like a word." Without waiting for an answer, he maneuvered her through the bar to the back door.

She tried to concentrate as the walls blurred by. Before she could protest, they stood outside on the steps.

He released her and whirled around. While he'd been calm inside, now fire lanced through his odd gray eyes. "What the hell did you think you were doing?"

She swallowed and stepped back. "Excuse me?"

He towered over her, hands on hips, all furious male. "Getting in the middle of a bar fight with men twice your size. You hired me for a reason, right?"

"Well, yes." Why was he so angry? She tilted her head to the side as irritation filled her. He had no right to question her. "If there's an altercation in my bar, I need to step in."

"No." His voice lowered to a growl. "If there's a fight, you call me over. You do not *step in*."

She frowned. Fury stretched awake inside her, but she kept it in check, keeping control. The idea of losing control of her environment worried her more than the rock-hard male in front of her. "You know you work for me, right?"

"Listen, lady"—red spiraled across his high cheekbones—"you hired me to bounce problems, which I can't do if your sweet ass is in the way."

Was that a fact? She took a deep breath and settled on the only solution other than kicking him in the shin. "You're fired."

Both of his eyebrows shot up. "Excuse me?"

Satisfaction tilted her chin. Not much probably surprised Matt Dean. "You're fired." As an exit line, it nailed the situation. Unfortunately, the toned soldier stood between her and the door. Just who the hell did he think he was? "Now move *your* sweet ass."

He slipped his hands into his pockets and leaned back against the door. As a move, it was intimidating. "Why am I fired?"

"You leave much to be desired as an employee." She eyed him, assessing the situation. Nope. The guy might be commanding, but she wasn't scared. He wouldn't hurt her. "All you've done since being hired is flirt with customers, order me around, and kiss me."

His chin lowered. "Which of those items is pissing you off the most?"

She narrowed her eyes as heat spiraled through her abdomen. "You can flirt with any dumb bimbo you want, and frankly, the kisses were all right. But ordering me around? Not a chance."

"All right? The kisses were *all right*?"

Figured the man would focus on that. She forced herself to lift a shoulder. "Eh."

His cheek creased, and his eyes warmed. "Maybe we should try again, then. See if I can do better."

"No." The spit in her mouth dried up. She hadn't meant to challenge him... had she? "I don't, ah, kiss fired employees."

"So that leaves Smitty." Matt grinned.

"Very funny." The tension slowly drained from her muscles in response to his instant humor.

He exhaled slowly. "Listen, I'm sorry if I scared you."

"You didn't."

"I'm also sorry if I was too bossy." He rubbed a hand through his hair. "It's just, after being in combat, orders come naturally. Seeing you, somebody so small near danger... well, it hits triggers. All sorts of triggers."

She could handle him bossy or charming. But sweet and honest? She shook her head and gestured toward his hard body. "You're just...too much."

He chuckled. "If you give me another chance, I promise I'll tone it down. All of it."

She'd be a fool to let this guy get close, but she knew better than to make a snap decision based on one moment or one emotion.

She studied him. Earnest eyes, relaxed shoulders, apologetic half smile. If he was working her, he was damn good at it.

Yeah, she liked him. Not only the look of him, but the self-effacing humor and ease of saying he was wrong. Most Alpha guys like him never admitted to being wrong. He'd had no problem with it.

Plus, she needed a bouncer, and he could certainly bounce. The tickle at the nape of her neck promised something bad was coming, and facing it with a guy who wanted to protect her? Probably not a bad idea, so long as he understood the rules. While she wanted to convince herself she was making a business decision, there was no doubt her feelings for him went beyond personal. But she could handle her own emotions. "Fine. One more chance, but if you order me around again, you're out of here."

"Fair enough." He opened the door.

Heat brushed her as she moved past him. "If I ever get lost in a snowstorm, I hope you're there," she muttered under her breath. The guy cascaded warmth.

"Huh?" Matt asked as he shut the door.

"Nothing." She shook her head and headed back to the bar to get to work. What would life be like if she could flirt a little and even hope for a future? One with a husband and even kids? But there were no kids in her future.

She plastered on a smile and began helping Smitty with drinks. The weekend chef manned the kitchen to prepare bar food, so she didn't need to cook that night.

The evening slid into closing time, and she shut the outside door with a sigh of relief. As usual, she double-checked the door locks and extra stoppers placed into the floor. The bikers had filled her till as well as the tip jars. "It was a good night." She smiled as she tossed a bar rag toward Smitty.

He caught it and grinned, lines fanning out from his bloodshot eyes. "Cleanup was quick. Ready for inventory?"

"No." She jerked her head toward the kitchen. "We're done for the night and will do inventory another time. Go home and get some rest since tomorrow night will be busier than tonight, probably."

He finished wiping down the bar. "You do look tired, boss. Feeling all right?"

"I'm fine." The flush filling her face resulted from Matt's loping in from the kitchen and not from any illness. "I'll see you tomorrow afternoon."

"Good enough." Smitty nodded to Matt on his way out. "Night, all."

"Night." Matt crossed broad arms. "Did I hear something about inventory?"

"Yes. I've got it." She reached under the bar for a notebook. "I'll see you tomorrow."

His smile was slow and way too sexy. "We could get it done in half the time if we worked together."

Well, at least he'd stopped issuing orders. She studied him for a moment. While she felt like she could sleep for a week, he looked up for running a few miles. Her eyes were gritty and her neck already ached, promising a headache would soon arrive. With her efforts in becoming part of the town and trying to learn how to make friends, she'd been working on accepting assistance and not being so alone. She really could use the help tonight, stubbornness aside. "Okay. Follow me to the storeroom."

A small room with a sexy ex-marine after midnight? What could possibly go wrong?

• • •

Matt followed the curvy bar owner into the room full of alcohol-lined shelves. Sawdust and faded rum filled his senses. He should get back to his investigation, but curiosity kept him in place.

Laney pointed to the top row. "We have to keep close records of sales in connection with our liquor license, so inventory is a must. You count the vodka bottles on the top row, and I'll mark them off on the sheet."

"Okay." He could see to the back without a stepladder, but Laney would've needed a lift. "Why don't you like help?"

"I don't usually need help."

Sure, she did.

He pushed aside two bottles. "I have seven bottles here."

"Great. How many tequila?" she asked.

A stack of photographs of different bottles sat over to the side of the gin. "Your pictures are great."

"Thanks."

"Ten bottles of tequila, two bottles of gin." Matt moved the pictures to a safer spot and then glanced her way. "How long have you been taking pictures?"

Her lips pursed as she marked on her sheet and looked up. "Forever. I mean, I tried sports as a kid but never really enjoyed playing. My mom gave me a camera for my twelfth birthday, and I was hooked." She grinned, transforming her face into something that stole his breath. "I even had my own darkroom for a while. Then, when digital came along, life turned fantastic."

He moved to the next shelf to count. "Why pictures? I mean, with all the hobbies you could've chosen, why photography?"

"I can't draw," she shot out.

He turned and raised an eyebrow. "Seven bourbons."

She scribbled, and her face heated as he kept his focus on her. "Fine. I like being able to capture a moment...to have proof it existed. Proof that will be here after I'm gone." A tinge of sadness flowed on her words.

The odd tone bespoke of possible health problems or a doubt of longevity. "Are you all right?" he asked softly.

"Fine." She pointed to the bottom shelf. "Keep counting."

He had no right to push her to confide in him, considering his falsehoods to her already. Plus, he'd be leaving town soon. "Three cases of ginger ale, two of Pepsi, and three of Wallace Brewing's Idaho Select Lager." Turning, he eyed the shelves on the opposite side of the room. "Why didn't you like sports?"

She shoved hair out of her eyes. "I was a bit klutzy, and it wasn't fun." Her eyes remained downcast.

"What else?" he asked, going on instinct.

She sighed. "Like I told you before, my mom drank. A lot. I never knew if she'd show up to games stumbling and swearing, or beaming with pride."

"That sucks."

"Yeah. It made for a lonely childhood." She turned and eyed him. "What about you? I mean, you have brothers, but what were your parents like?"

The question somehow caught him unaware, but he answered naturally. "My father was in the military, and we moved a lot. No mother." The lie bothered him all of a sudden. He wanted to be as honest with Laney as she was with him, but he had his brothers to protect. That vow trumped his wishes.

Laney's eyes narrowed. "What else?"

He shrugged. The woman was smart and could sense a lie. Interesting. "Nothing else. My dad was never around, and I pretty much raised my brothers."

"That's probably why you feel so guilty losing one." Those eyes softened.

The woman had no clue. Guilt didn't come close to the devastation he lived with daily. "You mentioned your mother. No father?" Matt asked.

"He died before I was born." Sadness tinged her smile. "For years I dreamed he was still alive and would show up, cure my mother, and take us somewhere exotic where I wouldn't have to act like a grown-up all the time."

He could relate. Time to get back on even topics here. "So, no sports, huh?"

Her shoulders visibly relaxed. "Well, except for track. I liked running."

He loved to run. "Do you still jog?"

"Sometimes. Lately I've been so busy, so no."

To jog, she must be fairly healthy. His curiosity reared up again. "How about tomorrow morning you take me jogging? Show me a good trail here?"

She frowned. "Well, I guess we could try. I'm not in training or anything."

"Neither am I." He'd slow down as much as necessary to spend time with her...and watch her move. If there was something going on physically with her, he'd figure it out. He wanted to convince himself that he just would like to see her hot and sweaty in tiny shorts, but it was more than that. He wanted her healthy and happy...and safe once he moved on. She mattered to him even if he never saw her again. "Tomorrow it is."

"I guess." Doubt filled her voice. "We could start out together, and if I'm too fast, I could meet up with you later."

Smart-ass. He grinned. "I'll try and keep up."

"If you say so." She crouched down to look under a bottom shelf. "There's the extra grenadine. I *told* Smitty that's where it was."

Matt maneuvered the small distance to the other shelves, easily keeping her from lifting anything heavy by predicting where she'd move before she did so. "How did you end up with Smitty?"

"He's lived in town forever and was retired. When his wife died, he was just lost." Laney grabbed the grenadine and plunked it on a higher shelf. "He has been invaluable, to be honest."

Sounded like she'd saved a lost soul. Just like the way she fed Rufus and Aaron... and half the town apparently. Matt stilled. *Shit.* Did she see him as another wounded orphan to be rescued? He frowned.

She chuckled.

"What's so funny?" he asked. The idea of her feeling sorry for him didn't set well at all.

"The look on your face." She dropped to her knees and reached both hands under the shelf. The little wiggle of her butt made him groan. "Like I see you the same as Smitty."

"Do you?"

She glanced over her shoulder, her pretty eyes darkening. "No. Not even a little bit."

Well, that was something.

What in the hell had Laney been thinking to agree to go jogging at freakin' dawn? The truth was that she'd been hiding inside her bar for so long that she'd forgotten how great it felt to enjoy a little bit of freedom. She stretched her calves and fought the urge to growl at the fit specimen currently stretching his arms.

Instead, she smiled sweetly. "When was the last time you jogged?"

He shrugged. "Last week."

Wonderful. "How far?"

"Dunno. Maybe ten miles?" He eyed the quiet main street of town. "Where is everybody?"

"Small town at dawn? Everyone is in bed." Laney shook out her neck.

"It's six in the morning—nowhere near dawn." Matt rolled his eyes.

It felt like dawn. "Well, try to keep up." She shot into an instant jog, wanting to be grouchy but enjoying the early sun, which was rare during storm season. The warmth caressed her face even as her muscles relaxed into the run. She hadn't done this in much too long.

Matt loped to her side, easily matching her strides. Fit muscles filled out his tank top and basketball shorts in a way that made her salivate.

They ran by tidy stores that sold everything from cupcakes to garden supplies, and block after block remained quiet. The small town was a haven to a lost woman like Laney, and she'd dug right in by joining the business group and feeding the needy—from the safety of her bar. Sorrow panged her at the thought that she'd have to leave soon. Finally, at the end of the street, they reached the local bank. The sheriff's station sat across the street, and squad cars were being exchanged at the change of shift.

Laney huffed out air and nodded toward the mountain. "Up for some trail climbing?"

"Absolutely." Matt's breathing remained even. The guy wasn't even sweating.

"Good." Laney increased her pace and veered down another street, this one lined with small homes and ruthlessly tended gardens. The movement felt good, and having Matt at her side felt even better. Safe and right somehow.

They moved in unison, as if a comfortable pair. She'd never been completely comfortable with a man, and she'd certainly never felt like a couple with anybody. As if she belonged and was special. If life were different, she could feel that with Matt.

She glanced his way, and her face heated. "Stop watching my ass."

He grinned. "You have a great ass."

That should not please her. Even so, she bit back a smile. "Take a right at the big rock."

Matt turned first, leading the way. The closest trail led up to a magnificent view of the small town, even as clouds began to roll in. They kept to the ridges, and one hour turned into two. Finally, Laney led the way down the mountain.

When they reached the residential street, Matt grabbed her hand and lulled her into a walk. "We ran enough. Time for a slowdown."

Sweat dripped down her back. "I could keep going."

"I know." He still wasn't sweaty.

"Whatever," she mumbled, shoving wet hair off her face. Movement behind a white picket fence caught her eye as she saw her friend gardening. "June? What in the world are you doing with a storm coming?"

June sat up, her bright pink hat hanging lopsidedly on her head. "Well, good morning." Dirt caked her hands as she patted soil around purple pansies. "It's nice to see you and your fella outside."

Her fella? Laney cleared her throat and kept her gaze away from Matt. "Um, it's storm season." While she didn't know much about gardening, she did know that storms destroyed flowers.

June clucked her tongue. "Silly girl. Pansies are tough, and the way I have them against the fence will protect them." She patted the ground around several batches of flowers, delight filling her papery skin.

Well, maybe. A large bag of mulch near the porch of the modest home caught Laney's eye. "Do you want me to grab that for you?"

"I've got it." Matt stepped over the fence and onto the grass, returning with the bag to place by June.

Yeah, Laney enjoyed watching him move. His sweetness in helping June warmed her way too much. How could such a sexy man be so kind and caring? He'd make a wonderful husband and father. At the thought, her stomach dropped. There would be no kids for her. She forced her attention to her friend. "Where's Phillip?"

"Sleeping." June wiped her forehead with the back of a

smudged hand. "You're so good with him, Laney. You'll make such a good mother someday."

Hurt slammed into Laney's chest so quickly she winced. "Thanks, June. Well, we have to run." Turning, she headed toward the sheriff's station.

Matt quickly caught up. "You okay?"

"Fine." She kept her head up.

"No kids, huh?" he asked softly.

Her stride hitched, and she quickly regained her footing. There was no way she'd have kids. "No."

"Sorry," he said.

"Me, too."

They walked the rest of the way back in silence.

CHAPTER
6

MATT FINISHED SLIDING empty glasses toward Smitty as the night droned on. He'd been wondering all day about Laney's statement that she couldn't have kids. Was it a medical condition?

Why did he care? He probably couldn't have kids, either.

And if he could, it wasn't like he'd have them with her.

What the hell was wrong with his brain this night? The longer he remained in Laney's world, the harder it would be to leave. He had to get a move on his mission and find the doctor before forcing her to deactivate the deadly chips.

Across the bar, the group of businesswomen tipped back cosmos in a wide booth, several of them checking out his ass at regular intervals once the night had worn on. They all wore bar-worthy tight jeans and low-cut tops. He kept his peripheral gaze on the veterinarian's assistant, who was weaving back and forth. She'd arrived with a female accountant driving a pristine SUV.

Next to her sat the coroner, a blonde with sharp eyes. She'd been sipping a glass of wine all night. The same glass.

Unfortunately, the family practitioner was a no-show. He'd have to seek her out.

For now, he captured a bottle of silver tequila and shot

glasses, approaching the table. He could've sworn the vet's assistant purred as he neared. So he flashed his most charming smile. "How about a shot? On me?"

"Awesome." The vet's assistant snorted. "I'm Claire." She pointed to the accountant. "She's um, Betty, and this is Tasha."

Tasha held out a hand. "Dr. Friedan." Culture sounded in her low voice.

"Doc." Matt enveloped her hand. Yeah. Snotty tone, smart eyes…definitely a doctor. Was she the one he needed to find? "Shot?" He quickly poured four glasses. "What should we toast?"

Betty weaved back and forth. "Sexy men." Grasping her drink, she threw the booze back, her eyes watering. "Yum."

Claire followed suit and immediately launched into a coughing attack. Betty smacked her on the back. Kind of.

Matt nudged a glass toward Tasha and took his own. "What kind of doctor?" he asked.

"Coroner." She eyed the liquor. "I don't drink hard alcohol." Her brown eyes lifted to rake him. "Although I do like it hard."

He leaned in and forced interest into his eyes. "I like the way you talk." His gaze dropped to the glass and traveled back up to her smooth face. "How about one tiny drink? It'd make my night."

She blinked. "Cheers." Taking the drink, she swallowed, her gaze remaining clear and on his.

"A coroner, huh?" He fetched the empty shot glasses. "That's interesting."

"It pays the bills." Gathering her purse, she scooted from the booth. "Thank you for the drink, but I need to go home. Night, everyone." Without a backward glance, she headed for the door.

Claire chortled. "She's funny, right?"

Matt nodded. "Thanks for the drink, ladies."

They probably would only stay for another round, so he needed to get a move on. He had a plan, and it'd be nice to rule out at least one of the women. Crossing behind the bar, he dumped ice from the glasses and inserted them into the dishwasher. "I owe you four shots, and am now heading to the can," he murmured to Smitty, who was pouring another round of cosmos.

"Sure thing," the bartender said absently.

Matt sauntered past the restrooms and out the back door. The accountant's SUV was parked down the alley, and within seconds, he had the hood popped and the carburetor cap off. The government had taught him more than guns and charm. He opened his senses to make sure nobody lurked near, shut the hood, and sprinted back to the door.

Laney stepped outside and stopped short. The scent of vanilla came with her. "Why are you outside?"

"Garbage." He eyed her carefully, his fingers itching to touch her again. "You okay?"

"Stop asking me that." She took a deep breath, outlining her breasts against the worn cotton. "I'm fine."

The woman was more than fine, yet she was pale. "If something's going on, I can help." It surprised him how much he wanted to help her.

She rolled her eyes. "Listen, I appreciate the concern, but we just met. That does bring up the topic of our earlier kiss: I think we should just forget our bonding moments earlier."

He studied her body language instead of her words. He sensed before she moved that her head would snap up. The pulse fluttered in her neck, and he could hear the quickening of her heart.

Not exactly a fair advantage, but one he'd take anyway. "Is that what you want?" he murmured, wondering if she'd deny the attraction between them.

She met his gaze, hers seeking. "It's the right move."

Interesting that she'd said move, like they were pieces on

a chessboard. "Is this a game to you?" Irritation filled him that she saw him so narrowly.

"No game." She swallowed, her fragile throat moving.

Right. Just a huge risk, and one he couldn't take. Even so, he ran a knuckle down the side of her face, the caress having become one of his favorites. For the first time in his life, he wished he didn't have a mission about to take him somewhere else.

She closed her eyes, leaning into the touch.

Tension centered low in his belly, and he stepped into her space. Grasping her chin, he leaned in and brushed her lips with his, keeping the moment light when all he wanted to do was strip her bare and feast for hours. "You're a sweetheart, Laney Jacobs."

"No, I'm not." She leaned back and smiled, the sparkle back in her eyes.

He'd done that. One kiss, and he'd made her sparkle. He could get used to this.

Laney made herself lean away from sure comfort. Yeah, she wanted to get lost in the ex-marine. But right now, she had a bar to run. "We need to get back inside and close down."

"Good point. Then maybe we should talk." Matt released her chin.

"About what?"

"Us. This. Tonight." His inscrutable gaze failed to give her an inkling of what he was thinking.

"Okay." She really wanted to get inside his head.

He turned toward the door and immediately stepped to the side as two women stumbled out.

Laney frowned at women who usually held their liquor better. Well, when Matt wasn't drinking with them. "How much did you two drink?"

Claire hiccupped. "Not much. Plus, tomorrow is a light day.

I only need to monitor a German shepherd that might go into labor." She squinted up at Matt. "You like dogs?"

"Love 'em." Matt scratched his head. "I'm not sure you two should be driving."

"We're fine," Betty said, marching down the steps toward her SUV. "I only had a couple."

"As an accountant, you should probably count better," Claire snorted, wobbling across the alley to fall into the backseat and lie down.

Betty hopped into her car, slammed the door, and rolled down the window. "Claire, get your butt up front." She twisted the ignition.

Nothing happened.

She hit the steering wheel, focusing out the window. "My car is broken."

Matt glanced down at Laney. "We can't let them drive."

"No kidding." Laney rubbed her nose. "Betty? Why don't you come back in, and I'll take you home?"

"But my car is broken," the accountant wailed.

Matt strode toward the car. "Pop the hood."

Laney followed in his wake. Not only did he have the body of a god, the fighting skills of an ancient warrior, and the face of an angel, but the guy could fix cars? "Who the hell are you?" she muttered.

He either didn't hear her, or he chose to ignore her comment. Regardless, after two seconds of peering under the hood, he twisted some knob to the left. "Try again."

The engine roared to life, and he gently shut the hood. "You had a loose cap. No big deal. But you're not driving home." Long strides had him opening the driver's door.

Oh, he was not taking two intoxicated women home. Laney rushed over and clutched his arm. "I'm taking them. Please go finish busing tables. We close in a few minutes."

Betty scooted over to the passenger seat, a goofy smile on her patrician face. "We want him to drive us."

"Yeah," Claire chirped from the backseat. "We want the handsome bartender taking us home. He makes us feel safe."

Frustration roared through Laney at Matt's amused grin. "Fine." She leaned up and put on her most fierce expression. "You come right back. I'm liable for anything you do, Prince Charming."

He stretched into the seat and shut the door before leaning out the window. "You're cute when you're territorial, boss. Very cute." A quick glance around the quiet alley had him focusing back on her. "Go back inside before I leave." At her raised eyebrow, he smoothly added, "Please."

"That was still an order," she muttered, pivoting on her heel and stomping up the stairs and inside where she took a deep breath and leaned against the door. Worse yet, he'd been correct. She had been feeling territorial.

Irritation flicked like ashes beneath her skin at her own weakness. She had no claim to Matt, no matter how much she liked him. How much she wanted him. Years ago she'd learned that fantasies were just that, and reality was much darker. She lived in the real world.

Sexy, dangerous soldiers didn't settle down and fix everything for somebody like her. Period.

As a cautious woman, she rarely made mistakes. But when she made them, they were monumental...and instinct whispered giving Matt Dean a second chance and allowing him to stay was going to be a whopper. Not only to her life, but to her heart.

The man called to her on a primal, feminine level. His strength, his loneliness, his over-the-top commanding attitude. She had to figure out a way to maintain space between them.

She'd been hiding from her last mistake for years. Something told her she'd never be able to hide from Matt, and she thanked whatever gods existed he wasn't after her. The man was a hunter, one who had shown no mercy when taking down the two drunk men in the bar the other night—and if he ever had cause to hunt her...he'd find her.

Betty eyed Matt from the passenger seat, her lips pursed, her eyes bright, and her curly hair a tangled mess. Claire sang an old Bon Jovi song from the backseat, her heels pressed against the roof of the SUV. All of a sudden, Betty gasped and sucked in air.

"I'm going to be sick," she said.

Matt pressed harder on the gas pedal. "Let's get you home first." Excellent. He needed to get the singing woman alone, anyway.

"Good idea." Betty plastered a hand against her stomach and pointed down the road. "Go into the River Creek subdivision, and I'm the fifth house on the right."

Within a couple of minutes, he'd maneuvered the vehicle into the driveway of a tidy white ranch-style house. Betty jumped out of the car and made it to a row of hydrangeas before throwing up. Apparently she'd eaten a salad for dinner. Finally, she turned and waved. She scaled three steps up the porch until tripping and landing in what looked like shrubs.

Damn it. He could just leave her there. But his sister-in-law was an accountant, a lightweight drunk, and he'd kill anybody who left her floundering in shrubs. He may not understand women, or people who had no regard for their own safety, but he didn't want to be a guy who left a woman helpless. So he put the car in park and glanced over his shoulder at the woman now singing "Living on a Prayer."

"I'll be right back."

She stomped her feet on the roof in time with her off-key song.

How the hell had he ended up in this mess? He stepped out of the vehicle and shook his head. Give him two drunk farmers who wanted to fight any day. Reaching the struggling accountant, he grabbed her under the armpits and picked her up, walked to the front door, and set her against it. "Keys?"

She handed him a key from her pocket. He opened the door and moved to assist her, but she stumbled against him, her palms spreading along his abs.

Tilting her head back, she gasped. "Are those real? I mean, *really* real?" She hiccupped and yanked up his shirt, ducking her face to his stomach. "Oh my. Wow." Her fingers dug into his ribs, and her breath brushed his skin. "Those abs should be on television. Or billboards. Or me." Her teeth snapped closed on his flesh.

Good God. The woman had bitten him. He jumped back, sending them both sprawling into the shrubs. Stems cracked as his weight landed, plunging him to the ground. Needles dug into his neck. "You're fucking kidding me," he muttered, reaching with one hand for the porch railing and one for the giggling woman.

A headache roared front and center. Frustration dried up his mouth.

He was one of the most dangerous men ever created by people who *studied* danger. If his brothers could see him now, they'd never obey another one of his orders. Ever. He hauled himself up, tossed the accountant over his shoulder, and stalked back up the steps.

She shoved her hands into his back pockets and dug in her nails, her jeans-clad legs happily swinging. "Here's my card."

He flipped her over, set her gently inside the front door, and then closed it. "Lock the door."

Once the bolt slipped into place, he turned and headed back to the SUV, yanking needles and shrubbery out of his hair. Upon reaching the vehicle, he hit reverse to the road as Claire sang "Runaway."

Once out of the subdivision, he cleared his throat. "Claire? I don't know where you live."

Her feet struck the window. Humming, she quickly popped up by his head.

Jesus. Only unnatural reflexes kept him from swerving. "Your home?"

She dove headfirst into the front seat. Her elbow nailed him in the ear, and he did swerve. Hell. Controlling the wheel with one hand, he settled Claire into the passenger seat as gently as possible.

Her boots hit the console as she wiggled into the seat and blew hair off her face. "I live in the same subdivision as Betty." Frowning, Claire looked around the car. "Where's Betty?"

Matt drew in a slow breath. "You live in the subdivision we just left?"

Claire rubbed her eyes. "Yeah, I guess. Two streets over from Betty." She turned toward him. "Did you get attacked by a tree?"

No. A horny, drunk accountant. He flipped a U-turn and drove back into the subdivision. "Which house?"

"Pebble Street, the third house on the left." A lopsided grin twisted Claire's lips. "You sure are pretty."

Whether he liked it or not, that was his cue. He returned the smile. "How long have you been a vet?"

"Assistant. Veterinarian assistant." She wiggled her feet on the dash. "About eight years, I guess. I mean, I really like animals, so I'm good at it. But I wouldn't want to do all the schooling . . . or have to actually do surgeries. I can hand over implements, but that's all."

"You didn't go to college?"

"Nope." She eyed him again. "Really pretty. Like on those romance novel covers." She slapped a hand over her mouth. "Not that I read those. I mean, okay, I read those . . . Don't tell. They can't know."

Heat flared down his back, and his instincts roared to life. "I won't tell," he lowered his voice to a conspirator's tone. "But...who can't I tell?" While he didn't think the commander would give a shit if his surgeons read books, maybe Claire felt differently. "Are you hiding from *them* in Charmed?"

"Kind of." She lifted a shoulder and turned to stare out the window.

If Claire was the woman he hunted, this was probably his only chance to get her to open up. A hiding woman didn't drink like this often. He pulled into the driveway in front of a two-story brick house. "Tell me more, Claire."

She swallowed and glanced back at him. "Do you want to come in?"

No. Absolutely not. He wanted to go home, get the shrubbery needles out of his skin, and take a shower. "I'd love to come in."

She clapped her hands together and scrambled for the door handle. The woman was still fumbling by the time he'd crossed around the SUV to open her door. She fell out, and he caught her before she hit the cement. Broad and bulky, she regained her balance.

"Um, thanks." She shook her head. "Come inside." Throwing back her shoulders, she led the way across the driveway, up the steps, until she opened the door.

He stopped cold on the front porch. "Your door isn't locked?"

"Nope." She glanced around the quiet neighborhood. "Are you gonna come in or just stand on my porch? I do, ah, you know."

"Do what?"

"Have a reputation and all of that. You know."

He had no freakin' clue. Scratching his head, he crossed the threshold and allowed her to shut the door. "Why don't you lock your door?" There was no way in hell somebody on the run from the commander and his colleagues would leave their door unlocked. No way.

She sniffed. "Habit. I mean, where I grew up, we didn't even have locks." Boots hit the wall as she kicked them off and fell into an overstuffed chair. "Sit."

He scanned the room. Plush, comfortable furniture, girly knickknacks, and pictures of animals all around. "Where did you grow up?" He slipped around and sat on the sofa, facing her.

"You'll think it's weird."

If she had any clue where he'd grown up, she wouldn't make such a statement. "Never. Come on, tell me." He lowered his voice to cajoling.

She blinked. Twice. "The Chipperanti Commune in Western Virginia."

His shoulders relaxed as a realization hit. That explained why she was so far off the grid. "You grew up in a commune?"

"Yeah. I love my family, I really do, but I wanted television and cars and stuff." She sank into the deep chair. "You know?"

"Sure." This was not the cold-blooded doctor he needed to find. But he had to ask. "Are you in danger? I mean, are they hunting you?" Though he doubted it, considering the unlocked door.

She wrinkled her forehead. "Oh no. Never. I could go home in a second. But sometimes, I feel guilty." Her words slurred at the end, and her eyes fluttered closed.

Slowly, he exhaled. Frankly, he was glad it wasn't Claire. The slightly snoring drunk seemed like a kind soul. He stood, unfolded an afghan to gently place over her, and slipped out the door, after engaging the lock.

He loped back to the car with a sigh. One suspect cleared. Two more to go.

CHAPTER
7

L ANEY SET UP the shot glasses and tried to cool her temper. While this wasn't the first time a bouncer had driven home inebriated customers, this was the first time the bouncer was sexy as hell ... and had kissed her. She wanted to be the one he was taking home—to his bed. Yet he was out with two other women.

She shouldn't care.

She didn't want to care.

She cared.

Matt Dean sure hadn't wasted any time in moving on ... if he had moved on. Maybe the guy was as sweet and protective as he seemed and taking drunken women home was a kind gesture.

Yeah, right.

Tipping back her head, she downed the tequila. Her second shot. She'd finished busing the tables and wiping down the bar before sending Smitty home.

Now she was drinking.

Matt had been gone for over an hour. What if he didn't come back?

She had always approached romance with a logical mind ... and she'd never gotten this upset about a man. Ever.

She'd had her first boyfriend in college, and even then, she'd liked the guy enough to hang out with him. Plus, she'd been curious about sex.

But her heart had never quite been involved.

Her heart needed to remain closed even now. No matter how appealing Matt could be.

As if her imagination had conjured him, he swept inside, a massive man wearing a scowl. Slamming keys across the bar, he growled, "You get to exchange the car tomorrow."

She took a deep breath. "Why are you so late?"

"Mainly? Your friend's treads are worn, and her spare sucks."

"You got a flat tire?" Laney narrowed her eyes.

"Yes. I did." He rubbed a purple mark on his hand. "I changed it after dropping the unsecured spare on my hand."

Relief lifted her lips as she eyed the long scratch along his arm. "Problems?"

He reached for the filled shot glass. "Yeah. Problems."

"Is that why you're wearing a tree in your hair and are scratched?"

"Shrubs. I was dumped into shrubs by an accountant." He downed the liquor and held out his glass for more. "According to your friends, I have great abs and am really pretty."

She snorted and poured them each another shot. While she liked those two women, they probably couldn't be considered friends. Friends were something she didn't quite do. Since she'd spent so much time avoiding friends as a child, she'd never quite learned how to make many. "Well, I can attest that you are both pretty and blessed with great abs."

The moment heated, as did his eyes. "Is that a fact?"

His voice should be labeled and sold with how fast his tone licked through her body. "That's not exactly a matter of opinion, so yes, it's a fact."

"Well, you've seen mine..."

Tempting. God, he was tempting. But self-preservation

was a skill, and she'd spent years honing it. "I thought we agreed to keep things professional between us."

"I've agreed to no such thing." He rubbed his chin and took another shot. "Though I do need to admit, considering I'm passing through town, temporary is best." The glass clanked when he set it down.

Warmth spilled through her followed by surprise at how tempted she was to accept. The man was correct in that temporary was probably good for her. "I'm considering it." Good God, had she actually just said those words? "But, well, there has to be something. Tell me something you either don't want to tell, or you've never told anybody."

"What is this, a slumber party?" A wry grin took the sting out of his words. "You go first."

When was the last time she'd trusted somebody with the full truth? Never, really. But something about Matt's level gaze inspired confidence, and she was so damn tired of holding everything inside. Some days she feared she'd just burst. "Smitty thinks I'm going to be arrested for how I came up with the funds for my bar."

Matt lifted his chin. "God. Tell me you're a bank robber."

She chuckled and tried to enjoy the moment. Sometimes there were so many layers upon layers of secrets she became lost. "Sorry to disappoint, but, ah, no. The money for this bar came from a dubious source."

The crestfallen expression in Matt's face lightened her mood. "I was hoping for a dramatic bank robbery, or at least a classic bait and switch."

"No. I mean, I borrowed from somebody I shouldn't have." She hated telling him only half the story. "I shared with you…"

He sighed, those incredible gray eyes darkening to slate. "I don't plan to live past the age of thirty." Surprise elevated his eyebrows as if he hadn't meant to confess.

The moment held truth, and she breathed it in. After his time in the service, had he given up? "How close are you?"

"About six weeks."

"It seems like a short time to give up, Mattie."

His head jerked back, and his eyes narrowed. Emotion flashed across the hard angles of his face. "Very few people in the world call me that."

She'd put no conscious thought into it. Yet the intensity pouring off the soldier caught her breath in her throat as a thrill swept through her. "Oh, ah, I'm sorry."

"Don't be." An unidentifiable light entered his eyes. The air in the room thickened. "I like my nickname on your lips."

The man issued one hell of an innuendo. Need flooded through her, softening her thighs. "This is a bad idea."

"I know." His direct gaze held blatant male hunger.

She liked that he didn't pretend to misunderstand her train of thought. Nobody had ever studied her so closely. A quivering warmth started beneath her breasts and spread down to her abdomen. So she poured them another shot. The night was hazing, and she needed to get out of her head. "Why aren't you going to live long?"

He tipped back the glass, muscled neck moving as he drank. Her toes curled in response. The glass clanked as he set it down. "I can't reveal all of my secrets in one night, darlin'."

"That's fair." She sipped hers, and her eyes teared from the potent brew. The shot heated her desire into lava. "Um, are you dying of something contagious?"

"No. I promise, it's nothing you can catch."

"What is it?" Curiosity battled with the need roaring through her.

He shook his head. "Let's just say the wrong people are after me."

She could relate to that. Thank goodness he was physically healthy. "I'm sorry. That's why you're a loner?"

"Yeah. I rarely make connections, but when I do, they mean something."

Sweet and probably a line. But sweet nonetheless. Her heart thumped. Hard. "How long has it been for you?"

His grin promised sin. "Too long. Way too long. You?"

"Quite a while." They weren't seriously talking about this, were they? She pressed her legs together and fought a groan of need.

"So, the pharmacist?"

"No way." She shuddered. "Not even close." A peck on the cheek at the end of the boring date was all she'd allowed. "I wish I could say differently, but temporary works for me right now."

"Temporary is all I have."

"I understand." She had her own ghosts haunting her, and she couldn't commit herself to anybody right now, and probably not ever. So she nodded and reached for the bottle, only to have him capture her hand and press it against the bar. His palm heated her skin and held with just enough pressure to show his impressive strength.

He leaned in. "I'm not one of the good guys, baby, but I'd prefer you somewhat in control of your faculties if this is going where I think it is."

Her gaze dropped to his full lips. "You're closer to a good guy than you believe."

For answer, he curled his free hand around her neck and drew her over the bar. "Don't look for traits I don't have. I know exactly who I am."

"Who are you?" she whispered.

"The guy who's going to have you screaming his name within the next hour." His lips took hers.

Raw fire burst through her so quickly the ground shifted beneath her feet. Heat zipped along her nerve endings, rippling fire into her veins and softening her sex. Her eyelids fluttered shut as she fell into the storm.

He angled his mouth more firmly over hers, his tongue sweeping inside. The hand at her nape tightened, the fingers long and strong.

Demanding.

The kiss was many things...but mostly demanding.

She'd known. Instinct had whispered he was a force of his own, an uncontainable male.

For the first time in her life, she wanted to get lost. Taken over.

Maybe because she was ready...most likely because that's the only way she could get Matt Dean.

And she'd never wanted anyone more.

Giving in to her own needs, she wandered her hands over his broad shoulders as his mouth worked hers.

With a low growl, he leaned down and wrapped an arm around her waist, smoothly lifting. Her knees hit the top of the bar, and she leaned into his strength.

He released her neck and skimmed both hands around to cup her ass. Heat rippled along her nerve endings.

Slowly, he drew back. His eyes had turned the color of storm clouds in a face stamped even harder than normal with desire. His hands flexed. "Are you sure?"

Oh, this was definitely a mistake. No question. She could barely breathe. "I'm sure."

A mere second later she was cradled in strong arms, being swept from the bar. "Man, you're fast," she breathed.

His cheek creased. "I'm hoping to revise your opinion on that score."

Humor bubbled up, giving her a brief reprieve from the painful desire, which still ebbed right beneath the surface. "Your place or mine?"

"I like your bed." His chest shifted nicely against her as he moved. "The colors are sensual and gave me ideas right off the bat."

She moved her hand up his chest to caress the hard cords in his neck. Only tough guys had necks like this. "What kind of ideas?" Was that her? Playing the flirt? Or perhaps not. She really wanted to know what kind of ideas a man like

Matt had. The need to be inside his head, inside his heart, flashed warning through her desire.

His stride hitched as he maneuvered the steps. "Some you probably wouldn't like."

"You have no idea what I like."

"No, but I know the kind of woman you are." He tucked his nose in her hair and inhaled. "Soft and sweet. You need to understand, I haven't known much of soft or sweet in my life. I don't want to hurt you."

Her heart thumped at such uncertainty from a guy who'd knocked her into oblivion with one kiss. "You should know, I'm neither soft nor sweet."

"Ah, baby. You're both." He dipped his head to take her lips again.

He turned the knob as they arrived at her door, and he broke the kiss. "Keys?"

Courage somehow filled her. "My back pocket."

She expected him to reach under her and should've known he'd do the opposite. The air moved, and she found herself upside down over an incredibly hard shoulder. Her ribs instantly protested.

He coasted his hand up the back of her thigh, igniting intrigue on the way until he drew the keys free. She plunged her hands into his back pockets and flexed her fingers on hard muscle. Her head swam. Her fingers dragged on something smooth, and she drew out…a business card. "Um, Matt?"

"Yeah?" he asked as he unlocked the door.

"Why do I think I'm not the only woman who's been over your shoulder tonight?"

The world tilted, and she regained her footing, facing him.

He grinned. "You're the only woman who matters."

Words like that from a man like this shouldn't make her heart leap against her ribs. But even so, flutters cascaded along her abdomen. "What exactly happened when you drove my patrons home?"

He reached behind her to shut and lock the door. "Until a few minutes ago, my night sucked and included shrubbery, Jon Bon Jovi, and drunken women I don't want."

She licked her lips. "And now?"

He focused totally and absolutely on her, and the world silenced. "A world of possibilities and a woman I've never wanted more."

Desire had claws. "You overwhelm me."

He threaded his hand through her hair. "You scare the hell out of me."

She blinked even as her thighs dampened. "How so?"

"I've lived a dark life, and you're all light. I'd break my own arm before I'd hurt you."

The man might be smart as hell, but he had her wrong. For the briefest of seconds, she wished she could be who he thought she was. "It's not going to happen—it can't—so don't freak out... but you'd be an easy man to love."

His upper lip twisted. "You need to read people better."

If he had any clue. "You might be right." But her heart secretly tried to hold him tight, to keep him. Years from now, she'd remember this night... She'd remember him. Even so, she tugged his shirt free of his jeans and ran her hands up those incredible abs. "Rumor has it these are classic." Of course, she'd seen them for herself, and they were beyond real. So she traced them with her fingers, gratified when his muscles shifted.

"Your bedroom."

It was an order she'd be happy to obey. But something kept her still. Defying him, she drew his shirt over his head, pleased when he ducked his chin to assist. Leaning forward, she kissed the tattoo above his heart. *Freedom.* He dug both hands into her hair.

She nipped his skin, biting hard enough it had to sting.

Drawing back her head, he lowered his face toward hers. "I like you playing, and I like you brave, but don't think for a second you're directing this."

Her eyebrow rose in challenge, feminine intrigue sweeping through her. "Prove it."

Dangerous words to say to such a man. But why not?

His smile showed both amusement and the confidence of a predator. "With pleasure." With superfast reflexes, he twirled her around to face the couch. Yanking her shirt over her head, he caged her with his body. Heated breath brushed her ear. "You ever begged, baby?"

"Never." She pressed back into the hard length of his erection. "Why? Are you planning to beg?" Yeah, she was pushing him. Something propelled her face-first into danger... Sometimes the reward was worth the risk.

Nimble fingers flicked open her bra. "If I were ever to beg, you'd be worth it." Calloused hands caressed her breasts. "But I think you're a woman who needs to be taken...and hard."

The words exploded through her veins, while the sentiment landed in her stomach with a fireball of desire. "You think you're up to the task?"

For answer, he pressed his impossibly hard erection against her buttocks. "You tell me." Those dangerous lips dropped to wander along the shell of her ear at the same time he tweaked both nipples, tugging strong enough to send electrical sparks to her clit.

As if he knew, he slipped one hand beneath the waistband of her jeans, caressing down tortuously slow, to press inside her panties.

Her body reacted without conscious thought, her butt pressing into his groin.

"Spread your legs," he whispered into her ear, the crass suggestion nearly throwing her into an early orgasm.

"I, ah..."

His other hand tethered in her hair and tugged her head to the side. Hot and firm, his lips traced her jugular until he spoke against her skin. "I believe the words were clear. Spread. Your. Legs."

A long shiver shook her body from the dominant tone. She wanted to refuse, to challenge him...but she wanted to continue far more. So she slid her feet farther apart.

"Good girl." She was rewarded by him delving deeper and slipping one finger inside her. Her eyes fluttered shut again at the exquisite sensation. So much need shot through her she would've swayed had he not caged her from behind. He started to play, exploring her, his thumb pressing against her clit. An unwilling whimper rippled up her throat.

He bent over her, his mouth at her ear. "That's a lovely sound, one just for me, and I will hear it again."

"Please, Matt..."

"You're right. I like that even better." He removed his hand and swung her around. "Take off your clothes."

She lifted her chin. "Take off yours."

He seized her hand and pressed her palm against the hard bulge vibrating in his jeans. "Why don't *you* take them off?"

He filled her palm with heat and promise. Swallowing loudly, she felt along his length. The sound he made defied description, yet infused her with power. So she released his zipper and tugged his pants down his muscled legs. Seconds later, he'd kicked off his boots and jeans after retrieving a condom from his front pocket.

"So, commando, huh?" she asked, her voice beyond husky.

His eyes somehow darkening more, he reached for the clasp of her jeans. They disappeared soon after.

Once she was fully nude, reality began to return to her brain.

"No." He pressed her against the couch, his hard length sliding along hers. "No thinking."

It was too late for thinking...too late for caution. So she stretched up on her tiptoes, manacled his shoulder-length hair, and yanked his lips down to hers.

He returned the kiss, taking over, his mouth destroying hers. His tongue stroked hers, and she moaned, tipping her head to take him deeper, to give more. A new desire, dark and with an edge, burned through her.

Finally, he lifted his head. "Bedroom. Now."

Now, that was an idea she could get behind. She reached forward to take his hand only to have him lift her once again and stride through the apartment to the bedroom. She expected a smooth lying down...and yelped when he tossed her across the room to bounce on the plush bedspread. Her laugh was genuine and filled with fun.

Who was this guy?

His smile warmed his face with amusement. "Your laugh both warms and arouses me."

Don't be sweet. Sexy, she could handle. Well, probably. Sweet? Not a chance. "You're too far away."

Most men were awkward walking naked. Not Matt. All male, all predator, he prowled forward with grace like the primal animal she suspected him to be. Hell. The animal she hoped he would be.

The entire time, he kept his gaze on hers. Confident, masculine, dangerous. Even relaxed and playing, an edge lived in him she hadn't seen for quite a while. If ever.

Was it happenstance he'd arrived in Charmed, Idaho? For the first time, she wondered.

Then he was on her.

CHAPTER
8

H E NEEDED TO touch her more than he needed to breathe. For years, when his subconscious had relaxed, he'd dreamed about love, about peace. Those fantasies didn't come close to the reality with Laney. She was kind, she was sweet...and for the night, she was his.

As a person, as a woman, she was breakable, and he needed to be careful.

He'd finish himself before he broke her.

So he settled over her and wanted nothing more than to lose himself in her. All of her.

He maneuvered up her body. The scent of woman and vanilla filtered through his senses and landed around his heart. Hard and absolute.

He'd trained to seduce women until he hated them as much as himself, and the idea of somebody good, of somebody kind, was a temptation he'd never resist. Add in courage and a lonely heart, and he couldn't turn away from this amazing woman.

Plus, he needed to taste her. Needed to know her.

So he slid up and angled his mouth over hers, trying to convey more than he'd ever be able to say. The words weren't his to give.

Manacling her hip, he plunged inside her with one strong stroke.

Her eyes widened, and she gasped.

He kissed her again, taking her under, waiting for her body to accustom itself to his size. Slowly, her muscles relaxed, and her internal walls gripped him with so much power it was all he could do to remain still.

He might quite happily stay joined with her forever. He reveled in the moment, in being so in tune with her. No dark thoughts existed for him when he was inside her. No danger, no despair. Only pleasure.

She took a deep breath, a tumultuous grin teasing her lips. Her eyes softened, and she reached around to skim her palms against his lower back, her fingers along his ribs. "This is nice."

"What is?" His biceps vibrated as he kept himself in check.

"You. Being inside me. Joined."

For the first time, he saw the real woman behind the brave and giving bartender. Vulnerable and open.

He wasn't strong enough to protect himself from such femininity, and he wasn't cruel enough to shut her down. It was a mistake they'd both probably pay for, but for the moment, he didn't care. He needed her. Even more, he got the feeling she needed him.

So he slid out and back in, losing himself in the sensation of heaven. Tight and hot, she gripped him like she'd never let him go.

For one moment, in one woman, he found home.

She arched against him and whispered his name.

The sound of her soft voice would stay with him. Through whatever the future held, he'd carry the moment. This woman should be savored, and there was no way he could keep her at arm's length. She'd slid right into his heart, and instinct told him she'd always live there. For the short time he had left, she'd be with him. Even if he moved across the world from her.

"Faster," she breathed.

He fought the demand, wanting to stay with the bliss.

But she grabbed his ass and squeezed.

His control snapped. Electricity danced in his balls. Gripping her, he began to pound...hot, fast, with just enough pressure to have her moaning beneath him. She met him thrust for thrust, her sighs mixing with his groans.

A white-hot burst of pleasure roared through him, and he spread her legs wider. Keeping her open for him. Tight. Wet. Hot. She was everything he could've dreamed. He lifted her so she could take more of him, so she could take all of him.

Suddenly, she tightened like a bow that had been struck, cried his name, and exploded around him.

The sensation was too much to resist. His heart exploded in unison with her body. He thrust harder, unerringly hitting her G-spot, prolonging her orgasm. As soon as she went limp beneath him, he let himself go.

Lava ripped down his spine to spark his balls on fire, and he came like a teenager. Hard, fast, and complete. The release blinded him, coursing through him, leaving him empty and panting. The moment left his legs trembling.

Finally, he lowered his forehead to hers. "You're perfect."

"Mmmm." She stretched against him like a lazy cat.

Her satisfaction filled him with pride. Sure, he'd slept with women. Either to get off or to gain information, and they'd both been satisfied. For the first time, he felt a sense of pride in supplying the satisfaction. Because it mattered, and this woman mattered.

He grinned at her whimper when he pulled out and disposed of the condom. "Are you all right?"

"Perfect." Almost naturally, she curled right into him. Seconds later, her breathing deepened.

Amusement filtered through him. She'd fallen right asleep. "Isn't that my role?" he whispered into the darkness.

For answer, she turned around and pressed her butt into his groin.

He hardened instantly but slipped an arm around her waist to tuck her tight. Holding her felt like something good, something he couldn't identify.

Sure, he'd screwed up. His plans to possibly seduce the other two women for information had just gone up in flames because he wouldn't hurt Laney. Not like that. So he'd have to think of another approach.

Contentment filtered through him followed by unease. Sex was one thing, but he was feeling something for this woman. He'd told her it was temporary, but for the first time ever, the thought tasted sour. Laney was a keeper. With his life, did he deserve a keeper? Most likely not. The reality sliced into his heart with the odd comfort of a familiar pain.

He slowed his breathing and heart rate in order to catch some sleep. With Laney in his arms, his body relaxed beyond the norm. Even so, his senses tuned in to the world around them in order to keep her safe.

The commander could never learn about Laney...nor could Emery. For years, Matt and Emery had battled out rank and superiority. Matt cared nothing about rank or pleasing the commander, but every time he won, he gained something for his family. A sense of safety for his brothers.

Emery didn't play fair...He never had. He'd broken Shane's arm when the kid was only eight, and Matt had instantly retaliated by breaking Emery's wrist. A year later, Emery had broken Jory's femur, and a femur injury often got a cadet removed from the facility.

While strategy dictated Matt go after Emery's youngest brothers, he couldn't do it. Couldn't go after kids smaller than he and hurt them.

But he'd hurt Emery. Badly.

Once recovered, Emery left the Gray brothers alone. As he trained and prepared, there was no question in Matt's mind someday they'd fight again. This time to the death.

News had reached Matt recently when Shane's wife had been captured by the commander that Emery was working with him.

God, when Josie had been taken, Shane had been beyond fierce.

As Matt held Laney, unease rippled through him.

He'd studied psychology, and he understood people. More important, he understood himself. As a personality type, he was a protector…probably because he was the oldest, and if he screwed up, people he loved died. From day one, he'd been a fierce and deadly protector of his brothers. He'd known. He'd known without a doubt if he ever found a woman to love, if he was ever weak enough to fall, he'd be caught forever. He'd live for her, and he'd die for her. God help the woman if she didn't understand him. God help them both.

Laney stretched awake, caught short by an iron band around her stomach. Her eyes flashed open. Oh God. A male body, hard as steel, cradled her from behind.

Matt Dean. No question, that body belonged to Matt Dean. She closed her eyes, and images from the previous night paraded through her mind. Five times. She'd orgasmed five times.

Matt had come three times.

Clearly, she'd won.

She snorted, although this wasn't funny. This was so far from funny she couldn't breathe. So she smiled.

The sex had been incredible.

Her heart thumped. Gosh darn it. Her heart needed to get a grip. Matt was dangerous, and he was temporary. No heart palpitations involved. Plus, it wasn't like she'd been completely honest with the guy.

She'd let him in—too much. Not only into her heart, but into her life. He couldn't stay, and she couldn't reveal herself in such a way again. Even so, the need to burrow closer to him, to really know him, ached within her.

His palm flattened against her abdomen.

Her breath caught.

"You're thinking awfully hard there," he rumbled, his voice rough with sleep.

She tried to cool her already heating libido. "You know. Morning-after stuff."

"Hmmm. Me, too." He maneuvered farther down and over her mound, one finger entering her. "Mainly, I'm thinking about how to best use the morning. Forget the stuff."

She wanted to say no, but the sound came out as more of a sigh.

His head dipped down, and his breath brushed her ear. "You know I like your legs open, darlin'."

God. The simple words from the deep voice with just enough of an order instantly made her wet. "I don't take orders from you." Yeah. The breathlessness of her voice may have ruined her defiance.

His index finger slid out and slowly circled her clit. "Is that a fact?"

Heat washed under her skin to pinpoint right where he played. The fierce line of his cock pulsed against her butt. "What are you, a machine?" she mumbled.

"Nope. Flesh-and-blood man. You can tell from the nail marks you left in my back," he murmured, continuing to torture her.

Unfortunately, they'd blend in with the rest of the old wounds on his back. She hadn't looked, but during the night, her touch had felt several healed bullet, knife, and other odd scars. As a soldier, he'd seen his share of battles.

He sank sharp teeth into the shell of her ear. "Give me one more, baby."

She turned into him and flattened her palms against his chest, careful to avoid the stitched wound, even though it had healed surprisingly fast. Maybe he hadn't been as injured as she'd thought. "Come with me."

"Fair enough." He rolled her onto her back and thrust inside her.

Her breath caught at the painful pleasure. Her body felt oddly relaxed and well used. They'd only had one condom, and after a frank discussion regarding recent medical check-ups for them both, Laney had admitted she was on the pill. Skin on skin had felt amazing. Sure, she shouldn't have trusted a guy she just met, but she did. Somehow, she did trust him.

He frowned and brushed hair off her forehead. "Are you sore?"

Hell yes, she was sore. The guy was hung like a stegosaurus. "I'm fine."

His eyes narrowed. "Hmmm." He withdrew, and his frown deepened as she winced. "I was too rough."

"You were amazing." Which was the absolute truth. The man started to glide down. "Where do you think you're going?"

His smile promised pleasure. "I can't leave you like this." Inching down her body, he kissed her navel and licked farther down. "I'll make it quick." And he did. He'd learned her body too well the night before.

In fact, somehow he'd been able to anticipate her every move, her every need. The man was immensely talented.

One finger stretched her as his rough tongue scraped her clit. Waves of pleasure rippled through her, and she rode out the orgasm, her eyelids fluttering shut. She came down with a soft whimper. "I think you killed me."

He nipped her thigh. "A guy likes to try. What's on your agenda today?"

She glanced at the clock. "I need to make more soup for

the testers. But, ah, what about you?" The guy still had a raging hard-on.

He rested his chin on her leg, gray eyes focusing on her. "I'm good and hoping we can do this again."

Even after the crazy night, her face heated. "Um, me, too."

Pleasure curved his lips. "You're blushing. I've kissed every inch of you, and you're still blushing."

"Yeah, well, I don't do one-night stands. Ever." While she only did temporary, she rarely involved other people. Casual sex didn't appeal much to her. She didn't want to know about him...She really didn't.

"You're special, Laney. Very."

How did he know just what to say? "So are you." In a different world, maybe they might have meant something to each other. "What's your plan today?"

He exhaled. "I thought I'd head to the family clinic and have a doctor take out these stitches."

Good idea. It was amazing the guy hadn't caught an infection already. She eyed the perfectly stitched fishing line across his chest. "You do good work, though."

"Thanks." He wiggled his eyebrows and pushed off the bed.

She chuckled. "That's not what I meant."

"Hmmm." He stood up, a naked modern-day warrior, scarred and magnificent. "I'll have to convince you later tonight."

"I think we've already run the gamut of possibilities."

His eyes darkened, and a wicked grin creased his cheek. "Oh, baby, we've barely started."

CHAPTER
9

MATT HELD HIMSELF still on the orange chair in the clinic's waiting room, hoping the cheap plastic would hold his weight. Shutting his eyes, he leaned his head back against the cedar-grooved wall. The receptionist's heartbeat alternated between slowing down and speeding up every time she glanced his way. He'd had to pour on the charm to get her to open up about which family practitioner was on duty and had finally caught a break. The doctor he needed to see, Millicent Vengas, was on duty and would see him soon.

His mind ran over the night with Laney. It had been perfect until the morning; then she'd withdrawn. No doubt the emotions swamping him had attacked her as well.

He hadn't been sure how to reassure her, considering he was leaving town as soon as he captured the doctor.

So he'd left, telling Laney he was heading to the doctor to get the stitches removed. Relief had filled her pretty eyes. So much so that even now, grumpiness rumbled through him.

He turned his attention back to the moment.

Several heartbeats echoed through the building, some torturously slow, probably from drugs. If he were Shane, he'd probably be able to guess at the drugs. Shane had the best hearing of them all.

Matt's gift lay in discerning movement before it happened. Maybe he read muscle movement, maybe he felt the slightest of air move. He didn't know, and he'd never trusted the people who might've helped him understand it. The bastards who'd created him.

Right now, they tracked him, probably hoping they could force him to do their dirty work some more. If he didn't eventually fall in line, they'd kill him. They'd also destroy anybody who knew about the program; anybody he'd become close with.

Sleeping with Laney had been a mistake. For one thing, she wasn't the type of woman a guy loved and left. She was one to be loved and tucked close. Even if he wasn't slated to die in less than two months, his past would always chase him.

Even one night with him might slap a bull's-eye on her smooth forehead.

He couldn't get her killed. The best course of action for them both would be for him to act the asshole and thank her for the quick lay. Piss her off, hurt her feelings, and get back to work.

No way in hell could he do it.

What a fucking mess he'd made of things. He'd kick his brothers' asses if they screwed up like this. In fact, if he confided in Nate, Nate would show up in town and punch him in the face. Not because he'd slept with a woman. Nate wouldn't give a shit about that.

He'd care that Matt was floundering. Completely confused by a woman he should be using as a cover. Matt couldn't even lie and say he was investigating her. The fact that she'd fainted when she'd seen blood proved there was no way in hell she used to be the mysterious doctor. Though owning a bar instead of being in the medical field would've been a good move. In his experience, people who cut into people seemed to need that type of power. The doctor he hunted still held a scalpel, he was sure.

High heels clicking down the hallway pulled his attention away from his failings. Centering himself, he listened to the rhythmic gait. The doctor was probably about five eight and one hundred sixty pounds. The door opened, and a woman glanced around, a file in her hands.

Yep. Right height and weight, and Shane had been correct about the blond hair. Taking in her color tone and bone structure, he figured she could pass for a natural blond.

She lifted her chin. "Mr. Dean?"

"Yes." He stretched to his feet.

Her gaze ran his length, appraising in a medical way.

He zipped back to times when Dr. Madison had studied him, and a ball of ice dropped into his gut. The doctor had been the closest thing he'd had to a mother, and she'd scared the hell out of him as a child. When he was a teenager, her gaze had warmed, and it had become worse. So much worse.

The bitch had made a move every chance she'd gotten. No wonder he very rarely trusted women. He'd ignored her until she'd propositioned Jory.

Matt had caught them in the clinic, Dr. Madison pressing against a terrified thirteen-year-old Jory. Matt had instantly ordered Jory outside before threatening Madison with a terrible death if she hit on one of his brothers ever again.

Her blue eyes had turned more calculating than afraid. She'd probably taken notes on the encounter afterward.

But she'd apparently believed him, because she'd stayed clear of his family from then on. Well, until she'd sicced her daughter on Nate.

Jerking himself back to the present, Matt plastered on a charming expression and moved toward the door.

Dr. Vengas motioned him inside. "We'll go into exam room three."

His heart rate slowed, and his emotions shut down as he entered the room and sat on the examination table, the paper crinkling. If he ever let madness consume him, the crinkle of the thin paper would be the ignition point, since the sound drove him nearly crazy.

Vengas shut the door.

He drew his shirt over his head. "No nurse?"

"We're understaffed." Vengas tossed the manila file to the narrow counter and quickly washed her hands in the always-present examination room sink. "Freedom, huh?"

He glanced down at the tattoo over his heart. "That's the goal." Would she understand the subtext to his statement?

She turned. "That is a good goal." Pursing her lips, she approached and glanced at the stitches. "Is that tackle line?"

"Yes. I was in a pinch."

"Interesting." She reached for a box on the counter and drew out latex gloves. "Your medical form is rather brief and uninformative. You're positive you have no allergies?"

"Yes, and it's brief because I merely need the stitches taken out."

She clipped the knotted end and smoothly pulled out the tackle line. "You really didn't." Intelligent eyes studied him. No judgment, just resigned curiosity. "We don't hand out unnecessary prescription drugs here."

"I don't like drugs."

Her eyebrow lifted. "Why are you here?"

He flashed his dimples. "My boss insisted."

"Your boss?"

"Yes. Laney Jacobs over at J's Bar. She said she'd fire me if I acted like a doctor again and took out the stitches by myself." He shrugged as the lie rolled off his tongue. "I need the job."

For the first time, the doctor smiled. "Now, that makes sense. I've met Laney, and she definitely takes care of people."

"Like you do. I mean, with being a doctor and all."

Vengas drew a can of antibacterial spray from the counter to cover his wound. "That's kind of you to say. To be honest,

I figured being a doctor would allow me to build a stable life someday so I could stay in one place."

He drew in air as the cold spray hit his skin. "You want to stay in one place?"

"Yes." She ripped off the gloves to toss in a garbage can. "I grew up an army brat, and we traveled the world my entire childhood." She glanced at a row of old bullet holes across his upper ribs. "You saw combat."

"Yes." If she was telling the truth, she wasn't the right person. "Was it your father or mother who was in the army?"

"My dad. He was a chaplain. What about you?"

"Marine." He might as well stick with his most current story. "Ah, do you mind checking out an old wound on my back? Just to make sure the scar isn't too much." Standing, he turned around. While he couldn't see her face, he tuned in to her breathing and heart rate. If she recognized the cut next to his upper vertebra, he'd know it.

"Which one?" she asked softly.

"Upper back to the right of the spine, diagonal cut."

She leaned in, her fingers tapping across the cut that guaranteed his death. "This is surgical."

Her heart rate and breathing remained constant. When he turned around, only curiosity sat on her face.

"Yes. A doctor removed a metal splinter from an IED." The lie came easily.

She lifted her eyebrows. "The doctor did a good job."

That's what she thought. He yanked his shirt back over his shoulders. Once he got back to the bar, he'd send Shane the information to see if this family practitioner was telling the truth. If so, he'd narrowed down his search.

The coroner and he were going to meet again soon.

Laney tossed more salt into the soup upon recommendation of Rufus and Aaron. While she prepared the food basically to feed them, they'd been surprisingly helpful the past year.

The soup did need more salt, a fact she'd confirmed after taking a quick taste.

She did a quick jig and then laughed at herself. Yeah, happiness felt good. Matt Dean felt even better. The night with him had been so full of passion, she wanted more. Sure, they were both lost. Maybe they could find each other.

Enough daydreaming. Glancing at her watch, she dropped the lid into place, fetched Betty's keys, and headed out the door. Betty had taken the day off to recoup from overindulging, and Laney had agreed to drive the Jeep out after lunch.

The car smelled like Matt. Male, wild, and free.

Her abdomen heated as images from the previous night zipped through her brain. While by no means a virgin, she'd never experienced such a night. He was amazing.

And temporary. Very temporary. She had to remember that fact and not start dreaming about the wounded soldier. There was no question he was wounded, and it wasn't her place to heal him. She had enough to worry about.

She ignited the engine and hummed softly until arriving at Betty's house. The accountant loped outside, her face pale, her gait stilted.

Laney leaned out the window. "The bar overserved you."

Betty grimaced. "No shit. I should sue."

"Very funny." Laney scooted over to the passenger side. "Take me back, and I'll feed you some delicious beef noodle soup."

"Ugh." Betty stepped into the Jeep, secured her seat belt, and backed into the street. "I may never eat again. I threw up in front of your sexy bartender."

Laney covered her mouth with her hand. "Oh God. How embarrassing."

"Then I knocked him into shrubs." Betty snorted and turned the Jeep. "Poor guy."

They turned another corner and both gasped at the myriad of blue and red swirling lights. Police vehicles, an ambulance, and even a fire truck all blazed with emergency lights.

Betty slowed. "That's Claire's house." She rolled down her window and gestured the sheriff over. "Todd? What's going on?"

Todd hitched his belt and walked over, hazel eyes sober. At about forty years old, lines of stress cut into the sides of his mouth. "Claire's cleaning lady showed up earlier today and found her. Dead."

Laney peered out the window at the body being rolled from the house, her heart thumping. A white sheet covered Claire but had slipped off her bruised and battered face. Lacerations cut into her chin, cheeks, and forehead. Clear strangulation marks marred her neck, and her nose was a broken mess.

Betty rubbed her eyes. "Oh my God. We went out last night and she was fine."

Todd narrowed alert eyes. "When did you last see her?"

"We dropped her off about midnight," Betty said, her voice cracking.

"Who dropped her off?" the sheriff asked.

"Um, Laney's new bartender and me." Betty's eyes widened. "He dropped me off and then took Claire home."

The sheriff's shoulders went back. "What time exactly?"

Betty's hands fluttered together. "I'm not sure. I think I went to bed a little after midnight." She looked at Laney. "Did you see Matt when he returned to the bar?"

Yes, and he'd been a mess of scratches and shrubbery from falling. "Yes. I think he walked in about two in the morning," Laney whispered. There seemed to be a gap in the timeline, but had Matt really had a flat tire? If not, why would the soldier kill Claire? It didn't make sense.

"I'm going to need this vehicle as well as statements from you both." The sheriff opened the driver's side door and assisted Betty out. "My deputy will take you to the station."

He waited until Laney had exited the SUV. "How well do you know your bartender?"

She swallowed. After the previous night, she knew what made him growl, what made him smile, and what made him come. "Not much. I only hired him two days ago." Yes, she'd need to tell the full truth about their sexual encounter at the station. Wouldn't she?

The sheriff sighed. "Okay. I'll be to the station as soon as possible to take your statements. The timeline is crucial, so please start thinking about last night."

Betty eyed Laney as they scooted into the back of a squad car. "You don't think—"

"No." God, no. Laney hadn't spent the night with a murderer. But really, what did she know about Matt except he was expertly trained, definitely dangerous, and just passing through town? Maybe he was a man on the run.

"Me, either." Betty's voice lacked conviction. "I'm sure it's a coincidence Charmed had its first murder in decades the same time the tough guy shows up in town."

Laney cut her a look. "I saw him last night, and there weren't any bruises on his knuckles. Anybody who beat a body like that would show some damage." Well, except for the massive bruise across his hand. But that hadn't been a defensive injury. Probably.

"So he was fine?"

"Except for some scratches from your shrubs." Laney settled back into the seat and tried to swallow past the lump in her throat.

"I'm not scratched at all from falling in those shrubs," Betty said.

Laney looked her over. She was telling the truth. Not one scratch or bruise marred Betty's pale skin. Skin much smoother than Matt's. "Matt didn't kill Claire."

He just couldn't have.

CHAPTER
10

MATT STALKED OUT of the clinic, instantly aware of two men flanking the doors. Cops.

"Mr. Dean?" A man in a brown sheriff uniform asked, his hand on the butt of his gun.

"Yes." Matt could easily take them both, but that would seriously break his cover. "Is there a problem?"

The sheriff settled his stance. "We need you to come in and answer a few questions."

"About what?" As an outsider in a small town, he shouldn't be surprised.

"About last night."

Matt stilled. Was Laney all right? "What about last night?"

The cop gestured toward a dented patrol car. "Let's talk at the station."

"I'm happy to, but I'm not leaving my bike here." Matt ran a hand through his hair. "How about I follow you?"

"We'll follow *you*." While the sheriff's eyes were tired, they were hard and sharp. The guy had seen some action before and wouldn't be easy to manipulate. Even so, Matt understood the law. If they had enough to arrest him on something, he'd be in cuffs. Of course, sometimes small towns didn't exactly follow the Constitution. "Sounds good to me."

He stalked over to his bike, his cell phone heavy in his pocket. While he could ditch the phone on the way, he trusted Shane had a decent cover in place for him. If the cop probed too much, they'd need to create a deeper history for Matt Dean the ex-marine. He didn't have time for this crap.

Laney had been fine earlier, so it was doubtful anything had happened to her. Even so, his gut began to churn as he started the bike and drove onto the road.

The main street of town was quiet, and the storefronts sparkled with clean windows. He arrived within minutes at the one-story log building that housed the sheriff's office.

The sheriff and his deputy, a guy who looked to be about twelve, followed him into the station. A teenager sat behind the receptionist counter, popping a bubble from purple gum. She waved at the sheriff.

The guy sighed under his breath and gestured Matt down a hallway to a comfortable conference room with a stunning view of the mountains out the window. "Have a seat, Mr. Dean."

Movement sounded down the hall, and Laney walked closer with Betty right behind her.

Relief filled Matt that was out of proportion with the reality of how long he'd known the woman, so he frowned.

Laney's pale face illuminated her wide green eyes. "Claire Alps is dead."

"Shit," the sheriff muttered. "Why are you still here?"

"Are you all right?" Matt asked.

She nodded. "No. Somebody killed Claire last night."

What the hell? Matt pivoted to face the sheriff. "How did she die?"

"Sit down." The sheriff widened his stance.

Matt eyed the gun and then focused on Laney. "Wait in

the reception room for me, and I'll drive you home." He turned into the comfortable room to sit down.

"No." Laney strode into the room and sat in an adjacent chair. "You're my employee, and I'm staying."

The sheriff scratched his head. "I need to speak with Mr. Dean alone."

"About what?" Laney lifted her chin.

"About his whereabouts last night," the sheriff said.

"He was with me. All night." A very pretty blush wandered over her high features.

Something slammed into Matt's gut with the force of an anvil. The sweet woman was defending him. Nobody but his brothers had ever stood up for him, and even though he didn't need her assistance, he couldn't help but smile. Who was this woman?

The sheriff's gaze narrowed with a calculating light. "Very well. You can stay." He turned toward Betty, whose eyes had widened at the news. "My deputy will give you a ride home." He shut the door with a decisive click.

He sat and pressed his palms against the table. "Mr. Dean, run me through your night."

Matt did so, impressed with the sheriff's calm gaze and lack of notes. The guy didn't *need* notes. Finally, he wound down with his return to the bar.

The sheriff lifted his head. "It took you an hour to change a tire?"

"No. It took me an hour to take both ladies home *and* change a flat tire," Matt said calmly.

"You have a record, Dean?" the sheriff asked.

"No." He believed his new cover remained crime free.

"Would you mind giving DNA so I can rule you out?" The sheriff tapped his fingers on the table.

"I would mind." Matt flashed a smile. "No offense, Sheriff, but after my time overseas, I don't exactly trust everyone involved in the system."

"I can get a warrant." The sheriff focused on Laney.

"Go for it," Matt said. The authorities lacked enough probable cause for a warrant, but that didn't mean a local judge would refuse to do the sheriff a favor. They couldn't get Matt's DNA, that was for damn sure. Not that they'd do the tests that would show the abnormality of his creation, but still. Nobody could get his DNA.

"I will get a warrant." The door opened, and a deputy handed the sheriff a manila envelope. The sheriff sat back, his chair creaking. "Now tell me again, how long have you been in town?"

"A few days."

"Where did you wander before you arrived here?" The envelope crinkled when the sheriff dropped it on the table.

"I've been all over the States." Matt leaned back and slid an arm across Laney's chair.

She jumped. What in the hell was wrong with her?

"I see." The sheriff turned the envelope upside down and dumped out a bunch of notes, each in a plastic bag. "Did you write these?"

Laney went completely still next to him.

Matt picked up a bag to read a handwritten note: *You look beautiful today.*

"Definitely not," he said quietly, reaching for more notes. All had poetic and slightly creepy messages. Nothing threatening, but an underlying danger hinted in the simple words. "What are these?"

"They were in Claire's house. We don't know how long she'd been receiving them." The sheriff focused on Laney. "Are you all right?"

"No," she breathed, her eyes wide on the notes. "I've been receiving notes, too."

Matt frowned as the world narrowed to the small woman now under his arm. "Where are the notes?"

"At home." She shrugged forward, looking soft and vulnerable. "I've received two of them. One on my car, and one at the bar. Sometimes I feel somebody watching me, but I figured it was my imagination."

"Why didn't you file a report?" the sheriff asked.

She sighed, and her gaze dropped to the table. "The notes seemed dorky, and I figured some goofball admirer wrote them. I did tell Smitty."

Yeah, like the sweet old guy would provide much protection. Matt leaned into her space. She was hiding something. "Could the pharmacist have sent them?"

"Greg?" the sheriff asked, even as Laney shook her head.

Laney shook her head. "I don't think so. I mean, he's socially awkward, and we did go on one date, but I think he'd sign any silly note he left." She picked at a loose string on her jeans.

Matt kept his face blank. Why hadn't she gone to the police? If she'd been frightened, she should've filed a report. Was it the loan shark she'd borrowed money from? If so, he needed to take care of the situation. It was the least he could do.

Well, after he took out whoever was threatening her with the notes. They'd spent a night together, and she'd burrowed deep into the realm of the few people he cared about. While they didn't have a future, they had a present, and nobody was going to hurt her in it. No matter how oddly she was acting. "Let's retrieve your notes for the sheriff." He pushed back his chair.

"Hold on a minute. How do I know you didn't send the notes?" the sheriff asked quietly, his gaze hard.

Laney swiveled to look at him.

Matt frowned. "I just got into town. Why would I send notes?"

The sheriff's gray eyebrow rose. "As far as we know, you've only been in town a few days. Maybe that's your MO. You arrive in a town, case it, send out weird notes, and kill people."

Laney swallowed. "That's crazy."

"Exactly." The sheriff shoved away from the table and stood. "I need your fingerprints, Dean, to use as a comparison for the prints we've taken from Claire's home."

"No." Matt stood and assisted Laney to her feet.

Laney faltered. "They'll find the prints anyway."

Not likely. He was always careful not to leave his prints anywhere. The second they turned up in the system, the commander would find him. While that showdown was coming soon, Matt wanted to control the location and timing. "That's all right." He took her elbow and steered her toward the door.

The sheriff blocked the path with his large frame. "It wasn't a request."

Enough was enough. Matt slid Laney to the side and stepped into the cop's space, glaring down at least five inches. "Either arrest me, or get the hell out of my way."

The sheriff held his gaze for several tension-filled moments. Finally, he stepped to the side. "Fine. Don't leave town."

"I have no intention of leaving town." At least not until he figured out who was stalking Laney.

"You know, there was no forced entry at Claire's. She let in whoever killed her." The sheriff peered around him. "You're in danger, Laney. Probably from this guy. I can tell you, after years in the military and then as a cop, this is a guy who's dangerous."

She looked Matt up and down, her green eyes softening. "I know."

Laney tucked her arms around Matt's rib cage and fought the urge to trace the abdominal muscles beneath his thin T-shirt as he steered the motorcycle toward the bar. Her mind whirled, and nausea filled her stomach.

Who had killed Claire?

Sure, Matt had taken the woman home. But that type of a beating took some time—more than an hour. Though Matt was incredibly fit and probably well trained. Darkness and secrets lurked in his gray eyes. Could he torture a woman in such a manner?

The night they'd spent together had revealed a lot about him. He'd been sweet, kind, and gentle. But an underlying tension, a sense of a contained animal, lurked within his hard body.

Even so, she was struggling to connect what she knew with what she'd felt during their short time together. He appealed to her baser nature and made her want to hope. To hope for something good, for something right, to emerge from the hell of real life.

The wind rushed through her hair, slapping her face. Sighing, she tucked her cheek against his broad back, allowing him to shield her. For the moment. When they arrived at the bar, they needed to talk.

They arrived too soon, and he assisted her off the bike. "Get the notes," he said quietly.

She stumbled. "I thought we agreed you wouldn't issue any more orders."

He swung his leg free and loomed over her. "That was before last night."

She backed up and tilted her head to better view his face. "Last night didn't change anything."

It was a challenge, and a good one. His eyes darkened to the color of a stormy sky right before thunder rolled. "Bullshit. Last night meant something, and you know it."

Vulnerability flashed across his strong face that gave her pause and cooled her temper. She sighed, her mind calculating best-case scenarios. "Okay. Last night meant something. But not forever, and one night of intimacy certainly didn't give you the right to boss me around. My life is private."

He dragged a hand through his thick hair, ruffling the

mass. "Listen, Laney. Your life *is* private, but I'm about the best trained investigator you'll ever meet. If somebody is threatening you, which we can now see is happening, you have to let me take them out."

She stilled. "You mean turn them in to the police, right?"

He remained silent for several beats. "Right."

A chill wandered down her spine, even as intrigue focused her thoughts. What would it be like to be loved by a man like Matt Dean? Probably overwhelming, safe, and exasperating. Surprise filled her at how appealing the thought suddenly became. But he wasn't for her.

"Stop shaking your head at me," he muttered.

"Then stop giving me orders." Make that *all* exasperating. She pivoted and yanked open the front door to the bar.

"I want to read the notes before we take them to the sheriff," Matt said, on her heels.

She reached the bar, leaned down, and secured the two notes. "Knock yourself out."

He took the notes, carefully reading each one. "I also want the name of the loan shark you used to buy the bar." His attention remained focused on the papers.

She stilled. *Shit.* "No."

"Yes." He didn't look up.

"No." She'd only given him half the story, and no way could he find out the rest. She had to believe he was one of the good guys, and she would not rain down trouble on him. He seemed to have enough of his own.

He glanced up, the angles of his face seeming sharper. "I want the name of the loan shark."

"My life, my issues." One night with the guy, no matter how amazing, didn't create obligations. "Sorry."

"We're not finished with this discussion." He studied her. "Do you have a copier in the office?"

"Yes. The printer copies and scans."

"Good." Turning on his heel, he disappeared into the office, returning mere minutes later. "I made copies for us, and now you can call the sheriff to pick these up." He rubbed his chin. "How well do you know Dr. Tasha Friedan?"

"Why?"

"She's the local coroner. We should go meet her and find out more about Claire's death." Matt tucked the copies in his back pocket.

Laney blinked several times, trying to focus. "Why? I mean, why are you suddenly so involved here? Last I heard, you were passing through town."

"Now I have my teeth in a mystery about somebody I care about." He spoke quietly and with calm control. "I know I'm passing through town, but I'm not leaving until you're safe, and you won't be safe until we catch this guy."

Sweet. The words were so sweet. For the first time in much too long, Laney felt like she was on the inside...and not alone. Which was false, because he didn't know her. He couldn't. "I can't ask you to go after what appears to be a murderer."

His grin flashed strong teeth. "Honey, after what I've seen, one little murderer in a small town doesn't faze me much."

"What have you seen?"

His smile slipped away. "Nothing I'd want you to hear about."

"My life hasn't always been safe. This isn't anything new."

"One loan shark after you isn't as scary as a guy who sends notes and kills people." Matt leaned forward, his jaw firming. "I promise you're safe. I won't let anybody get to you."

Warmth slid right under her heart. "One night creates such loyalty from you?"

His upper lip quirked. "No. But one night *with you* creates such loyalty."

Desire burst through her veins like a robust bourbon. "You're a dangerous man, Matt Dean."

"You have no idea, sweetheart." He nudged the original notes across the bar. "Why don't you call the sheriff to pick these up, and we'll go talk to Tasha. Please? I'd like to get a handle on this case."

Going on instinct, she nodded. If something was going on, she needed Matt's assistance. "Let me run upstairs and get a jacket. I, ah, appreciate your help."

He leaned in for a quick kiss that warmed her head to toe. "Anytime, green eyes. Anytime."

CHAPTER
11

Matt waited until Laney had run upstairs before yanking out his phone and dialing his brother. The security checks took a bit longer, since apparently Shane was tweaking the system. Finally, he could talk.

"I need a deeper cover," Matt said.

"How deep?" Shane asked, the sound of typing keys echoing over the line.

"Deep enough for possible fingerprints."

Quiet reigned for a moment. "Do we need to extract you?"

"No, Sally. I'm fine—just make the portfolio deep. The local sheriff will be running my name at the very least. If he can find a judge buddy to sign a warrant, there may be an arrest and DNA issues."

"Get out of town. Now." Shane's typing stopped.

"Can't. I think I found the surgeon and will go confirm now." Plus, he wouldn't leave Laney in danger.

The outside door opened and Smitty strolled inside, wearing his usual suspenders and bright flannel shirt.

"Gotta go." Matt hung up and leveled a look at the bartender. "Claire Alps was murdered last night, and apparently she'd been receiving notes similar to the ones your boss has been receiving."

Smitty stopped short. "Really?"

"Yes. Any clue as to who's been sending them?"

"No." Smitty rubbed his belly. "Shit."

"What's the name of the loan shark Laney used to buy the bar?" Matt asked.

Shrewd blue eyes narrowed. "She told you about the loan?"

"Yes."

"You think the notes might be related?"

"No clue. But I'll take care of the problem regardless." Matt kept his voice mild and truthful.

Smitty grinned. "You got money to take care of it?"

"Yes." And he did. "Family money." True enough. "It's the least I can do for her. I don't need the money and will probably never use it." If the loan shark didn't take cash, he'd no doubt want to live.

"She let it slip one day the guy's name was Joe-Joe from Philly." Smitty shrugged. "Don't tell her I told you. She'd probably be pissed."

"I won't say a word." Matt walked around the bar and headed for the front door. "Have Laney meet me outside." Stepping onto the sidewalk, he quickly dialed Nate's number.

"This is Vinnie's Pizza," Nate drawled.

"How's business?" Matt asked.

"Just fine. A bit slow, but I'm hoping a new advertisement brings in business."

So Nate hadn't found anything but did have a new lead. "Good. Ah, I need a favor."

"Anything for my favorite pepperoni salesman."

What a smart-ass. "How secure are we?"

"Completely. Shane set me up with a new system," Nate said.

"Then why the fuck are we talking about pizza?" Matt asked.

"Why not?"

"Jackass. I need you to pay off a loan shark named Joe-Joe in Philadelphia. How soon can you be there?"

"Five hours." Birds squawked in the background and a door closed. "Who borrowed money?"

"Laney Jacobs."

"Who the hell is Laney Jacobs? The surgeon?" Nate asked.

Hell, no. "She's a friend."

Only chirps from birds came over the line for a few moments. "What kind of a friend?"

"A friend I want to help. Pay off whatever her debt is," Matt said. They had tons of money from their security business, and Nate had invested the profits extremely well.

"We're paying off some random woman's debt now? What's going on, Mattie?"

"What's going on is that you have your fucking orders. Pay off the man." All he needed right now was a lecture from his younger brother.

"Wait a minute. Shane was bad enough. We don't have time for you to mess around with some small-town chick." Anger rode the low consonants of Nate's tone.

"I'm aware of that. Do your job."

"If the shark doesn't want payment?" Nate asked.

"Make sure he does."

"On it. Will text you as soon as I learn anything. For now, get your mind back in the game. We don't have time for mistakes." Nate clicked off.

Nate was right. They had six weeks until the chips in their spines exploded and severed their lives, and he needed to concentrate solely on survival. But at least Matt could take care of the cloud hanging over Laney's head. Now he needed to find the surgeon he hunted. Chances were, they were about to meet face-to-face again.

The door opened and Laney stepped outside. "I asked Smitty to hold the notes for the sheriff, who said he was on the way. Tell me again why we're going to meet your most recent drinking buddy."

Laney's voice held a hint of jealousy, and that shouldn't warm him so much. "I want to find out who's threatening you before I leave town." Might as well give the woman the truth. "Do you want to drive?"

She shuffled her feet, a small smile playing on her fragile face. "Um, I wouldn't mind riding the bike."

He grinned. "Really?"

"Yeah. I like to go fast and feel free."

Now, that was a woman. "Hop on." He sat on the bike and waited until she'd settled in behind him, her grip strong around his waist. Once again, the moment struck him as . . . right.

The coroner's office was in the basement of the clinic he'd just left, and the return trip seemed to go too fast. Maybe he could talk Laney into a longer ride that weekend—if he was still in town.

She hopped off the bike and led the way inside and down a row of stairs. Almost naturally, she reached out and slid her hand into his.

His heart thumped, and the world softened. The constant vigilance in his head mellowed.

The scents of formaldehyde and bleach yanked him back to reality. Even so, he tightened his fingers around hers.

They approached a steel double door, and suddenly, he didn't want to be there. He sure as hell didn't want Laney going into an autopsy room. He gestured toward a row of cheap metal chairs. "Why don't you wait out here?" What the hell had he been thinking to drag her to the coroner's office?

The door opened, and a tall woman in clean scrubs walked out. She blinked and stopped moving. "Matt? Laney? What are you doing here?"

Laney moved forward. "We came to see about Claire."

Tasha frowned. "What about Claire?"

Laney lowered her voice to a whisper. "Claire was receiving frightening notes, and I've been receiving the same ones. So, I asked Matt to help me figure out what's going on. He's an ex-marine who worked in investigative services for the military."

Matt kept his expression placid. *Investigative services?* The little brunette created quite the convincing lie when she wanted.

Tasha smoothed back curly blond hair and sniffed. "I see. Well, I haven't talked to the sheriff yet."

"I know." Laney patted Tasha's arm. "I wouldn't ask, but I'm scared, and Matt agreed to help me. What if this guy comes after me?"

Tasha shook her head. "I'm sure the sheriff is better equipped to figure this out than a bartender and her bouncer." Condescension dripped from her tone as she glanced at her watch.

Laney's chin rose. "Perhaps, but you owe this bartender one, and I'd like an answer."

Tasha's lips drew in a white line. "Fine. This makes us even. Just don't tell Todd. Claire died from strangulation after a violent beating."

"Was she raped?" Matt asked.

"Yes, but there's no fluid or DNA—the guy used a condom," Tasha said, slipping her hands in her pockets.

"Time of death?" Matt asked.

"Between midnight and four in the morning. I can't be more exact."

Shit. He'd been with the accountant after midnight, but he sure as hell hadn't killed her. The poor, lost woman. Anger began to boil in his gut. He'd find this murderer and take him out before he hurt anybody else. But for now, Matt had to figure out if this was the doctor who could save his brothers' lives.

She was tall and stood to about six feet. Brown eyes,

blond hair, and delicate bone structure. Snotty and arrogant. Exactly the type of person who could still sleep after implanting kill chips in a man's spine.

Matt nodded. "How long have you lived here?"

Tasha leaned against the dingy wall. "I've lived here my whole life, pretty much."

That was impossible. "In town here?"

Her eyes narrowed. "Yes. Even went to school with the sheriff."

Bullshit. If she was the woman he hunted, she'd lie. But why tell a lie that would be so easy to dispute? Unless she had the sheriff covering for her, or unless she was even trickier than that, somehow. In his life, he'd seen some amazing cover-ups. "I see." He tried to look sympathetic.

She pushed off the wall. "I need to file my report."

He slid his most charming smile into place. "I'm sorry to question you, doctor. It's just, this seems so crazy to have happened in a small town. You can't get many murders here, right?"

Tasha brushed her hair away from her face. "That's true. Once in a while we get a hunting accident, and every so often we get a murder among friends or family. But a murder from a probable stranger? This is my first."

Matt studied the doctor. Every line of her stature showed fatigue. It was a common mask for somebody lying. Either that, or the woman was tired and he'd descended upon the wrong town.

He didn't think so.

Every instinct he had whispered Charmed, Idaho, was the right place to find the surgeon, and the woman looking down her nose at them was the only possibility still standing.

So he smiled. "Thank you for your help."

Back at the empty bar, Laney poured two sodas and handed one to Matt. "Um, I feel like I should tell you I don't, um, usually..."

His grin loosened the tension in her. "I know you don't sleep around. Believe it or not, I'm a decent judge of people."

To survive in the military, he'd probably had to have been. She shouldn't care what he thought, but somehow, she did. But he'd misread her, hadn't he? "Okay."

He took a drink, the muscles in his neck moving nicely. "Will you tell me why Tasha owed you one?"

"Nothing big. She drank too much one night and passed out in the back booth. I let her sleep it off on my couch that night." The poor woman had been almost speaking in tongues by the time Laney had helped her upstairs.

Matt shook his head. "She doesn't seem like the type to let go and get drunk."

Yeah, the woman was a cold fish. "It was some anniversary of her escaping something." Laney lifted a shoulder. "I got the feeling she had an ex out there she got away from, but who knows."

"What was the anniversary?" Matt asked.

Laney paused and focused on the handsome soldier. "Why?"

He shrugged. "Just curious."

Laney frowned. He sure asked a lot of questions, now didn't he? "Why do I get the feeling you're not some drifter?" She tried to probe beneath the surface of those intriguing gray eyes. Just how much would he admit?

"I'm not just a drifter." His cheek creased. "I'm drifting right now. At one time, I was a soldier, and I actually did investigate crimes. This is old hat to me, and it feels good to be focused on something."

He always had a good answer—almost too good. Laney nodded. "It was a few months ago, maybe in February."

"I see." He finished the soda and slid the glass across the bar.

"What are your brothers like?" Laney asked. She'd love to get him to open up a little.

He paused, his gaze lifting to hers.

The outside door opened, and Greg hurried inside. His polo shirt hung awkwardly out of his pressed dress pants. "Did you hear about Claire?"

Laney leaned back from the bar as irritation batted through her. The pharmacist was not welcome to just drop by. She had enough problems. "Yes. Poor Claire."

The pharmacist jumped onto a stool next to Matt. "I can't believe it. The sheriff contacted me this morning and asked me about some notes you've been receiving." He pushed wire-rimmed glasses up his nose. "I haven't sent you notes. Why haven't you mentioned threatening notes?"

Because she didn't want anything to do with the asshat. "They're not exactly threatening, and I didn't think you'd sent them." Laney retrieved a rag and began wiping down the bar, hoping he'd get the hint and leave.

"That's good to know." Greg tapped his manicured nails on the smooth wood. "The sheriff was a bit rough because I was home alone. I mean, if I'd planned to kill somebody, I would've thought of a good alibi, you know?"

"It's nice to know you've given this some thought," Matt said, annoyance tightening his full lips. "How long have you lived in Charmed, anyway?"

Greg tugged on the collar of his golf shirt. "I moved here five years ago after graduating from Washington State. My mother died while I was in school, so there was no reason to return to Seattle."

"Why Charmed?" Matt asked, his gaze piercing.

"The pharmacy offered me a job." Greg glared at Matt. "I find it interesting a murder occurred right after you arrived in town."

"I find it interesting that a guy who secretly copies a woman's apartment keys and breaks into her place isn't a bigger suspect in this case," Matt drawled.

Greg flushed an angry red. "My gesture was romantic, and frankly, none of your business."

Matt leaned toward Greg, threat and tension in every line of his face. "Wrong. Laney is my business."

Greg gasped, his gaze slashing to Laney. "What does that mean?"

Heat spiraled into her cheeks, and she focused on scrubbing the bar. The silence dragged on until it became heavy.

Finally, Greg pushed off the stool, his lips twisting. "I see. Well, I also came here to ask you to the Elks dance tonight, but I can see now you wouldn't be interested. However, once you come to your senses, you know where to find me." His stride hitched as he hurried out of the bar.

Laney threw the dishcloth in the sink and crossed her arms.

"What?" Matt asked.

"You know what. Why would you do that?"

Matt unfolded his impressive length from the stool and maneuvered around the bar—toward her. "For two reasons. One, I wanted to gauge his reaction, because I'm not sure he's in the clear for Claire's murder. And two?" He reached her and skimmed a hand around her neck. "This is why." His mouth slid against her, engulfing her in instant fire. He turned them, putting her back against the wall.

He slipped one knee between her legs, pressing up with enough pressure to catch the breath in her throat.

His tongue swept inside her mouth, while the hand at her nape angled her so he could go deeper. Need rippled through her, pebbling her nipples and softening her sex. Finally, he lifted his head, allowing her to breathe.

Her mouth tingled, her breasts ached, and her clit pounded. She stared at his darkening eyes, bemused. "We're in the bar," she murmured. Her mind went blank, her body taking over.

Challenge and amusement filtered across his face as he slowly, deliberately, slid a hand under her shirt and wandered up to palm her breast. "I know."

She blinked several times to keep her eyes from rolling back in her head. She arched against him, wanting more. "We, ah, shouldn't..."

"Ask me to stop, and I will." He rolled her nipple, leaning in to scrape his teeth along her neck. "This is dangerous, and this is fun. Anybody might walk in, Laney." His talented mouth found her earlobe, and his thigh flexed against her cleft.

She gasped, her mind swirling. God. The man was correct in that anybody might walk into the bar and catch her making out with her new bouncer. Her body didn't care. Not even a little bit.

But her mind did. Self-preservation reared its head. Finally.

So she swallowed and sucked in a deep breath. "Please stop."

He released her and stepped back. "Are you sure? I could have you coming in about a minute." His grin was almost boyish, while the glint in his eye was anything but sweet.

She shook her head. "You're terrible. Just terrible."

"I could have you changing your opinion there...in about a minute." Good humor quirked his lip.

She tilted her head to the side and tried to control her breathing and rioting body. The man was sexy, dangerous... and likable. For a few moments, he'd taken her mind off the danger around them, as he'd no doubt meant to do. "I've already changed my opinion. You're a good guy, whether you want to be or not."

He exhaled. "I'm not even close to a good guy, but the fact that you believe so makes me happy."

Smitty chose that moment to wander in from outside, his fluorescent pink suspenders nearly overpowering. He glanced from Laney to Matt. "Happy hour is almost upon us. You okay, Laney? You look flushed."

CHAPTER
12

M ATT FINISHED DELIVERING another round of drinks to some college kids home for the weekend, his gaze again turning toward the group of bikers at the far pool table. They were having a good time and seemed like decent guys. He glanced at his watch, surprised how the night had flown by. He'd need to make a move while the bar remained busy, and now was the time.

He'd questioned Laney a bit more about Greg after the pharmacist had stomped out of the bar, discovering the guy lived in one of the houses scattered a few blocks away in an older subdivision. A quick flip through of the local phone book, and he'd found an actual address. Small towns—no real security. There was something off about the guy, and since Greg supposedly was at some Elks dance, now was the time for Matt to investigate.

Tossing the tray across the bar, he gave Smitty the high sign. "I need to make a phone call—be back in a few."

Smitty nodded, his attention remaining on a woman sitting at the bar chatting with him. The gal had to be about fifty, and wore heavy blue makeup, which enhanced her sparkling brown eyes.

Laney was in the kitchen scaring up some pizzas for the

crowd, so Matt slipped out the back door and jogged down the sweet-smelling alley. He kept to the shadows, his senses tuned in to the night.

Greg lived in an unassuming white cottage with over-grown grass and weeds. Apparently the guy didn't like lawn work. Matt glanced around the quiet neighborhood and then quickly vaulted over a rickety fence to the backyard. Weeds and crumbled bricks made an odd pathway to a sliding glass door. He drew on leather gloves and tried the door. It was unlocked.

What the hell was it with people who didn't lock their doors? While even an excellent lock was only a minor deter-rent, still, it was something.

Matt slipped inside and waited for his eyes to accus-tom themselves to the dim light. No sounds echoed in the house—no breathing, no heartbeats. Good. Greg was out somewhere. A dog barked in the far distance, and wolves mourned in the hills.

He used his phone as a flashlight to search the kitchen drawers. Old bills, parking tickets, and lottery tickets crammed the drawers full. A cursory glance at the liv-ing room illustrated leather chairs and yellowed news-papers. Continuing through the house, Matt trod lightly over scratched wooden floors and headed down a narrow hallway. The smell of copper hit him just as his foot slipped.

His gloves smacked the wall to keep him from going down.

Regaining his balance, he reached behind himself and shut the hallway door before flipping on the light, already knowing what he'd find. A large puddle of blood now held his perfect footprint. Arterial spray decorated the wall, which showed the shape of his hand.

Damn it all to hell.

His mind needed to get back into the game. He tugged off his boot and stepped over the blood and beyond a small bathroom into the home's sole bedroom, which had been torn apart. The body had been tossed on the floor in a heap. Dropping to his haunches, Matt leaned close. No heartbeat.

Greg's blue eyes were open in horror and death. His hands revealed no bruising or defensive wounds. The guy hadn't seen it coming.

Matt straightened and surveyed the room. Drawers had been yanked from dressers, the contents spilled. His attention jerked to the photographs spread across the bed. All black-and-white, and all of Laney. Had Greg been stalking her? They were all simple printouts, probably from a home computer. A desk sat in the corner without a computer or printer. Had the killer taken them? If so, why?

He glanced at his watch. Damn it—he needed to get back to the bar. After he erased any sign of his presence.

The cleanup took about five minutes, and he tried to leave the crime scene as close to untouched as possible. He paused as he surveyed the pictures. They showed Laney at the bar, around town, even through the window of her apartment. The digital camera or phone that had been used to take them was missing, as was the computer that had printed them out.

Fury filled him, and he wasted precious moments shoving it down.

Taking the pictures was a risk to him, and so was leaving them at the crime scene. The murderer had obviously rifled through them, and the sheriff knew Matt was sleeping with Laney. Since Greg had dated her, Matt would already be a suspect in Greg's death. The pictures of Laney would focus the sheriff on Laney, and in turn, the cop would take a closer look at Matt. He couldn't afford a closer look right now.

Without the pictures, Greg was just a dork who'd taken Laney to dinner once. With the pictures, Greg was more than that—an intense stalker who may have gone too far, or who may have seen something he shouldn't have.

Matt needed to take the photographs, just to buy himself more time.

So he gathered the pictures together, tucked them at the back of his shirt, and quickly exited the house, careful not to come in contact with any more blood. Once outside, he jogged down the street before replacing his boot on his foot. He'd cleaned the bottom with bleach, but he wouldn't mind giving it another soaking soon.

Sticking to alleys and the darkness, he arrived at the back of the bar just as his phone rang. He glanced down at the face and then answered. "Hi, Nate."

"Hi. What's wrong?"

"Nothin'." Oh, hell. The Southern accent gave him away.

"What the fuck is going on?" Nate asked, his voice dropping to a growl.

The outside door opened, and Laney stuck her face out. "You're still on the phone? You've been gone almost thirty minutes."

Actually, it was closer to an hour, but maybe she hadn't seen him leave. He gave her the high sign that he'd be finished in a minute. She rolled her eyes and disappeared again.

Man, she was cute. But he needed to step back and fully focus on Tasha to confirm she used to be Dr. Peters.

"A lot is going on, but I can't talk right now. I'll call you later," Matt said.

"Wait. I paid a visit to the loan shark," Nate muttered.

"Good. Did he take the money?" At least that was one less item to worry about.

"No. In fact, Joe-Joe said he'd already been paid in full." A police siren sounded through the line.

Matt straightened. "Where are you?"

"Downtown Philly. No worries."

His mind focused automatically, as they'd been trained. "When was the loan shark paid?"

"Apparently a cashier's check arrived every month, just like clockwork, until the entire loan and compounded interest were paid in full. Took over a year," Nate said. "I questioned him, but the guy had no clue who'd sent the checks."

"Where was the postmark from?"

"Dunno, but he said he'd look through his old files to see if he'd kept an envelope, though he doubted he did. I told him I'd pay for the envelope if he finds one, so he's inspired. I'll check in with him tomorrow."

"Thanks," Matt said. Who the hell would've paid off the loan shark? Laney didn't know anything about it, or she wouldn't still be lying low. Her brother was killed right after they'd taken out the loan, but maybe he'd had a friend with money? But if so, why not borrow from the friend and not a loan shark? None of this made any sense, and he had the oddest feeling that Laney was keeping something from him. What frightened her so? "I swear, the longer I stay in this town, the more bizarre everything becomes."

"Do you need to be extracted?" Nate asked.

"No."

"Do you need backup?"

"Not yet." If things kept going downhill, he might need help. "Wait to hear from Joe-Joe, and then get back to chasing down Jory's last location. If we're ever to find out what happened to our brother, we need to know where they killed him."

"*Shot* him. Where they shot him," Nate said.

Matt closed his eyes and exhaled slowly. "Nate—"

"No. Until I see a body, my brother isn't dead."

Matt nodded. "Fair enough." When they found Jory's body, Nate was going to fall apart. Matt would have to figure out a way to put him back together. But for now, he had enough to deal with. "Check in tomorrow." He ended the phone call and quickly dialed Shane.

"What?" Shane asked after a series of clicks.

Matt leaned against the brick wall. "I'm calling for updates."

"Claire Alps checks out. I found her cult—nice group of

people it seems. The family practitioner also checks out—I dug up her father's records and traced her whole life. She's allergic to nuts and most deodorants."

Only Shane would find that interesting. Matt shook his head. "What about Dr. Tasha Friedan?"

"She's full of shit. The name has only been used for six years...Before that, she didn't exist. Wherever she bought the new identification owes her money back—it's a bad cover."

Adrenaline flowed through Matt's veins. "I knew it was her. Okay, before I take her, I need a breakdown of where she's been since leaving the compound. Everything."

"You got it. Anything else?"

He should say no. But his instincts were humming, and that meant something. If Laney was in trouble, he needed to help her while he still could. "I want you to run a background check on Laney Jacobs," Matt said slowly.

"Already ran a surface check, and she seems all right."

Matt drew in a breath and eyed the door, gathering his thoughts. His shoulders went back. "Go deeper. I want to know everything." He clicked off and headed back into the bar.

After closing, Laney stepped around the snoring cat and set the pool cues back in the wall mount, her gaze on Matt as he finished cleaning bleach off his boots. The guy had accidentally spilled the bucket while mopping. "You don't seem like a clumsy man."

He plopped the mop in the bucket. "Wasn't paying attention."

Laney nodded. He'd been distant and preoccupied all evening. Unease and embarrassment filtered through her. She'd slept with a guy she'd just met. Did he think she was easy? Surely he felt some of the same emotions she felt while they'd been together. "Did your phone call upset you?"

"No." He rolled the moving bucket to the back room, returning and eyeing the room. "We're all cleaned up."

"Yes." She swallowed, a humming tickling her abdomen. She barely knew him, they didn't have a relationship, and she wasn't sure what to say. "Well, um, I guess I'll head up since we need to start early tomorrow."

"Laney." His low timbre wafted across the room as he focused on her. "I'm sorry I've been short tonight. It's just, I don't like what's going on here. With the notes and Claire's murder."

She tilted her head. "Me, either."

Lazy strides maneuvered him around the tables, where he wrapped his hands around her waist. Two seconds later, she sat on the bar, her legs on either side of his hips. "If you're in trouble, you can trust me."

"I-I know." He'd lifted her so easily, the power in his body intriguing her. Setting her blood on fire. They only had a short time together, and real trust wasn't something she did. "You don't have to worry about me." Frankly, it wasn't his place. But the need to protect seemed to be ingrained in the man, and something deep in her wanted to jump right into that strength. To keep herself from doing so, she slid both hands through his thick hair.

His eyebrow rose.

She leaned forward to brush his lips with hers. They had more time together, and she wanted it. She wanted him.

His smile against her mouth warmed her throughout and made her dream. He levered away, at the same time tugging her closer and tilting her hips until he pressed against the apex of her legs.

He grinned, already hard and throbbing against her sex. "Are you trying to distract me?"

"I'm just trying to enjoy the moment," she murmured. Finally, a truth she could give him. "Life is short and apparently getting more dangerous. Moments count."

His lids dropped to half-mast. "Moments count," he repeated, licking his lips. A hard edge still lived in his eyes, which revealed none of this thoughts. He seemed even further away than usual. "I'm not going to let anybody hurt you."

"Are you going to tell me what else is bothering you?" she asked softly.

"Life in general, sweetheart." He smoothly lifted her from the bar and waited until she'd tightened her thighs against his before heading to the stairs. "For one thing, I appreciate when my lover is honest with me."

Her body instinctively stilled. She dropped her hands to his shoulders so she could meet his eyes. "I'm not lying."

"The hell you aren't." His smile held both charm and challenge. "I've been trained by the best to discern shades of truth, and you're not being completely honest."

Terror stilled her limbs. "Completely honest? About what? Not that it matters. You're temporary, and as such, you don't get a free pass into my life."

His eyes darkened, his hands flexing. "The money for the bar. I don't know how, but that's the key to the notes and recent murders."

"Murders?" What the hell was he talking about?

"Murder," he growled. "Though I expect more bodies soon, considering the notes were sent to both you and Claire—probably to other women in town, too." He smoothly unlocked his apartment door, having them inside within seconds. "Considering my sleeping with you makes me a suspect, I want the truth."

She kept his gaze. "I told you the truth." Her stomach lurched as she lied her ass off.

His chin lifted as his hands dropped to cup her butt. "Try again."

Heat cascaded from his palms, and her eyes wanted to roll back in her head. "Put me down." She so did *not* mean those words.

"No." Her back hit the wall, held in place by a body harder than any other surface in the room. "You're not moving until you tell me the truth." He slid his lips along her jaw, sending her senses reeling.

They had too many clothes on. She sighed, arching into his touch. "I knew you were a throwback Neanderthal the first night I met you, but this is ridiculous. Put me down, or I'll scream," she said. Even though anger threatened to swamp her, desire slid through her blood.

"Go ahead."

Damn it. She didn't want anybody to come running, and he knew it. He had her legs secured, so she couldn't kick him. They were too close for her to get in a good punch, and he wasn't taking her seriously. So she levered back and went for his eyes.

His head jerked back, his hand instantly manacling her wrists. A grin flashed across his face. "Did you just try to poke my eyes out?"

She struggled in his grasp, her sex rubbing against his pulsing shaft, even through their clothing. "I saw the move on an episode of *Bones*."

"*Bones*." His smile widened, even as he lifted her arms above her head, pressing them against the wall.

Her back arched, her nipples scraping against his chest. She bit back a groan. This was pissing her off, not turning her on. Heat spiraled through her body and proved her a liar. Raw need clawed through her abdomen. What was *wrong* with her? His show of dominance should be a splash of cold water on her desire, not a freaking accelerant. Besides, she knew deep down it wasn't a *show*. Not at all. "I promise my bar has nothing to do with the notes."

He angled closer, his eyes right above hers. For several quiet seconds, he studied her. "You knew."

She swallowed and fought the urge to rip off his shirt. "Knew what?"

"That the loan was paid off," he drawled.

She frowned and tried to ignore the hard length of him pressed against her. "Do you have an accent?"

"No."

Sounded like a Southern accent for a moment. She shook her head, her mind scrambling, her body rioting for relief. "What are you talking about? The loan was never paid off."

A muscle visibly spasmed in his jaw as his gaze dropped to her needy breasts. "Stop lying."

"Fine." She relaxed against him. "I won't lie. Now mind your own fucking business." That was the second time she'd used the *f* word in the last few days. She never swore.

His head jerked back. "You've made this my business."

"No, I haven't." Wait a minute. "Why do you think the loan was paid off?" How had he found out?

"I had a colleague of mine meet with Joe-Joe the loan shark."

Heat drained from her face. "Why would you do that?"

"To help you out before I left town."

Damn, damn, damn. She shook her head. "I didn't ask for your help."

"I like you." The words rang true, but the pissed tone of voice didn't reassure her much. "I wanted to help."

She took a deep breath. "Listen, I'm sure your heart is in the right place, but I don't want your help."

He blinked, and erotic tension filled the room. "Fine. Who paid off the loan shark?"

She held his gaze and tried to put an apology in her eyes, telling him the less he knew about her past, the safer he'd stay, wouldn't help with a guy like him. "I can't tell you. Please, let it go."

For once, his feelings showed on his face. A combination of regret and relief. "So we agree we're limited."

She nodded. "We both need to understand the temporary nature of our, ah, relationship." She gyrated against him, appeased by the quick flare of hunger that lightened his odd eyes to a determined gray.

"Fair enough." Something in the tone hinted he wasn't finished with his search for the truth. "Promise if you need help, you'll ask."

"I promise." Yeah, she lied again, and by the flare of irritation across his face, he knew it.

His mouth slammed down on hers. Firm and angry, he kissed her hard, his body against hers and his hand holding her wrists captive. He was a storm, fully unleashed.

Thank God. Finally.

Desire crashed through her, weakening her muscles and shutting down her mind. She should get the hell away from this guy. Even so, she pressed against him, a whimper lodging in her throat.

At the sound, he gentled. Slow, soft, the kiss turned devastating. Hot and sweet, he drugged her with his taste, making her want. Making her hunger.

Maybe one more night together. Then she'd end it. She'd have to.

He finally released her wrists and strode toward the bedroom, his mouth working hers the entire time until he set her on the bed. Gentle hands tugged her shirt over her head and unclasped her bra to toss across the room.

"You're beautiful," he murmured, his gaze warm and his tone lazy.

She needed to tell him the truth. "Matt, I—"

"Shh." His hand flattened across her upper chest and pushed. "You said we have this, and I want it. I want tonight."

She fell back on the bed, her mind reeling. One night. Okay. One night.

He leaned over her, his mouth wandering from her neck, down between her breasts, to the clasp of her jeans. He unhooked it with talented teeth, and seconds later, her pants and underwear flew across the room. Her heart clutched, and her legs trembled. She'd never be able to find all of her clothes in the morning.

Her breath caught in her throat as he stood, so tall and formidable, fully dressed.

She was completely nude—vulnerable and feminine.

He yanked his shirt off, the dim light showing hard muscles and old wounds. She reached for him. He shook his head, desire and wonder creasing his cheeks in a soft smile. "Let me play, Laney. Let me show you what you do to me." A flash of teeth provided erotic warning before he dropped to his knees and his mouth found her.

CHAPTER
13

THE WOMAN TASTED like sunshine and spice, and Matt let himself get lost for a moment. It hurt that she didn't trust him, but he understood.

He'd all but told her they'd never see each other again when he left town.

He wouldn't trust him, either.

For now, they had this night, and he wanted to make sure she'd remember him.

Forever.

So he enjoyed himself, memorizing the way she moved, the small sounds of pleasure she made. His shoulders held her legs open as his mouth covered her.

She bucked, and he slid a hand over her hip to hold her in place. Her taste clouded his head, and he lost himself in the moment. Turning his head, he nipped her thigh, and slid one finger inside her to torture her G-spot. She gyrated against him, her muscles straining, small whimpers echoing on her sighs.

The sweet sounds roared his blood into the need to take. To possess and keep safe. Things he wanted to do so badly.

Her thighs tensed and trembled. She was so close.

She arched against him, her body going rigid, and he tightened his hold, refusing to let her go over.

A fleeting thought occurred to him that he could probably get the answers he sought right now. She was strung tight, and she'd give him what he wanted.

Something in him, a force he didn't recognize, stopped him. He wouldn't manipulate Laney like that. She wasn't part of a mission, and his reasons for wanting to know were personal. He'd learned to care, and nothing would destroy that. Not even his need to know the truth.

"Say my name," he murmured against her mound, his accent breaking free.

"Matt," she gasped.

He sucked her swollen clit into his mouth.

She arched against him, crying out, her body undulating as she came. He prolonged her orgasm as long as possible, finally granting reprieve when she settled back against the bed with a sigh of relief.

Maneuvering up her body, he lowered his against her softness, pleasure filling him. "You're stunning when you let go."

She blinked several times, her eyes slowly focusing on him. "You're just stunning." Her legs spread farther apart. "I need you inside of me."

The words slammed into his heart with surprising strength. "What the lady needs—" He grasped her hip and plunged inside her with one hard thrust. She arched, elongating her neck.

Heat surrounded him like a vice, and he dropped his forehead to hers, his muscles vibrating as he held himself in check. The softness of her skin, the sweetness of her taste, drove him wild. But he couldn't hurt her—he'd never hurt her.

She dug her fingers into his butt. "Don't hold back, Mattie. Let go."

It was the nickname that did it. Only family called him that, and for one second, he let himself go. He pounded hard, closing his eyes, letting the heat of the moment catch him. The world narrowed in focus to one small woman. No outside sounds, no internal awareness of danger...nothing existed but Laney and passion.

The heaven he found by being inside her was so perfect it hurt. Maybe because the moment held the first hint of peace he'd tasted, or maybe because the good never lasted—at least not in his life.

Either way, when her internal walls rippled around him and she cried out his name, he thrust harder, faster, and fell into the storm. He came hard, grinding into her, his heart ramming against his ribs. His heart swelled until his ribs ached.

Finally, he slowed and slid a gentle kiss on her mouth. One he hoped conveyed more than a simple thank-you. She was real, and good, and feminine...and he'd never forget the time he'd spent with her. Once away, he'd remember her scent, her sounds, her skin. So soft and kind, she'd let him in for a brief time.

She sighed and then winced as he withdrew. Turning, she shoved her butt into his groin and was sleeping within a minute.

He grinned into the darkness and tucked her close. Taking a moment, he tuned in to the universe outside of the apartment, identifying people, animals, and vehicles. Nothing seemed threatening, so he allowed his mind to drift.

His woman sure fell asleep easily.

He jerked fully awake. *His* woman? Not only was the thought impossible, he wasn't a caveman. But the feelings she evoked were raw and primal...and he wanted to keep her safe.

For an hour or so, he measured her heart rate and breathing. He'd learned to exist on little sleep, and genetically he was fairly certain the scientists had helped him along there. He should get up and contact his brothers, but instead chose to enjoy the sleeping woman in his arms.

So he knew the second her dreams turned frightening.

She twitched. He could hear her heart rate increase and her breath shallow into pants. She cried out in a small voice filled with terror. "Blood. God, make it stop. So much blood."

"Laney, wake up. You're safe." He ran a palm down her side.

She screamed and lurched across the bed. Only his enhanced reflexes kept her from dropping to the floor. She struggled against him, fighting hard, nailing him in the thigh.

"Laney. Now." He put the bite of a command in his voice, and she stilled. Then he flipped on the light and released her.

She sat in the middle of his bed, nude and fragile, her eyes opened wide, her breath panting out.

He waited until recognition filtered through her eyes before holding out an arm. "Come here."

She immediately launched herself at him and tucked her head beneath his chin. The small whimper she gave as she tried to get inside his skin sliced his heart in two.

Slowly, he turned off the light and snuggled them both down beneath the bedclothes. He kept his voice calm when all he wanted to do was kill something. Whatever had frightened her so badly, he'd take down. "Bad dream?"

She snorted against him, holding him tight. "You could say that."

He focused and relaxed as her heart rate returned to a normal level. "Want to talk about it?"

A long shudder shook her body. "No."

"I get nightmares, too. It helps to talk about them." He smoothed hair off her damp shoulder.

Her shrug was the only response he received.

He shut his eyes and exhaled slowly. Now wasn't the time to push her. "Go back to sleep. I swear to God nothing will hurt you on my watch."

As a vow, it was a good one. Apparently, she believed him, because soon she was back to sleep. This time peacefully.

He kept track of the world as she slept, wondering whose

blood she'd seen in her dreams. Who had scared such a kind woman? If he managed to track down a way to save his brothers and himself, the very next mission would be to help Laney. Yeah, it was a big if. For the first time, he wondered if he would have a life after the next six weeks. Since he'd discovered Tasha, the coroner, was the surgeon he hunted, did they have a chance at surviving?

He allowed himself to drift off into a light sleep to recharge his energy. Since he slipped barely under, he failed to shield himself from the terrors of the past.

The dream took shape as a memory from five years previous, when he and all three of his brothers trained at headquarters. It was the first time all four of them had been in the same place at the same time, since their trainers always had one or two of them out on a mission, the threat of death hanging over the others.

He'd loped into a jog to make a squad leader's meeting when a hard body slammed him into the cinder blocks. He turned and shoved a shoulder under his attacker's chin, not surprised to see it was Emery.

Even as an adult, Emery was an asshole.

Emery fell back, a malicious smile on his smooth face. "I watched training earlier. Have to say, your brother is out of control."

Matt growled and refused to rub his aching shoulder. He didn't need to ask which brother Emery had watched. Ever since Audrey had dumped Nathan, he'd been out of control. Reckless and dangerous. "Worry about your own brothers. I'll take care of mine."

Emery's dark brown eyes gleamed with an odd light. "Your loyalty makes you weak."

"If you don't understand, I can't explain it to you." Matt studied the man he'd known as a mean kid. Time to tip his hand a little to get information. "Don't you want out of here? Want to find peace?"

Emery threw back his head and laughed. "Peace? Hell, no. Fighting, killing, being a machine? That's who we are." He eyed Matt, probably looking for an opening to strike. *"Your weakness for Nathan will take you down. Soon."*

Ah. There was the opening Matt had been searching for all week. Something was up. He lunged and shoved Emery hard against the wall. *"What do you know?"*

"Nothing." The lie held a dark tenor.

"Liar." Matt shoved harder. There was only one reason all of his brothers would be in the same place at the same time. The commander had something planned. Something bad. Pure instinct told Matt it was about Nate, considering he was plunging off the deep end. *"If anything happens to Nate, I'm taking you out,"* he said quietly to Emery.

Emery pushed him. "You can try."

Matt released him. Yeah, it was time to blow the place to hell and find freedom—now might be his only chance. *"Don't make me kill you, Emery."*

Emery smiled again. "Someday I'm going to bury you—after I get to your brothers and everything you ever cared about."

Five years later, Matt forced himself to awaken. Without question, Emery would come after Laney if he knew about her. Matt's heart thudded, and he took several deep breaths. He'd always wondered if he had made a mistake in allowing Emery to live when the compound blew. While the commander had been safely underground at the first hint of trouble, Emery had been vulnerable in one of the weight centers.

But Matt couldn't kill him. Everyone deserved a shot at freedom. Hopefully Matt hadn't made a mistake that would get one of his brothers, or now Laney, hurt.

He tucked her closer, allowing the scent of woman to calm him.

Dawn arrived with the cacophony of robins outside the window, and he let Laney sleep. The sounds of the carnival rose in force outside as early booths were set up. The bar didn't open until later that morning, so there was no need to hurry.

She awoke and shoved hair away from her face. "Race you to the shower."

He grinned and gave her a head start. Yeah, he wanted to push her for answers about her dream—hell, he wanted her to trust him. But that took time. Instead of pushing her, he washed her head to toe and enjoyed every single second. He tried for more, but she slapped his hands, saying they had to get down to the bar.

So he dried her and quickly yanked on jeans to pad through the apartment.

She threw on one of his old shirts and hustled toward the door. "I'll go get dressed, and then we can head downstairs." She frowned. "Where's my bra?"

He turned his back to her and headed into the bedroom to fetch it from the top corner of the bookshelf. Apparently he'd thrown it rather hard. Returning to the room, he stopped short at the sight of her face.

She'd lost all color. Her pupils were dilated, and her hands shook around her shoes.

He stepped toward her. "What's wrong?"

She stepped back. "Um, nothing. I mean...well... cramps. They hit hard. Really hard." Her gaze dropped to his abs as she spoke.

How cute. She was embarrassed by cramps. He tossed her the bra. "No worries. I'll meet you in a few minutes."

She fumbled for the door, all but running out of the apartment.

He blinked, frowning. Now, that was confusing. With a shrug, he went to dig out a shirt to wear. It was time Laney Jacobs leveled with him.

CHAPTER
14

LANEY SCRAMBLED INTO her apartment, her breath rushing out. God. When Matt had turned around, she'd seen his bare back for the first time. Shock had filled her at seeing the scars along his back, and then her heart had stopped as she'd noticed the surgical slice adjacent to his 4C vertebra.

How was that even possible?

One look and she'd known exactly what the cut meant. Exactly what killing device lay just under his skin—ready to detonate and kill him.

If he realized who she was, he'd kill her. Or rather, he'd dump her in the back of his car and return her to hell. She knew his training, and she knew she'd never escape him if he figured out who she was. *What* she was.

She had to run.

She yanked on clothes and headed for the go bag in her closet.

He knocked on the door.

She twirled around, and a rock crashed into her gut.

The door opened, and he poked his head in. "Smitty's yelling for us. It's time to open."

When she swallowed, she tasted blood. Had she bitten her lip? "Oh yeah. We should go." Fetching a hair clip off the counter, she fastened her hair up and forced herself to walk toward Matt. The first break she got during the day, she'd run. Hard and fast.

She shot him a smile and almost yelped when he grabbed her arm.

"Are you sure you're all right?" he asked. "You're white as paste."

Numb, she nodded. "Yes. Really bad cramps."

"Oh." He led her outside and shut her door, waiting for her to lock it with fumbling hands. "If you start feeling poorly, you need to go rest today."

"I'll be fine. No worries." She swallowed. The scars on his back didn't lie. He stood next to her, suddenly large and formidable. Dangerous. Deadly, even. They reached the bar, and she all but ran for Smitty.

He snapped his lime green suspenders. "Everything is ready. I have soup on and burgers ready to go. Open the doors, Matt."

Matt loped over to unlock the main doors. "I'll get beer in plastic cups ready," he said, returning to the bar.

The first few customers wandered inside, many carrying balloons and stuffed animals. Apparently the carnival had been going for some time. Laney kept to pouring drinks, her gaze on the exits. She had to get out of there.

An hour in, Smitty asked Matt to help with the garbage, and she found her chance. She moved to retrieve her purse from under the bar.

A cry of angst filtered through the crowd. Laney turned, her heart kicking into gear. June rushed inside, carrying her limp grandson.

Laney's feet rooted in place. Fear roared her heartbeat through her ears. "June?"

"It's Phillip," June rushed, her eyes filling with tears.

Panic raced down Laney's spine as she looked at the little boy. His lips were turning blue, and his eyes were fluttering shut.

What the hell?

Laney hurried around from the bar, her gaze on the little boy. "What's wrong?"

June started crying. "I don't know. He fell down the street, and he's having trouble breathing."

As they came closer, panic cascaded off them. Phillip's eyes flipped open, filled with fear. Laney stepped back, her stomach revolting. His lips shouldn't be that color. She searched frantically for help. Smitty and Matt had taken out the garbage. There was only her.

June lay her grandson on the bar. He gasped for breath.

"Oh God," Laney murmured. How hurt was he?

It had been too long.

She swallowed down bile and launched into action. There was no choice. If she didn't do something, the boy might die. So she shoved all thought, all feeling out of the way to be dealt with later.

"Call 911," she ordered, reaching for his abdomen. "What did he fall on?"

June patted his legs. "The crane operator already called the paramedics. They're coming." She battled back tears. "He was running and tripped, flying into the fire hydrant."

Laney focused on the now-wheezing boy. She couldn't let him die. "It's okay, Phillip. We're going to fix this. We probably have a rib fracture, but let's check out the rest of you." That quickly, she fell right back into the jargon. "Okay. Inhale, and let's check your pain level."

Phillip frowned. "Huh?"

"Breathe." She ran her hands over his neck and head, peering closely at his pupils.

He sucked in air and winced. "Hurts."

She nodded. "Okay. Breathe again." She leaned in and listened for crepitus. Yep. Crackling. She gently slid her fingers along his upper ribs. "Does this hurt?"

"Yes." Tears filled his young eyes.

The sound of sirens trilled through the day. Thank God. An ambulance screeched to a stop outside in the alley, and two paramedics carrying a stretcher rushed inside followed by Matt and Smitty.

Laney focused on the medical personnel and tried to use layman's terms. "Broken rib, most likely the second one. Local tenderness and crackling over the fracture along with pain when inhaling. No allergies, no known medical problems. He's going into shock," she said tersely to one of the paramedics.

They kept moving forward. One turned toward her. "What kind of crackling?"

She leaned in. "Definite crepitus."

The first man grunted as they lifted Phillip onto the stretcher. "Nice job. You a doctor?"

"N-no." She shook her head. "I just watch a lot of television."

The paramedic nodded and quickly rolled Phillip out to the ambulance with his grandmother following.

The bar quieted. Laney looked down at her trembling hands, and a roaring filled her ears. Then she glanced up to find Matt watching her. Betrayal glowed in his eyes only to be quickly veiled.

She thought when she'd seen the scar next to his spine there would be time to run. Apparently not. "What?"

"Definite crepitus?" he asked. His gaze remained closed, but a heart-stopping tension spiraled out from him.

How in the hell had he heard that? There was no way he could've heard. She opened her eyes wide. "I heard the term on *Dr. Oz*."

His eyes narrowed, and his nostrils flared.

He knew. He definitely knew.

The soldier wasn't stupid, now was he? Heat filled her face so quickly her cheeks burned. Damn it. So she lifted her chin. There was no way to hide now.

His lip curled in almost a snarl.

Yeah. She'd seen that expression before.

The sheriff rushed through the front door, gun drawn.

Laney edged closer to the cop. "The ambulance already left, Todd."

He pointed the gun at Matt as a deputy hurried over with handcuffs. "Matt Dean? You're under arrest for the murder of Greg Garrison."

Matt allowed the deputy to cuff his hands behind his back, his face remaining placid. "Greg is dead?"

"Like you didn't know that," Todd said.

Laney staggered back against the bar, her breath heating. How could Greg be dead? "When did he die?"

"Last night," Todd said, holstering his gun.

"Matt worked all night." She spoke without thinking. A frantic hope burst in her chest. If they took him in, she could flee. "But, well, he did disappear for a while—maybe an hour."

Matt's gaze remained on her, his chin lifting. The deputy grabbed his arm and began pushing him toward the door. As Matt neared her, he leaned into her space. "You run from me, *Dr. Peters*, and it'll be the worst day of your life when I find you," he whispered before the deputy yanked him away. Matt looked back over his shoulder as they reached the door. "And I promise, I will find you."

Laney blinked as the door closed, fighting down shock and fear. There was no time.

She had to run. Now.

A series of low hums filled the one interrogation room in the sheriff's office. Matt searched for the camera, finally finding the lens hidden in an air vent on the ceiling. Smooth cedar planks made up the walls, dingy tiles spread across the floor, and a scarred wooden table sat in the middle.

They'd secured his cuffs to a ring set into the table.

He could be free in seconds if he wished.

Instead, he waited until the sheriff finished reading a rather thin file. As an interrogation technique, it sucked. If the cop wanted to wait for Matt to speak first, he'd wait all day.

Except Matt needed to get out of the station and find Laney. How the fuck could she be the surgeon? But she was. Not only had she handled Phillip's injury like a pro, the truth had shimmered in her eyes when she'd looked at Matt afterward. She knew who he was...what he was. Hell, maybe she'd even implanted the device that would soon kill him.

Anger rode through him, and he channeled the fury into ice. He could control his body, his mind, and his emotions. *Shit.* He wasn't supposed to have emotions. So the ache in his chest was not from her betrayal. Not at all.

The sheriff gave in first. "I understand why you killed Greg, but why Claire?"

"I haven't killed anybody." Not true, but adding the qualifier "in your town" would sound wrong.

"We have a witness who saw you leave Greg's home within the time frame for death."

Matt shook his head. "Impossible. I've never been to Greg's. What did your witness say?"

The sheriff shrugged. "He described you really well, height and weight. We'll plug you into a lineup later."

Bullshit. If a witness had accurately identified Matt, he'd be under arrest right now. The sheriff was bluffing and doing a decent job of it.

"We also found your prints," the sheriff said, shutting the manila file and smiling.

Excellent—the cop was lying in order to trap Matt. For a brief moment, Matt had wondered if a witness could identify him as leaving Greg's. Sure, he'd been cautious. But a soldier never knew who was hanging out on a roof watching a neighborhood. Of course, he would've heard a heartbeat.

"That's impossible, because I've never been to Greg's house." Or rather, he'd been wearing gloves while at Greg's house.

The sheriff narrowed shrewd eyes. "How did your prints end up in his house?"

Matt leaned forward. "I understand you're doing your job, but lying to me won't work. There are no prints because I've never been to Greg's." More important, he hadn't been arrested. The cuffs were for show. "Now either arrest me, or uncuff me."

"Know the law, do you?"

"Yes, and I also figure you're trying to get a warrant right now to arrest me, which you won't get, because you have no probable cause." *If* everyone follows the law. "I'd bet you're also trying to get a search warrant for my place. Again, no probable cause." Matt sat back.

"I don't like you."

"Why would you?" Matt asked. "I'm a new guy in town, and you don't know me. But I had no reason to kill either Claire or Greg."

"You know what I think?" The sheriff tapped his fingers on the table. "I think you're a whack-job who sends creepy notes to women, stalks them, and later kills them. Claire was victim number one in my town."

"And Greg?" Matt asked.

"Greg probably saw something he shouldn't have. He was infatuated with Laney and everybody knew it. In fact, I wouldn't be surprised if he was a bit of a stalker. So, what did he see? You leaving notes for Laney? For Claire?"

Not a bad interpretation, actually. Of course, since the killer wasn't Matt, that left a problem for the sheriff. Unless the sheriff obtained the search warrant, because then Matt was screwed. He hadn't had a chance yet to dispose of the photographs he'd stolen from the crime scene at Greg's. He'd planned to take care of them during the carnival, but everything had gone to shit too quickly. "I didn't even know Greg had been killed until you faked my arrest earlier."

"There was nothing fake about your arrest. I felt you were dangerous to those around you, and I took precautions." The sheriff tossed bullshit with the best of them. "If you didn't kill Greg and stalk Laney, then who did? You've been around Laney all week. Who else besides Greg has been watching her?"

"Nobody I noticed." Matt would've felt if something was off. Well, probably. He'd definitely been off his game since meeting Laney, and he deserved the shock he'd gotten. The woman had been lying from day one, and yet he'd never suspected her of being the commander's surgeon.

The faint that first night had thrown him completely off. It had been real, and the blood across his chest had caused it. Was that why she'd fled the commander and his organization? A doctor afraid of blood wouldn't have been useful to them. What had caused her fear?

Matt allowed the chains to clank together. "Look me in the eye, Sheriff. Can you tell when a guy is lying?"

"Yes." The sheriff leaned forward. "You're full of shit and have more secrets than a guy running for office."

"Perhaps, but do you really think I killed either Claire or Greg?" Matt asked.

"I don't know. My gut tells me you'd have no problem killing."

Matt nodded. "I've done plenty of things to answer for—mostly under orders. But killing an innocent woman? Never." He let the truth show in his eyes. "Claire was a sweet, helpless woman, and I wouldn't have hurt her."

"What about Laney?" the sheriff asked.

Matt forced a fond smile, when all he wanted to do was growl. Of course, he'd thought Laney innocent and helpless, too. Turned out the ex-doctor was anything but sweet. For the first time since meeting her, Matt's world centered and refocused. No emotion existed—only the mission. Whatever it took, he'd make her talk. "I'm hoping Laney and I have a future." They damn well had a future—one that consisted of her saving his brothers' lives. Whether she wanted to or not.

"A future?"

"Sure." Matt lifted a shoulder. "I've been looking for somebody like her for a very long time."

"I see." Someone knocked on the door, and Todd hitched his way to poke his head out the door.

Matt could clearly hear the deputy whisper that the judge had refused both warrants based on lack of probable cause. Well, chalk one up for a judge who followed the Constitution.

The sheriff loped back around the table and took out a cell phone, snapping Matt's photograph.

Damn it. "What the hell was that for?"

"Just in case." The sheriff stretched across the table and unlocked the cuffs. "Don't leave town, or I'll plaster your picture all over the news in order to get you back here."

"I have places to be." He had to get the phone away from the cop.

"Not until I wrap up this investigation. Besides, you have a future to plan with the bar owner, right?"

Matt stood and stretched his neck. "I'm not going anywhere. If you need me, I'll be with Laney." The truth of the words had an ominous ring to them, so he tried for a disarming smile. "I'll need a ride back to the bar."

The sheriff yanked keys from his pockets. "I'd be more than happy to take you back. Any chance you'll invite me in for coffee?"

"You're not my type." Matt had to get to those pictures and destroy them before the sheriff managed to wrangle a warrant. It was probably a matter of time. He gestured the sheriff in front of him and ignored the pointed looks from deputies as they maneuvered through the station and out to the car. He chose to sit in the front seat.

The sheriff sighed and twisted the ignition. He drove

quickly and with sharp movements down the street. "Why do I get the feeling you know more than you're saying?"

Matt glanced out the window at the passing storefronts. "You'll want to drive into the alley to avoid the carnival."

"No shit, Sherlock. I've lived here since birth."

Speaking of which. "The coroner said you're old friends—that you've known her forever." While Matt had found the surgeon he hunted, he still wondered at Tasha's false background.

"I have." The sheriff's consonants lifted as he told a lie.

Matt turned toward him. "You're not a very good liar."

"Sure I am." The sheriff turned down the alley. "Why are you asking about Dr. Friedan?"

Matt shrugged. "Laney met with her about Claire's death, considering Laney is getting notes, and I could tell the woman was lying about her background. Curiosity had me asking."

"You're a human lie detector, are you?"

Hell, no. Nathan was the human lie detector. "I'm trained, Sheriff."

Todd pulled to a stop. "Well, in this case you're wrong. Stay where I can find you, Dean."

"No problem." Matt unfolded from the car and didn't look back as he headed through the bar, where Smitty was finishing setting out another plate of hamburgers.

The bartender lifted bushy eyebrows. "You break out of jail?"

Matt snorted. "No. They didn't actually arrest me…just wanted to rattle my cage. Where's Laney?"

Smitty rubbed his forehead. "She headed up with a migraine after you were taken to the pokey. Haven't seen her since."

"I'll go check on her." The woman had run. He'd told her not to flee, and she'd done it anyway. Damn it. He took the stairs three at a time and stopped at her open doorway. A cursory glance around her apartment showed nothing out of place. She'd probably already had a bag ready to go.

Straightening his shoulders, he stalked toward the near-est photograph of Laney and her brother. He ripped off the back and studied more closely. Manipulated. The picture had been altered. All of the pictures had been manipulated. Laney probably didn't even know the guy in the pics.

Matt should've looked closer.

Yanking his phone from his pocket, he dialed Shane.

"Hi, Matt. I have news," Shane said.

"What?"

"Nate called in, and the postmarks from the payoff for your friend's loan were sent from Charmed. Somebody in town helped her out."

Matt closed his eyes briefly. "She helped herself out. Laney Jacobs is the surgeon." Matt yanked open drawers in a systematic search of the apartment. He found her phone crumpled and smashed in the garbage. "She's on the run now."

Quiet cascaded over the line for several beats. "Laney is the doctor? Are you sure?"

"Positive." The woman had hidden her tracks well. There was nothing left to find in the apartment. He hurried out the door and into his own place to fetch supplies. "I need to find where she's gone."

"Let me bring up the satellite I hacked into a few days ago," Shane murmured.

"Call me when you find her." Matt clicked off.

Striding through the apartment, he threw clothes and necessities into his backpack. Finally, he hurried toward the hidey-hole he'd created under a cupboard in the sink. He might as well destroy those pictures on the way to find Laney. He reached in . . . and stilled.

The photographs were gone.

CHAPTER
15

LANEY DOUBLE-CHECKED THE lock on the front door of the rustic cabin. An owl hooted at the moon outside, and a fire crackled quietly inside.

He'd find her. Without a doubt, Matt would find her.

But not tonight.

She'd prepared her getaway from the first day she'd arrived in town and even paid cash for the remote cabin from an old trapper who had no intention of recording the sale or exchanging deeds. Who knew if he had even really owned the land? But he'd built the cabin, and now it was her temporary shelter. A weathered tarp outside safely hid her car as she gathered her wits. Sure, she'd have to move soon.

She'd spent precious moments calling the hospital to check on Phillip, but the peace of mind was worth the risk. The child had broken his second rib and would be fine.

Thank goodness.

Smitty would take care of Eugene when Laney didn't return. She'd have to drop him a line once she reached safety.

Thunder echoed through the mountains, and lightning lit up the forest outside. She shivered and drew a blanket around her shoulders before sitting near the fire, careful not to jostle the knife she'd tucked at the back of her waist. The one-bedroom place held a bed, sofa, fireplace, and make-shift kitchen. But it was off the map for now.

Midnight drew near, and her eyelids grew heavy. Sawdust dried her eyes. She was so tired.

She understood a little of the training Matt had as a soldier, and she knew his body as a specimen. Created in test tubes with the finest genetic splicing available, he had skills beyond a human man's. As did his brothers. How had she not recognized him? He was beyond real with that body—and his mind was incredibly sharp.

Thus she truly had a small chance of outrunning him. But she only needed another six weeks, now, didn't she? Those chips would activate at that time.

Her breath caught, and nausea spiraled into her stomach. God. The horrific chips.

Thunder bellowed outside, and she jumped.

Maybe she should've stayed and faced Matt. But he'd been trained to kill any threat, and once he learned she had nothing to help him with, she'd just be a liability. Would he really kill her?

A stick cracked outside the window. She jumped up and clutched the blanket to her chest. Taking a deep breath, she shook her head, peering over the couch and out the window. The storm slashed rain against the glass and stirred pine needles in a mini-tornado. It was just the storm. When she turned back around, the door stood open.

"Matt," she murmured, dropping down to sit.

A formidable man backed by a dangerous storm, he stood in the doorway, legs braced. Wet hair curled at his nape, and droplets fell from his leather jacket to plop on the rough floor. He closed the door and engaged the lock before tossing his bag on the table. His ominous gaze never left her face.

She swallowed. Fear seized her lungs.

He shrugged out of his jacket and draped the leather over

one of two chairs bracketing the tiny table. Then he shoved
up his sleeves. "What weapons did you bring?"

Although his voice remained low and controlled, she
jumped. The knife she'd hidden pressed against her skin
in a deadly reminder of the danger now surrounding her.
"Weapons?"

His gaze ran over her form as he strode toward her.

Her heart may have stopped, and fear tingled through her
veins. She pressed back into the worn cushions.

Arriving within her space, he glanced around her imme-
diate area and finally dropped to his haunches. A quick
search, and he pulled the nine-millimeter out from under the
sofa. She'd purchased the gun several years previous—from
a back room. No records. Quick, economical movements
had the weapon dismantled within seconds. "What else?" he
asked, tossing the useless pieces onto the other end of the
couch.

"Just the gun," she managed to say as her breathing sped
up. She had to control her lungs, or she'd hyperventilate.

His chin lifted slightly. "Do you want me to search you?"

The deep timber of his voice rolled over her skin, igniting nerves. It was the same tone he'd used in bed, and her
body reacted instantly. Sure, she was scared. Even so, a very
unwelcome desire awakened in her abdomen. "No."

He stood and held out a hand. "Weapons."

She drew in air for courage. "Where are *your* weapons?"

"In my bag. I don't need them for you." His face remained
expressionless, which was so much more frightening than if
he'd been angry.

However, deep down, she couldn't believe he'd harm her.
"I'm not afraid of you."

"Liar," he said softly. "Stand up, Laney."

She should've brought her phone so she could call for
help. "How did you find me?"

"Now."

There was no choice. She stood and reached for the knife.

Without seeming to move, he pinned her arms against her sides with broad hands around her biceps. "Knife or gun?"

"Knife." Lying to him seemed pointless.

His palm skimmed down her arm in almost a caress. He drew the knife away from her, and the steel glinted yellow in the firelight. "You ever stab anybody?" he asked.

"No," she whispered.

"It's not as easy as you'd think." He casually threw the knife, and the blade embedded in the wall across the room.

She flinched as wood sprayed. "I don't think it'd be easy."

"Turn around."

Her shoulders went back. "I'd rather see it coming, thanks."

For the first time, emotion filtered into his eyes. Anger and something darker. Hurt.

She opened her mouth to say something, anything, when he jerked her around to face the couch. She caught her balance by grabbing the armrest. Heat rushed down her spine. This was the same position he'd put her in when he'd taken her by the couch in her apartment. "Matt—"

His hands along her flanks stopped her. Firm and knowing, he slid his hands over her hips and along her buttocks. Heat cascaded from his calloused palms. Fire licked along her skin. Oh. He was frisking her. Her muscles tensed as he touched her.

His hands enveloped her thighs, patting down to her boots. While short and businesslike, his search nevertheless awakened every pulse point she had. Warmth settled in her abdomen with claws. This was so wrong. Her body was well accustomed to his touch and didn't care. She had to get control of her libido and her brain.

He turned her back around. "Sit."

The movement didn't hurt her, but the hint of underlying violence caught her unaware. Her knees buckled before she even thought about refusing.

The rough floor protested when he dragged a chair across it and settled down, his knees bracketing hers. "Now we talk."

She clasped her hands together on the blanket, grateful to have even the thin cotton shielding her. "When did you know?"

"When you saved Phillip. When did you know?"

"When I saw your back this morning. I'd felt the scars, but there were so many, so I didn't..." She wanted to look away, but his hard gaze held her captive.

"Right," he said. "Did you know who I was before I fucked you?"

She barely kept from flinching at the harsh question. "I don't even know who you are right now."

"Answer me."

The desire flowing through her chilled. "I didn't realize until this morning, when I saw the scar adjacent to your 4C vertebra. What are you going to do with me?"

"That depends on you." Firelight flickered across his angled face, leaving deadly shadows. He turned and glanced at the still burning pictures in the flames. "You went through my apartment."

"Yes. Where did you get the pictures?" She'd stolen them to destroy immediately.

"I found them at Greg's."

She gasped and leaned back. "You killed Greg?"

"Of course not." Matt frowned. "The guy was a stalker, I think. Whoever killed him left the pictures scattered across Greg's bed. I found Greg and took the pictures, not needing any more police scrutiny."

Sounded like a decent explanation. Maybe. Perhaps Matt had killed Greg, but she doubted it. "Why keep them?" she asked.

"I hadn't had a chance to destroy them." Matt turned his formidable focus back on her. "What was your name before you went to work for the group?"

"Eleanor Roberts."

"When you were with the group?"

"Dr. Peters." She shrugged. "The missions were top secret, and nobody was supposed to learn our real identities . . . which had been scrubbed anyway."

"I know. How do I deactivate the chips?"

"With a code." If she'd known the code, she would've chased him down to give it to him already. "The chip holds a receiver. You need the right transmitter, hooked up to the right computer, with the correct code typed in. A wireless signal goes out, and the chip dies. The technology is light-years beyond anything our military has . . . Just the small size of the chips would seem impossible to most experts."

"What's the code?"

"I don't know." She bit her lip at the instant fury that leaped into his eyes. "I promise."

His mouth twitched in barely a snarl.

Okay. So her promises lacked depth with him. An apology would probably send him over the edge, so she kept quiet.

His phone buzzed, and he lifted it to his ear. "What?" He listened and then nodded. "Interesting. I may need to use that later. For now, I have the surgeon—her name was Eleanor Roberts before. She probably purchased the new identification in Philly. Trace back what you can, and we'll check her story with your research later. Oh—she'll tell me the truth. Bye." He slipped the phone back into his pocket, not having moved his gaze once.

"Use what later?" God. What had he found?

"Your friend the coroner has a false background because she fled from an abusive husband." Matt's smile failed to brighten his face. "Unlike you."

How odd. Maybe Laney wasn't the only person who'd seen small-town Charmed and found it was a good place to hide. "I spent half the money I borrowed from Joe-Joe on a new background," she said. There was no reason to lie now.

"You paid him back?"

"Yes."

"Why lie?"

She tried to keep her hands from trembling. "The lie kept Smitty from asking too many questions about my past, and it gave me an excuse to stay out of the limelight and away from the law."

"What about the fake photographs of *your brother*?" Matt's voice hardened at the end.

She lifted her chin. "Unlike you, I've never had family, which would've been in my employment file that you certainly dug up. I created a family with pictures from a free sharing site on the Internet. And no, I don't know who the guy was."

"Employment file?" Matt's chair creaked when he sat back, as if he had to distance himself from her. "Killing us was merely a job to you."

"No." Heat rushed up her throat. "Not at all. I didn't know—"

"Stop." He held up a hand. "I don't want explanations, and I don't want apologies. I don't give a shit what your reasons were, or how badly you want to live now. All I want to hear is how to defuse the chips."

"I told you how." She barely understood how the terrible things worked and had never seen the code. "I can't help you."

"Oh, you're going to help me." He rubbed his chin. "When was the last time you had contact with the commander?"

Just a mention of the man roared terror between her ears until they heated. "Five years ago. When the facility blew up, I fled." Somehow, she'd gotten away.

"Why?"

"Are you kidding? I was as much a prisoner in that hell-hole as you were." Fatigue swamped her, and she allowed her body to relax. If Matt decided to kill her, he'd be quick, and she probably wouldn't see death coming. Why tighten her muscles to the point of pain?

"How so?" he asked, his expression betraying nothing.

"That's a long story."

"Then I suggest you start talking."

She scrubbed both hands down her face. "Then stop being so scary."

One dark eyebrow rose. "I thought you weren't frightened."

She met his gaze evenly. "You sound scary, and that's annoying. I don't think you'll kill me." God, she hoped not.

"Why?" His upper lip twisted. "Because I've been inside you? Baby, that doesn't provide you one bit of safety. That just means I know where you live."

Anger shoved away the fear. "What you felt was real, jackass." Ah. There was some emotion from the soldier. Sure, it was anger, but it was something.

His nostrils flared. "You try to manipulate me, and you'll regret it." That elusive Southern accent sprang forward in full force.

She glanced at her watch. "You've tried to frighten me for a while now, and I'm done. What happened between us? It was fast, unexpected, and real. Like it or not, it was you and me...the real us. So fuck you."

Fire leaped into his eyes to be quickly squashed. "You've pushed enough. Where did you go to medical school?"

"Johns Hopkins." She'd been so proud when they'd awarded her the scholarship. "Top of my class."

"But no family?"

She shook her head. "No. Just a couple of friends, too. It's hard to get As in medical school and have a social life, so I, well, didn't." Frankly, she was the perfect recruit for a black-ops military organization. "They offered me a job making a difference to our country and soldiers, and I bit. The second I was on board, they erased my life."

The idea of how easily her past had been erased made her

wonder if her life had mattered at all. Nobody had missed her or come looking. Pain and loneliness echoed through her. Even her feeble attempts to make friends from the safety of her bar mocked her. She'd been fine all alone until Matt Dean had blown into her life and made her wish. Made her want and need. Now she had an idea of what she was missing.

"What else?" he asked.

She shook her head. "What do you mean?"

"Motivations. You had more—I can tell."

She sighed. He just had to dig into her as deep as he could go, now, didn't he? "My father was in the military and died in action when my mother was pregnant with me. My, ah, life would've been different had my father lived, I'm sure."

"So you thought helping other soldiers was the solution?" No expression crossed Matt's face.

She shrugged. "Maybe. If some of the research would keep someone's father alive, then it was a good cause, right?" She had felt closer to her own father, even though she hadn't met him, during her time with the military. At least she'd glimpsed how he'd lived.

"Did you see the risks with the experiments?" Matt asked.

Her shoulders hunched. "I did. I mean, I saw the possibilities of our research and findings being used to harm instead of heal. But I pushed through anyway, sure the people I worked with would do the right thing."

"You were wrong."

"I know," she said softly.

"Did you plant the device in my spine that's going to kill me?" Matt asked.

"No." She sighed and stifled a yawn. The adrenaline had disappeared, leaving exhaustion.

Matt's phone buzzed, and he lifted the device to his ear with a growl. He stood and glanced down. "My bike is visible through the clouds? Okay. I'll find a better hiding spot."

He slid the phone back into his pocket before digging into his bag. Shiny cuffs glowed in the firelight.

She tried to scramble away, but he grasped her wrist and secured the cuff to the wooden portion of the armrest. "Asshole."

"My bike is a couple of miles away, so this might take a little while. Stay here." He turned and stomped from the cabin.

Like she had a choice. Through the clouds? Somebody had access to high-level satellites, apparently. So that's how they'd found her. She snuggled down and watched the fire. Sure, Matt was mad at her, but he didn't understand the entire story. Against all rational thought, she had feelings for the guy. Even more so now that she knew who he was and what he'd endured.

Guilt spiraled through her. She shouldn't have run. Yes, she'd panicked. Had she had time to think, she would've realized that staying in town and facing Matt, telling him the truth, was the only solution for her. She'd worked for the commander, she had training as a surgeon, and she'd do whatever she could to help make things right for Matt and his brothers.

The fire crackled inside while the storm continued to rage outside. She shut her eyes and practiced deep breathing to calm herself.

She didn't know what to do, but she knew without question she wanted back into his realm of trust. The shield provided by Matt had been strong and sure, and she wanted that again. She needed him to look at her the way he had, as if he cared. As if she mattered.

She'd never truly mattered.

Now she'd give anything to feel that again with him. But even if he never trusted her again, she'd help him. How, she didn't know. But she'd figure out something to save his life.

Even if she lost hers.

CHAPTER
16

MATT STRODE BACK into the cabin and stopped short. The woman was sound asleep on the couch. Out cold. Her lips were pursed in sleep, and heat from the fire had pinkened her smooth skin.

Yeah, she was scared of him. Not.

If she'd been truly frightened, she'd be wide-awake.

A warmth he didn't appreciate unfolded in his chest. On some level, she trusted him. That fact shouldn't matter to him—at all.

Yet it did.

She'd been correct in that his feelings had been real. Sure, they were fast and inexplicable. But he'd cared for her in the short time they'd both pretended to be someone else.

But now he knew the truth. He had no doubt the commander and his scientists had tricked her into working for them by using patriotism. But once she'd discovered the truth, she'd stayed. While he didn't want to wake her, he had to uncover the extent of her involvement in the program. Something in her memories might help him save his brothers.

She was a damn good liar, and he should've seen through her from the start. The fact that he'd missed signals proved beyond any doubt his emotions were fucking with his instincts. Laney had him all twisted up, and he needed to get himself centered before he went at her again. So he allowed her to sleep and turned instead to his laptop. Now that they'd figured out who'd she'd become, Shane was able to trace back her old identity. Her name had been Eleanor Roberts—and she'd made a mistake choosing Laney as her new name. It could've easily caught up with her, and she was plain lucky it hadn't.

Shane was sending through more information on her, and Matt would need all the facts he could get. Her transcripts and IQ tests came first.

The woman was a fucking genius with steady hands that often held a scalpel. A surgeon whose skills were praised up and down by experts in the school.

He liked her better as a hardworking bar owner. A hell of a lot better.

Her psychological reports arrived next. Matt read them by firelight, memorizing her past. Laney had been all alone. She'd told him the truth about her childhood and that her mother had been an alcoholic. She'd survived her childhood by throwing herself into photography—another truth she'd shared with him. Her first job was babysitting when she turned eleven, and it looked like she'd taken care of herself from that time.

The drunk mother died before Laney's seventeenth birthday, and by the time the courts got around to supplying her with a guardian, she'd turned eighteen. Full rides to college and then medical school.

She was an easy target for the commander, to be sure.

Matt tried to stifle any sympathy he had for the little girl Laney must've been at one time, his gaze often straying to the sleeping woman. Asleep, at peace, she appeared fragile and innocent. For the briefest of moments, he allowed himself to be confused. What if she was innocent? It was entirely possible.

Or, what if his dick and heart were messing with him?

His past colored his view, but he'd never met a doctor who had a heart. All they did was experiment on him...which often involved some type of pain. Rationally, he understood there were probably good doctors out there who wanted to help people.

He'd never met one.

She breathed out and twitched on the couch.

He straightened up, his senses going on alert.

A low moan filtered up from her throat. *Shit*. She was having another nightmare. He pushed the laptop away and approached the couch, touching her shoulder. "Laney?"

She bolted upright and screamed, her eyes flipping open. Then she winced as the cuffs pulled. Tears gathered in her eyes and spilled over as she looked at him. Vulnerable and wounded—defenseless.

He hurried to unlock the cuffs. Against all reason, he lifted her to sit on his lap. "You're all right. It was a dream."

"You hurt my shoulder," she murmured, her gaze going to his neck.

"I'm sorry." He rubbed her shoulder and tucked her into his chest. Damn it. This was no way to interrogate somebody. "We need to get a move on, anyway. Do you want to talk about your dream?"

"No." She sniffled into his neck, sounding like a petulant teenager.

He couldn't help but smile. "Then we have work to do."

She lifted her head, tears clinging to her eyelashes. In the dim light, her eyes took on the hue of a meadow after a storm...soft and green. "I've been so scared."

His heart thumped, and the need to protect roared through him. His brain was short-circuiting, and he had to get a grip on himself. He wanted to trust her—too much. Way too much. "Laney—"

"No. You need to understand. I never implanted those

devices. Sure, I worked for the organization, and I helped concoct the steroids and drug regimen—"

Matt's shoulders shot back as a rare temper flared at the base of his neck. His feelings for Laney still lived, and the thought that she'd harm one of his brothers cut deep. Deep enough to take his breath. "Those fucking steroids and drugs almost killed my brother Jory. I had to put him in a headlock once, just to keep him from tearing off his own head." As a doctor, she should've known better. Plus, she was a good liar. If she had planted devices, she wasn't stupid enough to admit the truth to him.

"We didn't know. We thought we were helping."

His low chuckle even felt ominous. "Helping? Right. Experimenting on us like lab rats helped a lot."

"I'm sorry," she whispered.

The apology pissed him off more. "It doesn't matter. What matters is finding the code to deactivate these things."

"I don't know the code."

"No, but you probably know more than you think. So here's the plan. We're going to wait until dawn breaks, and then we're going back to the bar as if nothing has happened. Got it?" He'd cuff her if he had to.

"I figured you'd want to run."

"Oh, we're running. The second I get my picture off the sheriff's phone, we're out of town." He figured it'd take a day at the most to erase any evidence of his existence in town.

She frowned. "Why care about a picture? The people after you know what you look like, and if you leave town, who cares?"

"None of your business." The sheriff hadn't been bluffing about plastering Matt's face all over the news if he left town. He looked too much like his brothers, and they'd all be vulnerable. Especially considering they couldn't just hide out...They needed the freedom to infiltrate whatever organizations were standing in their way in finding that code. He lowered his face toward hers. "Have I made myself clear?"

She rolled her eyes.

The breath caught in his gut. The woman had dared to roll her eyes at him. "You understand what I'm capable of, right?"

"Sure. But I don't think you're going to hurt me." Confidence now shined in her pretty eyes. "I mean, I know you're dangerous and well trained. Your reflexes and strength are enhanced, and you probably know a hundred ways to kill somebody."

He tried to focus. "Okay."

"But you won't kill me."

He frowned. "How do you know that?"

She shrugged. "I just do." She wiggled a little on his lap. "Finding out the truth probably ruined anything we might have had, and I'm sure you're no longer interested, but I don't see you strangling me."

His balls leaped to life from her sweet butt on his groin. She was wrong. He didn't trust her...but damn, he still wanted her. Shit, he'd slept with plenty of women he didn't even like. In spite of everything, he wanted to like Laney. But he was losing control of the situation, and that wouldn't do. He needed her help.

So he clasped her waist and turned her to straddle him.

She caught her breath, and her eyes widened.

His palms slid down, and he cupped her ass. "You've misread me." He allowed the natural dominance he'd been born with to echo in his voice.

Her face flushed, and her pupils dilated. While her voice could lie, those eyes spoke the truth every time. She wanted him. "Stop."

"Are you sure?" he asked, tugging her closer into his erection. He'd been trained by the best in sexual manipulation, and he could seduce her to orgasm within a minute. But as his hands tightened on her fragile bones, he couldn't do it. "Here's the deal. I do want you—that hasn't changed. No, I don't trust you, and frankly, I'm still pissed."

"I know." She flattened her hands on his chest.

"I love my brothers, Laney. From the time I realized they were mine, I've done whatever I had to do to keep them safe." He needed her to understand the truth. "You will help me save them."

She dropped her hands. "What are you saying?"

"If you run, I'll find you. Do you believe me?"

She studied him for a moment. "Yes."

"Good. Besides, if I've found you, the commander will find you, too. I'm your best bet for surviving the next six weeks." He'd keep her safe while they found the truth. "Do you know who the commander is?"

"Yes." Fear filled her voice.

Irritation slammed into him. He didn't like her afraid. "How did you get away?"

"I transferred from the base in Colorado to the one in Tennessee right before the whole place exploded."

He stilled. "What base in Colorado?"

"Headquarters for the organization was actually in Colorado. I was only in Tennessee for a week to replace a doctor who'd had his hand broken."

"Crushed." Matt swallowed, his ears ringing. "I crushed Dr. Rodriquez's hand when he injected Nate with a concoction that almost put him in a coma."

She glanced at the door and back. "I'm sorry."

"So you showed up to continue his work? To implant us?"

"I said no. The second I found out about the chips, I refused. Which is why I was locked up when the whole place exploded." She shuddered. "I should've stayed and helped the wounded, but I ran . . . and I kept running."

"You're done now." Even if she hadn't had a choice, she'd worked for the commander for at least a year. The damage she must've wrought. He released her hips and sat back. "How did you find Joe-Joe in Philly?"

She licked her lips and tried to scoot back, relenting when he held her in place. "A kid I went to college with came from that neighborhood and used to tell fun stories about Joe-Joe and his pals. I headed that way the first second I could."

That was slightly plausible. "And then? Why Charmed?"

A small smile lifted her pink lips. "Why not? I wanted a small town, away from Tennessee, and figured a place called *Charmed* had to be a good choice. It was a whim, and I've enjoyed my life there."

"I see." Was she telling the truth? He wanted to believe her so badly.

"Do we have a chance of surviving this?" she asked, her voice soft.

"Yes. If you help me, I promise I'll make sure you're safe. Even if we don't find the code, and I, ah—"

She grabbed his shoulders. "I'll help you in whatever way I can. You can't die, Matt. You just can't."

The desperation flashing across her face warmed him way too much. "Then I need to know everything you know...from the time they first approached you in medical school until the time you escaped. But first, tell me all about Colorado."

Laney dropped her bag on the main couch in her living room, acutely aware of the man at her back as he shut the door to her apartment. He dropped his bag next to hers, and her mind reeled. "You're not staying here."

"Sure I am. We're dating, it's been a whirlwind, and we're moving in together." His voice remained level as he fastened the locks and maneuvered around the apartment, checking all of the windows. "You might as well start believing it so others will, too."

Matt in her space? All day and night? She shook her head

even as tingles wandered through her abdomen. Sure, she still wanted him. The guy was sexy as hell, and he'd brought her to orgasm multiple times during their nights together. Now she knew he was strong and brave...and wounded. So terribly wounded as a kid in the horrible place. He'd survived, and that impressed her. Even so, they couldn't stay together. "You're not sleeping here."

"I am." He finished his tour and returned to pat a couch cushion. Dare and determination hardened his cut jaw.

"I am not sleeping with you again." She said the words with force, reminding them both.

He shrugged a massive shoulder. "Your choice." A slight Southern accent lifted his consonants. "The sofa will do fine."

She put her hands on her hips. "My choice? Sex is fine with you?" Against all logic, she was furious. The man could just sleep with her without any emotion—without it meaning anything. Without trust?

His eyes turned to slate and gleamed in assessment. "Darlin', I could happily fuck you three ways to Sunday...just say the word." The accent broke completely free this time, and hunger streaked across his face.

She reacted without thinking, tightening her hand into a fist and aiming for his mouth. He could've easily blocked the hit. His gaze remained steady on hers, and he didn't even flinch as she connected. Pain ricocheted up her arm to land hard in her shoulder. His jaw was made of rock.

Slowly, deliberately, he wiped a spot of blood off his bottom lip.

No anger, no expression crossed his face.

For some reason, that was terrifying. Her breath panted out, and a roaring filled her ears. She'd never hit another human being in her entire life, and so she stepped back.

"Stop moving." His soft order held enough of an edge that her feet instantly halted.

She swallowed.

"Feel better?" he asked with a raise of one eyebrow.

"Not really." Her palms were suddenly sweaty. Hitting him had been incredibly stupid. The guy could probably kill her with his pinkie.

"We should probably have some ground rules if we're going to be roommates," he said, his reasonable tone a deadly contrast to the tension emanating from him.

She cleared her throat. "No more hitting?"

"Yes. I'm not a guy you hit." He cocked his head to the side. "Understand?"

"You're fine. Don't be a baby." He was trained. And big. Really big.

He inhaled as if trying to draw in patience. "Just no more hitting. You're better than that."

Heat spiraled into her face. "You don't know me."

"Don't I?" He slipped out of his leather jacket, his voice rumbling low in a tone that licked down her spine with heat. "I believe I know a lot about you. In addition, I suggest you play the part of the doting girlfriend until I get my picture from the sheriff. If anybody suspects the truth, I'll have to take them out."

Her stomach dropped. "You'd hurt Smitty?"

Matt blinked. "In a heartbeat. You understand my motivation here."

His brothers. He'd do anything to save his brothers, including harming somebody innocent. "You can truly be an asshole."

His chin lowered. "I'm glad we're seeing eye to eye. Smitty's safety is in your hands. You control who gets hurt here."

"I'm not that good of an actress."

"Bullshit." Fire leaped into his eyes. "You had me fooled from day one, and that's not easy. Which brings to light my final rule."

Rule? The anger returned full force. "Which is?"

He manacled her elbow. "No more lying. Period. If you even think of lying to me again, I promise you won't like the result. You won't like me."

"I don't like you already." She jerked her arm free. Anger and hurt ached through her. "Let's go get the sheriff's phone so we can forget all about this charade. I'm not a good enough liar to pretend I'm dating you. Not even close."

"Fine by me." He reached back into his bag and tugged out a masculine silver bracelet. "Give me your wrist."

She faltered and then held out her hand. "You don't seem a bracelet kind of guy."

"I'm not." He wound the heavy silver twice around her left wrist. While chunky, the jewelry was surprisingly intriguing. "Do not take this off."

She shook out her arm. "Why not?"

"The clasp has a transmitter so I can find you." He took a deep breath. "Let's go find the sheriff's phone."

"You got it." She'd remove the bracelet the first chance she found.

Somebody rapped several times on the door, and they both turned.

"Laney?" Smitty called. "The police are here and need to talk to you."

She gasped and cut her eyes to Matt. He drew his gun from his bag and slipped the weapon under his shirt against his lower back. Finally, he nodded toward the door. "Answer it."

CHAPTER
17

LANEY'S KNEES TREMBLED as she pulled open the door to reveal a man in a dark blue suit.

Smitty tilted his head, Eugene sprawled in his arms. "FBI guy."

"Agent Patterson," the man said, holding out a large hand. He had to be about thirty with numerous laugh lines that spread out from hazel eyes. He stood to about six feet tall with lean muscles.

She shook his hand. "Laney Jacobs."

Matt stepped to her side and slipped an arm around her shoulders. He extended his free hand. "Matt Dean."

They shook.

"Nice to meet you," Patterson said. "May I have a few moments of your time?"

"Of course." Matt pulled Laney to the side. "Come on in. We were moving my things over." He tugged her to sit on the sofa.

Her mind spun, and she tried to keep from blanching.

Patterson sat on the matching floral chair and drew out a notebook.

Smitty shuffled his feet. "The cat and I are going back to work." The door shut behind them with a decisive click.

Patterson clicked a Cross pen into action. "You're moving in, hmmm?"

"Yes." Matt drew her closer, his tone the right amount of truth and anticipation. "Do you believe in love at first sight, Agent?"

Patterson glanced around the apartment. "I don't know, but I'm not opposed to the idea." He surveyed Laney. "What about you, Miss Jacobs?"

The solid arm around her shoulders provided both security and threat. She had no doubt Matt would take out the FBI agent. Even if Patterson was trained, Matt had learned from birth to fight. Matt's casual mention of love spiraled through her, leaving an odd hurt.

She'd never admit it out loud, but being loved? Yeah, she wanted that. Even more so, being loved by a man like Matt would be all-encompassing. She was just realizing that she had love to give, and she could do that. Could actually give part of herself to somebody else.

Now she did have other feelings for him, and right now, they were edging toward homicidal, so she dug her nails into his thigh and plastered on her sweetest expression. "Please call me Laney. I fell for Matt the first second I saw him." There was enough of a ring of truth in the statement the hurt spread.

"See why I love her?" Matt smiled and adjusted their position so he could clasp her shoulder...beneath her hair. His grip tightened until she retracted her nails.

Patterson nodded. "Uh-huh."

Matt released her and played with her hair with a warning tug. "I'm confused as to why the FBI wants to speak with us."

"The notes Laney has received are part of a case I've been working on for more than five months." Patterson scribbled something in his notebook. "We've been tracking a serial killer in the Pacific Northwest who leaves romantic notes for his victims, rapes them, and kills them."

Her body went cold. Head to toe, ice flushed through her. "Serial killer?"

Matt stiffened. "Are you serious?"

"Yes." Patterson tapped his pen on the notebook. "My partner is with the sheriff right now analyzing the notes, and we have an expert profiler flying in hopefully tomorrow."

"How many women has he killed?" Laney asked, her breath catching.

"Five, counting Claire Alps," Patterson said soberly.

"Commonality between victims?" Matt asked, suddenly all business.

Patterson shook his head. "Young, professional, beautiful. And—their domiciles. Towns in the west like Charmed, Faith, Serenity, Peaceful Valley..."

Seriously? Her choice of a sweet-sounding town had put her on a killer's radar? Laney instinctively snuggled closer into Matt's side. He might not like her, but he wouldn't let anybody beat her to death. God. She'd been afraid of the commander and his followers for so long, it was surprising she could feel this new wave of fear.

"You're safe, Laney," Matt said, running a reassuring hand down her arm. "I promise."

"Actually, you're in danger." Patterson clicked the notebook closed. "I'd like to put you in a safe house while we hunt this guy."

Matt lifted his chin but remained silent while tangling his fingers with hers. The message was clear, however. He'd let her be the one to refuse protection, and she didn't have a choice.

She needed to take control of the situation. "I appreciate the offer, but I'm staying right here. Matt is a former marine, and I feel safer with him. This killer isn't going to make me abandon my life like this—it's time he was caught." She sounded so much braver than she felt.

Plus, right now, the biggest threat in her life was currently holding her hand.

Patterson shook his head. "I'm sure you're trained, Mr. Dean, but we can keep her safe."

"I appreciate your offer," Matt said calmly. "But she's staying here with me."

Yeah, right. They were skipping town the second Matt got his hands on the picture.

"Okay," Patterson said, his tone implying the refusal was anything but okay. "I understand you've been questioned by the sheriff, Laney, but I'd like to nail down the timeline a little bit. When did you receive the first note?"

She recalled the events methodically for the agent, answering each question, trying to remember anybody who'd seemed threatening. There wasn't a soul. Matt remained silent during the interview, his solid presence oddly comforting.

Finally, Patterson wound down and turned toward Matt. "You arrived in town just after the notes started?"

Matt shrugged. "I don't know when the notes started. I arrived in town last week."

"Uh-huh." Patterson's eyebrows drew together. "Do you have a criminal record, Mr. Dean?"

"Nope."

"How long have you been out of the service?" Patterson asked.

"About two years." Matt tugged Laney's hair again.

"I see." Patterson's smile didn't reach his eyes. "What have you been doing for the last two years?"

"Traveling. Trying to find myself," Matt said easily. "As luck would have it, I found Laney. All I ever wanted."

Laney's smile was beginning to hurt her jaw. *All he ever wanted?* Yeah, right. He was full of crap. The words sent an initial happiness through her, but they were a lie. Hurt and anger comingled through her until her head ached. "What a sweet thing to say." She shifted her weight and dug her elbow into his ribs. Hard.

Not by one inch did he react to the dig. "No, *you're* sweet."

Patterson's phone buzzed, and he read the face. "The local sheriff said you refuse to provide either DNA or fingerprints to rule you out for Claire Alps's murder."

"Yes." Matt drew Laney close enough she couldn't jab him with her elbow again. "I'm not exactly trustful of the small-town sheriff or his labs."

"How about the FBI's lab?" Patterson asked smoothly.

"Sorry." Matt didn't sound sorry. "I've had enough experience with big government to be cautious; and since I didn't harm Claire in any way, you don't need my prints or DNA." He turned toward Laney. "Right, sweetheart?" A promise of retribution for the jab glinted in his eyes.

"I totally agree," she said.

Patterson cleared his throat. "Miss Jacobs? Please don't take this the wrong way—" He paused as Matt turned his attention back to him. He swallowed. "But, well, you don't know Mr. Dean. It is quite the coincidence this murder occurred when he'd arrived in town...and the series of murders are in different towns. Probably committed by somebody 'traveling and trying to find himself.'"

A chill swept through her. Was it possible? There had been time for Matt to have killed poor Greg...and even Claire. "Matt is innocent, Agent." If nothing else, she had to keep the FBI guy safe. If he suspected Matt, he wouldn't make it out of the apartment.

Patterson's lips drew into a fine line. "All right. I'm sure you understand to be careful, and please contact me if you receive another note or if something else concerning the case occurs to you." He stood and headed for the door. "We aren't finished, Mr. Dean."

He let himself out.

Silence encompassed the apartment for a moment, and she refused to look at Matt.

He drew his cell phone from his pocket and pressed speed dial. "Shane? My cover needs to be deep enough to withstand FBI scrutiny. So does Laney's. Shore them both up—and get the files on a possible serial killer in the northwest murdering women who live in quaint-sounding towns. I'll give you a call later to explain." He disconnected the call. "So, lover. What now?"

She ignored the sarcasm. "I can't believe any of this."

Matt rubbed his chin and shoved to his feet. "Me, either."

She frowned. "You think Patterson was lying?"

"Maybe, maybe not. But by tomorrow morning, I'll know everything the FBI does about the case." He took the gun from his back and checked the clip. "Why are there so many serial killers in the northwest?"

"It's the rainy season," Laney muttered before she could stop herself. "Not enough sun."

Matt raised an eyebrow. "Vitamin D deficiency, huh?"

"Maybe." She hated that he actually got her odd sense of humor.

"You chose Charmed because of the name. I guess it's possible a serial killer is drawn to the same weird name."

Her mind struggled to realign the facts. "I know it's possible, but how could I have the commander, you, and now a killer hunting me?"

"Born under a bad sign?"

She coughed out a laugh. Yeah, she understood his sense of humor, too. "Were you serious about believing in love at first sight?" She hadn't meant to ask the revealing question.

He shoved the clip back into place. "Hell if I know. Truth be told, I'd have figured we weren't genetically disposed to have love, or feel love, or whatever you do with feelings."

"But?"

"One of my brothers found love—the real kind. He even got married." Matt put the gun back into place. "So, I guess it's possible." Concern filtered through his eyes for a moment.

"Why is that bad?" she asked.

"Because there's a good chance we're all dead in less than two months, and who will protect her? She'll be all alone, and if anybody is left from the organization, they'll hunt her. She knows too much." Matt scrubbed both hands down his face. "So we either need to survive this, or I need to destroy the organization to the point it'll never recover."

"What's her name?"

He shook his head, and Laney tried not to let the rejection sting. Trust didn't exist between them. What would it be like to have Matt's trust and loyalty like the mysterious sister-in-law had?

A shudder wound through Laney. "How many people will you kill to ensure her safety?"

He studied her for a moment before answering. "All of them."

Matt crouched behind the tree and handed the binoculars to Laney. He felt fucking stupid forcing her to accompany him on the midnight mission, but he didn't trust her not to flee him again. When given the choice between being handcuffed to the bed or joining him, she'd chosen to tag along.

Which was a good thing. Because if he'd cuffed her to the bed, he wouldn't have wanted to leave her. Not only because there was possibly a serial killer after her, but because Laney spread out on a bed was a temptation he couldn't resist.

She was so damn cute his teeth ached.

Once learning they were going on a clandestine mission after closing the bar, she'd dressed all in black, including a cap that covered her hair. If she'd had camo paint at the apartment, she probably would've slathered her stunning face with it. Even now, when she was pissed at him and scared of a serial killer, her eyes gleamed with fun as she eyed the cabin.

"They're still awake," she whispered.

A moan echoed through the night.

Laney choked. "Oh. They're, ah, busy."

Yeah. The sheriff was putting it to Tasha Friedan for the third time that night. "I gotta give it to the guy—he has some stamina." Matt turned around and leaned his back against the tree. "I can't go in until they freakin' go to sleep."

Laney pivoted and sat next to him. "Promise you won't hurt them."

He'd do what he had to do in order to secure the phone. "I won't hurt them." The lie cut through him and made him frown. "Promise you'll stay right here."

"I will." She shrugged. "Running doesn't make sense any longer. You found me, the commander will find me, I'm on the FBI's radar, and apparently a killer wants me. I'm out of safe places to go...so I need to finish this. One way or the other."

"Been giving it some thought, have you?" While he appreciated her logic, he didn't like the fatalistic tone of her voice.

"Yes."

"You're going to survive this." He'd make sure of it.

Her smile was sad, especially in the soft moonlight, as she wrung her hands together. "It's doubtful any of us are going to survive this. I've had three good years here, and that's more than some people get." Her gaze ran his face in an almost physical caress. Sorrow echoed in her tone, nearly palpable with her regret. "It's probably more than you've had."

His five years of freedom had been good, but he'd been working hard the entire time to position himself and his brothers in a way to help them survive. "Is that what you meant in that you can't have kids? I mean, that you knew the commander would find you?"

"Yes." Her voice softened. "I couldn't bring a child into the world knowing I was going to die soon. The commander will find me, and you know it."

"No, he won't. My brothers and I will make sure you live." His feelings were convoluted and confusing as hell, but he wouldn't let the commander or Emery hurt her. He'd spent time protecting her, caring for her, and he couldn't just let that go.

"What's it like? I mean, having brothers?" The wind picked up, and pine needles settled across her legs.

He brushed them away. "It's good. I had to train them harder than the commander realized, and sometimes they hated me. But that was okay. We survived, and now Shane is happily married."

"What about the other living brother?" she asked, curiosity in her voice.

Matt shouldn't trust her. He couldn't tell her anything about Nate. But he found himself answering anyway. "He's on the edge...always. Drinks too much, fights too much, and plans to sacrifice himself to save us."

"Same as you. Well, without the drinking and fighting." She wrinkled her nose and glanced up at the full moon. "Maybe that's what it's like to have brothers—to be willing to die for somebody else. To plan on it."

"I guess. We were raised as soldiers and studied as brothers. They used us against one another—if one of us escaped, the others would be killed. So we didn't escape until we all could survive." He plucked a weed by the tree. The woman was too easy to talk to, and the desire to share with her clouded his mind. "Thanks for giving me the location for the sheriff's fishing hut."

"No problem. When he skipped work today, I figured he'd gone fishing." She peered around them to the quieting cabin. "Though I had no clue he was seeing Tasha."

"At least that explains why he'd cover for her about her past." Matt grimaced. "Though why they just don't go after the bastard who hit her, I don't understand."

"Perhaps she's too afraid," Laney whispered. "If the

sheriff loves her, he'd understand and let her choose her own path." Then she grinned as more pine needles scattered around them. "I guess I'm not the only one drawn to Charmed."

"Apparently not. You should've changed your name more."

"Why? Laney is a far cry from Eleanor."

"No, it isn't. You should've changed your name to something completely different." No reason existed for him to be so irritated with her choice of names, or for her courting danger when she shouldn't have. If the commander had found her before Matt had, she'd be dead. But, that wasn't his business, was it? Laney Jacobs didn't belong to him, and he needed to stop acting like she did.

"I disagree with your assessment of my choice of fake names." Her stubborn chin poked out. "I've been fine flying under the radar until you found me, and the search took you five years. So suck it."

His head jerked up. "Did you just tell me to suck it?"

"Yes." She turned back to watch the cabin.

The woman had grit, that was for sure. And no sense of self-preservation. When she forgot how dangerous their situation was and challenged him, he couldn't decide whether to kiss her until she submitted, or flip her over his knee. God help them both when his temper decided for him. "Behave."

"*You* behave," she retorted.

That did it. He shot an arm around her waist and tumbled her to the ground, stretching out atop her. While his elbows bracketed her and sustained his weight, he allowed enough pressure against her to keep her in place. Intensity poured through him with raw, living need at the contact. "I think we need to go over the rules again."

Her eyes darkened to the shade of a pure, deep riverbed. Her lips parted. Indecision wavered across her face. With a smile that was all female, she leaned up and placed a soft kiss at the base of his throat. "No rules."

Fire shot through him. His heart slammed hard enough that he was sure she could feel it against her breasts. He tried to breathe, tried to keep in control.

What in the hell was she doing?

She slid her fingers through his hair, scraping her nails along his scalp.

"Laney," he breathed, her name a warning on his lips.

Her eyelids dropped, and she licked her way along his jaw to nip at his ear. She shifted beneath him, opening her legs and making room for them to get closer, her thighs bracketing his.

His cock sprang to full life, and his mouth took hers. Hard, demanding, he put the feelings he couldn't recognize into the kiss. Gone was indecision, gone was anger, all burned away by a soft kiss to his jugular. His body went up in flames, and he didn't care. He grabbed her ass, his hand scraping dirt, and rubbed her against his raging erection.

A soft sigh from the back of her throat yanked him back to reality.

Then her small hands banded around his back, and her body softened against him. She returned the kiss, her tongue stroking his, her thighs tightening against his.

Electricity roared down his spine to spark his balls.

He lifted his head, taking a deep breath and trying to regain control. They were on a mission, about to commit breaking and entering. She stared up at him, her eyes unfocused, her lips nicely swollen.

A part of him wanted to snap at her, to rage at the way she could light him on fire. But no matter what she'd done in the past, she was his responsibility now, and hurting her was out of the question. "I like kissing you."

The surprise that flashed across her face mirrored the one inside of him. Now he couldn't even control his speech.

She blinked, her tongue darting out to wet her lips. "I wish we could go back to you liking me."

"Me, too." He rolled to the side and helped her into a seated position. The hurt that shot into her eyes hit him right in the chest. He blinked, the idea of causing her pain slamming denial through him. Through who he needed to be. "Okay. I still like you."

"Do not." Her lip pouted out and tempted him far too much.

He blew out air. "You don't sound like a doctor." She sounded way too down-to-earth and real...no snotty opinions or medical jargon.

"I can speak to you in Latin, if you wish." Her slight grin still held sadness.

"Thanks, but no." Latin would sound sexy coming from her, and he had enough problems.

She shrugged. "I was raised pretty much on my own. My friends were poor, and their families were poor. So once I went to college and medical school, I decided to sound like a real person and not an overeducated butthead. I decided to just be me." A dark flush wandered from her chest to cover her face. "Well, until I decided to become somebody else. You know."

He did know. Every time she explained her past, he wanted to like her more. "Tell me the commander forced you to work for him."

Her lids dropped to half-mast. "I'm sorry, I can't. Truth is, I willingly went to work for the organization, and I enjoyed the job for the most part. For the first year, I worked on finding drug regimens to help soldiers survive injuries. I really thought I was helping."

"You didn't question the experiments? Not once?" Those drug regimens had caused more problems than the training exercises.

"Sure. I have a brain, Matt. I knew the incredible results we gleaned could be misused. The science could be misused. But we were allowing people to live. To walk after spinal trauma, to think after brain trauma. I saw the danger and still participated." She ran a hand down the side of his face. "I'm sorry, Mattie. I really am."

The use of the nickname dashed cold water through him. While he didn't believe she was trying to manipulate him, the fact that it'd be easy for her to do so caught him up short. "Okay. Let's figure everything out later." He turned to survey the now-darkened cabin. "I'm going in to get the phone."

She grabbed his arm. "Won't the sheriff notice his cell missing?"

"Yes, but hopefully I can just screw with the memory chip enough that he'll think the phone malfunctioned and not question the missing pictures."

She arched both eyebrows. "You're going to replace the phone after you erase the picture?"

"That's my plan." He should cuff her, but to what? "I want your word you'll be here when I get back."

She nodded solemnly. "I promise."

He studied her, his gut churning. He had no clue whether or not she was lying. "This trust is a one-shot deal you don't want to blow."

She rolled her eyes.

Damn it. "Fine." He stood and strode silently through the trees and toward the darkened cabin. Rough steps led to the wraparound porch, which had old tackle gear and fishing poles hung for decoration. The place was rustic and didn't even have a lock on the door.

He opened the door and slipped inside, taking several moments to accustom his eyes to the darkness. Two heart-beats pumped slowly from the cabin's only other room—they were asleep. Good. He didn't want to blow his cover—or have to hurt the sheriff.

Moonlight illuminated the main room to show a small kitchen and slightly bigger gathering room. A woman's purse sat on the counter, surrounded by fishing paraphernalia.

A stereo system was shoved to the side of the counter, and a smartphone had been plugged into the base.

Excellent.

He hustled over and lifted the phone. The sheriff's screen-shot was of a ten-pound bass, and the guy apparently didn't believe in passwords. Matt scrolled to the photo screen and looked through the pictures.

The breath caught in his throat. Holy crap. The pictures were of Tasha in various stages of undress and— He shut his eyes. God. The woman had been smiling as she'd posed, so the couple had probably been having fun. But...ugh. He didn't need to see some of those shots.

Swallowing, he ran through the remaining pictures—all were taken that day of the woman, the lake, and some fish they'd caught.

Matt replaced the phone in the holder and exited the cabin. Time to configure Plan B. He reached Laney and was surprised by the rush of relief that filled him.

She stood and gave him a questioning thumbs-up signal.

His grin came naturally even as he shook his head.

"Why not?" she whispered, glancing back toward the cabin.

For answer, he took her arm and led her back through the forest toward where he'd stashed his bike—a mile down the way. "The sheriff purged his phone before today, apparently. I need a whack at his computer." Which would be beyond difficult considering the sheriff's station was staffed twenty-four hours a day.

Laney bit her lip as he straddled the motorcycle. "That sucks."

"I know." He held out an arm to help her mount the bike. She hopped into place behind him like she belonged there.

They rode back to the bar, and he paid close attention to sights and sounds around them. Nothing seemed out of place. After parking the bike, they headed up the stairs to her apartment.

The note taped to her door caught him up short. Slowly, he tugged the paper away from the wood and unfolded: *Did you like my present? She wasn't as lovely as you are, and thus she had to go. She tried, but her love wasn't enough. We have much to accomplish, you and I.*

He handed the note to Laney, and the anger in him grew in direct proportion to the color that drained from her face. "I won't let him near you."

She swallowed. "Ah, should we call the FBI?"

The less interaction he had with governmental agencies, the better. Laney was safer with him, and notifying Patterson wouldn't accomplish anything. "Let's call them tomorrow. That way we won't need to explain where we've been tonight."

She paused and then nodded, unlocking and pushing the door open.

He caught her arm and drew her behind him as they moved into the apartment. No heartbeats, no breathing. He closed his eyes and listened. No humming of any type. The apartment was secure. "Okay." He herded her inside, turned, and locked the door.

She brushed the cap off of her head, and her brunette hair framed her face. "So, um, I guess I'll go to bed." Desire and need shimmered in her eyes, even as she faltered near the doorway. "Are you coming?"

CHAPTER
18

N O. YOU GO TO BED." God, he wanted her. Matt gestured
Laney toward the bedroom. Her natural vanilla scent
was killing him, and if she didn't get away, he was going to
tackle her into the couch. "Sleep well. I'm going to call my
brother and see if he's hacked into the FBI files yet."

Her bottom lip trembled, and she turned to head into the
bedroom. Her shoulders dropped to a dejected slant. Did she
not want to be alone?

It took all of his formidable will not to call her back…
or follow her inside. He'd almost lost it in the forest, almost
let down his guard again. But lines had been drawn, and
sleeping with her would screw things up more. He'd slept
with her, and that meant something even to a fucked-up guy
like him. It meant he'd make sure she lived through this and
could start over afterward.

That's all he had to give.

So he sat on the sofa and booted up the laptop until Shane
came into view. A shadow covered his brother's jaw, and
dark circles lined under his eyes.

"When was the last time you slept?" Matt growled, not in
the mood to see his brother disintegrate.

"You sound like my wife." Shane shoved unruly hair

away from his face. "We only have six weeks. Sleep is a luxury I can't afford." Anger and determination glowed strong in Shane's gray eyes...along with fear.

Matt had never seen Shane truly afraid until he'd married Josie. Now he had something to lose. "I know. Stop worrying poor Josie—she deserves peace for now. I mean, just in case."

Shane flashed twin dimples. "Josie is worried about you. She thinks you're in over your head and need backup. In fact, she packed a bag."

God, Matt loved his sister-in-law. "Tell her I'll call the second I need help."

"I will."

Right. There was no way in hell Shane would allow Josie to leave the safety of the ranch in Montana, but the feisty blonde probably didn't know that. Her security meant everything—to all of them. "Is she asleep?"

"Yes." Shane sighed. "Nate has fallen off the grid again. He's obsessed with finding out if Jory is dead or not. I wish I hadn't shared the memory of the video where Jory might have moved. What if he was dead, and I imagined him moving because that's what I needed?"

That's probably exactly what had happened. "Where was Nate's last location?"

"Philly."

Shit. "When?"

"Yesterday. I've called several times, and he hasn't called back in. I've left messages about what's going on with you... and he hasn't called in." Worry lowered Shane's voice. "He's on the edge, Mattie. We need to pull him back."

"I will. You worry about Josie and our next step." Shane had followed the money that funded the commander's organization, Matt had followed the doctor, Jory had infiltrated the scientific agencies, and Nate was supposed to infiltrate the military organizations that conspired with the commander. Their jobs were clear. "Maybe Nate dropped under cover."

"I hope so. If not, the jackass had better check in." Shane typed in keys on his computer. "I'm sending you the rest of Laney's file—her history after she purchased the new identity in Philly. I haven't been able to find her records from when she worked for the commander."

"Don't." Heat filtered down Matt's gullet. "Don't look for them right now. We'd make them aware we have her, and we don't want him to realize we're getting close."

"I understand." Shane nodded. "I also finished a perfunctory search into Dr. Tasha Friedan's background and found a file containing medical records where she'd been harmed."

"Beaten?"

"I think so. She had a different name...and I can go deeper."

"No need." Matt eyed the quiet bedroom. Laney's heartbeat hadn't slowed enough for her to be sleeping. "I know enough there. Concentrate on finding Nate, and on finding out what happened to Jory."

"What about you?" Shane asked quietly. "Are you all right?"

"I'm fine. This is business—always has been." He kept his face stoic as he tried to convince himself.

"Okay." Shane frowned. "If you say so. I'm also sending you the files I stole from the FBI. The case is legitimate... There's a serial killer targeting women in sweet-sounding towns. A total freak."

"You're kidding. I mean, *you're kidding*." Matt shoved an impatient hand through his thick hair. "I swear to God, if we get a break, it's usually a compound fucking fracture."

Shane grinned. "Yeah, I know. Maybe that's what happens when man instead of God creates you."

Matt rolled his eyes. "Shut up. God created us, too." He'd tried to give his brothers that sense of comfort from the beginning, but sometimes, when nobody else was watching, he wondered. Did they have souls?

Had the things they'd done stained their souls, if they had them? Without doubt, letting Jory die alone had destroyed Matt, and he wasn't sure if he wanted a soul any longer. Emotions were weak, and he was now broken. A soul would only get in the way of finishing out what he needed to do.

Shane nodded. "Okay. Call me if you need me. I'd be there in hours."

"Thanks." He forced a smile and said the words that would help Shane deal with the upcoming fight, even though each syllable was now a knife to Matt's gut. "Never alone, right?"

"Never alone." Shane repeated the mantra that had helped them to survive their childhood. "Night, Mattie." He clicked off.

"Night." Matt closed the laptop and dialed Nate's cell phone.

He reached a recorded message. "Nate? It's Matt. Fucking check in, or I'm coming to find you." Disengaging the phone call, he eyed the bedroom. Why wasn't she asleep?

Movement sounded, and the air shimmered before she appeared in the doorway. She'd donned a white tank top and pink pajama bottoms, her hair was up in a ponytail, and she'd removed all her makeup.

She was the most beautiful woman he'd ever seen.

His dick stretched awake while his heart thumped. "Why are you up at two in the morning?"

She shoved an errant curl off her face and steeled her shoulders but kept huddling by the bedroom door. "I've been thinking."

He tilted his head to the other end of the couch and shoved down irritation. "Stop cringing over there like I'm going to hurt you. You know I'm not."

Her head snapped up, and a light pink rose began to cover her face. "I'm not afraid of you." That dainty nose in the air, she flounced over to sit.

No, but something was making her cautious. "Thinking about what?" He closed his laptop and pushed it onto the coffee table.

"The truth," she said softly.

He stilled. "Which is?"

"You're going to need me when you find the right computer and code to deactivate the chips in your spines."

"No." The response came naturally. The mission would be a suicide one, and he couldn't guarantee her safety. Even though she'd lied to him, he'd allowed her in, and he'd allowed himself to care about her. There was no turning that off, and there was no being somebody other than whom he'd become so many years ago. He protected the people he cared about, and although it tore him in two, he couldn't sacrifice her to save his brothers. They wouldn't want him to, either. But he'd figure out a way to save them...maybe with her help so long as she remained safe.

"You don't have a choice." She met his gaze head-on, which couldn't be easy. "The medical computer system is calculated to accept voice command from very few people, and I'm one of those accepted." She shrugged. "There's also a fingerprint scanner and an iris reader involved."

"I know, but we're trying to duplicate the system, so all we need is the code for the chips."

She shook her head. "They wrote an entire program for the chips. You trying to deactivate them, even with the code, would be like trying to open a Word document in Power-Point. It wouldn't work."

The woman was damn smart. "Yes, but we're trying to duplicate the actual program."

"Duplication is impossible. You'll need the exact program. In fact, there's a chance I'm not cleared for use with the chips, since I never implanted any. But I'm the best you've got."

The reminder that she'd held a position of trust at the

facility contrasted with her honest eyes and fragile body in a way that confused the shit out of him. He wanted to hate her, and yet every instinct he had was pushing him to draw her near and offer shelter. Protection from the world. "The best I've got?" he asked.

She nodded. "Maybe I can find some redemption. I definitely worked for the people who hurt you, and I knew the risks of what we were doing. At that time, the good outweighed the risks. Now I'm not sure. But I did refuse to implant chips."

For the first time, he could hear the analytical education in her tone. Her statement came out as more of a challenge, and the primal being at his core reared up to accept it as such. So he tamped down on all emotion. "What's your point?"

"My point?" *Haughty* was the only way to describe the tilt of her chin. "You want my help? Then I want yours first."

Is she fucking kidding? "I already told you I'd protect you from whoever has been sending you notes. If we figure out how to deactivate the chips, I'll go after the guy immediately."

"I know, but that's not what I want."

He kept still to refrain from grabbing her. "Do tell."

She shifted her weight, her gaze finally dropping. "You're probably the best-trained soldier I've ever met."

"True." Did she want him to take somebody else out? The thought settled hard in his gut that she'd send him into a fight. Who was this woman?

"I want to survive this, Matt." She leaned toward him and clutched his knee. "So I'll help you deal with the security when we find the right computer, if you'll train me to survive."

His temper smoldered. "You'll help me deal with the security regardless, baby."

"Will I?" That quickly, she went arctic cold, her expression hard as slate. But those eyes. Dark, green, and teeming with emotion. Oh, she wanted to be tough. She wanted to bluff to get her way.

He appreciated her effort, and even more, the fact that she couldn't quite pull off mean and frosty warmed him in places he needed to protect. Her very failure in trying to be uncaring unfurled something wound tight inside him.

Intrigue and desire began to warm his blood, slowly this time. Taking the moment and gaining depth. "Blackmailing me won't get you what you want, Laney. I could gain your cooperation easily, and you know it." *She wants to play, does she? Fine.* He let his gaze wander down her thin shirt, appeased when her nipples hardened. "You have better ways to gain my help."

She sniffed, fire flashing in her eyes. "I think I'll stick to blackmail, thanks."

The woman had thrown him, and he didn't like it. Not one bit. So he studied her, trying to get inside her head. She stared back, her face pale, darkening circles under her eyes.

"What's your game, little one?" he asked, finally giving in to curiosity and giving up pretext.

"No game. You're trained, I'm not, and I want to learn some self-defense for next time I run." She rubbed her eyes. "I have something you want, and you have something I want... so we make a deal."

Relief finished calming him when he realized she just wanted help. Even so, fairness dictated he provide warning to the sexy little bartender. "I'm an asshole when I train somebody."

She appraised him, biting her lip from the obvious opening he'd just given her.

Yeah, he could be an asshole anytime. He admired her restraint in not stating the obvious. But she should learn some self-defense. Realization finally dawned on him. If the idea of making a deal helped her to feel more in control with the crazy situation they'd found themselves in, how could he refuse? He chose not to question why he wanted her to feel better. "All right."

Her shoulders relaxed. "Good. Let's get started."

He shook his head and fought a grin at her eagerness. His hands clenched with the thought of tossing her down in a move and covering her, but the circles under her eyes worried him. "You need sleep. We'll begin tomorrow."

"I'm not tired." Her lids were half-dropped, and her words had begun to slur.

"Go to bed, Laney."

"No," she said, looking so small and vulnerable his gut hurt.

He frowned. "Are you afraid of another nightmare?"

"No." Her pupils dilated as she lied.

He could handle her stubborn or righteous, but fragile and feminine? He didn't stand a chance. So he stood and lifted her.

She gasped. "What are you doing?"

"I'm tired, and the couch isn't big enough for me. We're sharing the bed." He strode through the apartment and into the darkened bedroom. The scent of vanilla and woman hit him right between the eyes, and the feel of her in his arms quieted the rioting thoughts in his head. Finally.

"No," she said, her cheek resting against his chest, her palm sliding over his shoulder.

He settled her under the bedcovers, scooching her over until he could get in behind her. "I won't touch you, but we're going to get some good sleep. There's too much danger around us right now to be at half strength."

She slid her cold feet along his calf.

"Jesus. Your feet are freezing," he grumbled, smashing the pillow behind his neck into a better configuration.

She chuckled. Her entire body moved when she sighed. Then she turned around, snuggled close, her hand on his abs, her knee pressing his thigh. "I was scared to go to sleep. Thank you."

Unguarded and sweet, she ripped out his heart. God, he needed to touch her. But they really did require sleep. He contented himself with placing his hand over hers.

Seconds later, she was breathing deep against his skin. His woman sure could fall asleep quickly.

The thought jerked his eyes open. His woman? No. What the hell was wrong with him? She muttered something in her sleep and flipped around, wiggling her butt against him.

He swallowed and tried to control his raging hormones. Turning, he wrapped around her, his arm at her waist, his nose buried in her hair.

She sighed and relaxed right into him.

A fierce wave of protectiveness surged through him. He tucked her even closer and decided to worry about it later. For now, his eyes closed, and he found peace.

CHAPTER
19

LANEY AWOKE TO the smell of fresh coffee. She stretched. No bad dreams. She'd finally gotten some good sleep. Turning over, she buried her face in Matt's pillow. His scent surrounded her, and a warming hummed in her belly. The man had slept with her last night, knowing she was afraid of the nightmares. He was one of the good guys, whether he knew it or not.

She slipped from the bed and sought socks from the dresser before heading into the attached bath to brush her teeth. She tamed her hair into a ponytail and headed out for coffee, stopping short at the sight of her living room.

All of the furniture had been pushed to the far walls, leaving a large clearing. *Oh.*

Matt loped out of the kitchen in sweats and nothing else. Smooth skin on his chest covered unrelenting muscle, his body moving with tightly controlled power. Sharp angles defined the tendons and muscles in his arms, and hard ridges made up his abs. His feet were bare and lent an intimacy to the moment.

Oh. Her mouth may have dropped open. Sure, she'd touched him. But she hadn't had a moment to study him... and the guy should be admired. Her fingers tingled with the need to trace each line of those ripped muscles. To feel him over her, thrusting inside her again. Taking her over, stealing her control, making her forget the danger and the past.

The various old wounds and scars enhanced his wildness. What she wouldn't give to jump into that storm again.

He held out a coffee cup, one eyebrow raised. "You okay?"

She wrapped her hands around the mug and nodded, not trusting her voice. Not at all.

"Good. Nice socks." Amusement lightened his eyes to an intriguing hue.

She glanced down at the purple and blue stripes through her thick socks and swallowed a drink of the potent brew. "They're warm."

"Good." He glanced around the room. "I figured we'd start training this morning before opening the bar."

"Why?" she asked, taking another sip.

"I've been thinking. If you're right, and I need to take you into the facility to use the computer, you need some training. Just in case." The determination in his hard jawline didn't bode well for her.

She scratched her elbow. "So this is about the mission. You training me."

"Yes, and I need to know you won't freeze if there's bloodshed, because there will be blood."

She coughed. "I won't freeze."

"Right. Tell me about the nightmares." He took her mug and placed both cups on top of the entertainment center.

"No." The idea of all of that blood made her want to vomit, and the last thing she wanted was to puke in front of him.

He stretched his torso one way and then the other. "You're going to have to talk about whatever happened. I'm assuming it happened in the facility before you escaped."

She jerked her gaze away from the ripple of muscle. "Yes,

and considering this is strictly business, I'm not opening up to you."

"Yes, you are." He drew in a breath. "The only way to deal with it is to talk about it, and we don't have a lot of time. Get your head wrapped around that truth, because next time I ask you, you're going into share mode."

The man had been right. He was an asshole when it came to training. Her chest already hurt. The previous night, when he'd slept in her bed, she'd thought maybe they had a chance...that he'd let go of his anger over her past. But that would mean his taking a chance, risking more than his body, and he wouldn't do that, now would he? To cover up her hurt, she donned anger. "Don't be so bossy. I just want to know how to punch somebody."

"Bossy?" He lifted an eyebrow. "Baby, we're past bossy. I'm training you, and that means you'll obey every damn order I give."

"Then I change my mind. No training." She pivoted to head back into the bedroom.

And didn't make it.

He caught her by the elbow and swung her around to face him. She gasped. His grip didn't hurt, but the restrained fury in the hold stole her breath. "Your choice in this matter ended the second you confirmed I'd need you on this mission. You will train."

Instinct ruled her, and she nodded.

Appeased, he released her. "What training with firearms have you had?"

"Um, none." Her feet arched with the need to retreat.

He shook his head like a dog with a faceful of water. "Yet you own a gun? Where did you buy the gun?"

She bit her lip. "Um, at a garage sale," she whispered.

He blinked as if she was speaking a foreign language. "Have you even fired the weapon?"

"No." She figured she wouldn't fire it unless she wanted

to shoot somebody, and so far, she hadn't wanted to shoot anybody. Until now. "I thought I'd shoot it when I needed to."

He studied her like she'd grown three heads. "You're kidding."

"No." Now she felt like a total dumb-ass, though it was interesting to see the unflappable Matt nearly speechless. His training with guns had probably begun in the crib.

He blew out air and reclaimed her coffee cup to place on the table. "You're supposed to be the smart one," he muttered.

Wait a minute. "I haven't had time to shoot." Although she should have.

"Okay." He loomed over her, looking more befuddled than dangerous. "Lesson one with guns...know that the one in your hand actually works."

She sighed heavily. "I know that." Great. Now he was going to treat her like some helpless female from the fifties.

He rubbed his chin. "You know where the bullets go, right?"

She snorted and laughed, quickly sobering. He wasn't messing with her. "Yes."

Relief crossed his hard face, and he nodded. "Good."

She shook her head, wondering how to redeem herself. "If you're finished with questioning me, maybe we should get to the hand-to-hand training." What she wouldn't give to knock him on his butt just once.

His gaze narrowed at her tough tone. "All right, Dr. Roberts. Or do you prefer Dr. Peters?"

"Actually, I like it when you call me *baby*," she said with a smile that even felt flirty.

"Okay, *baby*. Stop me." He lunged at her, a powerful man with grace.

She yelped and tried to jump away, tripping over her feet and plunging to the floor. He caught her, one hand behind her head, the other wrapping around her waist. He turned, and she landed on top of his chest, her breath rushing out. The carpet probably would've provided a softer landing place than his hard body. She sucked in air, trying to fill her lungs.

He lifted his head, more surprise lightening his eyes. "Your self-defense move is to yelp and fall."

She frowned, her face an inch from his. "You took me by surprise."

"Most attackers do," he said wryly. His broad hand settled at the small of her back. "You've had no training. I mean, none." His eyebrow quirked in shock.

The muscled angles pressed into her flesh, showcasing their differences. Where she was soft, he was hard...and she softened even more against him. "No training," she affirmed, her voice husky. While his heart beat slow and steady beneath her, hers ran into a full gallop.

His eyes darkened. He blinked once. Slowly. That heated gaze dropped to her mouth.

Panic and anticipation raced up her spine, followed by a tingling need for self-preservation. It would be way too easy to get lost in him...to forget the danger and the fact that he didn't trust her. He couldn't trust her, nor could he be blamed for the sad fact. She knew how much he had to lose.

"Wow. You're thinking way too hard there," he murmured lazily.

"Our previous sexual relationship muddies the water." Could she sound any more prim and proper? God.

His cheek creased. "Every once in a while, I can hear the Ivy League education in your voice." He sounded more thoughtful than irritated, so she chose to accept his statement as fact instead of insult.

"I lost the doctor-speak within a few months of working with soldiers," she said softly, gauging his reaction.

"Good. Doctor-speak scares the hell out of us." He lost his smile even while making the joke. Yeah, there was the guy who couldn't forget she'd worked for his nemesis. He tapped her back. "Okay. Let's get you ready to rumble."

She rolled off him and shoved to her feet. "I don't want to throw a wet blanket on your plan, but if we actually break into the facility, those guards are trained. Really, really trained. The little time we have isn't going to prepare me."

He stretched to his feet, all male grace. "I don't need you to take out a guard. I just need you to be able to throw any threat off balance until I can get to you."

"To take out the guard?"

"To take out anybody in our way." He frowned and surveyed her body. "Your strength is in your legs, so we're going to work on kicks first. Now bend your knees." He dropped into a fighting stance to demonstrate. "Kick me."

She couldn't help the small smile. "With pleasure."

Laney masked a wince as she leaned over to slide a beer across a table. Her legs protested every movement. When Matt had warned her about training, he hadn't been joking. They'd worked on kicks for nearly two hours before moving on to arm blocks. Her entire body felt like it had been tossed over a waterfall.

But she could kick.

The sense of power that came with knowing even a little bit of self-defense surprised her.

The bar was hopping, and most of the patrons were having a great time. Several groups of bikers milled around and brought a sense of good-natured fun to the evening. Midnight had passed, and she was counting down the minutes until closing so she could go soak in a nice, hot bath. Apparently her morning yoga routine hadn't been getting her muscles into shape like she'd hoped.

A whistle caught her attention, and with an inward sigh, she maneuvered around tables and bodies to three men who'd just finished playing darts. They had ridden in earlier on rustic bikes and didn't seem to know any of the regular bikers.

"What can I get you?" she asked the guy who had whistled.

He ran a hand through his beard, his gaze dropping to her chest. "What are you offering, hot lady?"

"Last call will be coming soon." She glanced toward the large clock over the bar. Maybe the casual dress she'd worn had been a bad idea. She felt tougher in jeans. "Would you like another round?"

He sat forward in his chair, his large bulk swaying. "I'd like a round of you." His two buddies guffawed, one of them swigging back the remnants of beer from a pitcher.

God. What morons. "Let me know if you'd like to order another drink." She turned to bus a table.

A beefy arm grabbed her around the waist and pulled. She windmilled, losing her empty tray as she flew back into the drunk's lap, her head thunking on his chin. *Ouch.* She struggled, trying to get free. He tightened his hold, cutting off her air.

"Release me," she gasped, her eyes watering.

A pair of long legs swam into her vision, and a long-boned hand reached for the band around her ribs. The drunk released her, and Matt gently drew her up by the shoulder to place behind him. She gulped in air and tried to keep from falling into a full-blown panic attack, pressing her hand against his back to keep her balance. Muscles vibrated beneath her palm like those of a furious German shepherd.

The snap of a bone fracturing halted her hysteria. Her eyes widened as she glanced around her rescuer.

The drunk howled as Matt yanked him from the chair with the damaged hand, his face sheeting white. "You broke my wrist!"

Good Lord. Matt had twisted the man's arm and broken his radius. The amount of force needed to do that with his bare hands was incredible. Laney latched on to his belt to pull him back.

Matt pivoted, jerked, and a loud pop filled the air before the drunk gasped and dropped back into his chair. "Your shoulder is out, too."

Laney released him and backed up, a roaring filling her ears. "You—you yanked the head of the humerus from the socket in the glenoid fossa."

"That's what I said. Dislocated shoulder." Matt kept his attention on the man now holding his arm and wheezing. "I suggest you refrain from grabbing women in the future." Low, controlled, his voice nevertheless held a promise of certain violence.

Laney shivered.

Fingers wrapped around her arm and yanked her against a bony chest. A knife slid against her throat. "Matt—" she whispered as the entire bar fell silent.

He pivoted, his gaze shooting above her head and to the right. "I just broke your buddy's hand for grabbing her. What do you think I'm going to do to you?" His voice softened with the deadly threat.

The body behind her trembled and tightened. "One move, and I cut her."

Laney's knees shook, and her vision wavered. God. Not now. Heat rushed up her body followed by chills. No panic. No panic.

Fire exploded in Matt's eyes. "One chance. Let her go now, or I will kill you."

So much truth lived in his words, Laney stilled. Even her panic was afraid of him.

The third guy went for Matt. Instantly, Matt dropped an elbow onto the guy's nose and punched him in the throat, his gaze never leaving Laney's attacker. The third man went down, his head smacking a chair on the way.

A loud swallow echoed from the man holding Laney.

The injured drunk stood, weaving as he regained his balance. He clutched his injured wrist, fear swimming in his eyes. "This is out of hand. Let's get out of here."

She had to concentrate to force out words. "If you let me go right now, I won't let him hurt you. I promise."

The man's breath hitched. Silence ticked tension-filled seconds. The knife slowly moved away from her throat, and the guy pushed her at Matt. Then he leaned down and hauled up his friend, who was gasping for air.

Matt caught her, smoothly setting her behind him. "You have five seconds to get out of this bar. If I ever see you again, no matter where, I'm breaking your neck in two. I promise." Anticipation lifted his consonants.

The three men quickly fled the bar.

Matt looked around at the quiet occupants. "Bar's closed. Go home."

People scattered like dropped nickels, heading for every exit. Within minutes, the place was empty save for Matt, Laney, and Smitty.

Smitty rubbed his chin from behind the bar. "Holy shit, you can clear a room."

Matt turned and grasped Laney's elbows. "Are you all right?"

She nodded, swallowing several times. The panic lingered just out of reach and waited to strike.

He drew her into his chest, into safety, and rubbed from her neck to her tailbone and back up. "Deep breaths, baby. Take the air in, hold it for five seconds, and then let it go." His warm palm continued to soothe her as she followed his orders. Finally, the buzzing in her head abated.

She stepped back. "I, um, forgot everything you taught me earlier." Not even a hint of an idea had occurred to her to kick or punch the first guy who'd grabbed her. She had just struggled like a flopping fish.

Matt brushed a piece of hair back from her cheek. "One day of training doesn't make you ready. You did fine."

Tears pricked the back of her eyes. After seeing what violence he could easily employ, his sweetness toward her was almost too much. "Thank you."

"I'm sorry I frightened you." A twist of his lips showed a vulnerability he probably thought he hid.

"I wasn't scared of you." Something in her wanted to comfort him.

He ran a thumb across her cheekbone in a soft caress. His gaze lingered on her eyes, as if trying to reassure himself she was now all right. "Yes you were scared, and your instincts are good. I was created to be violent even before I learned to fight. Killing is in my DNA." Sadness and regret darkened his eyes to a mysterious gray.

"No." She grabbed his hand and squeezed. He'd taken over and protected his younger brothers in an honorable way he'd learned on his own. She couldn't allow him to think poorly about himself. "DNA is an acid—heredity material that determines traits like hair color…maybe strength. Killing is a choice, and one you didn't make tonight. You let those morons go." Going on instinct, she stepped into his space and cupped his strong jaw. His rough shadow tickled her hand. "You're more than they made you to be—much more. Don't let them win. Not now, when you're so close."

He closed his eyes and turned his head to place a soft kiss on her palm. "I wanted to kill them, Laney. The second they put their hands on you, I was all right with ending their lives."

The fierce words spiraled down deep into her heart and took hold. He cared about her, and he wanted to protect her. Nobody had ever tried to protect her. "Why didn't you?" she asked, wondering at the pain riding his words.

"Because you were behind me, and I didn't want you to see me kill." His eyes flashed open, so much pain revealed that she caught her breath. Then he drew down the veil. "I easily could've ended them, and I wouldn't have lost a minute of sleep for it."

He would've killed for her, and the thought brought a primitive thrill. Being loved by a man like Matt Dean would carry risks and responsibility. She stiffened and dropped her hand. Where in the world had that come from? He didn't love her, and he never would. A sharp pang slashed into her heart. "Thank you anyway for saving me." She bent to retrieve her tray from the floor. "Let's finish and get cleaned up." Keeping her gaze away from him, she gathered glasses and empty bottles to take to the bar.

"Laney." His deep voice stopped her, and she turned around. His gaze was thoughtful, knowing. "We need to talk about this. Whatever it is between us, we need to talk . . . and I mean tonight."

CHAPTER
20

LANEY'S EYES WIDENED. "We have nothing to discuss."

Ah, there was the educated tone Matt was beginning to actually like. "Yes, we do." He'd almost killed
three men for threatening her, and he had to get himself
under control before he blew the mission any more than
he already had. The feelings coursing through him were
real and new. If he didn't deal with them, somehow figure
them out, he might be too distracted when he needed to be
focused. So she'd damn well help him figure out what was
between them.

The front door opened. "We're closed," he said.

"Ms. Laney Jacobs?" the newcomer asked.

Matt turned to view a lean man wearing khakis and a
polo shirt. "Who's asking?"

The guy smiled perfectly even teeth. "I'm Zeke Frant
from ATW News Source, and I've been covering the Sleepy
Town Serial Killer case for three months now. Rumor has
it Miss Jacobs has been receiving notes, and I was hoping
I could interview her." He dug a tattered notepad out of his
back pocket and promptly dropped it on the ground. "Sorry."
Snagging the pad, he straightened back up.

Matt frowned. Those had to be crowns, right? Nobody

had teeth so perfect. "Sleepy Town Serial Killer? You come up with the moniker yourself?"

"Yes." Frant's narrow chest puffed out. "Catchy, right?"

A reporter was all Matt fucking needed. The kid looked to be about twenty. "Is this your first big story?"

"No. I broke a story about the meatpacking plant in Helena using too much filler." He reached into his other back pocket to fetch a pair of glasses, which he perched on his nose. "Another story about the mayor of Blankstone growing pot in his basement in southern Idaho."

"Ahh. Well, no interviews tonight, pal." Matt glanced at Laney, who was staring at the reporter like a rabbit caught in a trap. "Right?"

She slowly nodded.

Damn it. Where was the woman who lied so easily? The fact that she didn't want to be interviewed was all but written on her face. He probably had worked her too hard in training, because she looked exhausted.

Matt strode straight at the reporter. "We've had a long night, and we're tired. Now is not the time for an interview."

Frant backed away, shoving his glasses up his nose. "What time tomorrow shall I come back?"

"We'll call you." Matt finished backing the reporter to the door, and he kindly opened it for him. Rain splattered the building, and the wild wind smashed water inside. "Good night." A hard clap to the shoulder had Frant tripping outside. Matt shut the door and locked up against the storm. "Unbelievable."

Laney nodded. "That's all we need."

If one reporter had caught the scent of a serial killer, more would be following. Matt had to get his picture off the sheriff's computer and then get Laney the hell out of town. Now.

Smitty whistled a jaunty tune. "More will be coming."

"Thanks, Captain Obvious," Laney muttered, wiping down the bar.

Smitty's gray eyebrows rose to his hairline. "Somebody's having a PMS moment."

Matt bit back a laugh at the murderous glint that leaped into Laney's eyes. "Be careful, Smitty. I taught her how to hurt a man earlier today."

"She'd have to catch me, first." Smitty threw the dishrag at Laney, who promptly threw it right back at his face. "I'm sorry about the PMS crack. I know you don't like me to point it out."

Matt coughed to cover his instant laugh.

Laney turned her glare on him.

He coughed harder.

A sharp rapping echoed on the other side of the door. What the hell? Sighing, he unlocked the door and poked his head outside. "What?"

Frant wiped rain off his face. "I had to call a cab, and it won't be here for ten minutes. Can I come back inside? I promise not to ask any questions." The storm picked up behind him, smashing leaves and pine needles against the building.

"Ten minutes?" Matt asked.

Frant shrugged. "The only cabbie in town is named Mario, and I woke him up when I called. He said it'd take him ten minutes to get dressed and drive here." The reporter hunched his shoulders against the pelting rain. "I'm staying on the other side of town over by the river and didn't want to walk through this storm."

"For Pete's sake, Matt. Let the guy in," Laney muttered from behind him.

He glanced over his shoulder and pinned her with a look. Rather, he *tried* to.

She rolled her eyes again and tossed napkins into the garbage. "Smitty? Help me with the garbage, will you?" she asked while tying a garbage bag.

The grumbling bartender hefted two bags and followed her to the back door.

Matt glanced down at the reporter. "You can stand inside

to avoid the storm, but if I hear one question from you, I'm tossing your ass back outside."

Frant swallowed, his protruding Adam's apple wiggling. "Not a problem. Really." Keeping a wary gaze on Matt, he shuffled inside the door. "I can help clean up, if you wish."

Matt shut the door. "We're good. Thanks." He leaned against the wall and crossed his arms. "What do you know about this serial killer?"

The reporter's eyes narrowed. "Why?"

"Just curious, considering my girlfriend is in his sights."

"Oh. Well, he stalks them by leaving notes, gets bored, and kills them after raping them. No prints, no semen... He's careful." Frustration wrinkled Frant's face. "The victims live in sweet-sounding towns, and they never see it coming. He has to be very meticulous and is an organized serial killer."

So Frant had done his homework into killer types. "How does he choose the victims?"

Frant lifted a shoulder. "I don't know. All the women are pretty, young, and professional. They're either business owners or have good careers." He sighed. "You know, women you'd like to be with. Good ones."

"How did you find out about the local murder already?" Matt asked.

Frant grinned. "Friend from school works with the FBI. Contacts are what you need as a reporter." He wiped rain off his forehead. "How long you been in town?"

"Long enough." Matt glanced at the back door. Laney needed sleep so they could train the next day. "I'd appreciate it if you left Laney out of the paper. She doesn't need any more interest from this psycho."

"Well, maybe. How about we reach an agreement?"

Matt turned his full attention back to the reporter. "Excuse me?"

"I'll sit on the story, on her name, if she'll give me an exclusive either the second the guy makes a move, or the second he's caught." Frant lifted a bony shoulder, his eyes gleaming. "That's the best I can do."

What a little weasel. Matt had never liked reporters. "I'll talk to her and see what I can do." He stepped into Frant's space and allowed the killer to show in his eyes. "Though I suggest you refrain from printing anything about my woman."

To his credit, the reporter kept his gaze. "We all have a job to do, Mr. Dean. This is my calling, and I do it well. Now, where is Miss Jacobs?"

Matt stiffened. Good question. Where the hell were Laney and Smitty? They should've been back by now. "Stay here, Frant." He turned and strode toward the back door.

Laney shot Smitty a hard look over her shoulder as she lifted the lid to the nearest garbage can, allowing the rain to fall on her face. The can was full. "Knock it off about the PMS."

Smitty shrugged and used another garbage can before loping back up the steps and under the awning. "Then stop being so cranky."

She shut the can and bit back a smart remark about bartenders being replaceable. Smitty was anything but replaceable. So, with a sigh, she lugged her heavy bag several yards up the alley to use Caffe Coffee's garbage cans since they were rarely full. Rain smashed into her, dampening her clothing. At this time of night, she really didn't care. Soon she'd be in a hot bath, soaking and relaxing. Dropping in the garbage, she turned and took a deep breath. Honeysuckle and angry nature. Yeah. Nothing like Idaho in the stormy season.

Thunder bellowed overhead, and lightning illuminated the angry sky. She loved a good storm but would prefer to head inside to watch. Skirting a mud puddle, she caught movement from the corner of her eye.

An ignition flared to life before a car door opened, and a body lunged for her.

A gloved fist swung for her face, and with a cry, she

ducked. *Oh God.* The commander had found her. Raw terror froze her for the slightest of moments.

The night narrowed into pinpoint focus. She turned to run, and strong fingers tangled in her hair, yanking her back.

Smitty bellowed and jumped the stairs.

The attacker turned and fired a wild shot.

God. He had a gun. But he'd failed with the shot. No way was this the commander or any of his soldiers.

Focusing, Laney threw an elbow, and her attacker protested with a guttural *oof.* She glanced frantically toward Smitty to see him on the ground.

Fire lanced through her along with panic. Struggling, she managed to throw another elbow. The guy yanked her hair, hard, and snapped back her head. Pain cascaded down her spine.

The bar door opened and Matt leaped outside with a primal roar.

The attacker turned and fired a volley of shots at him. With a cry, Laney jerked her head and shoved back, trying to dislodge the gun.

Matt stalked forward through the storm, toward the shooter, no expression on his deadly face.

The attacker shoved Laney at him and continued to fire.

Laney hit Matt midcenter, and he immediately dropped them both behind a row of garbage cans.

Tires squealed, and the blue SUV ripped down the alley. Black paint covered the windows, and the license plate had been removed.

Matt rolled to his feet and ran after the car, his strides long and sure.

Laney scrambled over to Smitty, who was groaning and sitting up. "Are you all right?" she asked.

"Fine." He pushed to his feet. "I ducked and hit my head. I'm fine."

Thank God. Laney stood and patted his arm. "Go inside

and get dry." She turned to follow Matt's progress, her heart beating so hard it was difficult to breathe.

At the end of the alley, the car zipped around a corner. Matt stopped and glanced back at her. Then, with a steeling of his shoulders, he stalked her way.

The reporter shoved open the door. "Oh God. Did I hear shots?"

"Yes." Laney gently led Smitty over to the kid. "Please take him inside and call the FBI guys." She had to yell to be heard over the rapidly strengthening storm.

"Will you talk to me?" Frant said with a calculating glint in his eye.

"Inside. Now." She put as much authority into her voice as she could.

Smitty grabbed the reporter's arm and all but shoved him inside. "I'm calling the sheriff. He can call the feds." The door shut with a hard bang.

Laney's knees gave out, and she dropped to sit on the bottom step, protected by the awning. She turned to watch Matt retrace his steps toward her. The serial killer had almost gotten her. Adrenaline shot through her veins, and her breath panted out. Safe. She was safe.

Matt strode through the rain, his shoulders wide, fury on his face. A man deadlier than the storm raging around them.

He'd saved her.

Without a thought for his own safety, he'd run straight for a shooting gun.

No fear. Only cold, deliberate intent lived in her savior.

He reached her and dropped to his haunches. Then those hands that had been clenched into fists slipped beneath her arms and lifted her with a gentleness that sparked tears to her eyes.

She swayed into him, grounded by his strength. Her hands slid up his chest, and she levered up to her tiptoes. Grasping his thick hair, she pulled his mouth down to hers.

He stilled.

She pressed her wet dress against his length. Heat washed along her front.

With a growl, he slapped both hands against the building, caging her. His lips slid over hers, taking over, taking control.

Fire flushed through her to pool between her legs. Her mind spun, and the world narrowed to razor-sharp focus on the mouth consuming hers. Heat and demand lived in his lips, in the sweep of his tongue through her mouth. He pressed her against the brick, his arm banding around her waist and dragging her closer.

She moaned, and he lifted her, his free hand shoving up her wet dress and caressing her thigh.

Her legs pressed his hips. A hard-as-rock erection pulsed against her panties. Need consumed her until all that mattered was quenching the fire.

He jerked away from her mouth, his chest panting. Slowly, he closed his eyes and lowered his forehead to hers.

His dick jumped against her, and she couldn't help gyrating along his length.

"Stop," he whispered, his voice beyond guttural, his heated breath brushing her face. The muscles in his arms undulated as he held himself in check. "Hold still, for God's sake."

"I don't want to." She tightened her grip in his hair. It felt too good to be alive.

He lifted his head. Lust, need, and regret swirled in his stormy eyes. "It's the emotion of the moment."

"No. I want you." She might not know much, but she knew her own body, and her own heart. "It's not fear, and it's not gratitude. It's you, Matt."

Sparks leaped through his eyes. Crimson spiraled across his rugged cheekbones as he searched her face. Finally, his lids dropped to half-mast. "Fine. We're going to call the cops and report this. Afterward...it's up to you." Stepping back, he allowed her legs to drop.

CHAPTER
21

A T THE MOMENT, Laney wanted nothing more than to get completely lost in the heat Matt created. She took his hand, needing to feel connected.

He led her back inside the bar and to a seat by Smitty at a table. "You okay?" he asked.

Smitty nodded. He'd already found a bag of frozen peas to press to his forehead. "I'm fine. When the guy shot at me, I fell and smacked my head on the stairs."

Laney kept hold of Matt's hand, all but pulling him into the free seat. "Did you see the guy? My back was to him the whole time. Who was he?"

Smitty lifted a shoulder. "He had on a ski mask that covered his entire head. In fact, the guy was in all black—heavy ski jacket, pants, and gloves. Maybe black boots?"

Dread chilled through Laney. "He was strong and maybe six feet tall?" The guy had seemed really tall and strong, but maybe some of that was the surprise of the attack. "He didn't say anything at all." She glanced up to see Frant rapidly writing in a notebook. "Hey. This is off the record."

The reporter kept scribbling. "No, it isn't."

Matt moved before Laney could argue, snatching the notebook and shoving the reporter into a chair. Matt leaned into him. "When she says it's off the record, it's off the record. Got it?"

The outside door opened, and the sheriff hustled inside followed by Agent Patterson. Todd hurried toward Laney and dropped a hand on her shoulder. "Are you all right?"

Tears pricked the back of her eyes. That was why she'd chosen a small town. "I am. Matt chased the guy away."

Matt stopped intimidating the reporter and retook his seat next to her, sliding a reassuring arm along her shoulders. He shook his head. "Laney fought well. The guy will have bruised ribs tomorrow, without a doubt."

Warmth filled her at his proud tone. Even now, she wanted to be strong but couldn't help leaning into his solid form.

Agent Patterson drew a notebook free of his jacket. "Describe the assailant."

They went through the list of what they'd noticed again. Unfortunately, the guy had been covered head to toe, and the car wasn't familiar.

Todd scratched his head. "Blue Jeep Cherokee?"

"Yes. Why?" Matt asked, studying the sheriff.

"Had one reported stolen earlier today." The sheriff shook his head. "So we don't really have much more to go on except that the guy is willing to kidnap people now."

"Actually"—Frant spoke up from where he'd leaned against the wall, away from Matt—"the killer kidnapped a woman in Faith, Washington, from outside of an ATM machine. They found her later in the forest, and not at her home."

Agent Patterson turned his full attention on Frant. "Who the hell are you?"

Matt frowned. "Who did you think he was?"

"Somebody who worked here." Patterson flipped back several pages in his notebook. "According to the background information my partner picked up, you have several part-time workers through the year."

Frant slipped a business card from his back pocket. "Zeke Frant. I'm a reporter with ATW News Source out of Seattle, and I've been covering the Sleepy Town Serial Killer since the beginning."

Patterson took the card. "Sleepy Town Serial Killer? Are you serious?"

"Yes. All famous killers have monikers." Frant revealed his perfect set of teeth. "Any chance the FBI would agree to an interview in this case?"

"No," Patterson barked. "What did you see tonight?"

"Nothing." Frant actually looked disappointed at the thought. "I heard the shots and ran outside in time to see this guy running after a speeding vehicle. The car was a dark blue, and there was no license plate, as they've already said."

"How many shots?" Agent Patterson asked.

"I don't know. Maybe six?" Frant pushed his glasses up his nose. "It all happened so fast. So, maybe your partner will consent to an interview?"

"My partner is currently trying to track down a witness from the Peaceful Valley crime scene. When he gets back, I'll get you two in the same room." Patterson flashed a hard grin. "He'll shoot you before he talks to you. I'm the nice one."

Frant's lips turned down. "The people have a right to know if there's a serial killer stalking them."

Patterson sighed. "When are you going to print?"

"Tomorrow is the first installment." Frant eyed Matt warily. "All I mentioned about the most recent crime is the location and that the FBI is in town investigating. I haven't written a word about Miss Jacobs. Yet."

Matt's low growl reminded Laney of a jaguar about to strike. She slipped her hand beneath his. "I appreciate that. Thanks," she said.

"Sure." Frant kept his gaze on Matt.

Yeah. Laney had learned the same lesson eons ago—to keep one's eye on the biggest threat. Matt was definitely the biggest threat in the room. Thank God he was on her side. Well, mostly.

Matt turned toward the agent. "Tell me you have some idea who this guy is."

"No clue." The circles under Patterson's eyes spoke volumes. "The guy seems to get better with each town he hits. Hopefully our profiler will get here tomorrow. We've been stretched thin."

Laney shivered in her wet dress.

Matt instantly stood. "We're done here, gentlemen. The second you hear anything, please call." He nodded at the sheriff. "I'd like to talk to you tomorrow about safety arrangements for Laney."

The sheriff stood. "You got it."

Smitty escorted the men out the front door. "Sheriff, give me a ride home, will ya? My head aches a bit."

"Me, too," Frant piped up. "The cabbie never showed."

Laney snorted. Mario was well known to hate calls after ten at night. She turned and tried to smooth down her wet dress. "Thanks, Matt."

He flipped off the lights and strode forward to take her hand to lead her through the bar and up the steps to the living quarters. "I didn't do anything."

"You saved me."

He stopped outside her door. "If I had saved you, the guy would be dead right now."

The harsh words rippled chills down her spine. She leaned back against the door, her head finally going quiet. "Why are you meeting with the sheriff tomorrow?" No way would Matt want anybody else to protect them.

"I'm hoping to get to his computer." Matt sighed. "Sorry I didn't catch that guy tonight."

"Why are you so hard on yourself?"

"I'm not."

Lightning arced outside the hallway window, illuminating the harsh planes of his face. The memory of him coming for her through the storm, walking toward spraying bullets as if they couldn't harm him, filtered through her memories. He'd been focusing on her and nothing else.

She dug both hands into his wet shirt, leaned up on her toes, and pressed her mouth against his.

He inhaled sharply and wrapped both large hands over her shoulders to push her back against the door.

She blinked.

Raw hunger glittered in his eyes. "Wait." Low, guttural, his tone licked right down her skin to part her thighs.

Her eyelids dropped to half-mast as need washed under her flesh. Breathing became unnecessary. "No. No waiting."

"Laney—"

"I want you, Matt. The real you . . . all of you." There were no more secrets between them.

"You don't know what you're saying." His tone dropped to gravel in a cement mixer . . . rough and ready.

"I do." She struggled against his hold until he loosened enough that she could reach up and tangle her fingers through his hair. "We don't have forever, and I know it. Hell, we may not have more than tonight. But I want it. Just you and me—the real us." When was the last time she'd let somebody know her? The good and the bad?

The idea that they were so temporary lent an urgency to the moment. To her need. Something flared to life inside her, filling those empty places she hadn't realized she'd had . . . until she'd met Matt. Until he'd filled them.

He licked his lips, and her knees weakened. Then his gaze dropped to her mouth, the darker flecks in his gray eyes becoming almost black. "I'm better at pretending. The real me? I'm not pretty, and I'm sure as hell not gentle."

"I don't want gentle." Taking the risk, she broke free of

his restraining hands and plastered her wet dress against his heated front. "I just want you."

His hard body shuddered as he fought the desire she could read on his face. "No—"

"Yes." Tightening her hold, she pulled his hair and took his mouth.

He fought her for all of one second. With a groan, he shook her grip and flipped her around to face the door.

One arm snaked around her waist and slid up to draw back her chin. She pressed both palms against the smooth wood. His erection pressed against her buttocks, while his hold arched her back.

She couldn't move.

Fire flushed through her so quickly she gasped.

"You want real?" His heated breath whispered against her ear, the tone dark and real. An offering...a surrender.

"Yes," she breathed. She wanted all of him with a desperation that had her nails curving into the door.

His fingers gripped her leg, skimming her dress up her thigh. She moved her butt restlessly against him, seeking any hint of relief.

"No." His other hand manacled around her hip, holding her still, his tone full of need. His hand continued up, over her belly, between her breasts, taking the material with him. "Arms up."

She faltered, her mind swimming, the words barely making sense. "B-but, we're in the hall."

"Now." The order held unrelenting command.

An erotic shudder wound down her back. Slowly, she inched her palms up the doorway, and he slipped the dress over her head. Her breasts sprang free.

"No bra?" he asked, his lips dipping to her ear, his hands covering hers above her head and holding tight.

She swallowed and bit back a whimper. "Shelf bra—in dress."

"Ah." His fingers curled over hers as he stepped into her, capturing her length with heat and unyielding muscle. There was nothing gentle about him—and he'd warned her. His hold on her was firm, controlling.

And she knew, with every instinct she owned, that he was just getting started. She'd unleashed something within him, and she'd done so on purpose. "Matt, please—"

"No, baby. You'll beg when you're on your knees. Later." His mouth found the sensitive spot beneath her ear in a full assault demanding her compliance. Her surrender.

His words permeated the fog in her brain even as she tilted her neck to grant better access. "I. Won't. Be. On. My. Knees." She panted the words out.

The male chuckle at her ear almost threw her into an instant orgasm. "You know not to challenge me."

Oh yeah? She rolled her hips against the hard ridge pressing into her.

His sharp intake of breath filled her with triumph.

"You wanna play?" he murmured.

"Yes." She did it again.

"You ever been taken from behind?" he asked, nipping her earlobe with enough of a bite to catch her breath in her throat.

"No." Sex had been merely a quick stress reliever while she was in school, and she hadn't been with anybody since fleeing the organization. "Not going to happen, Matt." Yes, she wanted him to change her mind. If he wanted such trust, he'd have to earn it.

He released her hands, opened the door, and banded one arm around her bare waist to walk her inside. Shutting the door, he flipped her around.

The glittering hunger in his eyes lit her on fire. She gripped his shirt and tugged it over his head, having to stand on her toes to make it work. Holding his gaze, she reached for his belt, her fingers fumbling as she slipped it free of his jeans.

Rain pelted against the windows in a full tantrum. The lights flickered, and she didn't care. Not at all. Unsnapping his jeans, she helped him to shed them. The guy had gone commando again. "Now who's nude?"

His arm snaked out and twirled her up and over, removing her panties before settling her back on her feet. "You are."

Her knees wobbled. God, he was fast. And strong. Incredibly strong. "So are you." She ran her fingers along the bottom of his shaft. The man was built.

His eyes darkened to masculine warning. "You have the softest touch." Threading both hands through her hair, he tilted back her head, his mouth taking hers. She parted her mouth to ease the pressure.

Matt thrust in and took firm possession with demanding strokes of his tongue. His scent surrounded her, filled her. The hands in her hair tightened, holding strong, keeping control. Her nipples scraped against his chest and sent raw tendrils of need to her cleft. God, she needed to be filled. She groaned, her hands gripping his waist, trying to get closer. So much closer.

He backed her through the apartment to the bedroom, his mouth working hers the entire time. Her feet slid on the smooth carpet, but she allowed him to steer her, sure he wouldn't let her fall.

They reached the bed and her knees buckled. He pushed her up the bed, moving along her, settling his bulk against her. His cock throbbed and pulsed right where she needed him, so she slid her legs apart.

His grin provided warning. "You're not ready."

"I'm so ready I may orgasm without you." She brushed his hair back, losing herself in all the silk.

He slid to the side, tweaking her nipple before caressing down to slip one finger inside her. "I think I was clear earlier."

Was he using words? Speaking something? Trying to communicate? "Um," she agreed, twisting against his hand. Another finger joined the first, and he rotated them, causing her to see stars.

"You're so wet for me," he said, his voice a deep rumble. "And I *was* clear."

About what? She frowned, trying to focus while he tortured her with that orgasm swirling nearer. "Clear?" she gasped.

"Yes." He leaned in, his mouth wandering along her throat. "Your knees. Begging." Strong teeth nipped her collarbone.

She arched into his hand, sighing deep. "No."

The tap to her clit had the room sparking into silence.

He slipped one arm beneath her and rolled them both onto their stomachs. Smooth and controlled, his knees pressed down on the backs of her calves, sliding her legs toward her chest.

One sharp yank back, and she found herself on her hands and knees. "Oh, I don't think so—"

He thrust two fingers into her from behind and scraped her clit with a fingernail. Sparks exploded behind her eyes.

"Oh God—" she moaned, her head dropping forward.

"Close, but not quite there." He released her. The hair on his thighs tickled her legs as he covered her, his cock pressing at her entrance.

Her nails digging into the bedspread, she shoved back against him. "Now—"

"Not quite..." He reached under her and palmed her breast, tweaking the nipple with enough pressure she whimpered. *For more.* "How about now?" His breath at her ear was heated sin.

Her entire body undulated with the need to come. "Now is good," she ground out.

He plunged hard and deep into her.

She cried out, her back arching, her sex vibrating.

His fingers found her clit, playing, tugging, torturing. She attempted to pound back against him, to find the friction to send her over, only to be thwarted by his sure hold as he continued to play. It was too much. Her abdomen rippled with hunger.

He pulsed inside her, so large, so deep. Another sharp tug to her clit.

"Oh God, Matt, now." Her eyelids fluttered shut as she balanced on the precipice.

"You're on your knees, just like I promised. Remember the rest?" His teeth sank into her ear. "Say *please*, baby. Say it now."

Her eyelids shot open to see a blurred world. He'd put her where he'd told her she'd be, and she didn't care. He was in control, and he held her tight. She couldn't move. One little word, and she could fall. She needed to fall. "Please."

At her word, a deep growl of surrender came from his chest.

Power infused her. He might think he was in control, but he needed her as much as she needed him. "Now, Matt," she whispered.

A heated breath at her ear was the only warning before he clamped both hands on her hips and started to pound. Hard and deep, he thrust into her, sending electrical sparks along the way. The headboard beat against the wall, and he pulled her back into his groin with each thrust.

So much pleasure rippled inside her she lost her breath. He angled deeper, and she exploded, screaming his name.

Flashes of fire zipped behind her eyes. Devastating sparks ripped through her in waves too intense to be pleasure. The sensations bombarded her, taking her over, taking everything. Somehow, he swelled even bigger inside her, prolonging her ecstasy, wringing every ounce of spirit from her.

Stilling, he tightened his hold as he came, her name a mere whisper on his lips.

She came down with a sob, going limp. He withdrew and flipped her around, his mouth finding hers.

Sweet, hot, and teeming with emotion, he kissed her until all she could do was wrap both arms around his damp shoulders and hold tight. Finally, resting against her, he let her breathe.

Her heart beat so rapidly her lungs compressed.

He dropped his forehead to hers, his eyes closed. "Laney."

CHAPTER
22

LANEY HELD MATT TIGHT as he slept, her chest aching. She wasn't sure she could forgive herself for working for the commander. There was no way Matt could forgive her.

Sure, the medical advancements had been impressive with the experiments and drug regimens. But she'd realized the dangers, and she'd pressed on. There was no undoing that fact. Life never really was black-and-white, now, was it?

She'd learned the hard way, as an adult, how evil ruled the commander. But being raised by the monster? How the hell had the Dean boys survived?

Laney struggled to keep her eyes open. After making love with Matt, she was raw and vulnerable...and the nightmare waited to claim her. So she allowed her mind to wander back to the best days of her life, when she'd started college.

She'd arrived early to her assigned dorm room with her neatly packed bag to find pure chaos. Music blasting, haphazard posters on the wall, and crazy mismatched rugs on the floor. A wild, unruly mass of red hair had popped up from behind a desk before sparkling blue eyes came into focus.

The girl hustled over the desk, hand out. "I'm Nancy, and I'm you're roommate, and I'm rebelling."

They'd been instant friends. The best of friends. They'd both majored in premed. While Laney had earned top grades, Nancy had struggled. Laney had helped her along the way as much as she could.

When Laney attended medical school, Nancy had decided to attend nursing school. They'd found an adorable apartment off both campuses to share. Life had been fantastic. When Laney had been offered the job with the military group, she'd agreed only if she could bring her own surgical nurse.

So Nancy had headed east with Laney. When Laney made a mistake, it was colossal. She'd killed her best friend.

At the sobering thought, Laney allowed Matt's heat to lull her into sleep. Usually if she acknowledged the truth before falling asleep, the nightmare left her alone.

Not tonight.

The nightmare hit close to dawn.

Over five years in the past, Laney glanced over at Nancy in the triage hospital waiting area. This was their first month in the new location, and she missed the routine of Colorado. "I'm not sure we should've agreed to come to Tennessee."

In adulthood, Nancy had tamed her crazy hair into a manageable bundle. She smoothed down blue scrubs. "Is that a gut feeling?"

"Yes."

"The same gut feeling you've been having about the recent drug regimens?"

"Yes." Laney drew in a deep breath. She was young, but she was smart. "Some of the side effects have concerned me."

"Me, too," Nancy said softly.

"Sorry about Adam," Laney said. The young soldier had reacted very poorly to a regimen and had been taken to another base somewhere.

Nancy shrugged. "We'd only been dating a month. It probably wouldn't have worked out anyway." She glanced at the blackened windows. "Maybe we should take some time off and go visit my granny. She'd love to see us."

The elderly woman had pretty much welcomed Laney into their family with apple-scented arms. She was the only family either woman had. Laney nodded. "Let's put in for vacation time tonight. We should rethink our plans here."

A nurse poked her head out of the surgical hallway. "Please scrub up—surgery in ten."

Laney led the way into the prep room, where they both scrubbed up. "Don't you think it's weird they won't tell us what the surgery is today?"

Nancy pursed her lips. "Yeah. Really weird."

Laney steeled her shoulders and headed into the operation room. She'd gotten her best friend into this mess, and she'd get her out. Dr. Rodriquez was waiting for them, wearing a cast on his right hand. She gasped. "What happened?"

His black eyes had seemed beadier than usual as he'd frowned over a bushy beard. "Risks of the trade." Then he'd stepped back as a patient had been rolled into the freezing room.

The patient was about six and a half feet tall, and weighed perhaps about two fifty. Short blond hair had been buzz-cut close to his head. He was out cold and stripped to the waist.

Laney frowned. "I don't understand."

Dr. Rodriquez wheeled a cart toward the patient's shoulders. Surgical implements and a rectangular silver disc were on the cart. "I need you to implant the disc as near to the C4 vertebra as possible."

Chills had slammed through her skin. "Wh-why?"

The door opened again. "That's irrelevant," said a hulking man with dead brown eyes. "Do your job."

This was wrong. On so many levels, Laney knew the chip would only hurt the patient. "Who are you?"

"I'm the commander. You could say I'm in charge here," he said.

Dr. Rodriquez laughed. "So true."

Laney backed away from the surgical implements. "What medical need does this serve?"

The commander narrowed his gaze. "It fills my need, which is all you should care about."

Fear trickled down her back. "What does the chip do?"

"It explodes and severs the spine if the soldier disobeys an order. All it takes is a code from my computer . . . or a lack of update every five years." No emotion filtered on the commander's words.

Laney squinted for a better look at the device. It was way too small to inflict the damage he claimed, yet she knew he was telling the truth. Whomever had designed it was a true genius. She swallowed. "So if somebody escapes you, they die?"

"Of course." Pure evil glimmered in his eyes. "You do understand that there's a nobler purpose here, right? We need these safeguards."

This wasn't a safeguard, it was slavery. She was too smart to fall for his line, and she'd followed blindly for too long, counting on patriotism. Counting on honesty. "No." She shook her head. While she had been a part of military experiments that appeared noble but could still be harmful, there was no nobility in the kill chip. "I won't do this."

The commander nodded. Quick as a whip, he grabbed Nancy and sliced the scalpel across her jugular. Blood sprayed in a graceful arc.

Laney screamed and rushed toward her friend.

Nancy slid to the floor, her eyes wide in death.

The commander kicked her out of the way and yanked Laney up with one strong hand. "Do the surgery, or I'll kill everyone you care about."

She shoved him, fury heating her breath. "You just did."

. . .

A small moan awoke Matt around dawn. The scent of woman and sex filtered around him, instantly hardening his cock. Laney snuggled into his side, her heart beating loud enough for him to time each pump.

Thunder rolled outside, and she jerked awake with a small scream.

He ran a hand down her arm. "Bad dream. You're okay."

She sucked in air, her entire back moving with the effort.

He turned her to hold close. "Tell me about your dream."

"No." She sniffled into his neck.

He couldn't help the smile. "Just tell me."

She drew in a shaky breath and told him the nightmare that kept her from resting peacefully.

He kept his face bland and ran a hand down her arm several times. The fact that the commander had killed the nurse without a second thought didn't surprise him one bit.

Finally, Laney wound down with a hiccup. "You were raised by that monster?"

He exhaled. "Yes. They put us into groups by family—my brothers and I all had the same sperm donor." He had always wondered what woman had carried him for nine months and then let him go so easily. Probably a surrogate. They'd never found any identities of the egg donors. "I think some serious genetic splicing went on. My brother Shane always thought we had some animal genes added." Matt smiled, hoping it was a joke.

He could lie to himself that he was sharing with Laney so she'd share with him as an investigative approach. But he'd be full of shit. He wanted to somehow explain who he was to her. However, he had to ask the question whirling through his brain. "The man on the table, the one you refused to harm. Was it me?"

"No." She ran her palm along the side of his face.

It was all he could do not to turn into her warmth. "How do you know?"

She shrugged. "He wasn't as big as you, and he had blond hair."

It shouldn't matter, but Matt was glad it wasn't him or his brothers. "When you refused to help, what did the commander do?" Rage all but wanted to eat Matt's skin off his body, yet he kept his voice low and soothing.

She bit her lip. "I ran out of the room, and next thing I knew, I was locked in a cell. The commander told me I would rot in there until I agreed to perform surgeries again, although he found somebody else to do those implants, as you know." She gagged and covered her mouth, sucking in several deep breaths. "I knew I couldn't ever return to surgery. Every time I see blood, I think of Nancy. And faint. I can't ever be a doctor again. I just can't."

"It's okay," Matt said softly. "You're safe." But she wasn't, not really. She wouldn't be any safer than he was until the commander was dead. "I'll take care of it."

She nodded, dark circles slashing under her pretty eyes. "I was there for a month...and then the world blew up."

"That was us." He forced a grin. "We blew the place up—computers and everything. That's when we fled."

Her cell phone buzzed from the nightstand, and he handed it over to her.

"Hello?" she asked quietly.

Even though she kept the device to her ear, Matt's enhanced hearing allowed him to hear the entire conversation. Apparently the FBI profiler was in town and wanted to speak with Laney. In fact, according to the sheriff, he was on the way.

She hung up and tossed off the blankets. "We need to get dressed."

A knock sounded at the apartment door. Matt exhaled. "The guy is in a hurry." He slipped from the bed and yanked on his jeans. "Get dressed and take your time. I'll handle him." He padded barefoot through the apartment to open the door and stopped cold. "What the hell?"

Nate's hand shot out to shake. "Mr. Dean? I'm Leo McGovern from the FBI. Can we talk?"

Matt took the offered hand and squeezed. Hard. "Now isn't a good time...Leo."

Nate's gaze dropped to his bare chest as his grip tightened in reaction. "I can see that." Even through the brown colored contacts, his eyes glinted with equal parts concern and irritation. "However, I'm here now."

Matt leaned in. "What the fuck are you doing here?" he whispered.

"I'm the profiler." Nate's lips quirked in his signature smart-assed grin as he yanked his hand free. "Apparently, you need a shrink, moron." The banter was light; Nate's demeanor anything but. The guy was pissed.

"I'm undercover here," Matt drawled. Sure, he'd slept with Laney, and he even liked her. But this was a job. Even as he tried to convince himself, he knew there was no fooling the human lie detector standing in front of him.

"Bullshit." Nate shoved him back into the room. "Shane and I agree you're in over your head, and this ends. Now."

Temper exploded in Matt's chest. "I'm in charge, and you two will follow every order I give. Right now, you're splitting town."

"That's proof you're not thinking," Nathan said. "I'm on the inside already. Any particular reason you don't want me here?"

"Matt?" Laney hesitated in the living room. "What's going on?"

"Ah," Nate said softly, a muscle twitch in his forearm broadcasting inevitable movement to the left.

So Matt edged to the side to keep Nate trapped.

His brother's eyes narrowed behind the dark contacts. "Does she know your special skill?" he asked softly...too softly for Laney to hear.

"No." Matt glanced over his shoulder. "This is Leo McGovern from the FBI, and he's leaving now."

"No, I'm not." Nate feinted left and then moved right so he could view Laney. "I need to interview you, Miss Jacobs."

Laney had donned faded jeans and a green T-shirt that brought out the different hues in her intriguing eyes. With her hair pulled back in a ponytail, she looked fresh and feminine. Delicate, even. "All right. Can I get you some coffee?"

Nate showed his teeth. "That's kind, but no thank you."

She gestured toward the chair angling the couch, her concerned gaze flitting from Nate to Matt and back again. "Would you like to sit, Agent?"

"I truly would." He shoved past Matt and took a seat. "No need for the title. I'm just an FBI consultant—not an agent. Their regular profiler had some sort of hunting accident, and they called me in yesterday."

Matt cut his brother a look. "The regular guy isn't dead, is he?"

"Oh no, of course not. Just laid up for a bit." Nate tilted his head toward the sofa and smiled. "Shall we get started?"

Nathan Dean shoved down anger and concern until the emotions no longer existed inside him. Focus was the key to getting Matt out of the mess he'd created. As the oldest, Matt was usually the cautious one. Not this time. Nate just couldn't understand it...until the woman had walked into the living room.

Laney Jacobs was beautiful. Not in a fancy, kick-your-ass way, but in a sweet, feminine, intelligent way. No wonder Matt was lost.

Time to get his brother back to earth. "So, you're a bartender?" Nate asked.

"Yes. I own J's Bar, which is downstairs," she said, settling closer to Matt on the sofa.

So far, true statement. Nate nodded. "Why own a bar?" he asked.

"What the hell does that have to do with the recent murders?" Matt growled.

Laney patted his hand, and he relaxed into the cushions, a muscle ticking in his jaw. Nate allowed enough of a sneer to cross his lips to piss Matt off more. Yeah, the woman had him leashed. "My brother wanted to own a bar, so we went in as partners."

Lie. Definite lie. "I see," Nate said. "I'm asking questions to get a feel for you, for the life you live." *In order to understand what the hell Matt is thinking.* "I need to get a handle on the guy sending you notes. Knowing you will help me to profile him."

"Okay." Laney drew circles across Matt's knuckles. "I like owning the bar. People come in to celebrate, to commiserate, to just relax. I get to be a part of their day."

Without being too involved. Interesting. God, Nate would love to understand why she'd become a surgeon. He purposefully moved in an unnatural way, so she wouldn't draw a comparison between his mannerisms and Matt's. "Do you think our professions are driven by needs or wants?"

She shrugged. "Both, I guess. Like you being a profiler. You must need to find the truth."

"I do." Nate switched his gaze to Matt's smoldering one. "The truth is often veiled, and once we get emotional, we lose all perception." He had to get his brother the hell out of town. Matt was spiraling, whether he admitted it or not. "Don't you agree, Matt?"

"I agree we need to get all important facts together before making snap decisions...and mistakes." Matt's tone couldn't be any more threatening.

Laney paused, her head turning in jerky movements to view Matt's face. Concern furrowed her brow. "Are you all right?"

"Fine. I don't like my morning interrupted by people asking stupid questions," Matt said.

Nate leaned forward, his ears heating. "You don't seem like you're in control right now, Mr. Dean. As a profiler, I have to wonder why."

Laney twitched, her hands fluttering. "Um, maybe we should do this later."

Nate waited until Matt realized he was scaring the woman next to him, and when Matt held his gaze, the truth hit. Matt didn't give a shit if Laney caught the undercurrents between them. Nate shook his head. "This is unbelievable."

Laney swiveled toward him. "What is?"

"A killer murdering people in quaint towns." Nate slid his most reassuring smile into place.

By the rapid fluttering of Laney's pulse, she wasn't appeased. "I agree," she said.

"Just a few more questions," Nate said. He ran her through her history with the notes, her thoughts, her feelings about the attack the previous night. While Nate didn't care about her responses, he cared how Matt reacted to every emotion or thought from the woman. They were in tune...too much so. Way too much so. Finally, Nate wound down. "I appreciate your answering my questions." He stood. "I'll be in touch."

Matt stretched to his feet. "I'll show you out."

Nate nodded and headed out the door and down the steps. Then he turned around to take the punch.

But Matt didn't swing. Instead, he gripped Nate's shirt and slammed him against the wall. Hard. Pain ricocheted down Nate's spine, and the roar of breaking wood echoed throughout the empty bar.

Matt leaned in, fury etched into his face. "What the fuck are you doing?"

"Saving you," Nate said simply. He'd kill for his brother, and he planned on dying for him. He'd willingly take the pain of a good beating if it'd help Matt get perspective. "Wanna hit me? Go ahead. But when you're done, we're leaving town."

Matt released him with a hard shove against the damaged wall. "I don't want to hit you. Much." He turned and dragged a hand through his hair. "I know she worked for the commander, Nate, but it's not like our hands are clean. While she repaired soldiers and even helped with the drug regimen, she didn't mean to hurt anybody—even if the procedures might someday. And she sure as hell didn't implant any chips in spines. She said no, and the commander is after her."

"So?" Nate asked.

Matt stilled. "So?"

"Yeah." Nate straightened his leather jacket. "Who the fuck cares if she's innocent or guilty? We have six weeks to live. Get the truth from her, get the codes from her, and let's get back to the mission." Why in the hell did he have to spell this out? He swallowed. *Wait a minute. No.* "You're not thinking—"

"No," Matt said savagely. "This is temporary."

Nate sagged back against the wall, his breath heating. *Impossible.* "You just lied to me."

Matt's jaw snapped shut. "No, I didn't."

"Shit, Mattie. You just lied to yourself." Nate shook his head. "I tried loving somebody from our past...somebody who the commander had gotten to. You know that. It almost killed me." Nothing could happen to Matt. Not Matt. He was invincible, and he had to stay that way. "You can't do this. Can't be lost."

"I know." Matt frowned. "I'm fine."

But he wasn't. Nate's gut clenched hard. "Shane is bad enough. I love Josie, I really do. But Shane doesn't sleep... He barely eats. He's consumed with the thought of the commander getting to Josie if we die. Shit, even if we don't die." Nate needed very little in life, but Matt being strong and whole was a must.

"I know." Matt's voice dropped to a tortured tone Nate had never heard before. "My focus is on the chips and on finding out what happened to Jory." Guilt and so much pain filled Matt's eyes that Nate's lungs quit working.

Nate shook his head. "Jory wasn't your fault—"

"Bullshit," Matt said savagely, his face contorting. "I promised him he'd never be alone, and he died without us there. Without—"

"*We* promised him that," Nate said quietly, his eyes filling. Shame and devastation made his voice hoarse. "I raised him as much as you did. *We* failed him."

Matt's chin dropped, and his eyes closed, the agonizing sound he gave defying description.

Nate reacted the only way he could and stepped into his brother, engulfing him in a hug. Matt reacted instantly, his broad hands clapping across Nate's back. For a moment in time, two of the deadliest soldiers ever created tried to offer comfort amid a whirlwind of pain.

"I'm sorry I haven't been able to grieve him. To help you grieve." Nate forced the words out, his voice cracking. "I've been clinging to the idea that he's still alive." Even now, a kernel of hope lived inside him. The second it died, he might, too.

"I know." Matt released him and levered back. "I try not to hope, but I can't help it. We need to find him, no matter what."

Nate inhaled and stepped back while nodding. "I agree." He took several deep breaths, calming himself. Time was running out. "Now, about Laney."

Raw emotion crossed Matt's face.

Reality hit Nate in the center of the head harder than any punch he'd ever taken. Heat filled his lungs, making them ache. "It's too late, isn't it."

Matt blinked. Twice.

Nate sighed, his brain rapidly calculating scenarios. "Even if you leave her, it's too late." His big brother had fallen in love, and hard. Completely. He shook his head. "God, Matt—"

"Shut up, Nate." Matt rolled his shoulders, using an old trick he'd taught them all to relax. From the look of his hard jaw, it wasn't working. "I've known the woman too short of a time." Desperation filled his eyes.

"So what?" Nate shook his head, pain for his brother washing down his back. "We don't live in the real world, in picket-fence places. We live the way we live—fast, hard, and bloody. Life is fast, and death is faster." He took a deep breath of lemon cleanser and gin. Jory was likely dead, Shane was consumed, and now Matt was lost. How the fuck was he going to fix everything? "If you love her, leaving won't help. Believe me, I know."

Matt eyed him, his pain palpable. "You still love Audrey?"

"No." The woman had tricked him and then betrayed him. "But I plan on meeting up with her again, if we survive the next six weeks. Just to settle the score." Just to prove he didn't still love her. He couldn't, right? "Do you love Laney, Mattie?"

Matt drew in air. "Feelings are irrelevant. Let's get to the plan."

"Actually, your brother asked you a question, *Mattie*," Laney said quietly from the stairwell. "Do you love me?"

Nate pivoted to face the stairwell along with Matt. *Shit.* They'd been so engrossed with their conversation, they hadn't heard her coming down the stairs. Instant fury ripped through him. "See why this is a bad idea? If she'd had a gun, we'd both be dead."

"I do have a gun." She yanked a nine-millimeter from her waist. "See?"

CHAPTER
23

T HE INSTANT ROARING through Matt's head didn't bode well for any of them. The woman pointed the gun at Nate, her gaze confused, her hand trembling.

"Put down the gun." Matt kept his voice calm and controlled to cut through her panic.

"No." She widened her stance. "I think it's time you introduced us."

Matt edged to the right and subtly shook his head when Nate moved the other way. His brother paused, one eyebrow raised. "I've got this," Matt said.

"Do you, now?" Laney changed her aim to him. "You let me sit through an entire interview with your brother without letting me know who he was."

Okay. So she had a right to be pissed. Kind of. "I said to put down the gun."

Nate chuckled and leaned against the wall, giving the impression he was relaxing. "Remember when Josie pointed a gun at us?"

"Yeah." Matt angled closer to Laney, his eye on the weapon.

Laney swallowed. "Who's Josie and what happened to her?"

"She's our sister-in-law, and she married our brother,

Shane," Matt said. Nate appeared calm, but he could strike without warning, and Matt didn't want him shot...or Laney hurt. "Nate? I need you to go to the sheriff's office and get a picture of me off his computer." The sooner Matt got Nate out of the bar, the better.

Nate frowned. "You let the sheriff take a picture?"

"Yes, and I hope it's on his work computer. Now that you're working with the FBI, you can get access to it." Actually, the situation was ideal.

Laney's nostrils flared. "Then what?"

"Then we're leaving town," Matt said. He was close enough to lunge and take the weapon, but he didn't want to frighten her. Too much. "All of us."

Nate let loose with a low growl and pushed off the wall. "We're not finished with our talk." Without looking back, he strode around the pool table toward the front door. Once close, he glanced over his shoulder. "By the way, *Eleanor*, I'm Nate. The brother who isn't going to let you take Matt down." He turned and shoved the door open before disappearing into the morning storm.

Laney cleared her throat. "I can tell he likes me a lot."

Matt eyed her. "Pointing a gun at somebody you don't intend to shoot is unacceptable and has consequences. Drop the gun, now." The bite of command echoed in his voice along with an anger he failed to mask.

She widened her stance. "I think you should answer your brother's question first."

Whether he loved her or not? Now wasn't the time for emotion. "Laney, you're two seconds from having an incredibly rough moment. I'm happy to deliver, but I feel it only fair to warn you. If I have to take the gun from you, I will, but I'm giving you one chance to choose your own result here."

Her eyes widened, and her pupils dilated. "I don't like threats."

"Consider it a promise." He eyed the gun. Yep. She'd released the safety. "What's the first lesson I taught you about guns?"

"Not to point one unless you intend to shoot, and not to shoot unless you intend to kill." Her voice cracked on the end.

"And?"

She sighed and lowered her hand. "If it helps, for a few moments, I considered shooting."

He snagged the gun. "Believe it or not, that doesn't help a bit."

She nodded. "So, Nate, huh? Those must've been colored contacts."

"Yes. We all have the gray eyes. It's a genetic marker used by the scientists." He slipped the safety back into place and slipped the gun in his waistband. "That was your one chance to hold a gun on me and still be able to sit for the next week. Don't do it again."

Her chin lifted. "Unless I intend to shoot, you mean."

He couldn't stop his grin. The woman had guts. "Yes. Unless you plan to shoot me."

"Your brother doesn't like me." Odd, but she sounded hurt by that fact, as if he'd taken her home to meet his family, and they'd disapproved.

Matt sighed. "Nate doesn't like doctors, women, or, well, people. Don't take it personally." Nate wouldn't like anybody who messed with Matt's focus, which Laney certainly did. Whether she realized it or not. "You need to pack. Once Nate has my picture, we need to get out of town."

"Won't the FBI follow us?" she asked.

He shrugged. "Yes, but we have better trackers after us, so the FBI is the least of our worries." His phone rang, and he lifted it to his ear. "What?"

"Nate said you're in over your head for this woman, and you're going to get yourself killed," Shane said. "He wants the full background on her sent to his phone."

Yeah, that sounded like Nate. He'd dig into Laney's past until he knew everything and how to get her out of Matt's life. "Send him the full package." Matt eyed the little brunette. She'd told him the truth about the commander, and Nate would have to reach that conclusion on his own. They'd all done things in life they regretted. He'd figure it all out later. "I know what I'm doing. Prepare for us to arrive sometime tomorrow after Nate fetches what I need."

Silence echoed across the line for several beats. "You're bringing her here, Mattie?" Shane asked.

"Yes."

"No."

Matt drew deep for patience. "Trust me, Shane. She's coming with me because we need her."

"We need her, or *you* need her?" Shane asked quietly.

Matt kept his focus on Laney as she tried to listen to his conversation. "Both," he said. Panic and fear swirled around his gut, making it hurt. His entire body ached. But he went with his instincts and solidified all emotion into a plan he could pursue. God, he hoped he was making the right decision. If trusting Laney harmed his brothers, he'd never survive the guilt.

Nate cataloged the number of weapons in the main hub of the sheriff's station. Three deputies stood in the room, and each had a holstered gun. At least one of the guys walked like he had another weapon secured to his ankle.

The gun at Nate's back provided safety for him.

With a nod at the men, he maneuvered past the desks to the sheriff's office. "I spoke with Laney Jacobs and her boyfriend," Nate said, striding inside and dropping into one of two wooden guest chairs.

The sheriff snorted. "I don't like the boyfriend." A beautiful picture window made up the entire wall behind him and showcased an abundant forest. A mounted trout took up another wall, and diplomas and awards the third.

Nate tapped his fingers on his pants. "The boyfriend seemed okay to me. Former soldier, trying to find himself. I'd say he's common." Yeah. Matt was anything but common.

The sheriff pushed back from his desk. "I don't know. He arrives in town, and women are attacked. Seems suspicious."

"My professional opinion is that he's not our killer." Nate slid on a charming smile. "Plus, he's stayed in town knowing you suspect him. That counts for something."

"Perhaps he's an arrogant son of a bitch who doesn't think we'll catch him. Or maybe he can't leave until he kills Miss Jacobs, considering he's been sending her notes." The sheriff revealed sharp teeth. "Besides, I took his picture and told him I'd send his mug to every law enforcement agency and every news outlet in the world if he skipped town."

"How?" Nate asked. Just how long had his brother been distracted?

"I interviewed him right after Claire was murdered and snapped a shot before he left."

Nate chuckled. "Good move. Have you sent the picture anywhere?"

"No. It's on my computer." The sheriff patted his protruding belly.

A whisper of cotton sounded at the door, and a woman rushed in. "Oh my God. I received a letter, Todd." Dressed in surgical scrubs, the woman waved a piece of notebook paper as she hitched across the room before dropping it on the desk.

The sheriff frowned and grabbed the paper: *You're lovely, and I can't wait to know you better. I feel you're the one.* He read the words slowly, crimson sliding across his face. "Damn it."

Nate leaned forward. "The guy needs to stalk two women at once." A primary target and a secondary. Unfortunately, the primary ended up dead quickly. "He'll try again for Miss Jacobs soon."

The woman fluttered her hands, her classic face pale. "Todd, what should I do?"

The sheriff stood and tucked the woman close for a hug. An intimate hug. "I won't let anything hurt you, Tasha. I promise." They stood about the same height, but next to the burly cop, the woman appeared lean.

Nate frowned. "Is this your first note?"

"Yes," she said.

The sheriff released her. "My apologies. Dr. Leo McGovern, this is Dr. Tasha Friedan, our local coroner."

And the sheriff's girlfriend, apparently. Nate smiled. "It's nice to meet you." He studied her.

Intelligent eyes dominated a classic face. She wore her blond hair straight to the shoulders in a no-nonsense style she could pull back when cutting into bodies. No wonder Matt had liked her for the surgeon he'd hunted... until he'd fallen for the actual surgeon.

She pushed back from the sheriff. "It's nice to meet you. What kind of a doctor are you?"

"I'm not. A profiler," he said.

Her head lifted. "I see," she said in the snotty tone only medical doctors could manage when dealing with other doctorates. "Why is this guy after me?"

Probably because she was a bitch. "He likes successful career women who live alone in quaint-sounding towns. You fit the bill perfectly."

"Wonderful," she said. "The FBI has been after him for some time, right? Shouldn't you have a better handle on who he is? I mean, our tax dollars do pay your salaries."

Nate shrugged. "I'm not with the FBI."

The reporter poked his head into the doorway. "No, but her question was a good one. Why *doesn't* the FBI have more on this guy?"

Hell if Nate knew. He wasn't a profiler. "Why don't you? I mean, you've followed the case for weeks now, right?"

"Yes, but I just report the news. I'm not involved in solving cases." Frant shoved his glasses back up his nose. "Though, frankly, I think I've provided more information to the FBI than the other way around. What is the status of this case?"

"None of your business." Agent Patterson shoved past Frant to reach for the newest note, which he read quickly. He eyed Tasha. "Where was this?"

"On my car at work. I left to go grab lunch, and the paper was secured under my windshield wiper." Her voice trembled at the end, and the sheriff reached down to take her hand.

Agent Patterson swore and yanked out his tattered notebook. "Tell me everything."

Nate listened as Tasha recounted her last week, noting several times she hadn't seen or even felt anybody watching her. The woman had terrible instincts.

Of course, apparently Laney hadn't noticed anything, either, and she probably had decent instincts. At least to have hidden from the commander for so long. Nate knew Matt would go after the guy hunting Laney, but hopefully it wouldn't be until they survived the damn chips.

Finally, Patterson wound down the interview and thanked Tasha Friedan. He turned toward the sheriff. "Do you mind acquiring the surveillance video from the coroner's office?"

"Nope. I'm on it," the sheriff said.

Patterson faced Nate. "My partner, Agent Cusack, will be back in town in about an hour. He interviewed all of the earlier witnesses from the last two towns and has a lot to report. How about we meet and plan our next step?"

"Sounds good." Nate hoped to be heading out of town at that point. "Let's meet at Swank's Diner, down the street. We can have a lunch meeting."

"Excellent. I need to make a couple of phone calls." Agent Patterson strode out of the office without another word.

The sheriff slid an arm around Tasha's shoulders. "Come on, Tasha. Let's go get the video, and then we'll figure out a way to keep you safe, sweetheart."

Nate stood. "Hey, Sheriff? I'd love a copy of the picture you took of Matt Dean. If I send the photo to colleagues in the FBI, they can give us a better idea of who he is. Just in case."

The sheriff kept his gaze on Tasha. "Go for it. The shot is in my computer in a picture file called 'Big Catches.'" He grinned. "I usually keep fish pictures in the file." Keeping a protective arm around Tasha, he ushered her from the office.

Nate skirted the desk to sit and find the file. He brought up the picture of Matt. Anger shone in his brother's eyes, while Laney stood right behind him. Interesting. They made a striking couple.

Shaking his head, Nate typed in a series of commands to corrupt the picture. After completing the task, he erased the photo and emptied the trash.

Good enough. Slipping away from the desk, he strode through the sheriff's department to his car waiting outside. Once inside, he dialed Matt. "It's done."

"Excellent," Matt said. "Thanks. Drop by and we'll load up your car before heading out of town. I'd like to be on the road within the hour."

"You got it." Nate disconnected the call. God, he hoped Matt knew what he was doing in bringing the surgeon they'd been hunting for five years to their safe house in Montana.

His big brother wasn't thinking clearly, but Nate had made the decision to trust Matt with his life more than once.

He couldn't stop now.

CHAPTER
24

LANEY THREW SEVERAL yoga outfits into a bag. "Where are we going, anyway?"

"Somewhere safe." Matt inserted bullets in an extra clip for his gun. "I appreciate you coming with us willingly."

The last word in his sentence dropped a ball of ice in her abdomen. "If I didn't want to leave my home here, would you truly kidnap me and force me to leave?"

"Yes." He didn't look up from his task. "Either the commander or the serial killer would catch up to you. It's too dangerous for you here."

"So the possible kidnapping is all about my safety." She allowed sarcasm to fill her voice.

"It's *partly* about your safety." Matt slid the extra clip into his bag, his gray gaze slamming into her. "The other part we've already discussed. I need your help with the chips, although I'm hoping I won't have to take you on a mission. Shane should be able to duplicate the computer program we need."

That was an ambitious and unlikely hope. "The program is as complex as possible, and without the code, there's no way to duplicate it exactly." She had better mentally prepare herself to go into battle. Would she faint at the sight of blood? More than likely, and what then?

She turned and tossed another pair of boots into a bag, trying to ignore the fact that he sat on her bed.

Serious and determined, he brought a sense of maleness into her space. He'd been inside her several times, but she wasn't sure how to reach him. How to convey the feelings bombarding her. She'd never needed anybody before, and vulnerability threatened to shatter her. "Are you still mad at me?"

His eyebrows lifted. "No. You had your dream job, and you did help people. While you understood the risks, you still went forward and worked for the commander. But you didn't hurt me or mine, Laney. Any forgiveness for your actions, you need to give to yourself. And believe me, I've done plenty of things I've had to deal with, so I do understand."

The words filled her with relief and hope. Could she forgive herself? Maybe helping deactivate the chips would lead to redemption. "Where does that leave us?" She had to go and ask the tough question, now, didn't she?

"You know I'm probably dead in six weeks, right?" he asked softly.

"Maybe." She wasn't willing to give up on him. He was one of the most well-trained soldiers on earth, and he'd be able to find the computer and save himself. "But what if you're not?"

"When we find safety, I'm going to take precautions to keep you safe, no matter what happens. That's what we have to work on right now." He shifted his weight on the bed.

She forced a smile as hurt wandered through her. "One step at a time is a good plan."

He stood. "Yes, it is." Grabbing one of the bags, he headed into the living room.

She looked at the empty doorway, her head slowly lifting. Enough of running, of being scared. Life was too short and uncertain to leave things so neatly. She followed him into the other room. "I have feelings for you, Matt. Real ones, and I don't want to pretend they're not there." God. Had she really tipped her hand like that? Heat spiraled into her face.

The front door opened and Nathan loped inside. "My car is at the curb, and we should get going before the sheriff discovers I deleted the photo."

Laney sighed. So much for the serious discussion she'd wanted to have. "I'm all packed. Are we taking the car?"

"Your bags are going in the car, but you're riding the bike with me." Matt tossed one bag toward Nate and lifted two more. "Are you sure this is everything you want to take?"

"Yes." She eyed the signed documents she'd left on the sofa table that turned the bar and apartments over to Smitty, as well as a plea for him to take good care of Eugene. "There's no returning, is there?"

Matt shook his head. "No. Even if we take out the commander and the entire organization, it's too risky for you to return here. Just in case we miss somebody."

Something in her chest hurt. She'd liked Charmed. "I understand. To be honest, I'm surprised I was able to stay this long."

Nate pushed the door open. "Then you shouldn't have sent another letter and more money to your friend's grandmother. It was a dangerous risk."

Laney frowned. "What are you talking about?"

Nate lifted an eyebrow. "You sent money and condolences to Nancy's grandmother when she died."

"Sure. That was the right thing to do." Laney reached for her purse.

"Yes, it was," Matt said. "However, you shouldn't have sent her more money last year—especially from Charmed. Even though you didn't write on the postcard or envelope, you became easy to trace."

Laney stilled, and her gaze slashed to Matt. "I didn't."

"What?" he paused, his formidable focus narrowing right to her.

Nate flipped around, his gaze intense.

She blinked several times, trying to make sense of the situation. "I didn't send Nancy's grandma another postcard or money. Not at all."

The world screeched into a pounding silence. Matt lifted his head as heat washed down his torso. As reality smacked him hard, he sprang into action and grabbed Laney's arm.

"Trap," he said to Nate, who was already heading for the door.

How in the hell had he missed it? Not once—*not once*— had he questioned Laney about the second note. *Shit.* She'd sent the first one, and it had made sense.

But if the second one had been sent by the commander, Matt had just walked his brother into a trap.

They hurried down the stairwell and into the darkened bar.

"Why not strike us by now?" Nate asked, his voice low with urgency.

"They've been watching me and waiting for you and Shane to show up. I'm sure they're done waiting now." They would've given Shane less than a day to show up before taking Matt and Nate. The hair on the back of Matt's neck rose. "Run."

The plan was brilliant, and even worse, he'd had to work at finding Laney. Hard. The note had been sent almost a year ago, and he'd taken months to find it, and then had wasted precious time in town narrowing down the search.

The commander had most likely found her years ago.

She stumbled on the last step. "I don't understand."

"You're bait, doc," Nate said as he tugged a gun from his waistband. He nudged open the door and viewed the quiet street outside. "I'll go for my car and meet you at the second rendezvous point."

Matt rushed Laney toward the back door. "Shoot first, Nate."

With a smart-assed grin, Nate dodged outside.

Panic rippled across Laney's face. "They're here?"

Matt couldn't hear much past the roaring in his ears. He needed to calm down. "Not yet. Let's get out of town and regroup." Hell, yes, they were there...probably planning an attack now. "Trust me."

She nodded and yanked open the back door.

A cocked gun in her face pivoted toward Matt as the sheriff dragged Laney outside.

Matt stiffened, his gaze taking in the scene within seconds. Agent Patterson held a gun on him from several feet away—much too far to take. Three deputies trained guns toward him from various positions in the alley.

Damn it.

The sheriff pulled Laney behind his back. "Matt Dean, you're under arrest for stalking and murder."

Matt couldn't disarm all of them, and he couldn't risk Laney being hurt in a firefight. So he held his hands up and walked out. "I didn't murder Claire."

"Ah, we have evidence you did." Agent Patterson stalked forward and motioned for Matt to turn around.

Matt turned, his mind calculating through the last couple of days. The cuffs clicked over his wrists with an ominous snap. "What evidence?"

"We'll discuss evidence at the station." The agent frisked Matt and removed the gun at his waist as well as the knife at his boot before tugging Matt around.

Laney shoved to the sheriff's side. "Matt was with me the night Claire died. He hasn't killed anybody."

Matt jerked his head in a motion to keep her quiet. The less she said right now, the better. "I'd like Laney to accompany us to the station." If he left her alone, the commander would make his move.

The sheriff nodded. "I'll bring Miss Jacobs. We need to work on her timeline of recent events."

Laney opened her mouth to protest, and Matt shook his head. "Good. Laney, I'll meet you at the station." God, he hoped Nate had gotten away. Now he had to figure out how to get Laney out of the station once they were there.

Two deputies and Nate strode around the end of the alley.

Agent Patterson tilted his head. "We had both entries covered, but I knew you'd go for the bike."

Nate reached the scene, his hands casually tucked in his pockets. "Agent Patterson? You sure you have the right guy?"

"Positive." Patterson's eyes gleamed in the early light as he surveyed Nate head to toe. "What were you doing here, anyway?"

"Interviewing Miss Jacobs again," Nate said smoothly. "I feel like the killer is going to strike again soon, and I wanted to know more about the progression of the notes."

"Dean is the killer," the sheriff said, a murderous gleam in his eye as he turned toward Matt. "And now we've got you, you son of a bitch."

Matt kept his focus on Laney. "Stay with the sheriff until we figure this out."

She nodded, her face so pale her lips looked blue.

Patterson turned toward Nate. "I could use your help with the interview, McGovern. Why don't you ride with me?"

"Sure thing," Nate said. "Let's get going."

The men ushered Matt down the alley and into the back of a patrol car, whereas Patterson and Nate sat in the front.

Matt kept his face stoic as he made plans to kick Nate's ass later for not fleeing town when he had the chance.

"So, what's the evidence?" Nate asked the agent.

The agent shrugged. "Let's discuss everything at the station. I'd like to go over the new evidence with you before we interrogate the prisoner."

Matt settled into the backseat. He could release himself

from the handcuffs, and Nate could take care of the agent. But as two patrol cars flanked them the several blocks through town, he relaxed. The escape would be easier at the station when they had him contained.

He glanced out the back window for the sheriff's car. Where the hell was Laney?

CHAPTER
25

Laney secured her seat belt in the backseat of the sheriff's vehicle. "Am I locked in?" she asked, gazing at the bare doors.

The sheriff chuckled and glanced through the bars separating the front from the back seats. "Yes, but don't worry, you're not under arrest." He shoved a pile of books and papers across the front seat before hitting a button and partially rolling down her window. "We've been moving the courthouse library to a bigger room at the sheriff's station, and somehow I volunteered to help. I apologize for the mess and the musty smell."

"It's okay." Laney cranked her neck to peer out the front window. Agent Patterson's vehicle was out of sight. Thank goodness Nate was able to go with Matt. "You really do have the wrong guy."

"I don't think so. Dean had time to kill Claire and Greg and still make it back to the bar within the timelines you've specified." The sheriff's faded eyes sobered in the rearview mirror. "When he went after Tasha, he started making mistakes."

Laney narrowed her eyes. "Are you seeing Tasha?"

"Yes. For about six months now." The sheriff scratched

his whiskers. "I thought she was such a cold fish at first, and I even ran her records."

"Isn't she here under a false identification?" Laney asked.

"Yes, and I agreed to cover for her once I learned the truth. She warmed up to me, and I realized she's just scared of men. Really scared."

"I heard she fled an abusive husband." Laney knew what it was like to be hunted. She should've reached out to Tasha earlier and not assumed the woman was rude. "That's scary."

"Yeah. But their divorce went through all right, and my sources have confirmed the guy moved on. So my Tasha is safe."

"Maybe you've misread Matt the same way you initially misread Tasha," Laney said. "I have good instincts with people, and I believe he didn't kill anybody."

"You're wrong." The sheriff turned onto the quiet main street in town. "Agent Patterson's partner is finally back in town, and supposedly the guy is a master interrogator. He'll get Dean to tell the truth."

Dread filled Laney with icy tendrils. They had to get out of town before the commander attacked. "Thank you for trying to keep me safe, Todd." She'd miss the small town and the kind sheriff.

"Of course." His shoulders tensed as he slowed down the car. "What in the world?"

Laney twisted to see out the window. Tasha and the reporter stood near a car with the hood up and steam escaping from the engine.

The sheriff stopped the car in the middle of the street and jumped out. "What in the hell are you doing back in town, Tasha? I told you to stay put at the cabin until we found whoever was sending you notes."

Tasha brushed her hair from her face. "Frant called me and asked for an interview. I needed to get more things from home, so I figured it'd be safe if I stayed in town."

Frant gestured toward the car. "Something's wrong with the engine."

"What?" the sheriff asked, ambling toward the hood.

"How the hell should I know?" Frant leaned to the side to look inside the patrol car. "Why is Laney Jacobs under arrest?"

"She's not," the sheriff muttered.

Frant leaned down to smile. "You look all captured back there." An odd gleam lit his eye and reminded her of a wolf about to strike. "Sometimes fortune shines on the chosen few."

"I'm not giving you an interview," she retorted. The guy looked too happy now that Matt had been arrested. "I'm surprised you're not at the station."

"Why would I be at the station?" Frant asked. "Everything I want is right here." He drew a gun from his waist and turned.

Panic flushed through Laney, and she yelled to warn Todd, but it was too late. Frant fired, and the sheriff fell back against the car, his eyes wide with shock. Blood burst from his chest and coated the window.

Tasha ducked forward and shoved Todd inside her vehicle before looking around. The street remained quiet.

Blood. So much blood. Laney flashed back to her friend being cut, and her mind blanked. Shock coursed through her to freeze her limbs.

Tasha yanked open the passenger door and pushed the books to the floor. "Let's go."

Frant rushed around to jump into the driver's seat.

Laney shook her head and scrambled for the door handle, only to find smooth doors. *God.* She was locked in the backseat. Claustrophobia swamped her, the resulting fear springing the hair up on her arms.

Panic trembled down her legs, and she fought the urge to kick the seat. She needed to keep a clear head. Panicking wouldn't help. Even so, her breath panted out, and she couldn't stop her seizing lungs. The window was still down but not enough for her to jump out.

Frant put the car into drive and quickly flipped a U-turn. "You were right. That worked perfectly."

Tasha sniffed and glanced into the backseat. "Told you."

"What the hell?" Laney asked, glancing around for some sort of weapon. Shock narrowed the world into a tunnel.

"Did you like my notes?" Frant asked, his eyes gleaming in the rearview mirror.

Realization slapped Laney in the face. "Those were from you? How long have you been in town?"

"I moved with my Tasha, although I do head to Seattle to work as a reporter. But I stay with Tash when I can." He brushed Tasha's cheek with his knuckles. "The couple who plays together, stays together, you know."

Laney's mind spun, and she tried to focus. "I don't understand. You're his partner, Tasha?"

Tasha glanced at Frant before turning back toward Laney. "I've been his partner for nearly eight years. We found we shared certain interests. We make each other happy."

Frant giggled and covered his mouth. "This has been awesome, sugar momma. Just awesome."

"My sweet boy." Tasha smiled.

"Eight years? What are you, about twenty?" Laney edged back into the seat as far as possible.

"Twenty-two," Frant almost sang. "I was fourteen when Tasha saved me. She was already twenty-five and knew so much."

"The silly boy was hiding from his damn drunk father and peeking into my window one night." Tasha's lips curved in a benevolent smile. "Frant was so lonely, and I saved him by inviting him inside."

Frant clapped his hands together. "For so much more than a show." He settled one hand back on the steering wheel.

"Tasha knows so much to teach... She's taught others for years. Years and years."

"I'm not that old," Tasha objected.

"No, you're perfect." Frant's eyes glowed with adoration.

"Yes. Yes, I am." Tasha settled back in her seat. "And I always wanted my own children to teach, but that didn't work out. Endometriosis." Fury and pain lanced along her words.

Frant sighed. "I'm so sorry, my love. You deserved better."

"I really did." Tasha sniffed. "But you fill the holes in my life, handsome."

Weird. Oddly sad how they'd helped each other by turning evil. But so damn weird. Wait a minute. "So you stalk women and kill them together?" How was this even possible? Fear filled Laney until her stomach rolled again.

"Yes. It's fun for us... to watch and hunt." Tasha wiped spittle off her lips. "I don't care about the rape, but it makes Frant happy, so I hold them down if he needs."

"Then I beat them until they stop breathing." Arousal flared Frant's nostrils.

Bile rose in Laney's throat. "Why women in sweet-sounding towns?"

Tasha lifted a shoulder. "When we arrived here, we thought it was so funny the name was Charmed. The rest flowed from there. I mean, why not?"

Laney shook her head to focus her thoughts. "You attacked me in the alley when Frant was with Matt in the bar."

"Yep." Tasha clapped her hands together. "We figured Matt would be a good alibi for Frant, and I could just take you. But stupid Matt ran outside too soon." She pouted her lips.

"You tried, mama," Frant patted her hand.

Another realization hit Laney. "Why did you kill Greg?"

Frant laughed. "Greg snapped a picture of me hunting

you . . . a week before I was supposed to arrive here in town. That guy was trying to stalk you—he had tons of pictures of you. Once I found the picture, I took care of him."

"You did good with Greg. Real good," Tasha said.

"I know," Frant said.

God. Laney swallowed down bile. "What about the husband you fled?" she asked.

"No husband." Tasha chuckled. "That was a story for the sheriff, to get him protective in case I needed help."

Frant's lips turned down. "I don't like that you were his friend."

Tasha played with Frant's ear. "He didn't mean anything to me. You believe that."

"I hope the bullet killed him," Frant muttered. "You're mine. All mine."

"Of course I am." Tasha turned calculating eyes toward Laney. "Though I'll share you with her later. You're going to enjoy her so much."

Frant nodded. "We do have special plans for you, Laney Jacobs. Your night will bring me and my love closer together. Each experience we share heightens our love." He turned onto the main interstate. "You're going to make us fly."

Matt's shoulder blades itched. He'd been created with deadly instincts, which intense training had honed. His plan was going wrong, and fast. He allowed Agent Patterson to lead him through the station to an interrogation room, where he sat facing a long two-way mirror. Within seconds he could hear his brother's heartbeat on the other side, along with those of two other men. Both in good shape with regular heartbeats.

Agent Patterson sat across from Matt. A television set with DVD player had been rolled into the room and left at the end of the scarred table.

Matt leaned back. "I'm not talking to you until I have

confirmation Laney has arrived safely at the station." His gut ached as if something was wrong, and he'd learned decades ago to listen to his gut.

The agent rolled his eyes. "My partner will be interviewing Laney in a moment. For now, why don't you explain this video?" He leaned over and pushed buttons on a remote control.

A morning scene of a parking lot swam into focus. Matt frowned and leaned closer. "Is that the parking lot of the coroner's office?"

"You should know," the agent said.

Matt cut a glance at the two-way mirror. What the hell was going on? Taking a deep breath, he watched the video show him arriving on his bike, placing a note under the windshield wiper of a blue compact, and then riding away. He shook his head. "The video was doctored." Who would manipulate the video like that? His mind clicked facts into place as rapidly as possible.

"That's the story you're going with?" Patterson asked, rewinding the video to pause on a close-up of Matt's face.

"Yes." Matt rattled the cuffs on the table. "I didn't leave a note for the coroner."

"Right. I have you leaving notes similar to those left for recent murder victims and now just need to tie you to each murder." Patterson's cell phone buzzed, and he glanced at the screen. "Cusack is here. Good. Let's see how well you lie to him."

The door opened, and a man in a full black suit walked in.

Everything in Matt went cold. He straightened his shoulders and lowered his chin as one of his biggest regrets moved to sit on the other side of the table. "Agent Cusack, is it?"

"Well, it is today." Emery flashed a quick smile, his brown eyes as blank as Matt knew his own to be. "I'm sorry I haven't made your acquaintance yet, but I've been busy staying under the radar. You know, investigating, that is."

"Clever." How long had Emery been pretending to be an FBI agent?

A rustle sounded beyond the mirror, and Nate's heartbeat spiked before slowing. Damn it. He'd been Tasered.

Emery didn't blink. But he didn't have Matt's superior hearing, now did he? As far as Matt knew, only the Gray brothers had ended up with special senses and abilities. Of course, they had hidden their abilities, so it was possible other soldiers did, too.

Matt eyed the file folder sitting in front of Patterson. There was probably a paper clip in there he could use to disengage the handcuffs so he could get to his brother. "You two been partners long?"

"No," Emery said flatly, scooting the file folder in front of him to open. He tugged a paper clip off a stack of papers and twirled the silver around and around. "Why did you kill all of those women?"

"You know I didn't," Matt said softly. Had they already gotten to Laney? If so, he'd kill Emery with his bare hands, like he should've done years ago. "What's your plan here?"

Emery unraveled the paper clip. "Plan? We're just waiting for all the pieces to be in place before we take you out of here."

Patterson grinned. "How do you feel about a trip to DC?"

"I'm thinking DC isn't in the plan," Matt said.

Patterson snorted. "Right. Like you get to choose the plan."

Moron. The guy had no clue he was sitting next to a killer who'd end him as easily as talk to him. In fact, if Matt remembered correctly, Emery enjoyed killing. A lot. "Patterson, you're an idiot."

Patterson flushed a bright red.

Emery smiled. "Calling names, are we? You sound desperate, *Mattie*."

"You wish." Matt allowed confidence to shine in his eyes. "You can't beat me." The unspoken words *and you never could* hung in the air between them.

"Really?" Emery tore the paper clip apart and tossed it across the room to land in a corner. "We have Laney Jacobs in custody, and she's going to give me everything."

Fire lanced down Matt's spine. "Laney is honest and will tell you the truth. I was with her when Claire was killed, and although Laney and I have parted ways, she won't change her story."

Emery leaned forward. "Oh, nice try. You and Laney haven't parted anything."

Patterson frowned and glanced back and forth between the soldiers. "Have you two met?"

"No," Emery said. "But I've met plenty of killers like Mr. Dean, here. They're all the same."

"Most killers are," Matt agreed. "You should know." The gloves were about to come off. While he didn't want to harm Patterson, if it was necessary, he'd do it. Nate's heartbeat hadn't picked up any, which meant they'd used too much voltage, and Matt had to get to him. Fast.

A commotion sounded outside the door, and a deputy poked his head in. He'd gone so pale the freckles on his nose stood out in a jumble. "Agent Patterson? May I speak with you?"

Patterson swore softly and hurried from the room.

Matt lifted his chin to study his greatest nemesis. "I should've killed you when I had the chance."

"True," Emery said.

"Why did you go back? We blew the place to hell, and you could've been free. You and your brothers." Matt shook his head, truly not understanding. "What's wrong with you?"

"The commander is the closest thing we have to a father," Emery spit out. "How could you betray him? You destroyed so much of his life's work."

"He isn't our father." Matt tuned in to the commotion outside. "My brothers are more important than anything else, as yours should be."

Emery reached for a phone in his back pocket to read the face. "Your brothers are going to die in less than six weeks. Mine will live." He glanced up, a twisted smile lifting his upper lip. "I win."

"Bullshit. You stay with that sadistic bastard, you'll never win." Matt slid his feet apart to strike for Emery's knees. "What are you waiting for, anyway?"

"Our forces are moving in." Emery slipped the phone back into place. "We have you and Nate, and I'd hoped Shane would pop in to save you both. Since that's not happening, we're surrounding the town before taking you." He leaned forward. "I know you've amassed an army."

No, he hadn't. Sure, they'd created a security company that worked all over the world, but the brothers had remained anonymous. More people meant more chances at being found. "My army will take out yours."

"I don't think so." Emery's face lost all expression again.

Matt glanced toward the door as it opened. "What the hell is going on?"

Patterson stomped inside, his strides angry. "Who is working with you, Dean?"

Matt frowned. "Nobody. Why?"

Patterson's hand trembled as he grabbed the file off the table. "The sheriff was shot and is in surgery at the local hospital."

The room silenced into sharp focus. "What about Laney?"

Patterson shook his head, anger darkening his eyes. "She's gone."

Emery smiled. "Now, that's a surprise."

CHAPTER
26

RAIN SLASHED INTO her face. Thunder rolled above, and the wind whipped leaves and debris into her legs. Laney struggled against Frant as he propelled her down the rough path and toward a darkened cabin.

Now was her chance. Taking a deep breath, she pivoted and jammed her knee into his groin.

The squeal he made sounded like a pig being hit by a truck. She pushed hard against his chest and turned to run.

A branch hit her squarely in the cheek, and she dropped to one knee.

Tasha dropped the branch and yanked Laney up by her hair. "Nice try, bitch."

Frant, still doubled over, grabbed Laney's arm and shoved her into the cabin door. Pain radiated through her shoulder. Tasha opened the door, and Laney stumbled onto the floor.

The lights flipped on.

Reality pricked her with sharp needles as she focused on the man lounging on a battered chair. "Dr. Peters, it's good to see you again," the commander said smoothly as he rose to his feet.

God. Laney scrambled to her feet and tried to balance on wobbly legs. The man hadn't changed a bit in five years. Tall, rip-cord fit, he moved with the grace of a striking snake. His buzz-cut silver hair gave him an air of danger instead of proclaiming age. His angled face was hard, his black eyes dead. Evil truly existed, and it stood in front of her in the body of a soldier—one who had killed her friend.

She swallowed. Too many questions ripped through her brain, so she remained silent. Her gaze turned toward a woman sitting quietly on a kitchen chair, blue eyes appraising, black hair up in a bun. Laney hadn't even noticed the woman at first.

Frant stepped to the side. "What are you doing here?"

Tasha strode into the cabin and stopped short. "Sir. We hadn't expected you so soon."

"Sir?" Laney turned to face Tasha. "You know him?"

Tasha maneuvered around Laney toward Frant. "I've worked for the commander for years as a surgeon, a coroner, and most recently, an undercover operator." She smiled, revealing yellowing teeth. "Who do you think implanted your boys with those handy chips?"

Fire flashed between Laney's ears, and she lunged for Tasha.

Frant stepped between them and shoved Laney. Hard. She landed on her butt and bounced twice. Pain rippled up her spine. Scooting to the wall, she set her back against the rough wood, keeping them all in her sights. What she wouldn't give for a gun. Instead, she cleared her throat and focused on the woman. "Who are you?"

The woman looked down her nose. "I'm Dr. Madison, the one who created the boys. So you're the doctor who escaped us five years ago?" She frowned. "You don't look like much."

The commander smiled. "Oh, she's plenty. Apparently Matthew has fallen, and hard."

Crimson spiraled across Madison's classic cheekbones. "My Matt? Intriguing."

The hint of possession in her cultured tone made Laney

want to puke. She ignored the evil wench and turned her attention toward the commander. "You're okay with this whole serial-killer hobby?"

He sighed, regret twisting his lip. "No. Tasha kept her relationship and extracurricular activities secret. Once we found out, she was already in place in Charmed and had developed trust with both you and the local sheriff."

Tasha clasped her hands together. "Everyone needs a hobby. I figured you wouldn't mind."

"You figured wrong." The commander drew a gun out from behind his waist and fired. The bullet hit Frant in the forehead, and he went down, his eyes wide in shock and death.

Dr. Madison didn't even twitch.

"No!" Tasha cried, grabbing her boyfriend by the armpits and helping him to the floor. "Frantsie? Wake up." Tears coursed down her face as she glanced up at the commander. "Why?"

"Why?" The commander frowned. "While I appreciate the need to kill for fun, the FBI is looking into Frant's murders. *Your* murders. We stay under the radar, or we jeopardize everything. Period."

"But you knew about us," Tasha wailed.

The commander breathed in, his nostrils flaring. "I allowed you to continue only because it created a nice diversion for the cops, letting my forces swoop in under the radar. You had to know I'd dispense justice once I got the chance."

The smell of blood and death permeated the small space. Laney breathed out evenly, trying to keep from vomiting. A buzzing sounded in her ears. "Does it strike you as worrisome that the people you're leading are stark raving mad?" she asked.

The commander lifted a muscled shoulder. "We live in trying times. Believe it or not, this isn't the first serial killer to be found in my ranks."

"I believe it." Laney sucked in air. "You sent Tasha to Charmed because you found me." Frant followed Tasha, and they killed locally. "Claire wouldn't be dead if I hadn't moved here."

Tasha wiped tears off her cheeks and smeared her face with blood. She released Frant and stood. "Claire was a dumb bitch who trusted the wrong people. If we hadn't found her, somebody would have cut her fool neck."

The commander chuckled. "You couldn't believe the coincidence that there happened to be a serial killer in the town where you'd hidden, Eleanor? Really?"

Well, actually she had. "No. I understood my past would catch up to me. My name is Laney."

"Sweetheart, your past is irrelevant, as is your name." The commander drew out a phone to read the face. "You're bait. Nothing else."

Dread cascaded down her body. "You sent the note and money to Nancy's grandmother. To show Matt and his brothers where I was." It was a good trap.

"Of course," the commander said.

Laney shoved her elbows against the wall to rise. If she was going to die, she wanted to be on her feet. "What are you waiting for?"

His sharp gaze raked her top to bottom. "I'm not going to kill you. Right now, anyway." He read his cell phone. "We've taken Nate out, and I'm waiting for confirmation on Matt. Then we're all heading home."

God. The bastard was going to use her against Matt. "You've misjudged the situation if you think Matt cares about me. You can't use me against him."

"Matt may care about you, or he may not." The commander dodged forward and gripped her arm. "But he won't want to see you hurt. That boy has always had a weakness for anybody soft and vulnerable. No matter how many times I tried to beat it out of him."

The words shot a chill down her spine.

The commander led her to his chair and zip-tied her hands to the wooden armrests.

Laney struggled and the ties cut into her flesh. "Why do you want them back so badly? They'll never work for you."

"They will." The commander strode toward the door and kicked Frant out of the way with one large boot. "I've always been able to manipulate them with each other. If I threaten Nate, Matt will do as I wish. As soldiers, they're the best. The absolute best, and right now, more than ever, I need them back."

Laney lifted her chin. "Why?"

The commander's jaw hardened. "Let's just say I'm not the only one fighting for military dollars—especially those under the radar. The Gray brothers are the best, and I need them to solidify my power base. For now."

The brothers were just tools to the bastard. Laney tested the ties. "You don't have Shane."

"No, but I will. He'll give himself up when he learns I have his brothers." The commander turned and handed his gun to Tasha. "Watch her, and perhaps you'll live through this. Dr. Madison and I are going to fetch Matt—and I'm taking your vehicle. My troops took mine." He turned and assisted Dr. Madison up. She lifted her nose and stepped over the body as she headed for the door. They disappeared into the storm.

Tasha shoved the door shut and turned bloodshot eyes on Laney. "Frant is dead." Shock colored her words.

"Yes." Laney refused to look at the body on the floor. "I'm fairly certain you're next."

"Good." Tasha fell to sit by Frant. She pushed his bloody hair off his face. "He was my soul mate."

Laney tested the ties again. "I don't know. There are tons of killers out there you could molest as children and train."

Tasha snapped the gun up to point it at Laney. "You might want to watch the sarcasm."

"The commander won't like it if you kill me. Apparently I'm bait." Laney slid her feet on the rough wooden floor, trying to find any type of weapon. "Considering your boyfriend wanted to rape and murder me, I may owe the commander one."

"Stop talking about Frantsie," Tasha cried, grief twisting her face. "You didn't know him. He was amazing."

The woman was crazy. "How did you end up working for the commander?" Laney asked.

Tasha sniffed and her shoulders slumped. "I graduated medical school at the top of my class."

Now, that sounded familiar. "Any family?" Laney asked.

"No. Well, just a stepfather who beat the hell out of me until I escaped." Tasha settled Frant's head on her lap. "Frantsie said he'd go back and kill my daddy once we were finished with this mission." She lifted tear-filled eyes to Laney. "Who's going to kill my daddy now?"

Holy crap. "I don't know," Laney whispered. "But if you let me go, I'll ask Matt to do it. You know, as a thank-you."

Tasha sighed, her gaze on her dead lover. "I'm not that stupid."

It was worth a try. "Please let me go, Tasha. The commander killed your soul mate. Why would you keep working for such a monster?"

"What else do I have?" With a resigned sigh, Tasha shoved Frant's head off her.

Laney gagged and swallowed several times to keep her breakfast down. Darkness crept over her vision.

Tasha rose to stand. "I'll kill your soul mate."

Laney shook her head and tried to focus. "I don't have one."

"I've seen how you look at Matt—how he looks at you when you're not watching. Soul mates." Tasha dragged her feet on the way to the sink, where she washed blood off her hands.

Warmth and concern filled Laney simultaneously. "You're crazy."

"Maybe." Tasha dried off her hands and turned around, picking up the weapon. "You love that man. I can almost smell it on you."

"What does love smell like?"

"Desperation, lilies, and chocolate," Tasha said.

"O-Okay," Laney coughed out. "How much do you know about the chips?"

Tasha clapped her hands together and then looked down in surprise at the gun between them. "Oh yeah. Gun." She pointed it at Laney's chest. "Ever play Russian roulette?"

"No. Though you have—with those devices you implanted near their spines." Laney fought to keep from squirming.

"Yes." Tasha tilted her head to the side, her gaze thoughtful. "Brilliant devices, actually. If they're touched, they detonate and split the spine in two. There's no way to remove them while they're active. Just brilliant."

"Can you deactivate them?" Laney asked, trying not to focus on the smooth barrel pointed at her.

"Sure. Anybody can with the right code and transmitter." Tasha put both hands on the weapon. "Boom."

Laney jerked. "You know the codes?"

"Nope. I just implanted the devices. If I had the codes, I could deactivate them. But they're kept top secret."

Fury tasted like metal. "You're twisted."

"Yes." Tasha inched a few feet closer. "I love powder burns, don't you?"

"Not really." Laney glanced frantically for some sort of escape. "I don't think the commander realized how crazy you were before he left."

"Arrogant bastard, isn't he?" Tasha said agreeably. "Didn't think a woman would defy his orders."

Laney measured the distance between them. Too far. Way too far. "You need to follow his orders if you want to live."

"Maybe, maybe not." Tasha scratched her nose. "I hope I get to keep working with the soldiers. It'll be nice to study the Gray brothers. They're a legend within the ranks—so physically superior. Even Jory grew into quite the specimen."

Laney moved her feet into position. "Who's Jory?"

Tasha's eyebrows lifted into her hairline. "Matt *doesn't* trust you, now, does he?" She leaned even closer, her mouth near Laney's ear. "Jory is the youngest brother. We captured him two years ago. He was shot."

A sharp pang slammed into Laney's heart. "So the youngest brother really is dead?"

"I didn't say that." Tasha bit into Laney's ear.

God. Laney's shoulders tensed with the need to move, but she couldn't quite yet. "So he's alive?"

"I also didn't say that." Tasha leaned back, her face inches from Laney's. "He was breathing last I saw him, but not very well. They took him to the other facility."

"What other facility?"

Tasha's gaze dropped to Laney's lips. "You know, I think I see what Frantsie saw in this part of the hunt. I wonder how you taste."

Yep. She was going to puke. Laney forced a smile. "You don't know anything about the other facility."

"Sure I do." Tasha's eyes opened wide, the pupils even looking crazy. "The facility where miracles happen." She snorted. "Or cremations. I just get those confused."

Laney wasn't going to glean additional information from the lunatic. So she propelled her forehead into Tasha's nose, while kicking for the woman's ankles. Her head impacted with a loud clunk, and blood sprayed across her face.

Tasha yelled and went down.

Pushing with her heels, Laney jumped the chair up and forward, slamming a wooden leg squarely down on Tasha's temple.

The woman's eyelids fluttered shut.

Laney's heated breath panted out, and her heart beat so quickly her ribs ached. Using her ankles and knees, she hopped the chair into the tiny kitchen. With her feet, she pulled open a drawer to dump on the floor. Towels. Old towels. Systematically, she opened each drawer, her feet cramping. Finally, she dumped cooking utensils onto the ground... along with one knife.

Okay. She could do this.

She pressed her ankles together and secured the knife. Scooting her butt toward the edge of the chair, she ignored the pull in her shoulders and lifted her legs. With a quick twist, she pushed the knife close enough to grab with one hand. Thank God for yoga. She began to saw and sliced right into her hand.

Pain ripped through her arm.

Tears sprang to her eyes.

Swallowing down bile, she tried again. Several bloody moments later, her hand sprang free. Pain ricocheted through her wrist. Shoving sensation away, she quickly used the knife to free her other hand.

Raw flesh rippled along her wrists. She wiped the knife off on the towels and tucked it into her front pocket before wrapping her injured hand. A quick check of Tasha's vitals revealed the woman was alive but out cold. So Laney took the gun and opened the clip.

Empty. The commander had left Tasha with an unloaded weapon. Maybe he hadn't been as foolish as he'd seemed.

Shoving the useless gun into her back pocket, Laney hurried out into the storm.

All alone.

CHAPTER
27

MATT TRIED TO keep calm as he faced his oldest enemy. He shifted his weight on the metal chair as the walls of the interrogation room began to close in on him. They had Laney. Without question, Emery had Laney. "Where is she?" Matt asked softly.

Emery smiled. "How should I know? But she has a rather *commanding* presence, and I'm sure we'll find her soon."

The commander had her. Matt's entire body went cold with a fear-filled rage. "Is that a fact?" Matt would kill them all with his bare hands.

"Yes, it is." Pleasure glimmered in Emery's eyes. He glanced at Patterson. "They're probably creating a manhunt for whoever shot the sheriff. Why don't you go make sure they're not going all vigilante on us."

Patterson eyed Emery and then Matt. "I don't think so. I'll stay right here."

Chalk one up for decent instincts. Matt forced all emotion into a box, becoming the killer his creators had wanted. "Things aren't quite what they seem, are they, Patterson?"

Emery glanced at Patterson. "Don't let this guy get into your head."

Patterson nodded. "I know he's trained, but my gut tells me something more is going on here. What is it?"

Matt wanted nothing better than to tell the agent the truth as a surprise tactic to jump Emery. But if Patterson discovered who they were, he was a dead man. The guy wouldn't survive the night. So Matt sighed. "What's going on is that you guys are chasing your dumb-ass FBI tails and have the wrong guy in custody."

Emery smiled. "Look at you being all confrontational."

"Very," Patterson agreed with a glance at his partner, back in sync. He moved around to retake his seat. "Tell us who tried to kill the sheriff, Dean. Let us find Laney and protect her. I believe you care about her."

Matt lifted a shoulder. "Laney was a sweet distraction as I played the part of a bartender for a while. But I didn't kill anybody and would like to be on my way."

"Now, why would you discount what you have with the pretty green-eyed woman?" Emery drawled. He turned toward Patterson. "She *is* lovely, isn't she?"

"Very." Patterson tapped his fingers on the manila file. "Help us save her. Please."

"I don't know where she is." Matt tuned in to the activity in the station house. It did sound like the deputies were heading out to hunt... and with a vengeance. "Did anybody witness the sheriff getting attacked?" he asked Patterson.

"Nobody saw anything." Patterson sighed. "If you don't have a partner, and you're not involved, why would somebody take Laney?"

"The serial killer?" Emery asked casually. "Maybe the serial killer or killers got her."

Patterson's eyebrows slashed down. "This attack would be different from the killer's MO. He likes to get victims alone and take his time."

Matt kept his gaze on Emery. "Kill*ers*? Plural?"

"It's a theory." Emery shifted his weight as he reached

for something under the table. "Makes an odd kind of sense, doesn't it?"

"How so?" Patterson asked. "Because Dean is here and Laney has been taken somewhere else?"

What the hell? Matt ran back the last week in his mind. So Emery knew about the serial killer. What did this mean? "I don't have a partner, but I'm interested in your thoughts about the serial killer having one."

A vein bulged in Emery's neck as he angled toward Patterson. "Why don't we go meet them?" Quick as a python, he struck with a syringe plunged into Patterson's neck. The guy was out immediately.

Matt reacted just as quickly, balancing himself with his cuffed hands and swinging his legs over the table to hit first Emery and then Patterson. Patterson flew to the side, his eyes shut, his head thunking on the table. With a primal roar, Matt landed on his feet and lifted the table into Emery, throwing them both into the two-way mirror.

Then he threw himself back, ripping the table over his head and twisting. He dropped to his knees and used his teeth to tug the keys from Patterson's pocket.

Emery regrouped and shot forward, so Matt kicked out with his boot and caught the bastard under the chin before falling and throwing the table over his head again. The cuffs ripped into his skin, and his shoulders popped from the effort.

The table hit Emery in the neck, and he fell back.

His mind calming, his body relaxing, Matt set down the table and spit the keys at his hands. A couple of twists, and the cuffs released. Just in time for Matt to throw an elbow into Emery's chest and avoid the syringe aimed at his neck. Being able to discern movement before it happened saved his ass again.

Ducking and reaching out, Matt grabbed the syringe and burst into Emery, injecting the needle and releasing the liquid. "I hope that's not a lethal dose," Matt said, allowing Emery to drop.

Matt leaped across the room and locked the door. A commotion sounded beyond the mirror. Taking a deep breath, he bent at the knees and lifted the table. Tucking his arms in, he burst through the mirror.

Glass shattered.

He landed on the other side and threw the table toward two soldiers trying to draw guns. The table legs impacted first, and Matt jumped to punch for throats.

Both soldiers went down and hard.

Gulping, Matt reached for their weapons before approaching his unconscious brother.

Nate lay on his side, his heart beating steadily again. Thank God.

Matt grabbed Nate's shoulders and shook. "Wake up, Nathan. Now." He shook harder.

Nate came to with a low groan.

Matt removed Nate's cell phone and dialed Shane. "We're in trouble. Lock on to Laney's signal, and when I'm safe, I'll call you back."

"Roger that," Shane said, his voice tense.

Matt slipped the phone into his pocket, thrust a gun into Nate's hand, and hauled him up. "Get ready. We need to go now."

After receiving a nod from his pale brother, Matt turned and slid open the door. Time to go find Laney.

Laney shoved wet hair off her face and tried to run under the heavier trees to block the storm. Rain smashed down, and the wind had picked up to the extent pine needles hampered her way. She shivered in her wet clothing, her mind going numb. What now?

She kept jogging through the forest, heading toward town. If nothing else, she needed transportation.

What about Matt?

She steeled her shoulders, determined to save him. But if the commander had gotten to her, he'd probably gotten to Matt. Though, with Matt's training, maybe he'd escaped.

God, she hoped he'd been able to escape.

Her entire life, she'd followed her instincts. Sometimes they'd helped her, like when surviving her lonely childhood. Often, they'd sucked, like when going to work for the commander.

So this time she followed her heart. Matt was one of the good guys, and if she had a chance to save him, she'd do it. She headed toward town and the sheriff's station, which had to be about fifteen or so miles away.

She managed to jog the first mile through the dark forest as the storm pummeled down. The second mile, she sprinted.

The third, she walked.

By the time she stretched into the fifth mile, weakened legs, upturned roots, and flying branches tripped her.

She landed hard, debris cutting into her already-wounded hands. Taking a deep breath, she leaned against the trunk of a pine tree being assaulted by the crazy wind.

Cold encased her wet feet until they cramped. Chills cut down her back, and her lungs heaved. She wiped her soaked hair off her face and tried to dig deep. The injuries to her wrists and hands screamed in agony, and she used that pain to center herself.

Furious clouds hid the sun, and the world continued to darken. Night would soon fall, and she needed to be out of the forest while she could still see.

A low-pitched whistle had her stilling and jerking her head to the side. She peered into the rain-drenched forest. Maybe it was some sort of weird birdcall.

Her heartbeat picked up in a way she respected. So she listened some more.

SWEET REVENGE   283

Another whistle.

The crack of a stick pierced through the storm. She leaped to her feet, her heart nearly stopping.

A man stood in shadow between two massive pines.

She blinked several times and took a hesitant step forward. "Matt?"

The rain had slicked back his hair to curl around his ears and run down the hard angles of his face. His black T-shirt clung to his broad chest, while mud and leaves coated his boots.

He looked like a pissed-off fallen angel in the middle of Armageddon.

Tears shot into her eyes. Bone-deep relief made her sway. He was all right. Thank God.

Long strides propelled him out of the darkness toward her, where he cupped her face. "Are you all right?"

She struggled to remain in control. Now wasn't the time to fall apart, no matter how badly her knees were shaking. "Fine. You?"

"What happened?" He whistled, and Nate instantly appeared to Laney's right.

"The commander is here," Laney said on a rush. "He has troops moving in from all sides to take us."

"I know." Matt glanced around. "Nate, how close are we to Backlebee Lake?"

"About five miles," Nate said, wiping rain off his forehead with his arm.

Matt nodded. "Thank God for tracking devices. That's how we found you, Laney." He fingered the bracelet still wrapped around her wrist that held the tracking device. Then he slipped his cell phone from his back pocket and pushed a number on speed dial. "Shane? Can you get a satellite view of the forest?"

Matt listened for a moment and then shook his head at Nate. "The cloud cover is too thick. We have to assume they're moving in, and quickly. The good news is if we can't see them or their heat signatures, they can't see ours."

He turned his concentration back to the phone. "How soon can you get an extraction team here?" Matt listened and cut a look at Nate. "Okay. Stay in touch." He disconnected the call.

Laney swallowed, and her teeth began to chatter.

Matt slid a wet arm around her shoulders. "The storm is too bad to land a team here. We need to ride out the next hour or so, and Shane will airlift us out as soon as possible."

"Let's go." Nate pivoted and disappeared behind a fir big enough to decorate Rockefeller Center at Christmas.

Matt turned and tugged Laney close for a hug. "Can you make it five more miles?"

She forced a smile and hoped he ignored the trembling of her lips. "Yes."

"Good." He slipped his hand into hers and led her onto a barely discernible path.

She could do this. Yes, the commander was scary and the men after her deadly. But the one in front of her knew how to kill, and he'd do so for her.

The least she could do was jog through a storm.

So she sucked in rain-filled air and ran like her life depended on it. Matt stayed close to her side, while Nate scouted ahead and often doubled back to check in.

Night began to fall, and the storm somehow increased in strength. She struggled to continue even as Matt blocked her from most of the wind.

An hour later, Nate reappeared. "There's a cabin about forty yards to the east."

Matt retook her hand and tugged her to the left. How he knew which way was east was a mystery, but Laney didn't have the time or energy to figure it out. She plodded doggedly along, her tennis shoes squishing in mud, her body more numb than cold.

The sound of waves battering the shore competed with the wind a second before a rough cabin came into view.

Shelter. She almost cried at the welcoming sight.

Matt herded her along the beach toward the front door as Nate ran around back.

The door was locked. Matt put his shoulder to it, and the wood crashed in with barely a whisper. He tugged her inside and used his cell phone as a flashlight to illuminate the small space.

A bed took up the left corner, a small kitchenette the right, and a sofa lounged in front of a stone fireplace with wood stacked to the side. An arched doorway had been cut into the far wall, and Laney immediately headed that way.

"The water pump is probably off," Matt said, heading toward the fireplace. "You can use whatever toilet they have, but don't flush until we fetch water from the lake."

She nodded and tripped inside a surprisingly modern bathroom. God, she was cold. After making use of the facilities and trying to wipe off mud and leaves from her tingling cheeks, she headed out to face Matt.

The roar of a fire caught her attention first, but his broad back enticed her more than the flames. He'd tossed his shirt over the back of a chair, and muscles shifted nicely as he tugged open drawers near the bedside.

He reached in and drew out a large flannel shirt. After shaking it out, he turned and tossed the worn material at her. "It's clean. You have to get dry."

So this was the soldier. Laney had seen glimpses of him during their time together, but seeing Matt in full concentration, all fighter, was something new. Intimidating and intriguing all at once.

She caught the shirt. "Won't they see the smoke from the fire?"

"Not in this storm." His gaze raked her head to toe. "Getting warm is too important, so the risk is worth it."

Her hands hurt, they were so cold, so she headed back into the bathroom.

"All clothes, Laney," Matt called after her.

"I know. I am the doctor here," she tossed back.

His barely audible "Smart-ass" made her smile as she removed her wet clothing to cover up with the soft flannel, which reached past her knees. She padded out barefoot and hung her clothes over chairs to dry as Matt finished going through all the drawers.

He turned around. "No weapons. Damn it."

The cabin's owners had probably closed the place down for the winter. Laney handed him the gun she'd taken off Tasha. "For bluffing. There aren't any bullets."

Matt took the gun and frowned.

Laney headed over to the small kitchen to open the remaining two drawers. "A couple of steak knives. Nothing impressive."

The door burst open, and wind rushed inside to scatter her clothing across the floor.

"Sorry." Nate elbowed the door shut and shook out his hair.

"No problem." Laney fetched the clothing and rehung it. The small room suddenly had way too much testosterone in it, with two Gray brothers.

"Okay." Nate wiped moisture off his face. "There are several cabins along the lakefront. I'll go search each one for weapons, and then I want to scout to the west to find how close the commander's troops are, and how many he brought."

Matt headed toward the door. "I'll walk you out." He turned around toward Laney. "Get warm by the fire. We'll plan when I get back." His gray eyes revealed nothing.

Laney took a deep breath and nodded. *Plan?*

CHAPTER
28

MATT KEPT TO the shelter of the rough porch, his gaze focused across the lake. "A row of cabins front the north shore. I doubt we'll find anything but a shotgun or two, but you never know."

"I'm more interested in how many troops the commander sent after us." Nate stretched his back with a loud pop. "Getting out of here with the surgeon is going to be tough."

"She's not a surgeon any longer," Matt said, the wind smashing rain up against his bare chest.

"Sure she is." Nate shrugged. "Maybe she's not cutting into people right now, but she learned the skills—and she has used them."

"Not on us." Matt didn't understand why he was defending Laney, but he couldn't stop. "The commander manipulated her like he did us."

Resignation shot through Nate's eyes before determination hardened his jaw. "Okay, then. I guess she stays with us?"

An unknown force filtered through Matt. What the hell was that? Panic? *Shit.* Had he just felt panic? If so, he didn't like it. At all. "Yes. I just almost had a panic attack at the thought of losing her, and I won't do it. Not because I need her to help us, but because . . ."

"You need her." Nate sighed. "I guess she's one of us, then."

Heated air rose up Matt's esophagus. "She is, and I need you to be nice to her."

Nate chuckled. "I'm always nice."

"Are not."

"Am, too." Nate sighed and leaned back against the weathered wood. "You love her."

Two of the deadliest soldiers trained by the commander shouldn't sound like arguing two-year-olds. "I haven't known her very long." Matt shook his head.

Nate rolled his eyes. "What does time have to do with anything?"

"I don't know." This couldn't be happening. Not right now.

Nate closed his eyes for a moment and pushed off the cabin. "Listen, Matt. I don't want you to be in love any more than you want it. Any distraction right now is bad. But if it has happened, we deal with it like we always have."

"Deal with it?" Matt shook his head. "You really don't understand."

"Sure I do." Nate swallowed. "From day one, you've lived for us. You were our brother, father, mother, commanding officer, and medic. We all know it. There's nothing wrong with having something for yourself. Having somebody."

But his focus had to be his brothers. He was the oldest, and they were his responsibility. Shit, he needed them. Without his brothers, he was just another killing machine. The thoughts raced through his mind as his brother waited him out. "Hell."

Nate smacked him on the shoulder. "Listen. If you decide she's family, she's family. We'll protect her until our last breath, which, unfortunately, may be soon. Very soon."

Matt shook his head. He'd never faltered in his path, never. Now he couldn't find his footing. "What if she, I mean, if..."

"If she doesn't feel the same?" Nathan shrugged. "Well, you say she's nice. Maybe she'll take pity on you. After all, you are the ugly one."

Matt coughed out a laugh. "You're such an ass."

"Yeah, and I'm good at it." Nate glanced toward the north. "Our chances of getting out of this forest are not good. You know it as well as I do."

"I know." Even if they caught a miracle and got to Montana, the Gray brothers probably only had six weeks to live. How could he ensure Laney's safety from beyond the grave, especially since his brothers would be dead, too? "We're going to take care of these chips. But first, we have to survive the night." Matt glanced back at the darkened cabin. "I'd like to go with you to scout, but—"

Nate shook his head. "Stay here, protect your woman. You'd be worried about her, and I don't need you distracted. I'll be back as soon as I can." He exhaled. "Take the time, Mattie. It may be all you have."

The truth in the words cut like a blade. "Thank you for being my brother, Nate."

Nate's smile held too much sadness. "Never alone." He turned and ran into the devastating storm.

"Never alone," Matt repeated quietly. His chest hurt. They'd survived their childhoods and found freedom together. In order to survive the next weeks and beat the commander, he had to become the worst part of himself. The part they'd created in a test tube to feel nothing and kill easily. In order to save his brothers, to protect Laney, he had to become all hunter.

A being Laney couldn't possibly love.

He appreciated Nate's push for Matt to find happiness. But happiness and the things he had to do didn't go together. He knew it, and deep down, he suspected Nate knew it, too.

Matt would make his stance in the forest. He probably only had a few more hours to live, and he was taking them.

So he pushed open the cabin door and headed inside to see what might have been. In a different time, in a different world, if he'd been a different man.

Laney stood near the crackling fire, her legs bare, the light shining through the thin cotton to illuminate her curves. She was so beautiful his gut hurt. Green eyes that hinted at Ireland, feminine features that whispered at fragility, and long legs meant to wrap around his hips all drew him forward. "Nate went to scout for more weapons and will be back shortly."

Laney's eyes widened. "Then what?"

"Then we run to wherever Shane is picking us up." They'd probably have to fight their way there. "No matter what happens, you head for the coordinates and get on the helicopter."

"Not without you." She lifted her chin, intelligence sizzling in her eyes.

Yeah, she'd read him correctly. He'd sacrifice himself to save her. "I need you on the helicopter."

"Then I suggest you be with me so I get on it." While delicate, her chin held a dangerous amount of stubbornness.

An image of a little girl with his eyes and her chin flashed through Matt's head, and he almost staggered with the need to have that life. To have that family. "I may not be able to have kids," he said. Jesus. Why the hell had he said that? They didn't have forever and sure as shit wouldn't be planning to procreate.

Laney's eyebrows lifted into her hairline. "Are you asking me to marry you or something?"

"No." *Hell, no. God.*

Feminine knowledge glowed in her eyes and scared the shit out of him. She glided forward and slid her palms along his wet skin. A roaring filled his ears and urged him to take her down and bury himself in all that softness. To beg her to never leave him.

She tilted her head to meet his gaze. "Why not?"

His mind fizzed. "Why not what?"

"Why aren't you asking me to marry you?" Those nimble fingers unlatched his belt.

He blinked. "Huh?"

"You love me, right?" She tugged his belt free.

His cock suddenly tried to punch through his zipper, and he bit back a wince. "What does marriage have to do with anything?"

She unsnapped his jeans. "Answer the question."

Oh, he'd left her way too long in the cabin to think. She'd been thinking, obviously. "Yes, I love you. But love doesn't change anything."

She slowly, way too slowly, released his zipper. "You're wrong. Love changes *everything*."

"Why?" He held her upper arms, wrapping his fingers all the way around and being careful not to bruise.

"Because I love you, too." She held absolutely still as she said the words.

His gut clenched, and his heart thrummed. Love. The real kind, and from Laney. His head spun. He didn't deserve her, but the idea of losing her sliced through him like a sword.

"I know it's quick, and it probably doesn't make a lot of sense, but with who we are? Who we've lost? I love you, Matt. I'm keeping you." She smiled, and the world narrowed in focus. "I always figured somebody was meant for me, and when I found him, I'd know it. The second I saw you in the alley, something in me recognized you."

The woman had a frightening way with words that made sense to him. Probably *just* to him. Adrenaline roared, forcing a primal need to claim her in the most fundamental way. He wanted to imprint himself so deep inside her, he'd always be there. They didn't have forever. They might not even have past the hour. But he wanted her to remember him until her last breath, and if he had his way, she'd live for decades after this. She ran her fingers along his cock, and his attention snapped back to her. "You're killing me."

"Keeping you alive is one of my biggest goals right now," she murmured, her voice husky.

"What are your other goals?"

"Getting you nude. Orgasming until we can't see straight." She stepped back and shoved his jeans down his legs. "Ohhh. Black boxers this time. You are full of surprises, aren't you?"

Her speech was way too clear, while he could barely form a grunt. Enough of that. "You have no idea." He reached for the hem of the flannel and tugged the material over her head. "Why don't I show you?"

Laney stood in the firelight and licked her lips when Matt tossed his boxers to the side. Her IQ lived well into the triple digits, and reality had always been her companion. There was little chance they'd make it out of the forest before the commander got to them. They were outmanned, outgunned, and out-timed.

Life was life.

But she had right now. There wasn't time for being coy or for worrying about the future. She had only her emotions, her intelligence, and her instincts. Those all told her Matt was a good guy, and he was *hers*. Being close to death made things so clear.

She loved him.

They had an hour or so.

So she stepped into him and played with those amazing abs. He dug both hands into her hair with just enough strength to be forceful and tugged back her head. A sexy growl rumbled in his chest before his mouth slid along hers.

Smooth, firm, his lips played as if they had all the time in the world.

She swayed toward him, her muscles going lax, her eyelids fluttering shut. Desire spiraled through her abdomen with heat and emotion. The moment held significance and somehow felt different. She opened her mouth, and his tongue swept in.

He kissed her like he did everything else, with control and heat.

This once, he needed to lose that control. She'd make sure of it.

So she stepped into him, ignoring the erotic pain at her scalp, and gripped his shaft at the base. Her fingers didn't wrap all the way around, yet she kept a good hold.

He stilled and released her mouth to lever back and study her. Desire darkened his eyes to a smoky slate. "In a hurry?"

"No." Her smile even felt challenging. "I thought I'd take control."

His chin lowered. Tension vibrated in the air between them with a masculine edge—a moment of breathless calm when the world goes silent before fire erupts. His fingers curled through her hair. "You think you can keep control?" His voice lowered past husky to pure sin.

Wetness coated her thighs. Her ab muscles trembled with need. She didn't need to look down to know her nipples had hardened to rock. No matter what the future slammed into her, she'd carry the tone of that voice into forever. *Male. Sex. Hers.* "Yes." She tried to tug her head free and wasn't surprised when she barely moved. "You think I can't?"

Hunger flashed across his angled face. "I think you've bitten off more than you've realized."

"How so?" She lightly caressed his entire length.

A dark flush wandered across his cheekbones. "Don't push, baby."

"Why?" She slid her thumb over the slit in his penis. "You afraid you'll let go? That I'll finally know all of you?"

"Yes." His nostrils flared, and the muscles in his shoulders flexed like a wolf's before striking.

Triumph filled her, along with a reasonable caution. *Screw caution.* "Too fucking bad. You want me?" She tried to toss her head, but his hold kept her in place.

"Yes."

"Then nut up, soldier boy." She gripped him harder as she allowed her voice to drop. "Look at you, all pumped up, waiting for the command to go. I think I have you leashed already."

She expected him to lunge. To take over. Instead, a slow smile lifted his sexy lips. A smile full of confidence and warning. The confidence, she appreciated, while the warning...instinct told her to heed. Her heart lurched against her rib cage. "I, ah—"

"No. Too late. Way too late." He moved his hands down her face, over her shoulders, along her arms, the movement gentle, yet with a hint of power. Of his incredible strength. Nerves shot to life beneath her skin. He grasped her wrists and used an effective pressure point to make her release him. "You were saying?" Gliding forward, he towered over her while securing her wrists against her lower back.

Her nipples scraped against his warm skin, and electric charges shot straight to her clit. She bit back a moan and fought to keep her eyes from rolling back toward her brain. "S-so you're stronger. Big whoop." She had to force the words out with little breath. It was all caught in her lungs.

"Ah, baby"—he dropped to one knee and released her hands—"I don't need to use muscle to receive your submission." His mouth found her.

Her entire body short-circuited. She arched against him and might have fallen if he hadn't gripped her thighs and held her against his devastating mouth. He slipped one finger inside her...and then two. His rough tongue lapped her clit, alternating between long passes and gentle pulls.

Glancing up, he spread her apart with his thumbs. With a lethal grin, he leaned forward to pleasure her with a vengeance. The fire warmed her from behind, while an incredible male built up the fire in her front. It was too much.

He was too much.

His touch, the intimacy of the cabin, the incredible need coursing through her all combined to steal her mind. To center her reality to the man on his knee, still so strong and unbeatable. He had to be invincible, didn't he? To beat what was coming?

He nipped her clit, and her head jerked back. "Stay with me, baby. Here in the moment." His words echoed through her mound to land somewhere deep inside her.

How could he read her so easily? The thought brought an odd comfort, even while her body flared with raw need.

Thunder bellowed outside but was no match for the storm going on within her body. Even the zig of lightning failed to jerk her attention from the mini-explosions rocketing her body. The carnal pleasure kept her on the edge, and her hands tangled in his hair, trying to force more pressure.

This time he chuckled against her. "Now who's in control?"

Who gave a whit about control? An orgasm lingered beyond the ridge she'd scaled, and she craved relief. "Stop playing," she gasped.

"Not until I'm ready." He continued to torture her, to restrain her right on the edge, keeping her from falling. Finally, after a lifetime where she forgot how to breathe, he sucked her clit into his mouth.

She cried out his name, her back bowing, the climax ripping through her in a whirlwind of ecstasy. He kept her from falling into the fire, even while the one within her burned. The waves took her over until the room sheeted white. Finally, he gentled her. Even when she came down, her heart thudding, her lungs aching...it wasn't enough. Nowhere near enough.

With a growl, he stood and swung her up, stalking toward the bed. Within a second, she lay flat on her back. He covered her, his fists on either side of her head, the veins popping out on his arms. He thrust inside her with one strong stroke.

She cried out as pleasure and pain combined into a clawing hunger. Her knees rose even as her back bowed and her thighs clasped his. "You're t-too big," she gasped.

"You'll take all of me." Dark, lazy, his gaze pierced into her mind as surely as his body had impaled hers. "You're mine, Laney."

She didn't want him to stop. Ever. As she took in the warrior covering her, her heart clicked into place. As if it had been slightly askew her entire life, it finally found home. Tears pricked the back of her eyes. "I love you, Mattie."

He dropped his forehead to hers, the gesture more intimate than she would've imagined. Slowly, he withdrew and slid back inside.

The sensation was as close to heaven as she could hope. She relaxed into the bed and caressed down his flanks. "You have an incredible body."

He lifted up and grinned, the cords of his neck standing out. "Ditto."

She laughed and dug her fingers into his fine butt.

He rewarded her with a low growl.

She flexed and wrapped her legs around his back. Rearing up, she nipped his bottom lip.

His eyes flashed a warning, and his shoulders stiffened.

"Control?" she asked softly, rubbing her breasts along his chest and gasping at the incredible sensation. Then, with a tightening of her legs, she flexed her fingers.

Any control he thought he had snapped into nothingness. Grabbing her hips, half lifting her from the bed, he plunged inside her hard. His other hand snaked up her side to clamp over her shoulder from behind, yanking her down to meet his primal thrusts.

She closed her eyes as incredible pleasure melded with pressure inside her. Each thrust, each pound, only increased the desperate craving. He hit nerves she didn't even know existed. She let him take her, helpless in his hold and her need. He moved her as he wanted her, his pounding fast and furious.

Electricity uncoiled within her, sending sparks to burn her from within. Her eyelids flipped open as the orgasm took her over, rode her, forced her to explode in a climax so violent she couldn't even whimper. She arched her back, her mouth open in a silent scream. Waves of pleasure rippled through her, touching more than flesh, more than right now.

He took everything she was.

Finally, the ecstasy released her. With a sigh, she softened against the worn bedspread.

Matt stilled and ground against her, his teeth latching on to her neck as he came.

The bite barely registered as Laney panted in air. Matt collapsed against her, his head in the crook of her neck, his heart beating so hard she felt it against her chest.

"You're going to survive this, Laney," he murmured against her skin. "I promise."

Tears pricked her eyes. "We both are." They had to. Now that she'd found him, she couldn't lose him. "Right?"

CHAPTER
29

THE WOMAN NEEDED a reassurance he couldn't give. "Right. But if I don't make it, I promise you'll be all right." If it was the last thing he did, he'd make provisions for her safety. Somehow. "So you getting on the helicopter is our primary focus. Got it?"

She didn't agree nearly soon enough.

"Laney?" he asked, lifting his head. Her stubborn chin came into focus first.

"We stick together." She met his gaze levelly, the firelight caressing her pretty features.

Shit. She hadn't agreed at all. He rose up on his elbows, his body caging hers. "Now isn't a good time to disagree with me." He allowed steel to enter his words.

She shrugged, her breasts sliding against his chest. "This is a perfect time. You look like a relaxed, lazy lion in the firelight."

His eyebrows lifted of their own accord. "Lions bite, baby."

"So bite me." She grinned.

He frowned, distracted. "I think I already did." He peered closer at the love nip at her shoulder. While he should probably apologize for his actions, the sight of his mark on her filled him with a primal satisfaction. An inappropriate throwback of a satisfaction. "I didn't break the skin, but, ah, my bite is there." For a few days at least.

"You're smiling." She tangled her fingers through his hair. "Neanderthal."

His woman had a point. "Good. We understand each other. I give an order and you follow it." Life would be so much easier if she'd agree.

"No."

Damn it. He needed to convince her. "I'm on board with equal rights, with trusting each other to make the right decisions." He sounded like a jackass who'd never been in a relationship. Hell, he *had* never been in a real relationship.

"Good." She stretched against him.

His cock perked up. "Except in battle."

This time her eyebrow rose. "Hmmm."

The fact that his temper roared so quickly after such amazing sex was proof of the danger in their current situation. He stamped down impatience. "Yes. In battle, one person has to command, or we all die. I have more battle experience, and right now, as we're fighting for our lives, you will obey." The *o* word was a mistake, and he knew it the second he said it. "Promise me."

She sighed. "If we're attacked by a squad of soldiers, I promise I'll follow orders to survive."

"But?" It couldn't be this easy.

"I'm not leaving you. Ever." Her eyes softened to the color of a summer meadow. "I've lost everyone I've ever cared about, and I've never loved somebody like this. I can't lose it, and I won't lose you." Determination lived in the lines of her fragile face. "This has nothing to do with equal rights or trust. This is life, and you're mine."

His heart swelled to the point his ribs hurt. Needles poked behind his eyes. Couldn't be tears, because he didn't cry. So he lowered his head and kissed her, accepting all she was giving. "I love you, Laney."

"I know." She hugged him, her arms not reaching around his back.

The idea of losing her terrified him, even as happiness he didn't deserve flowed through him. He ran his hand through her hair, marveling at the softness. He wanted to pet her forever. "I'll never let you down."

She murmured sleepily into his skin.

He rolled to the side and tucked her close. "Get some sleep. Nate will be here any time, and we'll need to head into the storm again." The fact that the storm had only increased in power was a lucky one. In his life, luck never lasted. So they'd have to run.

"Okay." Laney snuggled her tight butt into his groin and was asleep within a minute.

He loved that she could fall asleep so easily . . . She trusted him. Matt held her closer, breathing in the vanilla scent of her hair. The need to protect her coursed through him stronger than any drug the scientists had plunged into his veins with their experiments. This need, he'd follow. Arguing with her was a waste of time, yet he couldn't be anybody other than who he was. He'd make sure she made it to safety, even if he had to sacrifice himself to do it.

A sound in the distance perked his ears.

Thunder. Lightning. Rain slashing down. *A footstep.*

He went cold, all senses focused a hundred yards to the east. More rain, more thunder, and more pine needles slashing into trees.

Another footstep.

Careful and cautious—loaded down. Probably with weapons and tactical gear. Definitely not Nate.

Matt swung his legs from the bed, careful not to awaken Laney. Quick strides had him across the room, where he yanked on his jeans before dialing Nate with his cell. No answer. Either Nate had gone dark, or the storm was messing with his phone. While Matt had a satellite phone, Nate's was a burner phone.

Instantly switching into hunter mode, Matt pulled on his shirt and stuck the unloaded gun in his pants. Planning ahead, he grabbed the two steak knives out of the drawer. They were as useless as the weapon, but he donned his boots and tucked a knife into one.

Turning, he stared at Laney.

The soft light from the fire turned her skin to burnished gold. She breathed softly, sleeping peacefully. He could leave her, take care of the threat, and arrive back at the cabin before she awoke.

Or he could be walking into a trap, might get killed, and she'd be sleeping in bed, completely defenseless.

Both options sucked.

He didn't want to do this, but survival was all that mattered. So he retrieved her wet clothes and approached the bed. "Laney? Get up and get dressed, baby. Now."

She blinked and sat up in bed. "What?"

He set down the clothes. "Get dressed."

Her eyes widened, and she jumped from the bed to yank on the still-dripping clothes. Her hands shook when she tied her muddy tennis shoes. "What's going on?"

"I heard somebody to the east." He tossed one knife on the bed. "Take the knife, and if you need to use it, don't hesitate."

"How far to the east?"

"At least a hundred yards." Way too close. He tried to appear reassuring.

She frowned. "Your hearing is that enhanced?"

"Yes. All senses are." He needed to get her moving.

"Okay." She grasped the handle, her eyes way too wide in her pale face. "We're going to fight, then?"

He paused. "Ah, no. You're hiding, I'm fighting."

She glanced in slow motion down to the knife in her hand. "Why do I have a knife?"

"Just in case." He moved toward her and grasped her

shoulders. "I'd like to leave you in the warm cabin, but if something happens to me, they'll find you. We need to put you someplace else while I go take care of whoever is headed our way."

"B-but I don't want to hide out in the storm." Her knuckles turned white on the handle.

"I know, baby." He dropped a soft kiss on her head. "I'll hurry back and get you warm."

She shook her head and pushed him. "No, I mean I don't want to hide while you fight. I can help. We've been training."

"No." He allowed no softness or understanding to enter his voice. "This is what's going to happen. We're going into the storm, and we're going to find you a place to hide near the lake. Nate or Shane will know how to find you if something happens to me." Taking her arm, he propelled her outside.

The wind slapped them hard, while rain cut through oxygen like it was pissed. He tried to shield her as much as possible as he led her down to the lake. Yeah, he thought so. He pointed down the shoreline to the west. "About ten cabins down, there's a shed near the dock. Crouch down as much as possible under the eaves, and I'll be back soon." Kissing her hard on the mouth, he stepped back. "Do what I say, Laney. If you see anybody headed this way who's not me, I want you to get in the lake and swim under the dock."

God, he hoped he made it back.

She glanced at the churning lake and swallowed. "Okay." She grabbed his shirt and yanked his head down. "Come back to me. I love you."

He deepened the kiss, taking over, trying to put everything he felt into it. "I love you with everything I am."

She wiped rain off her face as the wind battered her. "I'd try to go, but I'd just get in your way. One week of training probably won't do much against those guys."

He forced a grin. "I don't know—you're fairly tough. Now go."

She nodded and turned, her feet slipping in the sand. But she lowered her head and fought the wind.

Matt waited as long as he could to make sure she was all right, but the sense of urgency at the base of his neck finally took over. Pivoting, he ran full bore to cut off the men headed toward his woman.

Laney clamped her hand around the knife handle and crouched down against the wooden boards. The small shack most likely held inner tubes and life jackets. She could kick the door in—maybe—but then she'd be trapped inside if the commander found her beach.

The storm continued to bluster, throwing sand to pelt her. Whitecaps smashed waves against the shore, and the nearest dock pitched wildly in the blackened water.

She'd never survive hiding under the heaving planks. No way.

Movement near the closest cabin caught her eye. She squinted through the darkness, her breath catching. The wind propelled a mass of leaves onto the porch. She relaxed.

A dark figure came into view.

Her heart clutched. So much for it just being the wind.

She couldn't discern his face, but he was big. He held something in his right hand—probably a gun. She peered around him for other soldiers. It was too dark.

Tightening her grip, she huddled back against the building.

The man stilled, his body turning toward her. *God.* Had he heard her move through the storm? No way. Unless he was engineered, like Matt.

The guy's shoulders went back, and he strode toward her through the billowing storm. She closed her eyes for courage, waited until he blocked the wind, and then lunged.

"Whoa," he muttered, catching her by the armpits and taking her down to the sand. "Doc. Take it easy."

She opened her eyes. "Nathan?"

"Yeah." He hauled her up. "Sorry to scare you. Where's Matt?"

"A hundred yards to the east." She tried to brush wet sand off her legs and quickly gave up the fight. There was no getting dry.

Nate lifted his head, his gaze to the east. He frowned. "The east is quiet."

"So the fight is over?" Hope flared in her chest.

"No. The fight hasn't started." Nate held a sawed-off shotgun in his left hand. "Can you move?"

"Sure. Any other weapons?" What she would give for a gun. Or an Uzi.

Nate shook his head. "Just this shotgun. Forces are moving in from the west and north, so I can't leave you here. We need to find Matt and now."

A ball of dread slammed into her gut. Even so, she turned to follow Nate along the shoreline, the sand sucking her feet deep. "They're coming from all sides. We'll have to fight our way out." Against the commander and his armed forces, chances were too slim to calculate.

Nate turned and smiled through the rain. "I have a plan, Doc. No worries."

"I'm not a doctor anymore, and I never will be. I'm a bartender." She liked her life, and she liked her job. Being a doctor had been a goal to make her somebody, and she had trained hard for it. But would returning to the world of medicine make her lose who she'd become? A part of a community that cared?

"Barkeep isn't as good a nickname." Nate angled his body to the right and provided her more shelter from the wind trying to kill them.

"Laney is." She put her head down to keep sand from her eyes.

"My brother, Shane, calls his wife Angel. Does Matt have a nickname for you?" Nate asked.

Nobody had ever considered her close to an angel. Laney wondered about the mysterious Josie. She must be the sweetest woman alive. Laney wasn't jealous. Not at all. Plus, Nate was trying to distract her from their imminent death, and she warmed toward him. "Yes. Either *smart-ass* or *baby*."

Nate chuckled. "I can't call you those. Mattie would kick my butt."

Smart-ass wasn't nearly as nice as *angel*. Laney tripped in the wet sand and quickly regained her footing. "True."

"What was your middle name—your real one?" Nate asked, his casual tone at odds with the at-attention set of his back.

"Um, Lou." Her mother had named her after her maternal grandparents, Eleanor and Lou. Of course, they'd died by the time Laney had turned three.

Nate tossed her a look over his shoulder. "We've got it. Laney Lou it is."

"Sounds like either a fat farmer's daughter or a porn star," Laney muttered, trying not to smile.

"Exactly."

"Are we bonding or something?" She'd have thought Nate would want her dead.

He shrugged. "Sure. Why not?"

"Um, because I was one of the doctors who worked for the commander." These men confused her.

"Did you do anything to hurt me or my brothers personally?" Nate asked.

"No."

"Well, life is too goddamn short for me to worry about who you might've hurt if it wasn't us. And it's too short to shove away love if it's real. Plus, as much as I hate to say it, we all worked for the commander." Nate eyed her.

"I guess." She really wanted him to like her for some reason.

"I get the feeling you'll fight with us, and I like that." Nate lifted his head and listened for a moment. "Plus, Matt seems at peace. Even with all of us about to die, he's found happiness. That's what I'd want for him."

Warmth bubbled through Laney, and she increased her pace. They had to win this.

Nate halted and held up a hand for her to stop.

She stilled, setting her stance to keep from falling over. Rain attacked her like they were enemies. When had she angered Mother Nature to such a degree? "What?"

Nate turned. "Twenty yards into the forest." He eyed her. "Come with me as far as the tree line, and then you hide."

Her knees wobbled, and her shoulders shook. She wouldn't get in his way, but she was ready to fight to the death if necessary. Chances were, even if she held back, it would be. "Okay. Just bring him back in one piece, will you?"

Nate nodded. "Of course. Let's find you temporary shelter."

CHAPTER
30

MATT LEANED AGAINST the ponderosa pine, his senses tuned in to the three men stalking him. He'd made enough sound for them to realize he was near as he led them away from Laney. In attack formation, they made barely a sound while moving through the forest.

They were good, but not as good as he.

Two of them had raised heart rates and breathing, while the other remained calm as death. Matt would bet his left arm the third guy was Emery.

Anticipation lit up Matt's spine. He'd waited for this day for as long as he could remember. When they'd blown the facility to hell, he'd had the opportunity to kill Emery, and he hadn't taken it. He'd given the guy a chance to find a life. Even now, years later, Matt felt for any kid who'd been raised by the commander and Dr. Madison. But Emery was now hunting Laney.

That meant death.

Matt's time on earth may be limited, but while there, he'd take care of any threat to Laney without mercy. None.

He'd done his best with Emery, and the time for mercy had passed. It was time to end this.

So he slipped around the tree and approached one of

the soldiers from behind. Shoving all emotion and thought into nothingness, Matt secured the guy in a headlock and twisted. The body hadn't hit the ground before Matt maneuvered several yards to the right.

The other two men stopped moving. *Shit.* They must've been using the sensor system Jory had developed years ago. On mission, their vitals were transmitted to each other. If one of them went down, the transmission alerted them.

Even so, he could hear their heartbeats, even through the damaging storm. So he angled toward the guy trying not to breathe and was on him within seconds. They landed on the wet pine needles, and the soldier caught Matt with an impressive choke hold.

Matt punched him in the eye, and the hold loosened. Death was quick and painless.

A crack sounded just before Emery ran around a tree, already firing. The first bullet impacted Matt's arm. The second, his shoulder. He rolled to the side and behind a tree, the rain piercing his eyes.

"You *shot* me?" he growled out. "Pussy."

Emery laughed, the sound grating above the rolling thunder. "I've always wanted to fill you with lead."

Matt glanced down at his bleeding right arm. "Guess you can't take me in a fair fight." Yeah, the bullet had surprised him. He'd always figured they'd do this hand to hand, and may the best soldier win. Measuring blood loss because he refused to feel the pain, he quickly slid between two trees and angled slightly to the north, his movements silent as he circled around his enemy.

Seconds later, several shots ricocheted off the tree where he'd caught his breath. He smiled.

Emery's muffled curse echoed beneath the rain pummeling down.

Matt hunted quietly and with determination, his senses

on high alert. He heard Emery before he smelled him. With a roll of his injured arm, Matt flipped around a birch and tackled Emery in the midsection.

Emery punched out even as they flew through the air, his fist catching Matt in the throat.

Matt jerked his head up and brought his forehead down on Emery's nose. The crack of cartilage breaking filled the air right before they crashed to the muddy trail. Matt's right arm was weakening, so he used his left to knock the gun from Emery's hand. The weapon spun through pine needles and landed at the base of a swaying conifer. Lightning struck a tree with a resounding clash, and branches pummeled them from high above.

The scents of ozone and blood permeated the night.

Emery bashed his knees into Matt's hips and threw him to the right. Matt rolled to one knee and kicked Emery in the face just like Emery had done to Jory once.

Matt shoved to his feet as Emery did the same. They both stood to well over six feet and had spent years honing their bodies into fighting shape. Except for the genetic eye marker that showed their lineage, they might have been brothers. But Emery had the deep brown eyes of his family, and they weren't brothers. Not even close.

"Why?" Matt asked, circling around, using his senses to predetermine every time Emery decided to move.

"Why do I hate you?" Emery dropped into a fighting crouch.

"Yeah." It didn't make sense. They'd both endured hell, and while Matt had fought their handlers, Emery had embraced them.

Emery feinted to the left and settled his stance. "You're an asshole who never got it. Never understood how fortunate we are. To be gifted. To be enhanced. To be gods."

Matt tested his damaged arm. *Not good.* "You're a god?"

Emery spit out blood. "We're as close as possible. Created by geniuses with superior genes? Yeah. Instead of fighting who you are, you ran."

"I ran to get freedom and safety for my brothers." Matt waited for the opening he knew would be coming. "Why didn't you? I've never understood why you'd sacrifice your brothers if necessary."

"We didn't have a choice." For the briefest of seconds, vulnerability flashed in Emery's eyes.

"Yes, we did." Matt shook his head, ready to strike. There had to be more to life than orders and killing, and he'd found that with his brothers. Love and loyalty had shaped them as much as military drills. Maybe more.

"No. You've always been headed down this path because of your self-destructive need to protect your brothers. They're your weakness, and now it's bringing you to heel," Emery spat.

Sorrow for Emery's younger brothers flowed unchecked through Matt. His family gave him strength and a purpose. "Even if I lose, I'm not alone."

"I won't lose." Emery smiled.

The soldier enjoyed inflicting pain and always had. "You like the killing."

"I have no problem being a soldier and fighting for our cause." Emery slid his arm behind his back.

Matt lunged for him before he could grab whatever weapon was stashed. They impacted a pine tree, and needles battered them. "What cause?"

Emery shot an elbow into Matt's gut and clamped on the bullet wounds in his arm. "Whatever the commander decides it is."

Matt bit back a growl of pain and wrenched his arm free to leap to his feet. He tugged the unloaded weapon from his waist. "You're crazy."

"We're all crazy." Blood dripped from Emery's teeth.

He kicked out faster than Matt expected, and the gun spun through the air. "Possibly we were designed that way. I mean, you have to be nuts to fight the way we do. To survive almost anything."

"Speaking of which, where's my youngest brother?" Matt reared up and kicked Emery in the chest with both feet and backflipped to land easily.

Emery flew backward, turned, and dropped to a crouching position before striking for Matt's knees. "Jory is dead. *Way* dead."

Matt's knee buckled, and he swung to the side. Pain slammed through him. "Bullshit. I already know he's alive. What I don't know is where he is."

"Come back, and I'll take you right to him." Emery fingered a cut along his jawline. "The shooter didn't aim as well as she should have."

So it was true. Jory was shot by a woman. Hope tried to flare in Matt's gut, but he couldn't allow it. Emery was as good a liar as a soldier, and he could just be playing with Matt. "Did Dr. Madison pull the trigger? She's a crappy shot."

"True. But she was an incredible fuck." Emery popped his shoulder back into alignment with his free hand. "Wasn't she?"

"Dunno. I always said no." In fact, the woman had scared the shit out of him.

Emery dropped into a fighting crouch. "You missed out. I'm not going to tell you who pulled the trigger—yet. Let's finish this so I can go find that bitch of a doctor you *have* been screwing."

Two men rushed out of the forest in full combat gear. Hell. Matt had been concentrating so hard on Emery, he hadn't focused.

With a battle cry, Nathan leaped from the west, straight at the soldiers, a sawed-off in his hand.

How many shells did he have? Matt kept his focus on Emery. Nate could handle the other two. For now.

Matt punched Emery in the jaw, and the fight was on.

The sounds of brutal punches, grunts of pain, and snapping bones filled the small clearing. Matt knew the second Nate snapped one of the soldier's necks, evening up his fight. Matt and Emery traded hits and kicks as Matt's arm slowly weakened. He needed to get those two bullets out. Now.

A rapid heartbeat caught his attention.

Around a tree, a soldier all in black dragged Laney into the clearing, a knife at her throat.

All movement ceased. Everyone still standing turned toward the duo.

Emery threw back his head and laughed, the sound gurgly from a lung that must be collapsing. "Where did you find our little rabbit?"

"Tree line by the shore," the soldier said, his brown eyes dead. "She tried to stab me with a steak knife."

Matt exhaled, his gaze on his woman. She stood, her face pale, wet hair matted to her head. Her pretty green eyes were wide with both fright and anger. She elbowed the soldier, and he tightened his grip.

"Are you all right?" Matt asked her.

"Yes. I'd be better if you just killed this guy," she said, her eyes full of apology.

He shifted his gaze to the soldier. "I plan on it. Let her go, now, and I won't break your neck."

The guy smiled and revealed a gold incisor. "I'm going to fuck her senseless after you die."

"I don't think so, G.I. Joe." Matt used the code word for Nate and silently counted to three. At three, both he and Nate struck.

Matt leaped for the soldier and used his superior strength to yank the knife away from Laney's throat. Shoving her to the side, Matt broke the guy's wrist and took the blade, slashing it across the jugular.

Pivoting, he stopped cold at the sight of Emery with a Glock pointed at him.

Nate finished off the other soldier and turned, his face a cold mask.

With a grim smile, Emery changed his aim to Laney.

She held out her hands. "Whoa, wait—"

Emery fired.

Matt exploded with a burst of energy and jumped in front of Laney. The bullet slammed into his upper arm and sliced an artery. Not feeling the pain—yet, Matt threw the knife as he pummeled to the ground.

The knife embedded in Emery's right eye, piercing to his brain. Emery stilled and dropped the gun, falling back. He hit the wet earth with a soft thump. Dead.

Matt's shoulders impacted first followed by the rest of his body. Pain lanced up his face.

Shit. He blinked rain and blood out of his eyes.

Laney skidded to her knees next to him, cradling his head. Nate dropped to his haunches, concern lightening his eyes.

Matt swallowed. He knew a kill shot when he felt one. He tried to speak to both Nate and Laney. "I'm sorry." The world wavered in front of his eyes.

Laney applied pressure to the wound in Matt's upper arm. Blood squirted out. "Oh God. The bullet sliced the brachial artery." Blood. So much damn blood. The liquid filled her hand, trying to escape through her fingers, still warm from Matt's body.

She pressed harder. Nausea filled her stomach, and bile rose up her throat.

If she didn't hold it together, he was going to die. A roaring rippled through her head, and she swayed. The forest went fuzzy.

"Laney." Nate's sharp tone jerked up her head. "Press harder."

She blinked rain out of her eyes. Or maybe that was tears. She yanked off her shirt and pressed it to the wound, trying to stem the blood. He'd lost too much already.

Matt swallowed and focused on Nate. "Plan?"

"Get your ass up, and I'll show you the plan." Nate grabbed his arm.

"Wait. We can't move him." Laney flattened her palm around the injury.

Nate lifted Matt up. "We have to move, now. More troops are coming."

Matt smiled at her, but with his face so pale, he looked more gruesome than reassuring. He slapped a hand over her drenched shirt and pushed. "I'm fine. Let's go."

He wasn't fine. Not at all. Laney nodded and stumbled, following Nate through the path. Matt followed doggedly after her, and she turned several times to view his progress. His face lost all color, but he kept moving.

The man was a machine.

Whatever genetics they'd used to create him were beyond belief. The guy should be passed out and almost dead. Instead, he sent her a smart-assed smile.

They reached the shoreline, and Nate had already uncovered a small wooden boat with three tiny benches stretching across. "I found it scouting last night."

Laney glanced out at the churning lake and dangerous clouds. She shivered in her wet bra as the rain drenched her bare skin. "We can't go out in that."

Nate yanked off his wet T-shirt and tugged it over her head. Then he grabbed her hips and plunked her on the middle seat of the boat. "We stay here, we die. I'd rather take my chances." Sliding his arm around his brother's waist, he helped ease Matt onto the third seat and shoved the boat out to the violent lake.

This was such a terrible idea. Laney reached for Matt to lean back against her. "Let me see."

"You'll faint," he murmured with a quirk of his lips.

"No, I won't." And she wouldn't. She'd suck it up and deal with ghosts in order to save him. "Let me see."

He moved his hand. Red coated the shirt. Bile rippled up her throat. She glanced at the wound and quickly replaced the shirt. "You're still bleeding, but it's stemming." Not really, but he didn't need to know that. She angled around toward Nate, who was rowing the boat against the wind with fierce grunts. "As soon as we dock, I need to tie off the artery." God. Could she do it? A real surgery in these conditions?

As she glanced at Matt's gray face, she realized she didn't have a choice. "Hurry, Nate."

The boat bucked and spun in the dangerous waters. Water poured from the sky, and lightning lit up the night. It'd be a miracle if they made it to the other side without being electrocuted. Water splashed over the sides, and the boat began to fill. Laney wanted to bail, but she had to keep pressure on Matt's wound. If the boat began to sink, she'd have to release him.

He glanced over his shoulder, flashed her a halfhearted grin, and his eyes fluttered shut.

"Matt!" she cried, grabbing his undamaged shoulder and yanking him toward her to prevent his falling overboard. His rear slid down, and she allowed his butt to fall into the waterlogged bottom of the boat, keeping his head elevated to avoid venous bleeding.

The boat pitched dangerously, and Laney glanced wildly over her shoulder.

Nate kept rowing, his face a grim mask. "Is he okay?" he yelled over the storm.

She shook her head and bit back a sob. "No. We need to tie off the artery. Now." The wind slapped her wet hair onto her cheeks.

Nate nodded and turned the boat just slightly. Rain

slammed into him, coating his bare chest and his tattoo, which was identical to Matt's.

Freedom.

The price they'd already paid for it stunned Laney. She turned back to Matt with determination. They wouldn't pay any more... not today.

Nate beached the boat, jumped out, and dragged it along the shoreline. Hustling over, he studied his brother, concern bright in his eyes. "If I throw him over my shoulder, he'll bleed out."

Yes. Gravity was a disaster they didn't need right now. Laney kept her hand on Matt's wound and stood, her shoes squishing in the water. "How about you take his torso, keeping pressure on his injury, and I take his feet?"

Nate nodded. "You keep the pressure on until I get him from the boat." Reaching for Matt's armpits, Nate turned his brother and lifted him over the boat with a fierce grunt and kept him in the bear-hug position. "Jesus. What has he been eating?"

Laney snorted and tried to ignore the fact that Matt might bleed out anyway. The guy was solid muscle. She gingerly stepped over the side, keeping the pressure strong. Finally on squishy sand, she took Nate's hand and put it into place. "We need to hurry," she yelled while running to grasp Matt's ankles. Wrapping her arms around him, she bent with her knees and lifted. He did weigh a ton, and his huge feet took up her entire torso.

Nate strode backward, up the embankment, keeping a quick pace.

Laney kept a strong hold of Matt, even while her shoes slipped in the waterlogged sand. Her knees and shoulders shook from the exertion of carrying Matt, although Nate had kept most of the burden. Even so, her breath panted out with the difficulty.

They arrived at a rough wooden shack, and Nathan

kicked the door open without even turning around. Matt
didn't make a sound as they carried him inside and all but
dropped him on a crude kitchen table.

"I need a knife." Laney took over again with the wound,
her mind fuzzing. Fear made her hands tremble, and that
wouldn't do. Matt deserved better. "And a light."

Nathan dug a survival pocketknife out of his left boot
and tossed it to her. Then he reached into Matt's pocket and
drew out a cell phone. "Go, satellite phone." He quickly
dialed. "Shane, lock on to this phone or on Laney's bracelet.
We need extraction now. It's Mattie." His voice cracked on
the end. "We're at the north end of the lake and might have
an hour before the commander's standing force of fifteen get
here. Unless they're dumb enough to come across the lake
like we did."

Tears filled Laney's eyes even as she glanced around the
space as she gently removed Matt's shirt. There was only
the table, so she yanked Nate's shirt off of her and slipped
it under Matt's head to minimize bleeding. "I need string.
Some type of string."

Blood slid down Matt's arm, and the room tilted. Laney
dropped to her knees, her forehead hitting the table.

"Damn." Nate hustled around and yanked her back up,
his breath brushing her hair. "You okay?"

She slid both hands onto the table and tried to tighten her
knee. "Yes." She loved Matt, and she was the only person
who could save him. The warrior was defenseless, and she'd
protect him, even if it meant cutting into him. She could do
this. "Get the string."

Nate released her and hurried toward a row of haphazard
cupboards, returning with a ball of twine. "It's thick, but it
won't cut him." Nate grabbed a half-full bottle of whiskey
and ran it over the knife.

Laney nodded. "Light."

Nate used his burner phone as a flashlight.

Laney glanced up. "Infection is a strong possibility."

"One thing at a time, Laney Lou," Nate said softly. "Stop the bleeding."

Swallowing, she nodded. Taking away the saturated cloth, she peered at the wound, the knife in her hand. She turned Matt's head to the side and extended his arm just enough. Nausea swamped her, and she swayed.

"Whoa, there." Nate clamped her shoulder. "You can do this. Talk me through the procedure, and you'll be fine."

She wiped away tears. "Okay. First, we make an incision just above the antecubital fossa, and we don't want to mess with the median nerve." Falling back into her old life, she slowly made the cut. "Sharp knife, Nate."

"Always."

She squinted to see better. "I'm extending the incision to see better." Whew. So far, so good. "Now, let's repair this ugly hole in his nice artery." Her hands stopped shaking. "Twine."

Nate handed her unrolled twine, and she slid it around the brachial and tied it as close to the origin as possible. She exhaled slowly and put everything back into place. "It's tied, but I don't have anything to stitch him up with."

Nate took duct tape off the small counter. "This will do until we're somewhere safe."

Laney's eyebrows rose. "I guess." She took the strip Nate offered and plastered it around Matt's arm, trying not to wince.

Her hands shook again when she stepped back. "If this works—"

"You saved his life, Laney Lou," Nate said somberly. "When he wakes, I won't even tell him you spent all night trying to show me your boobs."

Laney coughed out a laugh. "What?"

"You took your shirt off. Twice." Lines of fatigue cut into Nate's strong face, but his tone was light.

"To save your brother."

Nate shrugged. "So you say." He stretched across Matt and gave her a half-armed hug, his gaze serious. "Thank you for saving my brother."

Laney glanced down at the silent patient. It was way too early to tell if Matt would survive or not. "We might as well dig those two bullets out while we're here." Angling for a better look at his other arm, she went to work.

CHAPTER
31

L ANEY KEPT AN eye on Matt's vitals. It was entirely possible he'd slip into a coma, and without medical help, real
medical help, he'd never make it.

Nate paced by the window. "Matt's tough. He'll be
fine."

"How do you know?" Laney asked softly, brushing her
hand against Matt's forehead.

"Because he's Matt." Nate ducked down to squint into the
still-turbulent storm. Confidence filled his words, but his jaw
was set and his shoulders tight.

Laney drew in air. Now surgery had passed, and any
calmness she'd claimed had deserted her. From head to toe,
her body ached from trying to navigate through the battering
storm. Even with all the bruises and scrapes, nothing hurt as
badly as her chest. Terror lived there. Fear she'd lose Matt
after finding him. She leaned down and pressed her mouth
near his ear. "Don't leave me. Not now. *Please.*"

Love was supposed to be romantic and sweet. Not so
painful her lungs hurt to breathe.

Nate's phone buzzed, and he listened for a moment. "I
hear you out there. How close until touchdown?" He waited
and then swore. "Shane—" Nate's breath heaved out. "Yes. I

understand. Hold tight." He hung up and strode toward Matt. "If I awaken him, can he walk?"

"No way in hell." Panic rushed through Laney. "I just used fucking twine to tie his brachial artery. In. A. Shack."

Nate pierced her with sharp eyes. "If we stay here, he dies for sure. Can. He. Walk?"

A normal man? No. But Matt? Laney shook her head. Now she was seeing Matt as invincible as Nate saw his big brother. "It's too dangerous."

"So is death." Nate grasped Matt's shoulders and shook. "Mattie? Time to go, bro. We have to flee—now."

Matt's eyelids fluttered open, and his gaze focused way too quickly. "Status?" he croaked.

"Shit storm. The doc tied off your artery, the commander's forces are close. He brought a definite squad of twenty-one that is moving as teams of three from every fucking direction, and Shane flew a helicopter through this storm to a landing spot about a mile away." Nate dropped his hands over Matt's shoulders and eased him to a seated position. "Dig deep. We have to move."

Matt growled low. "Shane flew a copter into this storm?"

Nate grimaced. "We'll yell at him later. Can you walk?"

"Did you say a full twenty-one?" Matt groaned.

"Yes. We've taken down six men. That leaves fifteen still vying to kill us," Nate said tersely.

Matt turned toward Laney. "Are you all right?"

She sniffed. "Yes. Much better than you."

"Did you actually perform surgery? With blood?"

"Yes. You're not dying on me, Matt Dean." She eyed the duct tape around his arm. How was the man even conscious?

He swayed. "Why are you shirtless again?"

She shook her head and took Nate's shirt from where it had supported Matt's head. Wet and now bloody, it nevertheless beat Matt's bare skin if they had to go back out into the rain. "Long story. Put this on."

He shook his head. "No. *You* put it on. Your skin is nearly blue."

She opened her mouth to argue, and the hard glint in his eye stopped her. The man would try to force the shirt on her, and he'd probably ruin her fine surgical work. "Fine." She gingerly slid the cotton over her head.

Matt cleared his throat. "How much blood did I lose?"

Too much. Way too much. Laney lifted his shoulder. "Eh. Maybe about a teaspoon?"

"Right." He pushed off from the table and kept going down.

Laney scrambled for him, but Nate caught him first. Fierce lines cut into Nate's hard face as he waited for his brother to balance. "Shane's out in the storm all alone, Mattie."

Matt's head jerked up. "Never alone." He pushed back from his brother, raw determination darkening his eyes to nearly midnight. Blood leaked from under the tattered duct tape. "You take the lead, and we keep Laney between us."

Nate nodded and grabbed the sawed-off shotgun he'd placed on the tiny counter. "If you need a lift, just holler."

Matt winced. "I don't need to be carried. Just go."

Laney peered closer at his arm. While the duct tape around the bullet wounds in his other arm remained dry, that artery couldn't start bleeding again. "I need to make sure your artery is still clamped."

"I'm good." Matt grasped her arm to follow Nate. "Let's go."

Laney's mind swirled as she headed back into the storm with a soldier in front of her and the man she loved behind her. Their chances weren't good, and she had so much to say to Matt. While he remained conscious. But, as he nudged her with a push to her lower back, she lowered her head against the driving wind and followed Nate into hell.

• • •

Matt tried to concentrate on remaining upright by putting one boot in front of the other, like he'd done so many times in his life. Each step was sucked into the mud while wind and sleet attacked his bare chest and arms with a vengeance. The tape pulled against his injuries, and more liquid than just rain coated his skin. He could control the pain until sensation didn't exist, but blood loss? Yeah. Even the genetically engineered needed blood for strength.

But if Laney could conquer her fear of blood and operate to prevent him from bleeding out, he could suck it up and walk to safety.

If they found safety, he would even wait until tomorrow to beat the shit out of Shane for flying a helicopter by himself into the deadliest storm Matt had ever seen. It was as if even the gods above wanted him dead.

Fuck the gods.

Matt had his brother and his woman in front of him, and if he had to beat the gods to get them to safety, he'd damn well succeed.

The forest pressed in on him, and he tried to tune in to the world beyond the nearest trees. Not much permeated the roaring in his head, but every instinct he'd honed whispered the commander was closing in fast. But the speed with which Nate rammed down the nonexistent trail, he felt it, too.

Had the commander found Emery's body?

Matt stumbled and quickly righted himself. He'd killed someone he'd known as a kid. True, they'd never been friends. But they'd shared a childhood that had shaped them differently. Even being raised by monsters, they'd had choices in life. He'd chosen his brothers and loyalty.

Emery hadn't been strong enough.

Doubt had often assailed Matt that he could be as bad as Emery ... that maybe they were alike. But his brothers made him human and kept him from evil.

He owed them for that, and he'd save them if it was the last thing he did.

He would've given almost anything to have saved Emery from the demons possessing him. But the man had tried to kill Laney. He died for that choice.

Still, a surprising sorrow welled in Matt's chest.

Laney slipped on pine needles and yanked his attention to her. He rushed to catch her, but she hit the ground before he could get there.

"Ouch." She shoved to her feet with mud covering her butt.

"You okay?" he asked.

She shot him a look. "You're bleeding again."

"Well, at least you're not passing out." His vision wavered. "Get moving, baby."

"Okay." She slipped her hand into his. "We can walk together, right?"

Since his senses currently sucked, there wasn't a reason to keep her at arm's length. He wouldn't know anybody was upon them until they came into sight. "Sure."

She tightened her hold and moved into a quick walk. "What are our chances here?" Her hip touched his, keeping them close enough she didn't have to yell.

Not good. "Great. We'll get to Shane, head home, and have breakfast."

"Right." She edged her shoulder into the undamaged side of his body. "I want you to know...The time we've been together? It's been the best of my life." Her head remained down, and wet hair covered her face.

Matt tucked her closer. "Me, too. What do you say we make this permanent?"

Her head shot up, her eyes glowing emeralds in the darkness. "Permanent?"

"Yeah." His gut lurched. Now probably wasn't the time. "I love completely, Laney, and I'm sure it's a pain in the ass."

He stumbled and she helped him to right himself. "You have my heart and always will."

She caught her breath. "You know we're not going to live through the night, right?"

"So say yes. What do you have to lose?" His vision kept graying, damn it.

"Yes to what?"

"Me. Marriage. Life." His right leg was beginning to go numb. This had to be the worst wedding proposal on record. But Nate had been right. Matt had found happiness, and he needed to hold on with both hands. No matter what happened. "We need something to live for, don't you think?"

She smiled and shook her head. "You're crazy. Definitely crazy." Taking a deep breath, she snuggled closer. "I say yes."

His head snapped up as his chest filled. Love. She'd said yes. "You're the crazy one," he said with a smile. "I'll keep you safe, baby. I promise."

"How about we start with breakfast?" she asked, peering ahead into the storm. "We lost Nate."

"He's scouting ahead." Matt's head wanted to fall back on his neck. How long would his artery hold out, anyway?

Nate brushed leaves aside and appeared in front of him. "This way. Forces moving in on all sides. Shane is setting down in one minute, and we need to load before he hits the ground." Urgency cut lines into Nate's face. "You up to it?"

"Of course." Matt blinked to clear his vision while he released Laney and followed Nate to the edge of a small clearing. A *very* small clearing. "How close are the forces?"

A man leaped around a bush and tackled Nate, sending them flying across muddy grass. The gun spiraled out of his hands.

Matt shoved Laney behind him and dropped into a slide to grab the gun. Coming up firing, he hit first one and then a second soldier coming from the east. Two shells only. He was out of ammo.

Helicopter blades rose over the sound of rain pelting the earth.

He glanced up, and the black bird wavered in the dark sky, bouncing dangerously.

Nate and the guy grappled on the ground, and three more soldiers rushed from the north.

Matt swung with the gun, hitting one guy in the neck. He went down, out cold. Dropping into a stance, Matt waited for the other to strike. The third man went to assist against Nate, kicking him in the temple as he arrived.

Nate snapped the guy's neck on the ground and rolled over to kick the newest threat.

Matt struck fast and hard, not having the energy or strength for finesse. He aimed for the jugular and eyes, taking the guy down and rendering him unconscious. Matt tried to regain his feet and fell back.

Laney instantly appeared at his side and clutched his arm. "Get up." She pulled, her arms straining with the effort.

Matt wavered, his head bobbing. "What?"

"Now, Matt," she ordered, falling back. Mud, debris, and blood coated her face and hair. She was too pale, her skin almost blue, and fear had widened her pupils. She was the most beautiful woman he'd ever seen.

He wouldn't fail her. He couldn't. So he shoved to his feet and slid an arm around her shoulder.

The helicopter plopped down with a loud thump, and the side door slammed open.

Matt turned as Nate finished off the final soldier and then pushed to stand. Blood ran down Nate's face, and he turned to heave into the bushes. Pivoting, he made it two steps toward the helicopter.

And fell.

"Nate!" Laney cried, trying to drag Matt toward his fallen brother. "The blow to the temple was a bad one."

Matt tuned in as his senses roared back. Seven attack

squads were heartbeats away...and coming from all sides. "Get in the helicopter." He pushed her toward the helicopter.

"No." She tried to take more of his weight.

He turned. "Trust me. I need you on there. Please."

She hesitated, her gaze going from Nate to the copter and back to Matt. "But—"

"*Trust* me." He meant it as an order, but the entreaty came out as a plea.

She swallowed and took a step back. Then with a nod, she turned and ran for the open doorway.

Thank God. Matt staggered over to Nate and dropped to his haunches. The world tilted. Damn it. He could do this. Sucking deep, thinking of a possible future, he dipped his head and hauled Nate over his good shoulder.

Standing up was the hardest thing Matt had ever done. Quite possibly the slowest. Inch by inch, he rose to a crouch. Turning, he secured Nate's legs and put one boot in front of the other.

His vision fuzzed. Determination and love shot through him, giving him strength. Nate had counted on him their entire lives, and Nate had kept Matt human. He'd helped bridge the gap between Matt and the younger brothers, keeping Matt from going too cold while training.

Nate would not die.

Another boot forward. Another. And another.

Men crashed through the brush.

He reached the hatch and dropped Nate onto the floor. Laney lunged for Matt, her face determined, her jaw set. He all but fell into her arms, swinging his legs inside. *His woman.* "Go, Shane. Go now," he ordered, his voice way too weak.

Bullets sprayed the side of the craft.

He turned just in time to see the commander dart out of the forest, firing wildly. At Laney.

Matt reared up, only to have Laney lean over him and shove the door into place. A spray of bullets shot through the metal above them. She ducked low, covering him with her body.

Warmth and the scent of vanilla encompassed Matt. Heaven. Laney and heaven.

The commander's roar of outrage reached above the storm.

Take that, asshole. Matt swallowed and tried to keep his eyes open.

Shane lifted the copter, the side of his face a hard mask as he fought the wind, rain, and bullets. "Hold on."

Laney felt for Nate's pulse. "Steady, but he's out cold. Definite concussion," she said, her voice nearly shrill. Then, on the freezing floor, she gently lifted Matt's head onto her lap. "Keep the artery elevated." Tears coursed down her face to land on his.

He blinked, his heart lurching.

The helicopter pitched, and she cried out.

"It'sss okay." His voice slurred, and he tried to stay alert. He had to be strong for her. "Love you."

I love you, she mouthed and secured a hand on Nate's prone back. "We'll be fine." She eyed Shane, obviously trying not to panic. "Shane looks like you, Matt."

"Matt looks like me," Shane said, his concentration remaining on the blackness outside. He banked a hard left, and they dropped about ten feet. Laney yelped.

Matt tried to smile to reassure her, but his jaw locked and his eyes filled with dust. He coughed. He had to get Laney to safety. Desperation competed with the need to pass out. "Stay under the storm so they can't track us."

"Good idea." Sarcasm filled his younger brother's voice beneath the tension.

Thuds and bumps shook the craft, and several times lightning split the night. Laney held Matt tight, and even wounded and in pain, there was nowhere else he'd want to be. He'd take any amount of pain to be close to Laney.

Finally, an hour later, the night quieted.

Matt relaxed into the cold floor. Now he really needed to pass out. But first, he had to tell her, "We're safe, baby. I love you and will keep you safe."

Laney leaned over and placed her lips on his. "I love you, Matt Dean. Forever."

CHAPTER
32

THE HELICOPTER HUGGED the tree line for quite a while and finally set down near a sprawling ranch house in the mountains. Rain continued to fall as dawn broke, but softly and without the tantrum. Laney's legs had cramped an hour ago, but she didn't want to disturb Matt.

She'd spent the trip alternating between checking his vitals and checking Nate's. Her heart ached for both of them. Caring about people hurt, but she could never go back to being all alone. She was keeping them, no matter how dangerous life became.

As they touched down, she tried not to wince as the bounce jarred both injured men. "We need a hospital."

Shane turned and viewed her, his gaze veiled. "There's a fully equipped medical room in the basement. What do you need?"

A petite woman barreled out the front door, blue eyes flashing, blond hair whipping in the wind. Shane was out of the cockpit before she hit the door, and he grabbed her in a hug.

She hugged him back. "I told you not to leave me. How could you leave me here?" She shoved out of his arms and moved to open the other side door.

Shane beat her to it and yanked it open. "I needed you safe."

"What if you weren't safe?" She looked into the back, her eyes widening. "Oh God. Are they okay? Tell me they're okay." Panic lifted her voice, and she started to scramble inside, but Shane stopped her with one arm.

"Let's get them out," he said. "Doc? What do you need?"

Laney took a deep breath. For today, she was the only doctor they had. She dug deep for courage. "Nate needs to be inside and warmed up...and hopefully awakened. Matt needs surgery to repair his artery—tell me you have zero silk and don't mind donating blood."

The blonde reached for one of Nate's arms, her lips trembling. "She's kinda bossy."

Laney gaped. "I just want to help."

The woman smiled. "I didn't say it was a bad thing." Then she sobered. "How hurt are they?"

Too hurt. Way too hurt. Laney kept Matt's head elevated with her hands and swung her aching legs out from under him. "I'd like for them both to regain consciousness."

Shane hauled Nate over his shoulder. Concern tightened his mouth into a white line. "I'll put Nate inside, and Josie can keep an eye on him while I assist in surgery." Without waiting for an answer, he pivoted and headed toward the house.

The blonde smoothed Matt's hair away from his face, her hands shaking, her gaze on his closed eyelids. Fear cascaded from her. "I'm Josie."

"Laney." Laney turned brisk and professional. "They'll be all right." God, she hoped that was true. She nodded for Josie to slide her hands under Matt's head. He was too pale. Why didn't he wake up? "Would you hold him so I can get out?"

"Sure." Josie's eyes softened as she glanced down at Matt, agonized love in her expression. "Please save my brother." Desperation deepened the quiet plea.

"I will. I promise." Laney swung to the ground just as

Shane returned. She had to save them no matter what. God. She couldn't lose Matt now. "Let's do this."

After cleaning up, Laney eyed Matt while he lay in an operating room that rivaled anything found in the biggest hospitals. The zero silk had done the trick, and she successfully stitched up both his artery and damaged arm. She'd fought nausea the entire time, and even now, she wanted to plunge her head in a bucket of cold water.

Shane flipped open Matt's eyelid. "Did I give him enough blood?"

"Yes." Laney slapped his hand. "Stop that."

Shane grinned and looked so much like Matt she could only stare. "You *are* bossy."

"Not usually." She returned the smile even as her legs trembled. Exhaustion would soon set in after the night they'd had. "Just when I'm revisiting my doctor days."

"You didn't plant the chips in our spines, right?" Shane's eyes darkened.

She sighed and grabbed a blanket off a low shelf to spread over Matt. "No. I'd never cause such harm. The oath I took—it meant something."

Shane nodded. "Do you miss being a doctor?"

She bit her lip and allowed herself to really examine the question. "I'm not sure. I became a doctor to give myself security and because I enjoyed learning at school." She brushed hair away from her face. "But I like being a bartender better. Or rather, I guess I like who I am as a bartender better. There's no ambiguity."

"Maybe once we take care of these chips, you can be a bartender in town." Shane smoothed the blanket over Matt's legs as if he couldn't help but stay close to his brother.

Laney stilled. "You think I'm staying?"

"Do you love my brother?" Shane's formidable focus narrowed right on her.

She fought the urge to squirm. "Yes."

"Then you're staying." Shane smiled. "We need you to cut out the chips, anyway."

Why was it the Gray brothers seemed more predatory than relaxed when they smiled? Must be something in the genetics. "That's true," she murmured. Might as well boss Shane around while she could. "Stay here and keep an eye on Matt. I need to check on Nathan's concussion." After waiting for Shane's nod, she pivoted on squishy shoes to head upstairs to her next patient. She found him seated in a chair upstairs in a main living area, pretty much growling at a glaring Josie, who sat on the sofa.

"How's your head?" Laney asked, tapping her fingers along his neck to feel for a pulse.

"My brain hurts." A sprawling purple bruise cascaded out from Nate's temple to his forehead and cheek. "But I'm fine."

Laney dropped to her haunches and pointed a penlight in his eyes. "Hmmm."

"I told you," Josie said, hands on her hips. "You have a concussion, and you are not going to sleep."

Laney patted his arm and stood. "Stay awake for two hours, don't throw up, keep your vision, and we'll talk."

"How's Matt?" Nate asked, dark circles forming bruises under his eyes. Even so, a deadly tension cascaded around him.

"I'm fine." Matt hitched into the room, his arm around Shane's shoulders.

Laney twirled around. "What the hell? You should be prone."

"Is that an offer?" he asked with a grimace.

"No." Laney helped ease him next to Josie on the couch. His color looked better. "How are you feeling?"

"Like raiding the facility in Colorado." Matt lifted an eyebrow and focused on Shane. "Find it yet?"

Shane nodded and headed for the door. "Yes. Right now, I need to secure the helicopter in the barn. Be right back."

Josie jumped up and hustled after him. "If we're raiding, I'm going, too." The door closed behind her.

Matt held out a hand, and Laney took it, all but falling next to him on the sofa.

She had no interest in raiding anything. Ever. "You'll need a doctor on the raid," she murmured.

"No," Matt said, tangling his fingers with her. "We don't need a doctor, we need soldiers. Right, Nate?"

Nate's eyelids flipped back open. "Right. Although Laney Lou *is* a badass on a mission."

Warmth slid through her with the compliment. She had a feeling Nate didn't give them often. "Thanks."

Matt shifted his weight and grimaced. "Did you two bond or something?"

"Yeah," Nate said softly. "I welcomed her to the family, Mattie. We're keeping her."

Tears pricked the back of her eyes. When had she ever been part of a family? Never. Surprise filled her at how badly she wanted to be part of this one. To be part of the Gray family. "You're sweet, Nate. Thanks."

"I am not." He shut his eyes again.

"Open your eyes." She put snap into her tone. He couldn't fall asleep yet.

He flipped one eye open. "Control your woman, Mattie."

She grinned. "If I had more energy, I'd take out your other temple."

"Later." Nate pushed off the chair. "Oddly enough, I'm starving. I'll go get breakfast going." He limped into the other room.

Matt played with her hair. "Thank you for saving my life."

"You saved mine, too." She snuggled into his good side. "Tasha said somebody shot Jory, and he was taken to another facility where miracles happen. I don't know if that means anything, and the woman was nuts. But I thought you should know."

Matt exhaled slowly. "Emery hinted at the same thing. I keep getting my hopes up about Jory, but I know he can't be alive. If so, he would've contacted me by now."

"More than likely." Laney couldn't take away all hope. Matt had lived without it for too long. "But you live odd lives full of danger and intrigue. So don't give up completely. Just be prepared."

"Good plan." He relaxed next to her, the muscles letting go. "The commander may know something, and I'll find out what it is while he's still alive."

Laney wanted to be kind and right, but deep down, she knew the commander had to die. So long as he walked, he'd hunt the people she loved. "I'll help you do whatever you need to do, Matt." Her loyalty and heart belonged with him, no matter how dark the world became.

"I have to go on the raid to Colorado," he said softly.

"I know." She turned her head to study his battered face.

His left eyebrow lifted. "You understand?"

"Sure." She slid her hand over his heart to feel it beat. "I love you—all facets of you. I'd never ask you to be anybody other than who you are."

"Who am I?" he whispered.

"A guy who'd give a damaged surgeon another chance." She blinked back tears. "A guy who'd spend his last ounce of strength dodging bullets in order to get his fallen brother to a helicopter." God, she loved him. More than she would've ever thought possible. "A guy who'd raid a facility with few weapons to search for the chance that his youngest brother still lived."

A hero. The real kind. Without a doubt, *hers*.

Matt's hold tightened. "I don't think you see the real me."

"You're wrong. I see you clearly." How could he not know he was a hero?

He ran his knuckle along her cheekbone. "You're the amazing one, Laney. The way you overcame your fear of blood and performed surgery in a shack? Incredible. And you weren't damaged, ever. What happened wasn't your fault."

"Maybe."

"Thank you again for saving me. For taking care of Nathan."

"I love you. How could I not?"

His eyes darkened, and he lifted her with his good arm to straddle him. "I promise. The second we get these chips out, you and I are going to live a wonderful life. Full of family, fun, and peace. If I accomplish nothing else, I'll find you peace."

If anybody could engineer peace, it'd be Matt. She cupped his face and gently kissed him. "Peace or no, I just want you. Forever."

He deepened the kiss until she pulled back, not wanting to hurt his arm. His eyes gleamed an unfathomable gray. "Forever. I'll make sure of it."

EPILOGUE

MATT LEAPED OFF the helicopter and headed toward the ranch house, his strides long and sure. The Colorado raid had been a success. An easy one, which concerned him. Sure, they'd gone in under the radar as soldiers, and they'd blended right in. The security had been complex, but they'd easily maneuvered into secured locations to find information.

Not a shot had been fired.

In fact, there was a chance the commander hadn't known the Gray brothers had infiltrated Colorado.

But Matt didn't believe in chance.

Laney slipped onto the porch followed by Josie. "Did you find anything?" Laney asked.

Matt nodded. "We copied a cache of files and will start going through them tonight." He tugged her close, and her vanilla scent wrapped around him. Comfort and home.

She levered back to study the healing scab on his arm. "I can't believe how strong you are in just a week. Seven days ago, I was sliding your arteries around."

"We heal quickly." Good thing, too. They had only five weeks until the chips detonated. He took in her clear green eyes. "What were you up to today?"

"Practicing dummy surgeries to remove the chips." She frowned. "And I lost at gin rummy with Josie."

"Josie cheats," Nate whispered as he strode past them with several flash drives in his hand.

Laney glanced over her shoulder as Josie slipped outside. "You cheat?"

Josie opened big blue eyes. "Of course not. Geez."

Matt pressed a kiss to Laney's forehead. "Yeah. She cheats." He took Laney's hand to go inside, where Nate was already inserting a flash drive into a computer hooked up to a flat-screen. A day of sitting close with Laney beat any other day, even if he had to go through data.

Tons of data.

They read reports, flipped through pictures, and watched videos showing the commander's plan. Through lunch, through dinner, through a popcorn fight Shane started. At one point, Laney dropped off to sleep, tucked into his side. Josie fell asleep an hour later.

About three in the morning, Matt stretched his legs onto an ottoman. "This is informative, but we already knew about funding. And research." Frustration lit down his spine. There hadn't been one mention of Jory. Not one. Nor had there been any concrete data on any of the Gray brothers or the genetic splicing that had occurred to create them. He'd love to find that data. Maybe he'd destroyed it all in his bid for freedom. If so, he could live with that.

Nate popped his neck and inserted another USB. "This is the last one. So far, nothing."

Dr. Madison took shape on the screen, from about twenty years previous. Even back then, the intelligence in her cobalt eyes overshadowed her classic face. With her black hair pulled back, she even *looked* like a scientist.

Matt shifted on the couch. God, he'd hated her. Always watching, always taking notes. Even when they were hurt, she took notes, never offering a moment of comfort. Until they'd grown into young men, and then she'd offered too much. Now, years later, he forced himself to watch her personal journal. From the beginning when she discussed the conditioning she and the commander had created for soldiers.

No mention of their names.

Had they been human to her?

Maybe not. Matt cut a look at Nate. He watched the screen, eyes hard, jaw set. Nate had fallen in love with Dr. Madison's daughter, Audrey, and she'd nearly destroyed him. As an experiment.

As the years wore on, faint lines appeared at Madison's hairline. Then near her eyes. Finally, she discussed an experiment in young love.

Nate stiffened, a veil dropping over his eyes.

Matt glanced at Shane, who looked beyond pissed off. Yeah. He agreed.

The final entry was Madison smiling into the camera, nearly giddy. "I have incredible news. I'm going to be a grandmother. My Audrey is pregnant." The screen went blank.

Nate leaped to his feet.

Shane's eyes widened. "What was the date on that?"

"Right before we broke up." Nate ran a rough hand through his hair. "This isn't real. It can't be."

Matt swallowed. "You're right. There's no way this clip was left by accident. They meant for us to find it...and to go after Audrey. Or Madison. It's a trick, Nate." But was it? Madison and the commander had tried repeatedly to use the genetic material from the Gray brothers for a second generation—with no luck. If they'd succeeded, they would have certainly hid that from the brothers.

Nate turned toward him, torment in his dark eyes. "I have to go after her."

"I know. We've always known she was the way to get to Madison...and to the commander. They know it, too."

Matt had known this moment was coming from the moment they'd escaped. Nate would have to get ahold of Audrey. With a sigh, Matt glanced outside as the sun poked above the horizon. "Let's get a little sleep, and we'll come up with a plan." God. How the hell was he going to protect Nate from this? From whatever they discovered?

Matt didn't want to find hope there, but what if? What if they actually could have kids? Was it possible?

He stood and lifted Laney. "Three hours, and we meet to start planning." Without looking back, he headed down the hallway toward his bedroom. He laid her down on the sprawling bed and tugged off his shirt.

"I do love your chest," she mumbled sleepily, holding her arms out.

He slid a knee onto the bed and allowed himself a moment of peace. Temporary, for sure. He banished the fear of the future, the terror of something happening to Laney, the ever-present threat to his brothers—the ones he'd vowed to protect. "I was going to let you keep sleeping," he whispered, slipping his hands beneath her shirt.

Her pupils focused. "And now?"

He tugged off her shirt to reveal the prettiest breasts in existence. "Ah, baby. Now you're gonna have to *earn* sleep." He moved over her, covering her, balancing himself on his elbows. Those yoga pants of hers were coming off next.

Her smile was slow and so sexy his cock flared to life. "Good thing I'm a hard worker. Maybe I won't let you sleep."

Who the hell needed to sleep? He lowered his head and kissed her, diving deep, trusting completely. When he finally lifted up, her eyes had gone unfocused, and her lips were so nicely swollen he groaned. "I really do want to marry you. Soon," he said.

Her breath caught. "Name the time and place. I'm there."

God, he hoped they had forever. "I'm not easy, Laney." She needed to know what she was getting into.

Her small hands smoothed along his shoulders. "No kidding."

He chuckled. "No. I mean I'm bossy, protective, and I hold on too tight. Way too tight." It was the only way he'd known to keep his brothers alive through the years. Now his life centered around one small woman he couldn't lose. He *wouldn't* lose.

She shifted against him, creating a more comfortable home in the vee of her legs. "Hold on as tight as you need, Mattie. I've got you."

And she did. He had no idea what the future held, but he'd do his damnedest to make sure they survived it. "I'll give you everything. I promise," he said.

She smiled. "You already have. I have you...and a family. Trust me."

"I do. Completely." He kissed her again. For his entire life, he'd never broken a promise. So he gave her one. "Forever, Laney. I promise."

Rebecca Zanetti's thrilling,
sexy series continues!

Please turn this page for

a heart-pounding

excerpt from

Blind Faith.

PROLOGUE

Southern Tennessee Hills
Fifteen Years Ago

NATHAN'S BOOTS ECHOED on the hard tiles, the deep sound thrown back by the cinder blocks lining the wall. He'd wiped the snow off before heading inside, but the soles were still slippery. His twelve-year-old gut churned, and his mind spun. His older brother, Mattie, was out on a mission, and shit was about to hit the fan.

The situation was totally Nate's fault, but he couldn't be taken from the facility. If he was forced out, Matt would blame himself. And who would take care of the two younger brothers when Matt was out on a mission? At around fourteen years old, Matt was often out on a mission, and somebody had to protect Shane and Jory. Nate had taken on the job years ago.

He paused outside of the office doorway and took several deep breaths. Then he smoothed his face into innocent lines and knocked on the door.

"Come in," came the low baritone of the commander.

Sweat dripped down Nate's back. He shoved open the

door and hurried inside to stand at attention. The scents of bleach and gunpowder nauseated him.

The commander studied him with black, fathomless eyes while sitting behind a metal desk. He wore a soldier's uniform, his hair in a buzz cut, his body lean and hard. Behind him sat a woman furiously scribbling in a notebook on a small table. Dr. Madison, the head scientist who studied the cadets at the facility, liked to scribble.

"We seem to have a situation, Cadet Nathan," the commander said.

Nate's spit dried up. "Yes, sir." God, please make the situation deal with what he'd done wrong and not with Matt's mission. Matt was invincible. Nothing could happen to him.

"We found your stash of tree, decorations, and presents," Dr. Madison said, her blue eyes narrowing in calculation.

Relief filtered down Nate's spine. Thank God. Matt was all right. "Yes, ma'am." Damn it. He'd hidden those items carefully in a storage shack on the outskirts of one of the training fields. How had they found everything?

"Cadet Nathan, this is a military facility. You are a soldier created from birth to follow orders and protect our country." The commander pushed back from the desk and rose to his full height. "How in the world did you learn about Christmas?"

Nate tilted his head to look way up at the commander's face. Someday Nate would be taller and bigger. Even tougher. But now, not so much. "I can't remember, sir." In truth, he and his brothers had snuck into computer rooms to watch television sitcoms via satellite. The idea of Christmas had struck a chord with all of them.

"Humph." The commander clasped his hands behind his back. "I take it you were planning some sort of celebration with your brothers?"

Nate's knees wobbled, but he stayed upright. "Yes, sir. I thought the younger brothers should have good memories of their childhoods." It was too late for him, and that was all right. But he needed to give his younger brothers something good in their lives. Plus, seeing them happy cut down on Matt's guilt over how hard he trained them.

"How did you procure the items?" Dr. Madison asked, her pencil poised to write.

Nate shrugged. "I cut off the top of a tree and made the decorations from old weapons." The presents, he'd either stolen throughout the compound or made himself, and those were hidden somewhere else. Hopefully safely. Jory would love the modified remote-control attack helicopter.

"I could have you hanged," the commander said thoughtfully.

Dread and fear heated Nate's lungs. "Yes, sir."

The commander scratched his chin and eyed Madison. "Well?" he asked her.

Nate gulped in air and looked toward the woman. Would she want him hanged?

Dr. Madison pursed red lips. "I think we should give Cadet Nathan a choice."

Great. Another one of her crappy experiments. "A choice, ma'am?" Nate asked.

"Yes. The first choice is that you relinquish all of the Christmas items, and we'll forget this ever happened." She tapped her pencil on the paper. "The second choice is that you go ahead with Christmas for your brothers, and we'll forget this ever happened."

Nate swallowed. "What's the catch, ma'am?"

She smiled, revealing sharp white teeth. "A few days after your pseudo-Christmas, you go onto the training field with the three oldest Brown brothers."

The three oldest were all around fifteen, and although Nate was a hell of a fighter, he'd get hurt. Nobody could take on all three of them.

His mind reeled as he considered his options. A little bit

of pain was worth giving Shane and Jory a small bit of happiness. Of thinking they were part of a real family with good times. Plus, Matt often came back from a mission angry and depressed. A happy memory would be good for him, too.

"I'll take the second choice—with one condition," Nate said, his chin lifting.

Dr. Madison giggled. "Listen to the boy, Commander. He's giving us conditions."

The commander lifted a dark eyebrow, curiosity twisting his lip. "What's the condition, Cadet?"

Nathan took a deep breath. Maybe the Brown brothers wouldn't break too many of his bones. "This deal is between us, and I don't get onto the field with the Browns until Matt is out on another mission." Hopefully by the time Matt returned, Nate would be mostly healed.

"Interesting." Madison smoothed-back black hair. "You don't want him to know you're sacrificing your health for your brothers?"

"No, ma'am." Hell no. Matt would blame himself and maybe go off the deep end and finally challenge the commander. None of them were ready for that. Yet.

Dr. Madison nodded. "You intrigue me, young man. Just how far would you go for family? For love?"

Nate frowned. "I don't understand the question, ma'am."

She smiled, her eyes lighting up. "You have a deal, Cadet Nathan. Have a very merry Christmas."

CHAPTER
1

S OMEBODY WAS WATCHING her.

Audrey Madison glanced around the opulent ball-room, her face remaining calm while her heart roared into overdrive. She had been raised by a psychopath and was alone in the world, and her instincts were finely honed. The need to fight or flee lived in her daily moments.

Now was the time to flee.

Elegant and sexy, her black cocktail dress wrapped tightly around her fit form and wouldn't hinder her escape. Unfortunately, the three-inch Jimmy Choo heels needed to be kicked off, a necessity made nearly impossible by the two U.S. senators currently debating tort reform to her left.

She automatically smiled at a pun from one of the men and took a sip of champagne while searching unobtrusively for the threat.

Men in tuxedos and women in stunning dresses were scattered throughout the most prestigious hotel ballroom in Washington, DC. Tension rode high in the party atmosphere due to the hint of power threading through the air. The attendees of the political fund-raiser either had power and were desperate to hold on to it, or they were clutching at tendrils and trying to claim more.

Her reason for being there differed. Somewhat.

As if drawn by a magnet, her focus landed on a man leaning casually against the doorway leading to the dance floor. Although he was in disguise, recognition slammed through her, heating her ears and weakening her knees. It couldn't be. It *really* couldn't be.

Her fingers lightened around the champagne flute, and she clutched tight to keep from dropping the delicate crystal.

How could Nathan be there? Heat flowed through her so quickly her lungs seized. Adrenaline flared into her veins, and panicked tears pricked the backs of her eyes. In a nanosecond, her entire central nervous system short-circuited.

His gaze held hers captive as he lifted one lip in a mocking grin.

That one minor, sarcastic move dashed any silly dream she'd kept of his finding her. Rescuing her. Declaring he still loved her, and offering her a chance at a life.

At the realization, a very welcomed anger swept away her panic. She lifted her flute and silently toasted him, taking a deep drink and keeping his gaze, no matter how much the contact stung. Then, with a gentle smile, she turned to the men and excused herself.

Slowly, as if she had all the time in the world, she maneuvered around people, her hips nearly swaying. After five years of physical therapy, she could almost walk without a limp. The high heels were in celebration of her doctor's visit two weeks previous, where the doctor proclaimed the last surgery had finally healed her internally. Concentrating on walking smoothly, she made her way toward the dance floor.

Even as she kept up a calm façade, her mind raced. He

had to get out of there. Didn't he realize the commander was still hunting him? For years she'd figured she'd be the bait to bring Nathan back, but she hadn't thought he was stupid enough to seek her out. Especially in public.

The commander would have no problem causing a scene if it meant reclaiming one of the Gray brothers.

She reached Nate's side and almost recoiled from the heat and familiar scent of the man. Male and spice, something undeniably dangerous—Nathan. All Nathan.

Instead, she held out a hand as if they'd never met. As if he didn't still occupy every dream she had after falling into an exhausted sleep. "Hello. I'm Audrey."

Nathan's hand engulfed hers in a touch so familiar her heart broke all over again, even while desire unfurled inside her abdomen. "Jason Murphy. I work for the Neoland Corporation."

Ah. Good choice. Several executives from very flush technology firms were in attendance at the ball. Audrey extracted her hand and forced an interested smile as she studied him. He had inserted brown contacts to mask his odd gray eyes, but the longer brown hair seemed to be his. She had wondered if he would grow it out after escaping the military group that had raised him. A shadow lined his jaw, also looking natural. He'd definitely hardened even more in the five years they'd been apart. "Your disguise doesn't disguise much," she whispered.

He lifted a muscled shoulder that revealed the true predator lurking beneath the classic jacket. "I'm done hiding."

Those three innocuous words flared her neurons awake in terror. He had to stay in hiding from the commander and his men. "You can't beat them." Nobody could beat them. "Leave now, Nathan. Please." She needed him alive, even if he hated her. The world had to keep him in it.

"Now, Audrey, you actually sound like you care." He claimed her flute and finished the remaining champagne in two drinks, his lips over the same spot she'd used. The hard cords of his neck flexed.

Feminine awareness zinged through her body and pebbled her nipples. The man had always been dangerous, yet an edge lived in him now that was as appealing as it was deadly. That edge tempted her on a primal level she'd hoped had disappeared when he had. Apparently not.

To mask her unwelcomed desire, she moved to go. "Well, enjoy your night." She expected him to stop her retreat and wasn't surprised when his calloused hand wrapped around her bare bicep, but she hadn't even considered his next words.

"Let's dance." He turned her toward the dance floor.

She balked. "No." God. She couldn't dance with him, couldn't be touched by him.

"Yes." His hold slid down to the back of her elbow, and he ushered her toward where the orchestra was playing "I Will Wait for You" by Michel Legrand. Nate's skin on hers quivered her nerves to life in an erotic need she'd worked hard to overcome.

She could either cause a scene or go along with him. Didn't he understand if she protested, he'd probably be a dead man?

He turned and pulled her into his arms.

The bittersweet moment her body met his stole her breath, while memories of passion and love assailed her. For the briefest of times, she'd belonged in the safe circle of his arms. The only time in her life she'd been truly happy and not alone. Ah, the dreams she'd spun, even though she'd known better.

Happily ever after didn't exist for her. Hell, it didn't exist for anybody.

The music wound around them, through them, proclaiming a romance that couldn't really exist. His heated palm settled at the small of her waist and drew her into an impressive erection.

She gasped, her face heating, her sex convulsing. Blinking, she glanced up in confusion to see if he was as affected as she was and stilled.

Furious. The man was truly furious. Even with the contacts masking his eyes, his anger shone bright.

She tried to step back and didn't move. Yeah, she knew she'd hurt him when she'd ended their relationship, but after five years, he shouldn't still be so mad. He'd had freedom for five years, which was a hell of a lot better than she'd had. She'd had pain and fear and uncertainty. She blinked. "What is wrong with you?"

His impossibly hard jaw somehow hardened even more. "Oh, we'll discuss that shortly." Threat lived strongly in the calm words. "For now, we're going to finish this dance. Then you'll take the north exit and meet me in my car so we can talk."

"If I don't?" she asked quietly, wings fluttering through her abdomen.

His hold tightened imperceptibly. "I know where you live, I know your daily routine in working for Senator Nash, and I know where you go when you need time alone. You can't hide, you can't outrun me—and you know it."

The hair rose down her back. "How long have you been watching me?" More important, why hadn't she noticed?

"A week." He spun her, easily controlling their movements.

Her leg hitched, and she stumbled against him.

He frowned. "What's wrong?"

"Nothing." None of his damn business, that was. "What do you want to talk about?"

His gaze narrowed, and he spun her again. She tripped again. Her damn leg didn't move that way.

"What's wrong with your leg?" he asked, brows furrowing.

Oh, they were so not going into her injuries on the dance floor. "You almost sound like you care, Nate." She threw his words back at him, gratified when his nostrils flared in irritation.

His gaze probed deep, wandering down her neck. He blinked several times, his chest moving with a harsh intake of breath. "I like your dress," he rumbled, his voice a low whisper.

With his tight hold, she had no doubt the tops of her breasts were visible. "Nathan, don't—"

"Don't what?" His gaze rose to her lips. A light of a different sort filtered through his angry eyes. She knew that look. Her body heated and her thighs softened. His erection jumped against her, and she bit down a groan.

"One kiss, Audrey."

Her eyes widened to let in more light. "No," she breathed. One of his hands held hers, the other pressed against her back. Thank goodness. He couldn't grab her and kiss her, no matter how appealing the thought. "Bad idea."

"I know." Nate didn't need hands. His lips met hers so quickly, she never saw him move.

His mouth covered hers with no hesitancy, no question—as if he had every right to go deep. His tongue was savage and demanding, holding nothing back and accepting no evasion. He tasted of loneliness, anger, and lust. Hard, needy, *demanding* lust.

Her heart thundered in her ears, and she fell into his heat, uncaring of whether or not he caught her. He wrapped around her, his unyielding body holding her upright. He caressed her with his tongue, and she met him thrust for thrust, fierce hot pleasure lighting her on fire.

She forgot where they were, who they were, everything but the desperate need he created.

He broke the kiss, blatant male hunger crossing his face. His breath panted out even as he moved them in tune with the music.

She softened against him, allowing him to lead so she

didn't collapse. Her mind whirled, and she shook her head to regain reality. "Nathan, what do you want?" The question emerged as a breathless plea she couldn't mask.

That quickly, all hints of desire slid from his face. His chin hardened. "Want? I want to know what happened to the child you were carrying five years ago when you ripped out my heart. Where's my baby, Audrey?"

THE DISH

Where Authors Give You the Inside Scoop

♥ ♥ ♥ ♥ ♥ ♥ ♥ ♥ ♥ ♥ ♥ ♥ ♥ ♥ ♥ ♥

From the desk of Debbie Mason

Dear Reader,

While reading CHRISTMAS IN JULY one last time before sending it off to my editor, I had an "oops, I did it again" moment. In the first book in the series, *The Trouble with Christmas*, there's a scene where Madison, the heroine, senses her late mother's presence. In this book, our heroine, Grace, receives a message from her sister through her son. Grace has spent years blaming herself for her sister's death, and while there's an incident in the book that alleviates her guilt, I felt she needed the opportunity to tell her sister she loved her. Maybe if I didn't believe our departed loved ones could communicate with us in some way, I would have done this another way. But I do, and here's why.

My dad was movie-star handsome and had this amazing dimple in his chin. He was everything a little girl could wish for in a father. But he wasn't my biological father; he was the father of my heart. He came into my life when I was nine years old. That first year, I dreamed about him a lot. The dreams were very real, and all the same. I'd be outside and see a man from behind and call out to him. He'd turn around, and it would be my dad.

I always said the same thing: "You're here. I knew you weren't gone." Almost a year to the day of his passing, my dad appeared in my dream surrounded by shadowy figures who he introduced to me by name. He told me that he was okay, that he was happy. It was his way, I think, of helping me let him go.

I didn't dream of him again until sixteen months ago when we were awaiting the birth of our first grandchild. I "woke up" to see him sitting at the end of my bed. I told him how happy I was that he'd be there for the arrival of his great grandchild. He said of course he would be. He wouldn't be anywhere else.

A week later, my daughter gave birth to a beautiful baby girl. When I saw my granddaughter for the first time, I started to cry. She had my dad's dimple. No one on my son-in-law's side, or ours, has a dimple in their chin. He used to tell us the angels gave it to him, and we like to think he gave our granddaughter hers as proof that he's still with us.

So now you know why including that scene was important not only to Grace, but to me. Life really is full of small miracles and magic. And I hope you experience some of that magic as you follow Grace and Jack on their journey to happy-ever-after.

Debbie Macomber

♥ ♥ ♥ ♥ ♥ ♥ ♥ ♥ ♥ ♥ ♥ ♥ ♥ ♥ ♥

From the desk of Kristen Ashley

Dear Reader,

Usually, inspiration for books comes to me in a variety of ways. It could be a man I see (anywhere), a movie, a song, the unusual workers in a bookstore.

With SWEET DREAMS, it was an idea.

And that idea was, I wanted to take a hero who is, on the whole, totally unlikable, and make him lovable.

Enter Tatum Jackson, and when I say that, I mean *enter Tatum Jackson*. He came to me completely with a *kapow!* I could conjure him in my head, hear him talk, see the way he moved and how his clothes hung on him, feel his frustration with his life. I also knew his messed-up history.

And I could *not* wait to get stuck into this man.

I mean, here's a guy who is gorgeous, but he's got a foul temper, says nasty things when he's angry, and he's not exactly father of the year.

He had something terrible happen to him to derail his life and he didn't handle that very well, making mistake after mistake in a vicious cycle he pretty much had no intention of ending. He had a woman in his life he knew was a liar, a cheat, and no good for anyone and he was so stuck in the muck of his life that he didn't get shot of her.

Enter Lauren Grahame, who also came to me like a shot. As with Tate, everything about Lauren slammed into my head, perhaps most especially her feelings, the disillusionment she has with life, how she feels lost and really has no intention of getting found.

In fact, I don't think with any of my books I've ever had two characters who I knew so thoroughly before I started to tell their story.

And thus, I got lost in it.

I tend to be obsessive about my storytelling but this was an extreme. Once Lauren and Tate came to me, everything about Carnal, Colorado, filled my head just like the hero and heroine did. I can see Main Street, Bubba's Bar, Tate's house. I know the secondary characters as absolutely as I know the main characters. The entirety of the town, the people, and the story became a strange kind of real in my head, even if I didn't know how the story was going to play out. Indeed, I had no idea if I could pull it off, making an unlikable man lovable.

But I fell in love with Tate very quickly. The attraction he has for Lauren growing into devotion. The actions that speak much louder than words. I so enjoyed watching Lauren pull Tate out of the muck of his life, even if nothing changes except the fact that he has a woman in it that he loves, who is good to him, who feeds the muscle, the bone, the soul. Just as I enjoyed watching Tate guide Lauren out of her disillusionment and offer her something special.

I hope it happens to me again someday that characters like this inhabit my head so completely, and I hope it happens time and again.

But Tate and Lauren being the first, they'll always hold a special place in my heart, and live on in my head.

Happily,

Kristen Ashley

♥ ♥ ♥ ♥ ♥ ♥ ♥ ♥ ♥ ♥ ♥ ♥ ♥ ♥ ♥

From the desk of Rebecca Zanetti

Dear Reader,

I'm the oldest of three girls, and my husband is the oldest of three boys, so we grew up watching out for our siblings. Now that we're all adults, they look out for us, too. While my sisters and I may have argued with one another as kids, we instantly banded together if anybody tried to mess with one of us. My youngest sister topped out at an even five feet tall, yet she's the fiercest of us all, and she loses her impressive temper quite quickly if someone isn't nice to me.

I think one of the reasons I enjoyed writing Matt's story in SWEET REVENGE is because he's the eldest of the Dean brothers, and as such, he feels responsible for them. Add in a dangerous military organization trying to harm them, and his duties go far beyond that of a normal sibling. It was fun to watch Matt try to order his brothers around and keep them safe, while all they want to do is provide backup for him and ensure his safety.

There's something about being the oldest kid that forces us to push ourselves when we shouldn't. When our siblings would step back and relax, we often push forward just out of sheer stubbornness. I don't know why, and it's sometimes a mistake. Trust me.

SWEET REVENGE was written in several locations, most notably in the hospital and on airplanes. Sometimes

I take on a bit too much, so when I discovered I needed a couple of surgeries (nothing major), I figured I'd just do them on the same day. Why not? So I had two surgeries in one day and had to spend a few days in the hospital recuperating.

With my laptop, of course.

There's not a lot to do in the hospital but drink milkshakes and write, so it was quite effective. Then, instead of going home and taking it easy, I flew across the country to a conference and big book signing. Of course, I was still in pain, but I ignored it.

Bad idea.

Two weeks after that, I once again flew across the country for a book signing and conference. Yes, I was still tired, but I kept on going.

Yet another bad idea.

Then I returned home and immediately headed back to work as a college professor at the beginning of the semester.

Not a great idea.

Are you seeing a trend here? I pushed myself too hard, and all of a sudden, my body said... *you're done.* Completely done. I became sick, and after a bunch of tests, it appeared I'd just taken on too much. So at the end of the semester, I resigned as a professor and took up writing full time. And yoga. And eating healthy and relaxing.

Life is great, and it's meant to be savored and not rushed through—even for us oldest siblings. I learned a very valuable life lesson while writing SWEET REVENGE, and I'll always have fond memories of this book.

I truly hope you enjoy Matt and Laney's story, and

don't forget to take a deep breath and enjoy the moment. It's definitely worth it!

Happy reading!

Rebecca Zanetti

RebeccaZanetti.com
Twitter @RebeccaZanetti
Facebook.com

♥ ♥ ♥ ♥ ♥ ♥ ♥ ♥ ♥ ♥ ♥ ♥ ♥ ♥ ♥ ♥

From the desk of Shannon Richard

Dear Reader,

When it comes to the little town of Mirabelle, Florida, Grace King was actually the first character who revealed herself to me, which I find odd as she's the heroine in the second book. I knew from the beginning she was going to be a tiny little thing with blond hair and blue eyes; I knew she'd lost her mother at a young age and that she was never going to have known her father; and I knew she was going to be feisty and strong.

Jaxson Anderson was a different story. He didn't reveal himself to me until he literally walked onto the page in *Undone*. I also didn't know about Jax and Grace's future relationship until they got into an argument at the beach. As soon as I figured out they were going to end up together, my mind took off and I started plotting everything out, which was a little inconvenient as I wasn't even a third of the way through writing the first book.

Jax is a complicated fella. He's had to deal with a lot in his life, and because of his past he doesn't think he's good enough for Grace. Jax has most definitely put her on a pedestal, which is made pretty evident by his nickname for her. He calls her Princess, but not in a derogatory way. He doesn't find her to be spoiled or bratty. Far from it. He thinks that she should be cherished and that she's worth *everything*, especially to him. I try to capture this in the prologue, which takes place a good eighteen years before UNDENIABLE starts. Grace is this little six-year-old who is being bullied on the playground, and Jax is her white knight in scuffed-up sneakers.

Jax has been in Grace's life from the day she was brought home from the hospital over twenty-four years ago. He's watched her grow up into the beautiful and brave woman that she is, and though he's always loved her (even if he's chosen not to accept it), it's hard for him think that he can be with her. Jax's struggles were heartbreaking for me to write, and it was especially heartbreaking to put Grace through it, but this was their story and I had to stay true to them. Readers shouldn't fear with UNDENIABLE, though, because I like my happily-ever-after endings and Grace and Jax definitely get theirs. I hope readers enjoy the journey.

Cheers,

♥ ♥ ♥ ♥ ♥ ♥ ♥ ♥ ♥ ♥ ♥ ♥ ♥ ♥ ♥ ♥ ♥

From the desk of Stacy Henrie

Dear Reader,

I remember the moment HOPE AT DAWN, Book 1 in my Of Love and War series (on sale now), was born into existence. I was sitting in a quiet, empty hallway at a writers' conference contemplating how to turn my single World War I story idea, about Livy Campbell's brother, into more than one book. Then, in typical fashion, Livy marched forward in my mind, eager to have her story told first.

As I pondered Livy and the backdrop of the story—America's involvement in WWI—I knew having her fall in love with a German-American would provide inherent conflict. What I didn't know then was the intense prejudice and persecution she and Friedrick Wagner would face to be together, in a country ripe with suspicion toward anyone with German ties. The more I researched the German-American experience during WWI, the more I discovered their private war here on American soil—not against soldiers, but neighbors against neighbors, citizens against citizens.

A young woman with aspirations of being a teacher, Livy Campbell knows little of the persecution being heaped upon the German-Americans across the country, let alone in the county north of hers. More than anything, she feels the effects of the war overseas through the absence of her older brothers in France, the alcohol troubles of her wounded soldier boyfriend, and the disruption of her studies at college. When she applies for a teaching job in hopes of escaping the war, Livy doesn't realize she's simply traded one set of troubles for another, especially when she finds herself attracted to the school's handsome handyman, German-American Friedrick Wagner.

Born in America to German immigrant parents, Friedrick Wagner believes himself to be as American as anyone else in his small town of Hilden, Iowa. But the war with Germany changes all that. Suddenly viewed as a potential enemy, Friedrick seeks to protect his family from the rising tide of injustice aimed at his fellow German-Americans. Protecting the beautiful new teacher, Livy Campbell, comes as second nature to Friedrick. But when he finds himself falling in love with her, he fears the war, both at home and abroad, will never allow them to be together.

I thoroughly enjoyed writing Livy and Friedrick's love story and the odds they must overcome for each other. This is truly a tale of "love conquers all" and the power of hope and courage during a dark time in history. My hope is you will fall in love with the Campbell family through this series, as I have, as you experience their triumphs and struggles during the Great War.

Happy reading!

Stacy Henrie

♥ ♥ ♥ ♥ ♥ ♥ ♥ ♥ ♥ ♥ ♥ ♥ ♥ ♥ ♥ ♥ ♥ ♥

From the desk of Adrianne Lee

Dear Reader,

Conflict, conflict, conflict. Every good story needs it. It heightens sexual tension and keeps you guessing whether a couple will actually be able to work through those serious—and even not so serious—issues and obstacles to find that happily-ever-after ending.

I admit to a little vanity when one of my daughters once said, "Mom, in other romances I always know the couple will get together early in the book, but I'm never sure in yours until the very end." High praise and higher expectations for any writer to live up to. It is, at least, what I strive for with every love story I write.

Story plotting starts with conflict. I already knew that Jane Wilson, Big Sky Pie's new pastry chef, was going to fall in love with Nick Taziano, the sexy guy doing the promotion for the pie shop, but when I first conceived the idea that these two would be lovers in DELICIOUS, I didn't realize they were a reunion couple.

A reunion couple is a pair who was involved in the past and broke up due to unresolved conflicts. This is what I call a "built-in" conflict. It's one of my favorites to write. When the story opens, something has happened that involves this couple on a personal level, causing them to come face-to-face to deal with it. This is when they finally admit to themselves that they still have feelings for each other, feelings neither wants to feel or act on, no matter how compelling. The more they try to suppress the attraction, the stronger it becomes.

In DELICIOUS, Jane and Nick haven't seen each other since they were kids, since his father and her mother married. Jane blames Nick's dad for breaking up her parents' marriage. Nick resents Jane's mom for coming between his father and him. Jane called Nick the Tazmanian Devil. Nick called her Jane the Pain. They were thrilled when the marriage fell apart after a year.

Now many years later, their parents are reuniting, something Jane and Nick view as a bigger mistake than the first marriage. Their decision to try and stop the wedding, however, leads to one accidental, delicious kiss, and a sizzling attraction that is as irresistible as Jane's blueberry pies.

I hope you'll enjoy DELICIOUS, the second book in my Big Sky Pie series. All of the stories are set in northwest Montana near Glacier Park, an area where I vacationed every summer for over thirty years. Each of the books is about someone connected with the pie shop in one way or another and contains a different delicious pie recipe. So come join the folks of Kalispell at the little pie shop on Center Street, right across from the mall, for some of the best pie you'll ever taste, and a healthy helping of romance.

Adrianne Lee

♥ ♥ ♥ ♥ ♥ ♥ ♥ ♥ ♥ ♥ ♥ ♥ ♥ ♥ ♥ ♥

From the desk of Jessica Lemmon

Dear Reader,

A *quiz:* What do you get when you put a millionaire who avoids romantic relationships in the same house with a determined-to-stay-single woman who crushed on him sixteen years ago?

If you answered *unstoppable attraction*, you'd be right.

In THE MILLIONAIRE AFFAIR, I paired a hero who cages and controls his emotions with a heroine who feels way too much, way too soon. Kimber Reynolds is determined to have a fling—to love and leave Landon Downey, if for only two reasons: (1) She's wanted to kiss the eldest Downey brother since she was a teen, and (2) to prove to herself that she can have a shallow relationship that ends amicably instead of one that's long, drawn-out, and destined to end badly.

When Landon's six-year-old nephew, Lyon, and a huge account for his advertising agency come crashing into his life, Landon needs help. Lucky for him (and us!) his sister offers the perfect solution: her friend, Kimber, can be his live-in nanny for the week.

The most difficult part about writing Landon was letting him deal with his past on *his terms* and watching him falter. Here is a guy who makes rules, follows them, and remains stoic...to his own detriment. Despite those qualities, Landon, from a loving, close family, can't help caring for Kimber. Even when they're working down a list of "extracurricular activities" in the bedroom, Landon puts Kimber's needs before his own.

These two may have stumbled into an arrangement, but when Fate tosses them a wild card, they both step up—and step closer—to the one thing they were sure they didn't want...*forever.*

I *love* this book. Maybe because of how much I wrestled with Landon and Kimber's story before getting it right. The three of us had growing pains, but I finally found their truth, and I'm *so* excited to share their story with you. If Landon and Kimber win your heart like they won mine, be sure to let me know. You can email me at jessica@jessicalemmon.com, tweet me @lemmony, and "like" my Facebook page at www.facebook.com/authorjessicalemmon.

Happy reading!

Jessica Lemmon

www.jessicalemmon.com